Greek Billionaires

Two billionaire brothers…brides wanted!

Gorgeous Greek brothers Akis and
Vasso Giannopoulos have the world at their feet.

They have everything they need…except love.

Until their lives—and hearts!—are turned upside
down when two feisty women arrive on their
luxurious Greek island…

Akis meets his match—and the only woman who
can discover the man beneath the suit and tie—in
The Millionaire's True Worth

And

Vasso finds the woman of his dreams, but dare
she love him? Find out in
A Wedding for the Greek Tycoon

Let Rebecca Winters whisk you away with this
riveting and emotional new duet!

A WEDDING FOR THE GREEK TYCOON

BY
REBECCA WINTERS

MILLS & BOON

Published in Great Britain 2015
by Mills & Boon, an imprint of Harlequin (UK) Limited,
Eton House, 18-24 Paradise Road, Richmond, Surrey, TW9 1SR

© 2015 Rebecca Winters

ISBN: 978-0-263-25164-7

23-0915

Harlequin (UK) Limited's policy is to use papers that are natural, renewable and recyclable products and made from wood grown in sustainable forests. The logging and manufacturing processes conform to the legal environmental regulations of the country of origin.

Printed and bound in Spain
by CPI, Barcelona

Rebecca Winters lives in Salt Lake City, Utah. With canyons and high alpine meadows full of wildflowers, she never runs out of places to explore. They, plus her favorite vacation spots in Europe, often end up as backgrounds for her romance novels, because writing is her passion, along with her family and church.

Rebecca loves to hear from readers. If you wish to e-mail her, please visit her website, www.cleanromances.com.

To my wonderful grandsons, Billy and Jack.

These two brothers show a love and devotion
to each other that touches my heart.

CHAPTER ONE

August 9, New York City

THE BEARDED OLDER DOCTOR looked at Zoe. "Young woman. You've been cancer-free for eight months. Today I can say without reservation that it's definitely in remission. We've already talked about the life span for recovering patients like you. But no one can predict the end of life for any of us."

"I know," she said as he continued to explain the survival expectancy statistics for patients like her. But she'd read about it all before and didn't really listen. The adage to take it one day at a time and rejoice for another day of life was the motto around the hospital.

Zoe's physical exam had gone without incident. Her labs looked great. But she would never outgrow her nervousness. Fear lurked in her that the next time she had to have a checkup, the cancer would have come back. She couldn't throw it off.

The therapist at the center had given her a book to read about dealing with the disease once it had gone into remission. Depression bothered many patients who feared a recurrence and that was a problem they needed to deal with. Since Zoe was a prime example, she could have written that section of the book herself.

But for today she was filled with relief over the lab results. In fact she was so overjoyed with the news she had difficulty believing it. A year ago she'd been told she had a terminal case, but now... She looked at the doctor. "So what you're saying is—it's really gone."

His brows furrowed. "Believe it, girl."

She believed it for today, but it would come back.

"I'm pleased that the terrible fatigue you felt for so long is now gone. You seem much stronger physically and emotionally. Your therapist and I believe you're ready to leave the center today if you wish."

That was the news she'd been waiting for. She had plans and there was no time to lose.

"Here's hoping that from now on you can live a normal life."

Normal... It would never be normal when she knew the cancer would return. But she smiled at him. "How can I thank you for everything you've done for me?"

"You already have by working so hard to get well. You have a beautiful spirit and are an inspiration to the other patients here in the hospital. All the friends you've made here will miss you."

Tears stung her eyes. "I'll miss them more." With this checkup behind her, she could put her plan into action.

"I doubt that."

Zoe folded her arms to her waist. "My bill has to be astronomical. If it takes me the rest of my life, I'm going to pay back every cent of it."

"It's been taken care of by the generosity of the Giannopoulos Foundation Charity."

"I'm aware of that." So aware, in fact, she needed to thank the members of the Giannopoulos family personally and one day she would. "But everyone who works here is an angel, especially you. I don't know what I ever did to deserve such care."

When she'd been admitted to the hospital, she'd read the material given to every patient. The first time she'd gone to the chapel inside the hospital she'd read the plaque. It had been named for the Church of Agii Apostoli in Greece.

In honor of Patroklos Giannopoulos and his wife Irana Manos who survived the malaria outbreak on Paxos in the early 1960s.

In honor of her brother Kristos Manos who survived the malaria outbreak and emigrated to New York to build a new life.

In honor of Patroklos Giannopoulos who died from lymphoma.

"I'm here by the grace of the foundation here in New York too," the doctor reminded her. "It was established for Greek Americans with lymphoma who have no living family or means for the kind of help you've needed. There are some wonderful, generous people in this world. Do you have a place to go?"

"Yes. Father Debakis at the Sacred Trinity Greek

Orthodox Church has taken care of everything. I've known him since I was young. Throughout my ordeal he's been in constant contact with me. I owe him so much, and Iris Themis too. She's from the humanitarian council at Sacred Trinity and has arranged to take me to their homeless shelter where I can stay until I find a job and a place to live. All I have to do is phone her at her office."

"Splendid. As you know, you'll need another checkup in six weeks, either here or at another hospital depending on what's convenient. It will include a blood test and physical exam for lumps. But you can contact me at any time if you have concerns."

Zoe dreaded her next checkup, but she couldn't think about that right now. Instead she stood up to give him a hug. "Thank you for helping me get my life back. You'll never know what it means."

After she left his office, she hurried through the hospital and walked along the corridor that led to the convalescent center. She had a room on the second floor. Having lost her family, this had been her home for twelve months.

In the beginning, Zoe didn't dream that she'd ever leave this place alive. At first the man she'd been dating had called her often, but the technology company Chad worked for transferred him to Boston and the calls grew fewer and fewer. She understood, but it hurt her to the core. Even if he'd told her he was crazy about her, if he could leave at the darkest moment of her life, then she couldn't expect any man to accept her situation.

Though there were family friends from her old

neighborhood who phoned her every so often, the in-mates had become her choice friends. With all of them being Greek American, they shared stories of their family histories and had developed a camaraderie so strong she didn't want to leave them. It was here that her whole life had passed before her.

Once inside her room, she sat down on the side of the bed and phoned Iris. They planned to meet in front of the convalescent center in a half hour. One day Iris and the priest would receive their crowns in heaven.

Zoe had emerged from her illness wanting to help people the way they'd helped her. College could wait. If she could go to work for the Giannopoulos Foundation, that was what she wanted to do. Of necessity Zoe would have to approach Alexandra Kallistos, the woman who managed this center, but any experiences with her were unsettling. The other woman was standoffish. Whether that was her nature, or if she just didn't care for Zoe, she didn't know.

Earlier today when they'd passed each other in the hall, Ms. Kallistos hadn't even acknowledged her. Maybe it was because Zoe was taking up a bed some-one else needed, but the therapist had insisted she still needed to be here. Because she'd lost her parents and required more time to heal mentally, the arrange-ments had been made for which Zoe would be eter-nally grateful.

Ms. Kallistos had an office at the hospital and was officially in charge. All the staff, doctors, nurses, thera-pists, lab workers, X-ray technicians, orderlies, kitchen help, volunteers and housekeeping people reported to her. She was a model of efficiency, but Zoe felt she lacked the bedside manner needed to make the inmates comfortable enough to confide in her.

Alexandra was a striking, brown-eyed, single Greek American woman probably in her early thirties. Her dark brown hair flounced around her shoulders. She wore fashionable clothes that made the most of her figure. But she seemed cold. Maybe that wasn't a fair judgment, but the thought of approaching her for a position made Zoe feel uneasy.

If there was a problem, maybe Father Debakis would have better luck in bringing up the subject of Zoe working here.

August 10, Athens, Greece

Vasso Giannopoulos was nearing the end of the audits on the Giannopoulos Complex in Athens, Greece he co-owned with Akis, his younger married brother, when he heard his private secretary buzz him. He'd been looking over the latest inventories from their convenience stores in Alexandroupolis.

"Yes, Kyria Spiros?"

"Ms. Kallistos is on the line from New York. She's calling from the hospital in New York, asking to speak to you or your brother. Do you want to take it, or shall I tell her you'll call her back later? I know you didn't want to be disturbed."

"No, no. You did the right thing." The Giannopoulos Hospital and Convalescent Center were located in Astoria. But why she would be calling when he was scheduled to meet with her tomorrow seemed odd. His head lifted. "I'll speak to her."

"Line two."

He picked up the phone. "Alexandra? This is Vasso."

"I'm sorry to bother you, Vasso. I thought I could catch you before you fly here. You're very kind to take my call."

"Not at all."

"Everyone knows that you and your brother established the Giannopoulos Greek American Lymphoma Center here in New York several years ago. This is the fourth time that I've been contacted by a major television network to devote a piece to your lives.

"The managing director of the network wants to send a crew here to film the facility and interview some of the staff. More importantly they want to interview you and your brother for the featured documentary. I told him I would pass this along to you. I know you've turned them down before, but since you'll be here tomorrow, would you be interested in setting up an appointment?"

Vasso didn't have to think. "Tell the man we're not interested."

"All right. When can I expect you to arrive?"

"By two at the latest. I appreciate the call. *Yassou.*" As he rang off, Akis walked in the office. "Hey, bro. I'm glad you're back. Alexandra just phoned. One of the networks in New York wants to do a documentary on us."

"Again?" Akis shook his head. "They never give up."

"Nope. I told her to tell them no."

"Good. How soon are you leaving for New York?"

"I'm ready to head out now. I plan to meet with some of our East Coast distributors early in the morning. Then I'll go over to the hospital and take a look at the books."

"While you do that, I'll finish up the rest of the inventories for the northern region. Raina will help. She's a genius with accounts. You won't have anything to worry about."

"How's her morning sickness?"

"It hardly ever bothers her now."

"Glad to hear it."

"Before you leave, I have a question." Akis eyed him with curiosity. "How did your evening go with Maris the other night?"

"So-so."

"That doesn't sound good. We were hoping she might be the one who brings an end to your bachelor existence."

"Afraid not. She's nice and interesting, but she's not the one." He patted Akis's shoulder. "See you in a couple of days."

Vasso hadn't been dating Maris that long, but already he knew he needed to end it with her. He didn't want to lead her on. But Akis's comment had hit a nerve. Both of them had been bachelors for a long time. Now that Akis was married, Vasso felt an emptiness in his life he'd never felt before. His brother was so happy these days with his new wife and a baby on the way, Vasso hardly recognized him.

August 12, New York City

"Vasso!"

"How are you, Alexandra?"

The manager got to her feet. "It's good to see you."

"I walked through the hospital and convalescent center first. Everything seems to be in perfect order. My congratulations for running an efficient center we can be proud of."

"Thank you. I know you're busy. If you want to go over the books in here, I can order lunch to be brought in."

"I've already eaten. Why don't I look at the figures while you're out to lunch? If I see anything wrong, we'll discuss it when you get back."

"All right. Before I leave, I wanted to tell you about a young woman who applied here for a job yesterday. I told her she didn't have the education or background necessary for the kind of work we do at the center.

"Later in the day I received a phone call from Father Debakis at the Sacred Trinity Church here in Astoria. He knows this woman and finds her a very capable person. He wanted to know if he could go to someone higher to arrange for an interview. I wrote the priest's number on my sticky note in case you want to deal with him."

"I'll take care of it now. Thanks for telling me."

"Then I'll leave and be back in an hour."

"Take your time." Vasso's curiosity had been aroused by the mention of the priest. As she reached the door he said, "I want you to know my brother and I are very pleased and grateful for the work you do to keep this center running so smoothly."

He heard a whispered thank-you before she left the office. Vasso phoned the number she'd left and asked to speak to Father Debakis. Then he sat back in the chair.

"It's an honor to speak with you, Kyrie Giannopoulos. I'm glad Ms. Kallistos passed my message along. Since I don't wish to waste your time, I'll come straight to the point." Vasso smiled. He liked brevity. "A very special twenty-four-year-old Greek American woman named Zoe Zachos here in Queens would like to work for your charity. I've taken it upon myself to approach you about it."

"I understand Ms. Kallistos had reservations about hiring her."

"When I spoke to her on Zoe's behalf, she said this young woman doesn't have the credentials and flatly refused to consider interviewing her for a position. I disagree strongly with her assessment and hoped to prevail on you to intercede in this matter."

Vasso and Akis had flown to New York ten months ago to find a new manager after the old one had to give it up due to ill health. Alexandra had come to them with outstanding references and was the most qualified of all the applicants because she'd had experience working in hospital administration.

Akis, who'd been in business with Vasso from childhood, had flown to New York five months later to check on her. So far neither he nor Vasso had a problem with the way she'd been doing her work. She must have had good reason not to take the other person's application.

"Obviously this is important to you."

"Very." Vasso blinked in surprise at the priest's sobriety. "Perhaps she could be interviewed by you?"

He sat forward. "That isn't our normal procedure."

"Ah…" The disappointment in the priest's voice wasn't lost on Vasso, who'd been taught by his deceased father to revere a priest.

His black brows furrowed. "May I ask why you have such strong reasons for making this call?"

"It's a matter of some urgency."

The hairs lifted on the back of Vasso's neck. After the priest put it that way, Vasso didn't feel he could refuse him. "Tell me about her background."

"I think it would be better for you to discover that information yourself."

At this point Vasso was more than a little intrigued. In all honesty he found himself curious about the unusual request. "How soon could she be at Ms. Kallistos's office?"

"Within two hours."

"Then I'll be expecting her."

"Bless you, my son." The priest clicked off while a perplexed Vasso still held the phone in his hand. For the next hour and a half he pored over the books. When Alexandra returned, he told her everything looked in order and listened to some of her suggestions to do with the running of the hospital.

During their conversation, a polite knock sounded on

the closed door. He turned to Alexandra. "That would be Zoe Zachos. If you'll give us a half hour please."

After a discernible hesitation she said, "Of course." She showed remarkable poise by not questioning him about it. He watched her get up and open the door. "Come in, Zoe," she said to the blonde woman before she left them alone.

Zoe? That meant Alexandra knew her.

Vasso didn't know exactly what to expect other than he'd been told she was twenty-four years old. He got to his feet as the young woman came into the office.

"Kyrie Giannopoulos?" she said, sounding the slightest bit breathless. "I'm Zoe Zachos. I can't believe it, but somehow Father Debakis made this meeting possible." In an instant a smile broke out on her lovely face. "You have no idea how grateful I am to meet you at last."

Tears had caused her translucent green eyes to shimmer.

When she extended her hand to shake his across the desk, he saw a look of such genuine gratitude reflected in those depths, it reached places inside him he didn't know were there.

"Please, Thespinis Zachos. Sit down."

Her lissome figure subsided in one of the chairs opposite the desk. She was wearing a print blouse and khaki skirt, drawing his attention to her shapely body and legs below the hem. She had to be five-six or five-seven.

"I'm sure he told you that I'd like to work for your foundation."

He felt an earnestness—a sweetness—coming from her that caught him off guard. "He made that clear."

She clasped her hands. "When he spoke on my behalf with Ms. Kallistos, she said I didn't have the kind of background she was looking for."

"But Father Debakis feels that you do. Tell me about yourself. Why would you want to work for the foundation as opposed to somewhere else, or do another type of work entirely?"

"He didn't tell you?" She looked surprised.

"No. He's a man of few words."

"But he makes them count," she said with a smile that told him she'd had a running relationship with the priest.

Vasso agreed with her assessment. The priest had an amazing way of making his point. It had gotten Vasso to conduct this interview, which was out of the ordinary. "Why not start at the beginning, *thespinis*?"

She nodded. "I've been a patient here with non-Hodgkins lymphoma for the last year and was just released on the ninth of this month."

A patient...

Knowing what that meant, he swallowed hard. Vasso had thought of several reasons for the possible conflict between the two women. He thought back to a year ago when another manager had to resign because of health issues. When they'd hired Alexandra, Zoe Zachos had already been a patient here. The two had seen each other coming and going for months. But it didn't explain the problem that caused Alexandra to turn down Zoe's request.

"I was thrilled to be told I was cured."

The joy in her countenance was something Vasso would never be able to describe adequately. "That's wonderful news," he said in a thick-toned voice.

"Isn't it?" She leaned forward with a light in those marvelous green eyes. "It's all because of your family. The foundation you established literally gave me back my life!" The tremor in her voice resonated inside him.

He had to clear his throat. "To hear your testimonial is very gratifying, Thespinis Zachos."

"There's no way to pay you back monetarily. But I would love to work for you in some capacity for the rest of my life. I'm a good cook and could work in the hospital kitchen, or in the laundry, or give assistance to those convalescing. Give me a job and I'll do it to the best of my ability. The trouble is Ms. Kallistos told Father Debakis that without a college degree and no experience in the health field, there was no point in interviewing me.

"She wondered if I might not be better suited to becoming a nun if I wanted to be of service to others." A *nun*? "I'm sure she was just teasing. Father Debakis and I laughed over that. I'm hardly nun material. But I do want to make a difference."

Vasso's anger flared. Not so much at Alexandra as at himself and Akis. At the time they hired her, both he and Akis had decided she had the best credentials for the important position even if she was younger. But Vasso could see there was a great deal more to finding the right person for this particular job than what was put on paper. Since Zoe had been a patient here for such a

long time, surely Alexandra could have shown a little
more understanding.

"Whatever was said, you have a great advocate in
Father Debakis. How did you come to know him?"

"My parents owned a Greek *taverna* and we lived
in the apartment above it here in Astoria near the Sacred Trinity Church. Father Debakis was serving there
when I was just a young girl and always took an interest in our family. If it hadn't been for him, I'm not sure
I'd be alive today."

"Why do you say that?"

An expression of unspeakable sorrow brought shadows to her classic features, changing her demeanor. "A
year ago I'd gone to a movie with some friends from the
neighborhood. We walked home after it was over. It was
late. My parents would have been in bed."

She paused before saying, "When we got there, it
looked like a war zone. Someone said there'd been an
explosion. I ran towards the fire chief who told me an
arsonist had planted a bomb in the back of the laundry next door to my parents' *taverna* where I sometimes helped out part-time. Fire spread to the *taverna*'s
kitchen. Everything went up in smoke. My parents died.
So did the owners next door who'd run the laundry for
many years."

"Dear Lord." Vasso couldn't fathom it.

"Everything burned. Family photos, precious pos-
sessions, clothes—all was gone. I've always lived with
my parents and worked in the restaurant kitchen to save
money while I went to college. The scene was so horrific, I collapsed. When I came to, I was in the ER at

the local hospital. Father Debakis was the first person I saw when I woke up.

"He told me the doctor had examined me and had discovered a lump in my neck." Vasso saw her shudder. It brought out a protective instinct in him he hadn't felt since he and Akis were on their own after their father died. Though Akis was only eleven months younger, their dying father had charged Vasso to look after his younger brother.

"Honestly, I'm still surprised I didn't die that night. I wanted to. I was convinced my life was over. He, along with Iris Themis, one of the women on the church humanitarian council, wouldn't let me give up.

"They are wonderful people who did everything to help me physically and spiritually in order to deal with my grief. The diagnosis of cancer added another level of despair. My parents and I had never taken a handout from anyone. For them to shower me with clothes and toiletries lost in the fire besides being there for comfort, meant I felt overwhelmed with their generosity."

Vasso got up from the chair, unable to remain seated. Father Debakis had told him she was a very special young woman.

"Before the fire and my illness, I'd planned to finish my last semester of college to get my English degree. I'd even thought of going on to get a secondary school teaching certificate. Because I had to work at night and go to school during the day, my education had to be strung out."

A sad laugh escaped her lips. "At twenty-four I would have been one of the oldest college graduates around, but the enormity of losing my parents this last year along with the lymphoma has changed my focus."

"It would change anyone's." When Vasso's father had died of the disease, the world he and Akis had grown up in was changed for all time. They'd adored their father who was too poor to get the medical treatment needed. As he slipped away from them, they'd vowed never to feel that helpless again.

He watched as she re-crossed her elegant legs. "While I was still at the hospital, I met with a cancer specialist who discussed my illness with me. My student insurance would only cover a portion of the costs. There was only a little money from my parents' savings to add to the amount owing.

"With their insurance I was able to pay off my student loan. What I had left was the small savings in my bank account that wouldn't keep me alive more than a couple of months. I was trapped in a black abyss when Father Debakis and Iris came to get me and bring me here.

"I was told the center existed to help Greek Americans with lymphoma who had few sources of income to cover the bulk of the expense. They took me into the chapel where I read what was written on the plaque."

As she looked up at Vasso, tears trickled down her flushed cheeks. "At that moment I knew the Giannopoulos family truly were Samaritans. You just don't know how grateful I am." The words continued to pour out of her. "As long as I'm granted life, I want to give back a little of what your foundation has done for me. It would be a privilege to work for you and your family in any capacity."

As long as I'm granted life.

What had Father Debakis said? It was a matter of some urgency.

Zoe Zachos's revelations had left Vasso stunned and touched to the soul. He sucked in his breath. "Are you in a relationship with anyone?"

"I had a boyfriend named Chad. But he got a job offer in Boston around the time of the fire. I urged him to take it and he did. We've both moved on. So to answer your question, no, there is no special person in my life."

Good grief. What kind of a man would desert her in her darkest hour?

"Where do you live right now?"

"I'm at the church's shelter. I'm planning to find an apartment, but I hoped that if I could work at the center here, then I would look for a place close by."

"Do you have transportation?"

"Yes."

"And a phone?"

"Yes." She drew it from her purse. "Iris will pick me up here as soon as I call her."

He pulled out his cell. "Let's exchange phone numbers." After that was done he said, "Before the day is out you'll be hearing from me."

She got to her feet. "Thank you for giving me this opportunity to talk to you. No matter what you decide, I'm thankful I was able to meet one of the Giannopoulos family and thank you personally. God bless all of you."

All two of us, he mused mournfully. *Four* when he included Raina and the baby that was on the way.

After she left the office, Vasso went back to the desk

and sat down to phone Akis. He checked the time. Ten o'clock in Athens. His brother wouldn't have gone to bed yet. He picked up on the third ring.

"Vasso? Raina and I were hoping we'd hear from you before it got too late. How do things look at the center?"

He closed his eyes tightly. "Alexandra has everything under control. But something else has come up. You're not going to believe what I have to tell you." For the next few minutes he unloaded on his brother, telling him everything.

"When we created the foundation, it felt good. It was a way to honor *Papa*." In a shaken voice he said, "But one look in her eyes taught me what gratitude really looks like—you know, deep down to the soul. I've never been so humbled in my life."

"That's a very moving story," Akis responded in a serious tone. "What do you think we should do? Since Alexandra has made her opinion obvious for whatever reason, I don't think it would work to create a position for Thespinis Zachos under the same roof."

"I'm way ahead of you. What do you think if we hired her to work at the center on Paxos?"

He could hear his brother's mind ticking away. "Do you think she'd be willing to relocate to Greece?"

"I don't know. She has no family in New York, but she's very close to Father Debakis and one of the women working for the Church's humanitarian program."

"What about a boyfriend?"

"Not at the moment. But I'm sure she has friends she met at college. There was the mention of friends she'd been out with the night of the fire."

"She's definitely one of the survivors of this world. What does she look like?"

How to describe Zoe Zachos…? "I can't explain because I wouldn't do her justice."

"That beautiful, huh?" Akis knew him too well. After a pause, "Are you thinking of asking her if she'd like to move to Paxos?"

It was all he'd been thinking about since she'd left the office.

"Just be careful, Vasso. I know you inside and out. If she does take you up on your offer of a job, you're going to feel responsible for her. Be sure that's what you want."

He lowered his head. Funny how circumstances had changed. Vasso used to be the one watching out for Akis. Now his little brother had taken over that role. It gave him a lot to think about, but there wasn't time if he expected to phone her before nightfall. "I'll consider what you've said. *Yassou.*"

On his way out of the office, Alexandra was just coming in. "You're finished?"

"That's right."

She looked surprised. "Are you staying in New York tonight?"

"No. I'm flying back to Athens." The beauty of owning a private jet meant he could sleep at night and arrive where he needed to be the next morning.

"I see. What have you decided about Ms. Zachos?"

"You were right. Her skills can best be used elsewhere." Her bilingual abilities in English and Greek played only a tiny part of what she could bring to the job. "That's what I'll tell Father Debakis. Keep up the good work, Alexandra. My brother and I are relying on you."

Relief broke out on her face. "Thank you. I hope the next time you come you'll arrange to stay longer."

Vasso nodded before leaving the center. After he got in the limo, he phoned the priest.

"Father? This is Vasso Giannopoulos. I've just come from the center and am pressed for time. Could I meet with you and Thespinis Zachos in your office ASAP?"

"That can be arranged. I'll ask Kyria Themis to bring her immediately."

"Excellent. In lieu of her parents who died in the fire, I look to you as someone who has her deepest interest at heart. I understand she has revered you from childhood. What I'd like to do is present an employment offer to her. I believe it's vital that you are there so she can discuss it with you." He paused, then said, "She regards you as her mentor."

"She's so grateful to everyone who helped her; her dearest wish is to work for your foundation. She lost everything. Now that she has survived, she wants to give back what she can."

"After talking to her, I believe that's true. I'll see you soon."

He hung up and asked the limo driver to take him to the Greek Orthodox Church a few blocks away.

CHAPTER TWO

ZOE DIDN'T KNOW what the meeting with the priest was all about. The incredible-looking man she'd met at the hospital earlier had told her he'd phone her before the day was out. Since leaving that office, she'd wondered if he'd really meant what he'd said.

But any concern in that department vanished the second she caught a glimpse of his black hair through the opening of the study door. Her pulse quickened for no good reason the second a pair of jet-black eyes beneath black brows zeroed in on her.

Both men stood when she walked in wearing the same skirt and blouse she'd worn earlier. She only had three or four outfits because no more was necessary living at the hospital. But now she needed to do some shopping for a wardrobe with the money she still had left in her bank account.

Over the years Zoe had been in the priest's study many times with other people, but she'd never laid eyes on any man as gorgeous as Vasso Giannopoulos. The thirtyish-looking male possessed facial features and a hard-muscled body that were as perfectly formed as her favorite statue of Apollo she'd only seen in pictures. No other man could possibly compare.

Her first meeting with him had been so important, she hadn't had the luxury of studying him the way she could now. He was probably six foot two and topped the priest by several inches, having an authority about him not even Father Debakis possessed. The dark gray suit toned with a lighter gray shirt gave him a rare aura of sophistication.

"Come in and sit down, Zoe. Kyrie Giannopoulos requested that I be in on this visit with you."

"Thank you." She found an upholstered chair next to the couch where he sat.

Father Debakis took his place behind the desk. He nodded to the younger man. "Go ahead and tell her why you've asked for this meeting."

Vasso sat forward to look at her with his hands resting on his thighs. Her gaze darted to his hands. He wore no rings. "After you left the hospital, I phoned my brother to tell him about you and your situation. We would be very happy to have you come to work for the foundation, but the position we're offering would be on the island of Paxos in Greece."

Zoe decided she had to be dreaming.

"Have you ever been there?"

She shook her head. "No, though I did go on a two-week university tour to England right before the fire broke out. As for our family, we took trips up and down the East Coast and into French Canada."

After a quick breath she said, "My great-grandparents left Florina in Macedonia to escape communism after the Greek Civil War and came to the US in 1946. It was in New York my father met my mother whose family were also refugees. They'd planned to take us on a trip back there for my graduation present, but it didn't happen."

"Maybe now it can," he said. "The center here in New York is fully staffed, and it might be a long time before there's a vacancy. But our center on Paxos has needed an assistant to the manager since the last one left to take care of a sick parent."

Zoe could feel her pulse racing. "You've established another hospital?" That meant she wouldn't have to work under Ms. Kallistos?

"Our first one actually. My brother and I have interviewed a number of applicants, but the manager hasn't felt he could work with any of them."

He? "What makes you think he would feel differently about me?"

"I have a feeling he'll welcome you because you have one credential no one else has possessed to date. It's more important than any college degree."

Her heart was pounding too hard. "What's that?"

"Compassion. You've lived through the agony of having been diagnosed with lymphoma, being treated for it and beating it. The year you've spent in the center here has given you the most valuable knowledge of what it's like to know you have the disease, and to have survived."

"Still, Ms. Kallistos said—"

"Let me finish," he cut her off, not unkindly. "For

that kind of learning experience, you've paid a terrible price. Yet it's that very knowledge that's needed to work with patients because you conquered the disease. Everyone in the hospital will relate to you and your presence alone will give them hope."

"She does that at the hospital every day," the priest inserted.

Her throat swelled with emotion. "What's the manager like?"

"Yiannis Megalos served as a rear admiral in the Greek Navy before his retirement."

A man who'd been an admiral. How interesting. "Then he must run a very tight ship."

The smile he flashed turned her heart over. "He's an old family friend and came to us about a position with the foundation after losing his wife to cancer, in order to work through his grief. In that respect you and he already share something vital in common by having a burning desire to help. I don't need to tell you his organizational skills and his work with the wounded during his military career made him an excellent choice."

"He sounds remarkable."

"Yiannis is a character too," he added on a lighter note. She felt his eyes travel over her. "If I have any concerns, it's for you. Leaving New York to live in a new country is a huge decision to make. If you've got anyone special you don't want to leave, that could prove difficult."

She shook her head. "There's no one."

"Even so, you may not feel that you can uproot yourself from friends. It might be hard to leave those here at the church who've helped you. That's why I wanted Father Debakis to be here in case you want to discuss this with him in private."

"Of course I'll miss everyone, but to be given a chance to work for your foundation means more to me than anything."

"We can come to terms over a salary you'll feel good about. You'll need a place to live. But all of those matters can be discussed once you've determined that you want this position. Talk it over with Father Debakis. Take as long as you need."

Zoe was so thrilled to have been offered a job it took a minute for her to comprehend it. She fought back her tears. "I'll never be able to thank you enough for this offer, not to mention the generosity of your family's foundation."

He got to his feet. Again she felt his scrutiny. "Be sure it's what you want," he warned in a more serious tone of voice. If she didn't know anything else, she knew deep down this was what she wanted and needed. "In the meantime I have to fly back to Athens tonight. You can phone me when you've made your decision."

Seize the moment, Zoe. "Before you leave, could I ask you a few more questions?"

"Of course."

"What's the weather like right now?"

"It's been in the low eighties all summer and won't drop to the seventies until later in September. Usually the night temperature is in the sixties."

"It sounds too good to be true. Are there shops near the hospital to buy clothes?"

"The center is on the outskirts of the small seaside village of Loggos. There are a few tourist shops, but I'd suggest you do your shopping in Athens first."

"Then that solves any problems I'll have about luggage. I lost everything in the fire so I'll replenish my wardrobe there."

He paused in the doorway, looking surprised. "Does this mean you've already made up your mind?"

She eyed the priest then glanced back at the other man. "I can't wait!"

"I can see you're a woman who knows her own mind." She thought his eyes might be smiling. "Under the circumstances, let's go out for dinner where we can talk over details. I'll drive you back to your shelter then leave for the airport."

She turned to the priest. "Oh, Father Debakis…I'm so happy I could take flight."

He chuckled. "I believe you could."

Vasso knew he'd never forget this moment. It was a nice feeling to make someone happy. He smiled at the priest. "It's been a pleasure to meet you."

"And mine, Kyrie Giannopoulos. Bless you."

"Shall we go, *thespinis*?"

After they walked out to the limo, he asked her to recommend a good place to eat.

Zoe swung around. "There's a Greek diner called Zito's a few blocks over. They serve lamb kebabs and potatoes so soft you can taste the lemon."

That sounded good to him. He told the driver who headed there, then concentrated on the charming female seated across from him. "We need to talk about your travel arrangements. There are dozens of flights to Athens every day. Once we know the date, I'll book a flight for you."

"Thank you, but I'll take care of that. This is so exciting, I can't believe it's happening."

Her excitement was contagious. He hadn't felt this alive in a long time. Once inside the diner they were shown to a table for two. The minute they were seated and Zoe ordered for them, she flicked him a searching glance.

"While I've got you here alone, I need your advice. If I were to take Kyrie Megalos a small gift from New York, what would he like?"

His lips twitched. "He collects naval memorabilia from all over the world."

That gave her a great idea. "Thanks for the tip."

"You're welcome. Before any more time passes, I need to know about your financial situation."

"I don't have one. I'm broke." A laugh escaped her lips, delighting him. "That doesn't mean I have no money, but it wouldn't be enough to keep me alive for more than a few months. That's why I can't wait to start work.

"When I look back, I'm pretty sure I know the reason why Ms. Kallistos didn't want me to work there. I took up a bed in the center for eight months after my first cancer-free checkup. That's because I was allowed to live in the hospital's long-term facility for the last eight months and get therapy to help me with grief issues."

Vasso surmised that was only one of the reasons Ms. Kallistos had problems with Zoe. No woman could compete with this female's effervescent personality. Her reverence for life sucked you in.

"After the chemo and bone marrow transplant, I was given all the time there I needed to recover, for which I'm grateful. I don't even have to wear a wig now. No one would ever guess that I'd once lost all of it."

Without her blond hair that had a slightly windblown look, she would still possess stunning classic features. "You seem the picture of health. If a long stay at the center was what made the difference in your recovery, then I applaud the therapist's decision."

She nodded. "I finally got it out of my doctor that the therapist was worried about my recovery. Losing my parents was so horrendous I had gone into a deep depression, and he could see I needed counseling. That part was certainly true. I was an only child and way too connected to them at the hip. They were wonderful and worked so hard, I tried to do everything I could to help them. In one night my whole world evaporated."

"That's the way my brother and I felt when our father died of lymphoma. The world we knew had gone away. Luckily we had each other."

"My therapist explained that if I'd had a sibling, it might have made a big difference. He made me realize why I had such a hard time letting them go. Grief hits everyone differently. In my case I was a twenty-four-year-old woman crying like a child for her parents. You don't know how much fun they were. We were best friends."

"Akis and I had the same relationship with our father." Everything she told Vasso rang so true with him about his own life he had trouble finding words. "I'm glad the priest prevailed on me to interview you. He's very persuasive."

Another quick smile appeared. "He is that. The other day when the doctor saw me for my six-weeks checkup and told me I was still cancer-free, something changed inside of me. I didn't want to stay there any longer and realized I'd come out of the worst of my depression. Father Debakis knew about my wanting to work for your foundation. So for you to give me a chance is like another miracle." Her voice trembled. "Thank you for this opportunity. I promise I won't let you down."

"I'm sure you won't."

The waiter brought their food, but Vasso hardly noticed what he was eating because emotions got in the way of anything else. Their conversation had reminded him of the father he and Akis missed. Their dad had treated them like buddies. He had laughed and joked with them.

Vasso always marveled over how smart he was. Their father knew everyone and had taught them to treat other people with respect. That was how you got ahead. He and Akis remembered everything their father had told them.

She finished her meal before looking up at him. "Your money saved my life and it's saving the lives of everyone at the hospital. Not just the patients, but the staff too. My oncologist is thrilled to be working there.

You and your family have done more for others than you will ever know."

"I hear you, Zoe. Now no more talk about gratitude. Because you'll be living on Paxos, I know of several places you can rent. By the time you reach the island, I'll have lined up some apartments for you to look at."

"That's very thoughtful of you, but I can do that myself."

"I'm sure you could, but you'll need a place close to the center and they're not easy to come by."

"Then I take your word for it. Thank you."

"If you've finished, I'll run you by the shelter."

She got up from the table. "I'll phone you as soon as I've made my flight plans."

"I'll be expecting your call and we'll go from there."

As he walked her out to the limo, he felt as if he too had undergone a life-changing experience. Of course he realized the foundation was helping many people. But for the first time since he and his brother had established the two centers, he had a personal interest in one of the former patients who had recovered.

She'd been so open about her family it triggered memories for him about his father and the life the three of them had enjoyed together before he'd died. Despite their poverty they'd had fun, too. He'd forgotten that aspect until Zoe started talking about her life. Because of her comments about family, he was seeing his own past through fresh eyes. Her story tugged at his heart and Vasso found he was no longer the same emotionally closed-up man who'd flown to New York on business.

August 17, Athens, Greece

Prickles of delight broke out on the back of Zoe's neck as the plane made its descent through a cloudless sky toward the runway. From her coach-class window seat she looked out at the sea, the islands. Closer still she made out the clay-roofed houses lining Athens's winding roads. This was Vasso Giannopoulos's world.

A sense of wonderment accompanied these sensations because she still couldn't believe she was coming to a place where she'd never been before and would be working. No doubt her ancestors experienced the same feelings when they arrived in the US, ready to embark on a new life.

How easy her life was by comparison! Instead of reaching the US by ship, she was on an airliner. Instead of having to undergo a holding time for immigrants, she'd been given safe passage right through to the Athens airport where she'd be taken care of. A job was waiting for her. So was the man who'd made all this possible. He was so wonderful she couldn't believe how lucky she was to have met him.

Kyrie Giannopoulos and his family were responsible for everything that had happened to her since she'd been admitted to the Giannopoulos Center in Astoria a year ago. Somehow he'd made it possible for her to work for his foundation. He'd said he'd be waiting for her when her plane landed.

The thought of seeing him again gave her butterflies. Surely meeting him a second time wouldn't cause her legs to almost buckle as they'd done the first time.

The mere sight of such a magnificent-looking man had haunted her thoughts whether she was awake or asleep.

After the plane touched down and taxied to the hangar, the seat belt came off and Zoe reached for her secondhand overnight bag. She followed the other passengers out of the plane to the terminal lounge where they went through customs. Her bag was searched. After she'd presented her passport and answered a few questions, a female airline attendant came up to her.

"You're Zoe Zachos?"

"Yes?"

"Come with me, please."

She got on a cart and was driven some distance to an elevator that descended to the ground floor. After another little ride the airline employee stopped the cart in front of a door. She got out and opened it. "Your ride is waiting out there."

The second Zoe walked through the door onto the tarmac where the hot sun beat down she saw a limousine in the distance. Once again her legs seemed to go weak when she spotted her benefactor lounging against the passenger side wearing sunglasses. This morning he'd dressed in a light blue sport shirt and tan chinos. He looked so wonderful she moaned before she realized he could have heard her.

"Thespinis Zachos, welcome to Greece."

No man should be this handsome. Zoe felt out of breath. "Thank you for meeting me."

"Of course. I hope you had a good flight." He took her bag and opened the rear door for her to get in.

"It was fine."

He went around the other side and got in with her bag so they sat across from each other. The interior smelled of the soap he must have used in the shower. Her reaction to him was over the top. Maybe there was something wrong with her.

"My driver will take us to the complex where my brother and I work. We'll stay in the penthouse. It's where we entertain guests and business people who must stay overnight. Tomorrow we'll fly to Paxos."

The limousine moved into the center of Athens. Another time and she might enjoy the scenery more, but right now she couldn't concentrate. After what he'd just told her, Zoe felt like a tongue-tied high school girl with a giant-sized crush on a man so far out of her league it was outrageous.

Glomming onto the safer subject of business she said, "Does Kyrie Megalos know you've hired me?"

"Not yet. I want him to meet you first."

She eyed him directly, but couldn't see his eyes behind the glasses. "Something tells me you're pulling the same thing on him that Father Debakis pulled on you." Vasso laughed hard. "He may not want me to be his assistant."

"In that case he'll give you another position. Don't worry. He won't suggest that you join a nunnery."

Laughter escaped her lips. His sense of humor was very appealing. "I shouldn't have said anything about Ms. Kallistos's remark. It wasn't kind of me."

"She should have known better than to say anything, so put it out of your mind."

"I have. Do you mind if I ask you some questions? Would you please tell me what kind of business you're in? I don't have a lot of information about you apart from your philanthropic work."

They'd driven into the heart of the downtown traffic. "If you'll look out your right window, you'll see a store coming up that says Alpha/Omega 24."

Zoe searched each shop. "Oh—there it is! *Everything from A to Z*. It's like one of the 7-Elevens in the States!"

"It's store number four, the first store we opened on the mainland."

"So you're a convenience store owner! Where are stores one through three?"

"On Paxos. My brother and I started our own chain years ago. They've spread throughout Greece."

"Now you're forcing me to guess." She eyed him with an impish expression. "Do you have as many as a hundred perchance?"

"We reached the hundred mark in Thessalonika."

Zoe gulped. "You weren't kidding, were you? Does your chain spread as far as Florina?"

"Farther, but it might interest you to know we have a store in Kozani. It's not far from the home of your ancestors."

She'd just been teasing, but he'd come back with an answer that filled her with awe. "So how many stores do you have altogether? Wait—don't answer that question." Heat filled her cheeks. "I'm being rude to pry. Forgive me."

"I don't mind. 2001, including the one we recently opened in Crete."

Zoe had tried to imagine the kind of money it took to run both centers. Now that she knew what kind of wealth was behind the foundation, she was blown away by the generosity of these men. "You really are perfect," she whispered.

"You have a lot to learn," he quipped, making her smile.

By now the limousine had turned down an alley and stopped at the side of a big complex. He got out with her bag and came around to help her. He had a remote on his key chain that opened the door to an elevator. They rode it to the top. When the door opened, she entered a glassed-in penthouse where she welcomed the air conditioning.

"If you'll come with me, I'll show you to the guest bedroom." She followed him through a hallway to a room with a fabulous view of Athens.

"What an incredible vista! Am I the luckiest woman in the world to sleep here tonight or what? You're far too good to me."

"We do this for business people who come to be interviewed for store manager positions."

"But I'm not exactly the kind of business person that generates a profit for you. I promise I'll do my best to help the patients at the hospital."

"I have no doubt of it." He put her overnight bag on the floor. "The en-suite bathroom is through that door. This area of the penthouse is all yours until we leave for Paxos. Now I'm sure you want to freshen up and relax, but first let me show you the kitchen."

She walked down the hallway to the other part of

the penthouse with him. "There's food and drink waiting for you if you're hungry. Please help yourself to anything you want while I go down to the office and check in. If you need me, just phone me, but I won't be long. After lunch we can go shopping if you're up to it."

"Thank you, Kyrie Giannopoulos." He was beyond kind and so many other things she'd lost count.

"Call me Vasso."

She smiled. "I'm Zoe."

He'd removed his sunglasses. "Zoe Zachos. Has anyone ever called you ZZ?"

Another laugh broke from her. He had a bit of an imp in him. "No. You're the first."

She felt the warmth from his black eyes long after he'd left the penthouse. Before doing anything else she walked over to the windows in the living room. The site of the Acropolis seemed as surreal as the whole experience of meeting Vasso Giannopoulos for the first time.

He had to be a very busy man, yet he'd taken time out to interview her himself. His insight about the emotions she would experience by moving to Greece revealed he was a man of empathy and compassion. Because of his goodness, her life was already being transformed.

CHAPTER THREE

"KYRIE GIANNOPOULOS?" Vasso's secretary spoke to him as he was passing through to his office. "Your brother said he'd be in after lunch. You've had two calls this morning from Maris Paulos who said it was urgent you get back to her."

In order to maintain his privacy, he gave out his cell phone number only to a few people. It forced Maris to reach him through his secretary. Until she'd mentioned Maris's name, Vasso hadn't thought about her.

"I'll call her now. Just so you know I'll be out of the office tomorrow. Akis will handle anything that comes up. If there's an emergency, he'll call me."

"Yes, sir."

Vasso went into his private office and rang Maris. After apologizing for not phoning her before his quick trip to New York, he asked if they could meet later that night. He'd stop by her condo. She sounded happy. That worried him because he didn't plan on seeing her after tonight. But Maris deserved the truth. She wanted more out of their relationship, but he didn't have it inside to give.

With that taken care of, he sequestered himself in his office for a couple of hours to do paperwork. Then he phoned Zoe.

"I'm glad you called. I've eaten lunch and was just leaving to go shopping."

"Then I'll take you."

"Oh no. You've done enough for me."

She was so different from other women he'd known whose interest in money seemed to be at the forefront. Both he and Akis felt the women they met were always assessing the worth of the Giannopoulos brothers, a real turnoff. But the Zoe he'd met so far seemed the exact opposite of a woman with that kind of hidden agenda.

"But you don't know where to go to shop."

"I'll be fine. I've lived in a big city all my life."

Vasso chuckled at her show of independence. "I realize that. But it would please me to accompany you this once. I'm coming upstairs now."

He was aware how grateful she was for everything. Pleased that she wasn't too tired, he arranged for his driver to meet them in the alley and drive them to the Attica department store near Syntagma Square.

She must have showered because she smelled sweet like a fragrant rose, dressed in a different skirt and blouse, when he helped her out of the limo. "You'll find everything you want here at a good price," he explained. "Shall we start in the luggage department? You'll need a large suitcase."

Her sculpted mouth curved into a smile. "You're reading my mind."

He liked the three-piece set of luggage she picked with a gold fleur-de-lis design on a dark red background. Vasso asked the clerk to find an employee to take their purchases out to the limousine waiting in front of the store.

Women's clothing was on the next floor. Zoe stopped him before they approached the counter. "Tell me something honestly. I saw Ms. Kallistos coming and going for a whole year. She only wore dresses or skirts and blouses. Would you suggest the same thing for me?"

"For work, yes. But you'll want other kinds of clothes, too. The island has a lot to offer when you're off of work. Among other things like jeans and shorts, you're going to need some good walking shoes and a bathing suit. Maybe a sweater or jacket when the nights cool down. Paxos is a different world from New York."

"I realize that. After living in the asphalt jungle, I'm relishing the quiet of a sun-filled island with no skyscrapers."

"You're going to undergo a big change. Tell me something. Do you have a laptop?"

"I had one for college, but it got destroyed in the fire."

"I was afraid that might be the case."

"Stop, Vasso. I know what you're going to say. I have enough money to buy another one."

"I believe you, but the foundation supplies all the equipment, so I have an idea. While you shop for clothes, I'll go to the electronics department and get you a computer. You'll need it when you're not at the center. It shouldn't take me long then I'll come back here for you."

"That sounds good. When we're through shopping, I'd like to take you to an early dinner. It will be on me. I'm afraid I won't have much money left to spend, so I'll let you pick a place my pathetic bank account can afford."

Those shimmering green eyes had him mesmerized. "I know just a spot in the Plaka. You'll love it."

"The old part of Athens," she mused. "To think I have Greek blood running through my veins, yet I've never been here. I promise to hurry because I can't wait to explore." Zoe's eagerness to live life made him see it through new eyes. "My father didn't like to go shopping with my mother because she took so long. I'll try not to be like her."

Amused by the comment he said, "Take all the time you need." He and Akis had grown up in a one-parent household, so he didn't know what it would be like to hear two parents going at it back and forth.

He left her talking to a saleswoman and headed for another part of the store. Besides a laptop, Vasso wanted her to have a new iPhone. He was still amazed by the extent of her loss, and even more astounded that she wasn't bitter or angry. She didn't know how to feel sorry for herself. That trait alone increased his admiration for her.

Fire had snatched away everything from her, including her parents. She was forced to build a life all over again. The woman was a survivor in more ways than one. He couldn't imagine another woman of his ac-

quaintance who would be eager to throw herself head-
long into an undetermined future.

She was beautiful inside and out. By some miracle
the lymphoma hadn't taken her life. Her gratitude was
over the top, yet it was that very quality that drew him
to her. You couldn't compare her to anyone else. She'd
maintained a great sense of humor even after the ordeal
she'd been through, which put her in a class by herself.

As Vasso had discussed with Akis, he was happy
they'd honored their father by creating the foundation.
But at the time, neither of them had any idea that their
money would be responsible for Zoe getting the medical
care she'd needed to whip the terrible disease. Today he
was thankful they'd had both centers built so he could
give her the job she wanted.

She's becoming important to you.

An hour later he found her and they walked out of
the store with their arms loaded. They were greeted by
a rash of photographers and journalists taking pictures
and calling out questions. Someone had tipped the paparazzi off that he'd come to the store. Vasso was furious this had happened, but Zoe seemed to handle it
well by ignoring them. He helped her into the smoked-
glass limo.

"You must be a celebrity," she said in a quiet voice.

"Anyone's a celebrity if they have money."

"There's a lot more to their interest in you than that!"

"It's because Akis and I came from a life of poverty. The media has been following us around for several years."

"How ghastly." He heard a sigh come out of her. "But

I think it's because you've done something extraordinary with your lives. To impart your fortune for the good of humanity puts you in a class all by yourselves. Surely you must realize how much people admire you for that. It's a great compliment to you, even if you don't like the publicity."

"Trust me, I don't," he muttered. "Let's forget them. I'm just sorry I couldn't protect you from them."

"I can understand that you don't relish being mobbed."

She understood a lot of things that made him feel closer to her. He was beginning to desire her company more and more. "It's one of the reasons why I don't spend all my time in Athens."

Her gaze darted to him. "I don't blame you. Under the circumstances, can we go back to the penthouse to eat dinner? Now that they've seen you, they'll probably follow us to the Plaka. If I can't pay for our meal, I can at least cook for you."

"I didn't bring you here to cook."

"You don't know how much I miss it. I was at the center for a whole year. No place of my own to have fun in the kitchen. Yours is a cook's dream, believe me! But please don't misunderstand me," she cried softly. "I just meant that now I'm well, I look forward to doing the things that once brought me pleasure. That is if you'll let me."

How could he say no to that? "Of course."

"If I say so myself, my parents' *taverna* brought in a lot of customers because of my mother's recipes that go way back."

Vasso couldn't hear enough about her life. "What was her specialty?"

"She had several, but my favorite main dish is *burek*."

His brows lifted. "You can make Macedonian *burek*?"

"So you like it?" Her eyes smiled.

"I had it once in Kozani and loved it."

"I'd like to make it for you if you'll let me loose in your kitchen. We'll see how it compares. But you need to start with an appetizer and some Mastika liqueur over ice. You probably don't have any of that on hand."

"Our number-four store should carry it. We'll stop there on the way back."

She reached in her purse and wrote something on a piece of paper before handing it to him. "Do you have all these items?"

He checked the list: dough ingredients, minced lamb, white cheese, spinach, *kasseri* yellow cheese, olives and tomatoes. They'd need to pick up at least half the items on her list. Vasso alerted his driver, then focused on her. "I'm already salivating."

"So am I." She chuckled. "There's nothing I'd love more than to fix you one of my family's specialties."

"Are you homesick for New York already?" He'd been worrying about that. To live on Paxos was going to be a huge adjustment for her.

"I'll never stop missing my parents, but there's nothing in New York for me now so I won't be missing it. Yet being able to cook up a meal in your kitchen will be a little like old times with my folks."

Her tremulous answer tugged on his emotions. He

had a longing to comfort her. "I can relate. So many times I've wanted to discuss business with our father."

"Every time I went into the hospital chapel, I would read the words on the plaque and wonder about him. When did he die?"

"Sixteen years ago."

She shook her head. "You were so young to lose him. That must have been terribly hard on your mother."

Vasso cleared his throat. "She died soon after I was born."

A slight gasp escaped her. "I had no idea. That means your father raised you and your brother alone. Did you have grandparents?"

"They died too, but that's another story."

"Will you tell me about it?"

"Maybe. Over dinner." Just then the limo pulled in front of the store. "I'll be right back." He got out and hurried inside the crowded interior.

"Boss?"

"*Yassou,* Galen. I'm here to pick up a bottle of Mastika liqueur."

"I think we've got one left. It's been on the top shelf in back for a while."

"The older, the better."

"I'll get it."

"Let me." Vasso found it and the other items needed. After putting some bills on the counter he said, "Talk to you later."

When he got back in the limo with the groceries, he handed the bottle to Zoe. "Is this what you wanted?"

She looked delighted. "I can't believe you stock it

here. No wonder your stores have been such a huge success. This is my lucky day. Now I'm going to have to produce a meal that will win the Giannopoulos seal of approval."

He laughed, realizing that she had a knack for bringing that out in him. When she'd walked into Alexandra's office last week, he hadn't been prepared for the effect this utterly feminine woman would have on him. But the first impression she'd made on him, with her wavy blond hair, had brought a spring-like newness into his life.

When they arrived at the penthouse, they loaded everything into the elevator and rode to the top. Before long they'd taken everything to her bedroom. Then they gravitated to the kitchen where he helped her gather all the ingredients to make their dinner.

It was fun working side by side. "This is a brand-new experience for me."

"How come?"

"I've never brought a woman to the penthouse, let alone allowed her to take over the kitchen."

"You're kidding! Not one girlfriend?"

"I have a confession to make. After Akis and I started making real money, we worried whether the women we met only wanted us for what we could do for them. We refused to bring them here. It was safer to take them to dinner. That probably sounds very cynical to you."

"No. Not after what you've told me about your life. There's a lot of avarice in the world. I imagine anyone who has the kind of money you make would have trouble trusting someone who wanted to get close to him."

"Akis had the same trust issues, but he's married now. When he first met Raina, he fell hard. But his fear of not being loved for himself caused him all sorts of pain."

"How did they meet?"

"She flew over to attend the wedding reception of her Greek friend Chloe who'd lived with her in California. Akis had been the best man. After running away from the maid of honor who was after him, he picked on Raina to dance with him until he could get out of the room safely. That accidental meeting changed his life."

Zoe chuckled. "When did he know she was the real thing?"

"He always knew it in his heart, but he needed a nudge. I did some research on her and learned she was Raina Maywood."

"What? Isn't she the famous American heiress to the Maywood fortune?"

He nodded. "When Akis found out, everything changed. He knew that she wasn't after his money, but he had another problem."

"Why?"

"He didn't feel good enough for her. Our lack of formal education made him worry that she'd soon grow bored of him. On the night she was leaving to go back to California, I called her and begged her to go to him. She was broken up, not understanding why he couldn't accept that she loved him. Luckily she took my advice and convinced him he was her whole world. They got married fast and I've never seen him so happy."

"Was that a little hard on you?"

He looked in those compassionate green eyes. "You have a lot of insight, Zoe. Until they said their vows, I never realized how connected we'd been throughout our lives. When you told me how close you were to your parents, you were describing me and Akis.

"I felt lost at first, but slowly that feeling started to dissipate. Raina has been a joy and makes my little brother so happy I can't imagine life without her now. With a baby on the way, Akis isn't the same man."

"A baby? That's wonderful!"

"When Akis and I were young and struggling, we couldn't have imagined this day."

She flashed him a smile. "And now there's a lot more to come. Your lives are a miracle, too."

The things she said...

They kept working in harmony. Zoe definitely knew her way around a kitchen. By seven o'clock, they sat down at the dining room table to eat the best home-cooked food he'd ever tasted.

They started with the Mastika poured over ice and served with a grilled *krusevo* cheese pie for an appetizer. The *burek* was out of this world. Layers of dough with white cheese, minced lamb and spinach garnished with tomatoes and onions marinated in a special herb sauce. It was so good he ate more than he normally did at a meal.

"You could open your own *taverna*, Zoe."

"What a lovely compliment. Before I decided to go

to college, I actually thought about it, but my parents insisted I try college first. You know the rest. Then the day came when the world as I knew it went away."

Vasso didn't want her to think sad thoughts. "We can be thankful you didn't go away with it or I wouldn't have been treated to such a feast."

"You're just being nice."

"Not true. Now it's my turn to pay you back by doing the dishes while you get your bags packed. Tomorrow we'll have breakfast here and fly to Paxos."

That was the plan, but he discovered he was loving her company so much he wanted to keep her here in Athens for a while and show her around. It shocked him that he could feel this attracted when they'd known each other for such a short while. How had he existed all this time before she came into his life?

"Before I do that, I want to hear about your grandparents. It's sad to think you didn't have them in your life either." She started clearing the table. It thrilled him she didn't want to leave him quite yet.

"Both sets of grandparents came from Paxos."

"Ah. I'm beginning to understand why the island has been so important to you."

"The grandparents on my father's side and their children—with the exception of our father—were victims of the malaria epidemic on Paxos. In the early sixties it was eradicated, but they didn't escape it."

"Amazing that your father didn't get the disease."

"No. Pockets of people were spared. No one knows why. Maybe he was naturally immune. A poor fisherman who lived on Paxos took care of my father. Together they caught and sold fish at the market in Loggos.

"After the fisherman died, our father continued to fish in the man's rowboat. It was in town he met our mother. She and her brother Kristos survived the epidemic that had killed her family. He emigrated to New York to find a new life, but was killed crossing a busy street."

"How awful. That explains his name on the plaque!"

"Yes. Apparently my mother grieved when he left Greece. In time she and my father fell in love and got married. She worked in the olive groves. Together they scraped to make ends meet any way they could.

"I was born first. Then Akis came along eleven months later. But the delivery was too hard on *Mama* who was in frail health and she died."

He could see Zoe was trying not to break down. "It pains me that neither of you knew your mother. That's so tragic. I at least didn't lose my parents until a year ago, so I have all the memories of growing up with them."

His eyes met hers. "In ways I think your pain has been much worse. We never knew her. She didn't know about her brother getting killed, which was a good thing. We were so young when she died we had no memories except the ones our father told us about. But you lived, laughed and cried with your parents for your whole life, doing everything together. That's a loss I can't comprehend."

"Thanks to the therapy provided by your generosity, I'm doing fine these days. Truly your father had to be a saint to manage on his own. No wonder you wanted to do something extraordinary to honor his name."

"To be sure, he was our hero. I was six when we helped him in the store where he sold the fish. Neither Akis nor I went to school regularly because we needed the money too badly. Poverty was all my father knew. I know it hurt his pride that we boys were known as the poor Giannopoulos kids.

"Most people looked down on us. But no one could know the depth of our pain when he was diagnosed with lymphoma and died. At that point we only had each other in order to survive. *Papa* asked me to look out for Akis."

Zoe gasped. "How old were you?"

"Thirteen and fourteen."

"Overnight you two had to become men."

"All we knew was that we only had ourselves in order to survive. The man who owned the store died and his wife needed help. We asked if we could stay on and work for her. By then the woman was used to us and she really needed the help. So she let us work in her store.

"Akis and I traded off jobs. He'd wait on the customers while I went fishing and picked olives. Then we'd turn the schedule around. We worked long hours."

"When did you fit in some time to play, let alone attend school?"

"Not very often."

"I'd love to meet Akis."

"That can be arranged. But enough about me. Now I want to change the subject. Have you ever ridden in a helicopter?"

She shook her head, still haunted by what he'd told her. "No. I've always wondered what it would be like."

"Does the thought of it make you nervous?"

"Kind of." A hint of smile broke the corner of her mouth. "Ask me tomorrow when I actually have to climb inside it."

"Once you get used to it, you won't want to travel any other way."

"I'll have to take your word for it." After a hesitation... "Vasso?"

He'd started loading the dishwasher. "What is it?"

"You've been so kind to me my debt to you keeps growing. I told Father Debakis what I'm going to tell you. If it takes me the rest of my life, and it probably will, I intend to pay back every cent your foundation spent on my behalf.

"Every inmate at the center would like to tell you of their gratitude in person. You've saved the lives of many people who had no hope. It's staggering the good you've already done." Her lower lip started to tremble. "You're wonderful."

Her words moved him. "If I started to tell you all the things I think about you, there wouldn't be enough hours."

Color rushed into her cheeks. "You're full of it, but it's nice to hear."

"How could the man you had been seeing before the fire have walked away?" he whispered. That question had been gnawing at him since she'd first told him she'd had a boyfriend.

"I don't know." She half laughed as she said it. "He broke my heart when he made the decision to move to Boston. I went through a lot of pain, but with hindsight I can see he didn't love me in that heart-whole way or he couldn't have left.

"After several months I decided I was lucky. If there'd been no fire, would he have eventually asked me to marry him? I don't have an answer. But the fact remains that he wanted to go to Boston more than he wanted to be with me. I certainly don't blame him. To be with a terminally ill patient would mean he had to forget his dreams. That's asking too much of a man unless he's met the love of his life."

"Was he the love of *your* life?" Vasso needed to hear her answer.

"Let me put it this way. I had boyfriends. Some meant more to me than others. But I met Chad while we were both on that study abroad program in England. That was his graduation-from-college present. It threw us together for two weeks. You can learn a lot about someone on a trip like that. We had fun and didn't want it to end after we returned to New York.

"The more I saw of him, the more I thought maybe he could be *the* one. But the circumstances that brought me to this hospital put an end to the relationship we'd enjoyed. Now you know the story of my life."

"But not the pain you suffered when he didn't stay with you."

She took a deep breath. "It was awful. I won't lie about that. If ever I needed someone who loved me that was the time. But his love wasn't the forever kind. That was a hard lesson to learn. It taught me not to put my faith in a man." She looked up at him. "That's as honest as I know how to be."

The man had been a fool. Vasso's black eyes burned into hers. "Just look what he missed. Thank you for telling me."

"I've probably said too much." After taking a few steps away from him, she turned around. "Thanks for listening. I've talked your ear off."

"It was my pleasure. Just so you know, I have to go out again for a little while. I'll try not to disturb you when I come back in."

"Please don't worry about me. Good night." In the next instant she'd disappeared into the other part of the penthouse.

While Vasso stood there overwhelmed by tender new feelings she brought out in him, his cell rang. He pulled it from his pocket. When he saw it was his brother, he clicked on. "Akis?"

"I thought I'd check in. How's everything going with Thespinis Zachos?"

He held his breath. "Fine."

Low laughter bubbled out of Akis. "Come on. It's *me* you're talking to."

"I'm aware of that. I took her shopping, then we had dinner and now she's gone to bed. Tomorrow morning we'll fly to Paxos."

"I can read between the lines, bro. Let's try this again. How are things really going?"

"The press intruded as we left the department store, so we came back to the penthouse and she cooked dinner. It was probably the best Macedonian food I've ever eaten."

"I guess that makes sense considering her parents ran a *taverna*."

"She only has one more semester before she receives her college degree in English, but Alexandra didn't know about that. It's just as well Zoe will be working on this side of the Atlantic. Tonight she told me she wants to meet you and thank you for saving her life. If you want my opinion, she'll charm Yiannis until she has him eating out of her hand."

"It wouldn't surprise me considering she's already accomplished that feat with you. A woman cooking in our kitchen? That has to be a first. I guess it's too late to tell you to go slow, the same advice you once gave me. *Kalinihta*."

"*Kalinihta*."

Zoe was still on his mind when he arrived at Maris's condo twenty minutes later. "Vasso—you're finally here!" she said after opening the door. "I've missed you."

But when she would have reached for him, he backed away.

A hurt look entered her eyes. "What's wrong?"

Vasso hated to do this, but for both their sakes he needed to break things off with her. Zoe filled his thoughts to the exclusion of all else, but that made him anxious when he remembered how he'd once felt about Sofia.

As for Maris, he didn't like hurting her when she'd done nothing wrong, but as he'd told his brother, she wasn't the one. Still, he couldn't help feeling a little guilty about doing this to her.

"Let's sit down."

"I don't want to." Her chin lifted. "Why do I get the feeling you're here to tell me it's over with us?"

Being a journalist, she had good instincts and was always out for the truth. "To be honest, while I was in New York I had a chance to think. I don't believe there's a future for us and I thought it would be better to tell you now. I like you very much, Maris. We've had some good times, but—"

"But you're ready to move on," she interrupted him.

"Surely you know I don't mean to hurt you."

"One of my friends told me this was how it would end with you, but I didn't want to believe her. So who's the new woman in the life of the famous Vasso Giannopoulos?"

He stared her down. "Would you have preferred that I told you this over the phone?"

She had the grace to shake her head. "No. It hurts no matter what."

Vasso admired her honesty. "I've enjoyed the times we've spent together and I wish you the very best in the future."

Maris walked over to the door and opened it. "I'm afraid I can't wish you the same, but one day I'll get over it. I thought we had a real connection. Being with you has meant everything to me. Too bad it was one-sided. *Adio,* Vasso."

He left for the penthouse. After reflecting on what had just happened at Maris's condo, he realized this had been the story of his life since Sofia Peri had rejected his marriage proposal. That was ten years ago after he'd finished his military service. It had taken a long time to get over the pain of her marrying someone else. From then on he'd buried himself in business with Akis.

Over the last few years he'd been with different women when time permitted, but he'd ended every relationship prematurely and had pretty well given up on finding his soul mate.

Then Zoe Zachos had walked in Alexandra's office, causing his heart to beat so hard he hadn't been the same since. In the last twenty-four hours her effect on him had been staggering.

After getting used to being in a helicopter, Zoe was entranced by everything she saw. They passed over so many historic places in the Ionian Sea she'd only read about in books or seen in the movies she was awestruck.

From the copilot's seat, Vasso looked back at her through his sunglasses. Today he'd dressed in a white crewneck and white cargo pants. It wasn't fair one man out of millions could be so attractive. Using the mic he said, "We're coming up on Paxos."

She looked down from the window. "But it's so tiny!"

"It's only seven miles by three. Too small for an airport which is just the way all of us who live on the island like it."

Zoe leaned forward. "What do you mean *we*?"

A dazzling white smile greeted her gaze. "As I told you last night, my brother and I were born here. We had the center built here. *My* home is here."

Her heart pounded so hard she was afraid he could hear it. "*This* is where you live when you're not in Athens or traveling for business?"

"That's right."

In shock that she'd be working so close to this fantastic man's home, she turned to the window once more.

"We're flying to the center now. I've phoned Yiannis to expect me. Once inside his office you two can meet and talk about the position."

As the helicopter dipped, she made out several fishing villages with colorful harbors. Lower and lower now, she took in the lush deep greenery of olive trees sprinkled with pastel-colored clusters of small villas. Quaint waterside cottages came into view. One stretch of fine white sand scalloped the green coves and gave way to another seaside village. On the outskirts now she realized they were headed for a sprawling white complex peeking out of the olive groves.

She held her breath as they were about to land. This time it set down on the hospital roof, but she wasn't as nervous as when the helicopter had lifted off the penthouse roof.

"Are you all right, Zoe?"

"Yes. I was just thinking how my parents and I would have loved transportation like this all the years we lived in New York City. I'm spoiled already."

But the minute the words were out of her mouth, it made her realize she did too much talking. He brought that out in her. Now that they'd landed, she didn't want to prolong the conversation and unbuckled her seat belt.

She thanked the pilot and climbed out of the helicopter wearing one of her new outfits. The navy cotton dress with the white print had a crew neck and sleeves to the elbow. It was summery light, yet had a certain classy look she felt would be appropriate for the job.

When Vasso walked her to the stairs that led to an elevator, she felt his gaze travel over her. Hopefully he approved of her choice of dress. But the second Zoe entertained the thought she was irritated with herself that he was on her mind way too much. The fact that his home was so close to the center meant she'd probably see him more often than she would have imagined. It shouldn't thrill her so much.

"This is a private elevator," he explained as they entered. "The hospital takes up three floors. On the second floor there's a walkway to the three-floor convalescent center. Yiannis's office is on the main floor off the foyer at the main entrance."

They exited the elevator and walked along the corridor of one wing, passing a set of doors with stained-glass inserts signifying the chapel. Zoe looked around. "I love the Hellenic architecture." Their eyes met for a moment. "It flows like the sculpture of a Greek temple."

Her comment seemed to please him. "When we had it built, we tried to preserve the flavor of the island. The kitchen and cafeteria are in the other wing. The eating area extends outside the doors to the patio overlooking the water."

"A hospital built in the middle of paradise," she mused aloud. "If I'd been privileged to recover here, I know I would have lived on the patio. To be near the sea would be heavenly."

When they came to the foyer filled with exotic plants and tubs of flowers, he smiled warmly at a woman probably fifty years old who appeared to run the reception area. "Hebe." He kissed her cheek.

The other woman beamed. "Yiannis said you were coming. It's always good to see you."

"The feeling is mutual. Kyria Lasko, I'd like you to meet Thespinis Zoe Zachos from New York City. She's here for an interview with Yiannis."

"Ah? I hope it means what I think it means." Her friendly brown eyes were so welcoming Zoe was able to relax a little.

"How do you do, Kyria Lasko?" She shook hands with her.

"Call me Hebe."

After being around a cold Alexandra for a whole year, Hebe Lasko was like a breath of fresh air. "Thank you."

"Hebe is the head of our business office located down the other hall," he explained, "but she's been doing double duty as Yiannis's assistant."

Zoe turned to him. "You mean this front desk is where I would work?" she asked quietly.

He nodded. "Yiannis's office is through that door behind the desk. Let's go."

She followed him around the counter where he knocked on the door and was told to enter. Vasso ushered her inside and her first thought was that she'd entered a room in a naval museum.

There were models of ships on the shelving and several framed photographs of the former military leader in dress uniform. Other small photographs showed him with his striking wife. What an attractive man he was with gray hair and dark brown eyes!

As the two men embraced, she noticed he was shorter than Vasso and was dressed in a short-sleeved white shirt and dark trousers. They exchanged comments and his hearty laugh filled the office. Then his eyes swerved to Zoe.

"So, Vasso… I see you've brought along a visitor. A very lovely one at that. Is this some kind of announcement you're making?"

CHAPTER FOUR

THE INFERENCE COULDN'T have been more obvious. Zoe tried to repress a groan.

"In a way, yes! I've found you the assistant you've been needing. Yiannis? Meet Thespinis Zoe Zachos. She was born and raised in New York City, and she's a bilingual Greek American. I was so impressed with her I plucked her away and brought her here. I'm going to leave the two of you to get acquainted and take a look around the facility, but I'll be back."

He disappeared so fast Zoe felt like the foundation had just been knocked out from under her.

The older man smiled at her. "Sit down, Zoe. How come you're still *thespinis*?"

He immediately reminded her of her father who was always outspoken. "I haven't met the right man yet."

He frowned before taking his seat. "What's wrong with the men in New York?"

"I'm afraid the problem lies with me."

"What are you? Twenty-two?" he asked with a teasing smile.

"I'll be twenty-five next weekend."

His brows lifted. "That old." Laughter broke from her. "All right. Let's start from the beginning. Vasso wouldn't do this to me if he weren't a hundred-percent sure you're the person I'm looking for to help me run this place. Tell me about your background."

Without going into too much unnecessary detail, she told him about her family and education. When she got to the part about the fire, she managed to stay composed. Then she told him about her lymphoma and the year she'd spent at the center.

"My family priest knew how much I wanted to work for the center to pay back all it had done for me. When the doctor gave me another clean bill of health, Father Debakis arranged for Kyrie Giannopoulos to interview me. He said your assistant had to leave and you were looking for a new one."

The older man suddenly sat forward. "You're cancer-free?"

"At the moment, yes. But there's no guaran—"

"Forget that," he broke in on her. "You're exactly what's been needed around here. How long before you have to go back to New York?"

"I—I don't plan to," she stammered. "I told Kyrie Giannopoulos I'd like to work for the foundation for the rest of my life. It will take that long to pay his family back for all they've done for me. If I'm given a job here, this is where I'll plant new roots."

"You're hired, Thespinis Zachos."

Zoe couldn't believe it. "But you hardly know anything about me."

"Of course I do. Vasso wouldn't have brought you

here if he had any questions. This center needs input. Who better than you to see what we're doing right or wrong? When I was in the navy, we had informers who quietly gathered information helpful to the brass. With you around, I'm already feeling like I'm back on duty with a crew I can count on."

To hide her joy that he'd accepted her on Vasso's say-so alone, she reached in her tote bag and pulled out a seven-by-seven-inch box wrapped in paper showing various American naval frigates. "This is for you." She handed it to him. "I would have given it to you whether I got the job or not."

Yiannis eyed her in surprise before opening it. "What's this?" He pulled out a creamware mug and read aloud the words printed in dark red ink. "*We have met the enemy and they are ours.*"

"That's the image of Edward Preble," she explained. "He was a naval hero at the time of the war in Tripoli. Kyrie Giannopoulos told me you're a naval hero and have collected naval memorabilia. I knew he meant Greek memorabilia, but I thought you could add this mug as a piece to show your appreciation for an American naval hero. A little diversity makes things more interesting, don't you think? If nothing else, you could drink coffee from it."

He burst into laughter at the same moment Vasso joined them. "It looks like you two are getting along famously."

Yiannis lifted the mug. "Did you see this?"

"No."

"Take a look. Our new employee just presented me

a gift to add to my collection." Vasso shot her a knowing glance before he took it to examine.

The retired admiral sat back in his chair, eyeing the two of them with satisfaction. "The only thing I need to ask now is: how soon can you come to work? I needed you yesterday. Poor Hebe has been run ragged doing the job of two people."

Zoe liked him a lot already. For years she'd worked with her parents at the *taverna*. It would be nice to feel useful again with someone dynamic like him. Despite his grief over the loss of his wife, he had a buoyant spirit.

"Tomorrow morning? Today I need to find a place to live."

"Tomorrow at eight-thirty it is. You've made my day."

She got to her feet. "You've made mine by being willing to give me a chance. I can't thank you enough and I'll try not to make you sorry." Zoe shook his hand and headed for the door. She needed to use the restroom she'd seen down the hall.

After she emerged, Vasso caught up to her. "We'll fly back to my house for the car and drive into Loggos. When we reach the village I thought we'd stop for lunch and check out several furnished apartments I told you about. Hopefully one will suit."

Things were moving so fast she could hardly think. "Do all the people working at the center live in Loggos?"

"They come from all over the island, but Loggos is a good place for you to start out. The only bus picks up

passengers in front of the main *taverna* and will bring
you to the center. It makes three stops a day there in
front of the fountain, so you'll always have a ride home.
I suggest you give it a month. If it isn't to your liking,
you can live wherever you want on the island, but you'll
need a car. I'll help you with that when you're ready."

"Thank you, but I don't have a driver's license, Vasso.
If I decide to buy a car, then I'll have to take lessons
first." He'd already spoiled her so completely she would
never be out of his debt. Vasso was so caring and concerned—the differences between him and Chad were
like day and night.

The flight back to his house passed in a blur. There
was too much to absorb. She couldn't take it all in.
Once again she felt the helicopter dip and fly toward
a charming, solitary white beach villa with a red tiled
roof. They landed on a pad in the middle of a copse of
olive trees, causing her breath to escape. There was no
doubt in her mind this was Vasso's sanctuary.

She spotted a dark gray Lexus parked nearby.

Once the rotors stopped spinning, Vasso unbuckled
the seat belt. While he removed her luggage, she jumped
down so he wouldn't have to help her and reached for
the train case. Without waiting for him, she headed
for his car.

"Zoe? The house is in the other direction. Where do
you think you're going?"

"To get in your car. I'm assuming I'll be able to move
into an apartment today and don't want to put you out
any more than necessary."

"We're not in that big a hurry."

"*I* am. Once I have a place to live and am on the job, I'm going to feel free. I don't expect you to understand. But being the recipient of so much generosity for so long has become a burden, if that makes sense. I hope I haven't offended you."

"Not at all."

Zoe tried to sound matter of fact about it, but it was hard to hide the sudden alarm that had gripped her. Vasso was already bigger than life to her. She'd been in the penthouse that he and his brother used for business. She'd even cooked a meal there! Because she was a future employee, Vasso had opened every door for her.

But to enter his home would be crossing a line into his private world she refused to consider. She might like it too much. No way did she dare make a move like that. Already she was afraid that her feelings for him might interfere with their professional relationship.

Yiannis Megalos had made an assumption about her and Vasso the second he'd seen them walk in the office. She could imagine how it looked. Obviously Vasso had gone out of his way to do something unprecedented to accommodate her desire to work for the foundation. But this last favor to help her get settled had to be the end of it. Her self-preservation instinct had kicked in to guard her heart.

If she came to depend on Vasso, how did she know he wouldn't be like Chad in the sense that he wasn't invested in the relationship to the extent that she was? Zoe refused to put her trust in a man again where it came to her heart. There was no point anyway since her cancer could be coming back. Better to concentrate on her work and give it her all. In the end she'd be spared a lot of heartache.

She waited for Vasso to bring the rest of her luggage to the car. He used a remote to open the doors and put the luggage in the trunk. Zoe took advantage of the time to get in the front seat.

When he got behind the wheel, he turned to her. Suddenly they were too close. She was so aware of him she could hardly breathe. "Why do you think you would be putting me out?"

Until now she hadn't felt any tension between them, but after what he'd just said, she feared she'd irritated him after all. "Because you've done much for me, it doesn't make sense that you'll have to come back here later for my luggage."

"I'm in no hurry. Have I led you to believe that?"

She moistened her lips nervously. "No. Of course not. You're such a gentleman you'd never make anyone uncomfortable. But you and your brother run a huge corporation. Everything was going smoothly until you were asked to interview me. I know Father Debakis laid a big guilt trip on you, so don't try to deny it."

"I wasn't going to."

She took a breath. "Thank you. Since then you've had to deal with me. As if I'm not already indebted to you several hundred thousand dollars."

"Zoe—have you considered the situation from our point of view? Our father died a terrible death while Akis and I stood by helplessly. To know that the foundation has helped someone like you means everything to us. It's a pleasure to see you get back on your feet."

Her head bowed. "You're the two best men I know."

"That's nice to hear. What do you say we drive to the village? After lunch you can take a look at the furnished apartments available. One is over a bakery, the other over a gift shop."

She flicked him a worried glance. "A bakery?"

The second Zoe's question was out, Vasso realized where he'd gone wrong and gripped the steering wheel so hard it was a miracle he didn't break it. "Forgive me for forgetting where you'd lived." She'd never forget the fire that had traveled to the kitchen of her parents' *taverna*.

"We'll cross that one off the list. You'll like Kyria Panos. She's a widow who's been renting the apartment over the gift shop since her son got married. You'll have your own entrance in the back. The only drawback is that it's a one-bedroom apartment."

"I don't need more than one."

"You're so easy to please it's scary."

"Not all the time."

"Give me an example."

"If I told you some of my hang-ups, you'd send me back to New York on the next flight."

"How about just one?"

"A couple of my girlfriends wanted me to room with them in college, but I'd always had my own space at home and didn't want to give it up. They teased me about it and tried to talk me into it. But the more they

tried, the more I didn't like it. I guess I'm really a private person and get prickly when I sense my space is
being invaded. That's why I lived with my parents."

"There's nothing wrong with that. But maybe the day
will come when you won't want to be alone."

"If you're talking about marriage, I'm not planning
on getting married."

"Why?"

"I like my life the way it is." She turned to him. "I
really like the way it is right now. I don't want some
man bossing me around. One of the older patients at the
center used to tell me about the fights she had with her
husband. For the most part my parents got along great,
so I couldn't relate to this woman's life. He pecked at
her all day long."

Vasso's black brows lifted. "Pecked?"

"Yes. You know. Like a hen pecks at her food. That's
what he'd do to her about everything. What she bought,
what she ate, what she did with her spare time. Peck,
peck, peck."

Laughter pealed out of Vasso. "Most of the older
women in the center made similar comments about
married life. I decided I was well enough off being on
my own."

"My brother loves married life."

"Maybe that's true, but what does his wife have to
say when he's not listening?"

She heard a chuckle. "I have no idea."

"Maybe it's better you don't know." He laughed
louder. She loved hearing it. "I could see in Yiannis's
eyes that he wonders why you aren't married, Vasso.

Admit you don't want some wife leading you around by the nose."

"Now there's a thought."

She laughed. "I'm only teasing." No woman would ever do that with a man like him. The female who caught his eye would be the luckiest one on the planet. No way did she dare dream about a romantic relationship with Vasso.

If it didn't work out, she wouldn't be able to handle it. Just admitting that to herself proved that her feelings for Vasso already ran deeper than those she'd had for Chad. The two men weren't comparable. No one could ever measure up to Vasso.

"You may be teasing, but I can hear the underlying half truths."

Time to change the subject. "Tell me about my landlady, Kyria Panos. Did she henpeck her husband?"

"As I recall they did a lot of shouting, but for the most part it was good-natured."

"That's nice. I bet you know everyone around here."

"Not everyone," he murmured, "but Akis and I rented an apartment along this waterfront when we started up our business years ago, so we're friends with many of the owners around here."

Vasso started the engine and drove them through the olive groves to the village. An hour later, after they were filled with spinach pie and ouzo lemonade, he carried the last of Zoe's luggage up the stairs to the furnished apartment. The front room window overlooked the horseshoe-shaped harbor. The minute he saw Zoe's expression, he knew she liked the view and the typical blue-and-white décor.

She smiled at him. "This place is really cozy and so colorful. I love it, and it's all mine."

After what she'd recounted earlier about needing her space, he could believe she was serious. But it bothered him that she was so happy about it.

"I'm glad you like it. Our number-one store is just a few doors down. You can grab breakfast there while you're waiting for the bus."

"If I do too much of that I'm going to get fat, but I want you to know I'm ecstatic to be here," she exclaimed. Vasso couldn't imagine her with a weight problem, not with her beautiful face and body. Her green eyes lifted to his. "Cinderella may have had a fairy godmother, but I've had the perfect godfather who has granted my every wish. Now that your mission has been accomplished, I release you to get back to your life."

Zoe could tease all she wanted, but he sensed she wanted him to leave. The hell of it was he didn't want to go. Since she'd flown to Athens, he'd been a different person and couldn't spend enough hours with her. She was so entertaining he never knew what was going to come out of her mouth next. The thought of her ever being interested in another man disturbed him more than he wanted to admit.

He'd only scratched the surface of her life, but she'd drawn the line at entering his home. Why? Was it because she didn't trust him after what Chad had done to her? Did she see every man through the filter put there by the other man's defection? Was she afraid of marriage because of that experience?

She didn't bat an eye over renting an apartment with one bedroom. Did that mean she really did like to be alone? He could hear Akis commenting on the subject. *Are you still feeling responsible for her, or is there something more eating at you?*

Vasso had to admit there were a lot of things eating at him. He sucked in his breath. "If you need help of any kind, I'm only as far away as the phone."

"You think I don't know that?" She walked him to the door. "I'm sure we'll see each other again. Hopefully by then Yiannis will have a good word for me."

As Vasso had predicted to Akis, she already had Yiannis eating out of her hand.

"Stay safe, Zoe."

"You, too."

He heard the slight wobble in her voice. It stayed with him as he left the apartment, taking with him the haunting image of her blond hair and sparkling eyes, not to mention the white-on-navy print dress that clung to her figure.

Once he reached the car, he took off for his villa. But he was too upset by emotions churning inside him to stay on the island till morning. If he did that, he'd be tempted to drop by the apartment with some excuse to see her again. Instead he alerted the pilot that he was ready to fly back to Athens.

After the helicopter touched down at the penthouse, he checked any messages his private secretary might have left. Apparently Akis had dealt with everything important. Grabbing a cup of coffee, he went back to his office to dig into the inventories still left to get through. But first he texted his brother.

I'm back in the office working. Zoe Zachos is living in the apartment above Kyria Panos's shop. All is well with Yiannis.

Not two minutes later his brother phoned him back. "Have you contacted Maris?"

"Yes."

"That's good. She phoned several times yesterday wanting to know about you."

"Sorry."

"I get it. So how are things with her?"

"I broke it off with her last night."

"I guess that doesn't surprise me. Whatever happened to 'slow down'?"

Vasso let out a morose laugh. "Look where it got *you*."

CHAPTER FIVE

August 26

ALREADY IT WAS FRIDAY. Five days without seeing Vasso felt like five years. In the time they'd been together, they'd confided in each other about the very personal things in their lives. He knew information about her she hadn't shared with anyone else. Zoe loved being with him. She ached for his company. He brought excitement into her life.

But she'd better get used to separations because the foundation was only a small part of the huge company he ran with his brother. And the more she heard about their generosity, the greater her need grew to do all she could to help in such a humanitarian effort.

Over the last five days Zoe had been able to introduce herself to every inmate except the twenty-four-year-old guy from Athens named Nestor. The resident therapist was worried about him. He'd been undergoing chemo in the infusion clinic and was in a depressed state, refusing to talk to anyone.

The therapist told her Nestor had been a receptionist

at a hotel that went bankrupt. He couldn't find a job and after a few months became homeless. Two months later, he was diagnosed with lymphoma. He usually lived on the steps of a Greek Orthodox Church but spent a lot of time under the nearby bridge with his other homeless friends.

This was the case of another kind priest who got in contact with the center on Paxos and arrangements had been made to get him admitted. Zoe found out that the helicopters owned by the Giannopoulos brothers helped transport patients like Nestor from all over Greece when there was no other solution.

Through Yiannis she learned more about Vasso and Akis. Born to poverty, they'd built a billion-dollar business in such a short period of time it stunned the Greek financial world. That was why the media was always in their face. It explained why Vasso made his home here on Paxos. Evidently his younger brother lived on the nearby island of Anti Paxos.

Just thinking about Vasso caused her breath to catch.

Already she was finding out that the homeless patients were afraid there'd be nothing for them to look forward to once they had to leave the center. That was an area needing to be addressed. Zoe had known the kind of depression that was drawing the life out of Nestor. Now that lunch was over, it would be a good time to visit him.

She took some oranges and plastic forks with her. When she reached his room she found him half lying in a recliner wheelchair. Every room had a sign that said,

"Reality is never as dark as the places your brain visits in anticipation." How true.

"Nestor?"

He opened his eyes. They were a warm brown. Despite his bald head, he was good looking, or would be if he were animated.

"If you're too nauseated to talk, I've been there. Mind if I sit down?" She pulled a chair over to him and set the items on the table. "I'm new here. My name's Zoe. I just got out of the hospital in New York City after being there a year. I had lymphoma too."

That brought a spark. "You?"

"I thought I'd be dead by now, but it didn't happen. I also lost my family in a fire, which made things much worse. I understand you don't have family either."

"No. My grandfather raised me, but he died."

"Well we're both very lucky that the Giannopoulos Foundation exists. They've given me a job here. What kind of a job do you want when you leave?"

"I won't be leaving," he murmured.

"Of course you will. As my priest told me, God didn't come to my rescue for nothing. I know how the nausea can make you think you'll never be better. But it will pass. I brought you some things that helped me.

"If you open and smell an orange before you eat, the aroma will make the food tolerable. At least it worked for me. Also, the metal forks and spoons sometimes make you gag. Try eating your food with a plastic fork and see if it makes any difference."

He eyed her with curiosity. Good!

"See you soon. Maybe one of these days we'll go

outside on the patio and have a game of cards. I'll bring a scarf and some snacks. I have an idea you'd make a dashing pirate. You know, young-Zorba-the-Greek style."

She left the room and continued on her rounds until the end of the day. Yiannis wanted her to be his eyes and ears. Besides keeping up on the paperwork, he expected her to make suggestions to improve their services. What was missing? That's what he wanted to know.

Now that she'd been hired full time, they would take turns covering for each other Saturday and Sunday. This coming weekend was his turn to work. Suddenly Zoe had more freedom than she knew what to do with.

When she walked out to catch the bus, the fountain of Apollo was playing. Again she was reminded of Vasso who, like the sun god in his chariot, was so handsome it hurt. She needed to get her mind off him. In the morning she'd take a long hike around the island.

On Sunday, she and Olympia, one of the cooks from the hospital, were going to take the ferry to Corfu from Loggos. While Olympia met with her relatives, Zoe planned to do some sightseeing on her own and was looking forward to it.

A group of workers got on the bus with her. They were already friendly with her and chatted. One by one they got off at different stops. Zoe was the only one who rode all the way into the village. By now the driver named Gus knew her name. Though she might be in Greece rather than New York, there was the same atmosphere of community she'd loved growing up.

When Zoe got off the bus, she headed for one of the *taverna*s that served *mezes* along the harbor front. At twilight the lights from the boats and ferry twinkled in the distance. It was a magical time of night.

Most of the tables outside were taken by tourists, but she finally found an empty one. She'd been anxious to try the various fish appetizers to see how they compared with her mother's cooking. The waiter brought an assortment of octopus, shrimp, sardines, calamari and clams.

Maybe she was biased, but she thought her mom's were better. Then again maybe she was missing her family. How they would have loved to come here for a vacation.

Don't look back, Zoe. You're the luckiest girl in the world to have been given this opportunity. You've been handed a second chance at life. You've been able to realize your dream to work for the Giannopoulos Foundation. You're living in one of the most beautiful spots on earth.

"Such a beautiful young woman sitting alone at the table looking so sad is a sin. Even if it isn't all right, I'm going to join you."

She'd know that distinctive male voice anywhere and looked up in shock. "*Vasso*—"

"Sorrow on a night like this is a tragedy."

Zoe made an odd sound at the sight of him. Tonight he'd dressed in a black silk shirt and tan trousers. Afraid she was staring hungrily at him, she averted her eyes. "I was just doing a little reminiscing about my parents. You caught me at the wrong moment."

He took a seat opposite her at the round table. His nearness did strange things to her equilibrium. "What's on that mind of yours?"

The waiter came, but Vasso only ordered a cup of coffee. She knew he was waiting for an explanation. "I've been sitting here counting my blessings."

"That sounds like you. So you're not missing home then?"

She sat back in the chair. "I stay in touch with my friends through email. As for Chad, he took my advice and is out of my life."

Her heart skipped a beat. "It was the right decision for both of us. Otherwise I wouldn't be sitting here on the island Kyria Panos calls the jewel of the Ionian, eating dinner with my benefactor. If you saw me in a sad mood just now, I was thinking how much my parents would have loved this island and how they longed to visit Florina. But my mother would whisper that these sardines were overly seasoned."

Following his chuckle, he took a sip of the coffee the waiter had brought to the table. "What are your plans for this weekend? I talked to Yiannis and learned it's your turn to be off work until Monday."

She glanced around as if she were afraid to look at him. "We've decided to alternate weekends. The security guards will take turns to cover for us while we sleep there."

"According to him you're turning the place around already."

"Yianni is just being nice."

"So it's Yianni now?" he questioned with a smile.

"The first time I called him that by mistake, he said his wife always dropped the 's' and he ordered me to keep doing the same thing."

"It's clear he's happy with you." Vasso finished his coffee. "How do *you* like your job by now?"

CHAPTER SIX

"I LOVE IT!" Zoe's eyes sparkled like the aquamarine sea around Akis's villa on Anti Paxos. "There's this one patient named Nestor I want to tell you about. But only if you have the time."

"I'm off work for the weekend too. If there isn't something you need to do, why don't we drive to my house to talk? There's a lineup of tourists from the ferry who would appreciate this table."

When she reached in her purse to pay the bill, he checked her movement and pulled out his wallet to do the honors.

"I don't expect you to pay for me."

"Not even when it's your birthday?"

She gasped slightly, but then she shook her head. "Why am I not surprised? You know everything about me."

"Almost everything," he teased. "This one is the big twenty-five. I remember having one of those five years ago."

"Did you celebrate with someone special?"

"If she'd been special, she and I would still be together."

She eyed him frankly. "Your fault or hers?"

"Most definitely mine."

"Don't tell me there hasn't been one woman in your life who meant the world to you?"

He helped her up from the table and they walked along the waterfront to the parking area near the pier. "Her name was Sofia Peri. I asked her to marry me."

After a measured silence, "How long ago?"

"When I was twenty. But the business Akis and I put together hadn't gotten off the ground yet. She needed a man with substance."

Zoe stared up at him before getting in his car. "Just look what *she* missed…"

Touché.

He closed the door and went around to the driver's seat to get in. They drove the short way to his house in companionable silence. "Where does that road go?" she asked before they reached his villa.

"To the pier where I keep my boat."

She turned to him. "Can we drive down to look at it?"

"If that's what you want." He made a right turn that led to the water's edge where she saw his gleaming cruiser.

There was an enchantment about the night. A fragrant breeze lightly rippled the water. This was Vasso's front yard. "It must be fabulous to go everywhere you want by water. Of course you go by helicopter too, but I can't imagine anything more fun than finding new coasts to explore."

Vasso shut off the engine and turned to her. "I had

those same thoughts years ago. When the rich people pulled into our little harbor to eat and buy things from the store where Akis and I worked, I always wondered what that would be like. That was long before it became an Alpha/Omega 24 store."

Her heart ached for how difficult his life had been. "Is that how you met the woman you proposed to? Was she a tourist who came in?"

"No. She lived in the village. We went to the same church and the same school, even though Akis and I were absent most of the time. Her parents didn't approve of me, but she defied them to be with me."

Zoe felt pained for him. "Was she your childhood sweetheart?"

"You could say that. I assumed we'd get married one day. We were crazy about each other, or so I thought. It helped me get through some difficult times, especially after our father died. Akis and I continued to work there and had saved enough money to buy it from the owner. By then I was nineteen and had to do my military service.

"While I was gone, we wrote to each other and made plans. At least *I* did. But I didn't realize that while I was away, she'd started seeing a local fisherman's son who was making a good living. She never once mentioned him to me until my return. The news that she'd fallen for someone else pretty well cut my heart out."

Zoe didn't know what to say. "My relationship with Chad never got as far as yours." The normal platitudes wouldn't cover it to comfort him because in truth, the woman sounded shallow. If she chose ready money over the true value of Vasso Giannopoulos whom she'd loved for years, then he was well out of it.

"Are you saying you were never intimate with him?"

"No. I was taught to wait for marriage. Guilt kept me from making that mistake. Thank goodness it did since Chad and I weren't meant to be. But I'm truly sorry about Sofia."

"That's past history. Fortunately for me, it was Akis's time to go into the military. I had to do the job of two people to keep our business running. By the time he got back, we went all out to make a success of our lives. Both of us were sick of being looked upon as the impoverished Giannopoulos boys who rarely went to school and had no education. I believe it was harder on Akis, but he's very sensitive about it."

"The poor thing," she said quietly. "Neither of you knew your mother who could have comforted both of you. I can't comprehend it."

"Our father made up for it."

"That's obvious. The two centers you've built in honor of him say everything." Her throat had started to swell. "If I could meet him, I'd tell him he raised the best sons on earth."

"If I keep listening to you, I just might believe it. As long as we're here, would you like to go for a boat ride?"

"I thought you'd never ask," she admitted on a laugh.

"I'll take us on a short drive to the harbor. It's very picturesque at night."

Zoe got out of the car before he could come around to help her and started walking to the boat dock. She turned to him. "What can I do to help?"

His white smile in the semi-darkness sent a rush of warmth through her body. "If you want to undo the rope on this end, I'll take care of the other."

His cruiser looked state-of-the-art, but small enough for one person to manage. She did her part, then stepped in and moved over to the seat opposite the driver's seat. Never in her wildest dreams would she have imagined spending her twenty-fifth birthday driving around an island in the Ionian Sea with a man as incredible as Vasso. If she was dreaming, it didn't matter. She was loving every minute of it.

He stepped in with a male agility that was fascinating to watch and handed her a life jacket to put on. As he started to sit down she said, "You have to wear one too. I'm not the world's greatest swimmer. If I had to save you, it would be kind of scary."

His deep chuckle seemed part of the magic of the night. When they were both buckled up, he started the engine and they went at wakeless speed until they were able to skirt the cove. Zoe got up and stood at the side. Other boats were out, but all you could see were their lights and other lights on the island.

She turned around and braced her back so she could look at Vasso. "I've been thinking about your childhood. Did they offer a class in English when you did go to school?"

He slanted her a glance. "Yes, but we were rarely there. Our major knowledge came from talking to the English-speaking tourists. The owner of the store gave us a book to learn from. Our father told us we had to learn it in order to be successful."

"My parents spoke English and I was lucky to be taught at school from day one. If I'd had to learn it from a book the way you did and teach myself, it wouldn't have happened, believe me."

"You would if it meant your living."

Her life had been so easy compared to Vasso's, she didn't want to think about it. "I'm sure you're right."

"What kind of books did you read?"

"For pleasure?"

He nodded.

"English was my major, but I have to admit I loved all kinds of literature. In my mind you can't beat the French for turning out some of the great classics. My favorite was Victor Hugo's *Les Misérables* about Jean Valjean, who listened to the priest and did good. One of my classmates preferred Dumas's *Count of Monte Cristo* whose desire for revenge caused him not to listen to the priest."

Vasso slowed the boat because they'd come to the harbor where she could fill her eyes with its beauty. "I've seen the films on both stories. We'll fly to Athens and take in a film one day soon, or we could go dancing if you'd like."

Zoe smiled. "That sounds fun, but finding the time might be difficult." *Don't torture me with future plans, Vasso.* "I have my work cut out here."

In that quiet moment Vasso reached out and caressed her cheek with his free hand. His touch sent trickles of delight through her nervous system. "Yiannis has been thanking me for dropping you on his doorstep. I do believe everyone is happy." In the moonlight his heart-melting features and beautiful olive skin stood out in relief. "Shall we go back to the house?"

More than anything in the world Zoe wanted to see his home, but there were reasons why she had to turn him down. He was her employer, but there was much more to it than that. She'd found herself thinking about him all week, wishing he'd come by the hospital. For her to be looking for him all the hours of the day and evening meant he'd become too important to her already.

She could feel her attraction to him growing to the point she found him irresistible. This shouldn't be happening. If she fell in with his wishes, she could be making the worst mistake of her life. And it would be a big one, because there was no future in it.

"I'd better not, but thank you anyway. This has been a thrill to come out in your cruiser. I've loved every second of it, but I've got a big day planned tomorrow and need to get to bed."

The oncologist had told her that because of her type of lymphoma, the odds according to the Follicular Lymphoma International Prognostic Index indicated she'd live five years, maybe more. No one could guess when there'd be a recurrence.

With that in mind, she needed to keep her relationship with Vasso professional. She was already having trouble separating the line between friendship and something else. By touching her cheek just now he'd stoked her desire for him. He'd mattered too much to her from the beginning and her longing for him was getting stronger.

Whatever the statistics said, Zoe was a ticking time

bomb. The breakup with Chad had been hard enough to deal with. But knowing the disease would come back had made her fear another romantic involvement. The only thing to do was stay away from any sign of emotional attachment that could hurt her or anyone else. Zoe had her work at the center and would give it her all.

On their way back to the car she hoped she hadn't offended him. He'd been so kind to find her at the *taverna* and help her celebrate her birthday. Yet once again she felt tension emanating from him, stronger than before.

When he helped her in the car he said, "Tomorrow I'm planning to look at a new property. I'd like you to fly there with me. It'll be a chance for you to see another part of Greece. We'll only be gone part of the day. Once we're back, you can get on with your other plans."

The blood pounded in her ears. "That wouldn't be a good id—"

"Humor me in this, *thespinis,*" he cut her off. "Since I came empty-handed this evening, let it be my birthday present to you."

She averted her eyes. "Did Yianni put you up to this?"

"No. I actually thought it up all by myself." On that note she laughed and he joined in. "I like it when you laugh."

Zoe didn't dare tell him how his laugh affected her... the way his black eyes smiled, the way he threw his head back, the way his voice rumbled clear through to her insides making them quiver. Oh no. She couldn't tell this beautiful Greek god things like that.

Her resistance to him was pitiful. "How soon did you want to leave?"

"I'll come by your apartment at eight-thirty."

If he was going on business, then she needed to dress for the occasion. When he went out in public he was targeted by the paparazzi. She wanted to look her best for him.

"What's on your mind?" he asked when he pulled up in back of the apartment.

"Things that would bore a man."

"Try me," he challenged with fire in his eyes.

"What lipstick should I put on, what shoes to match my dress, what handbag will be better. Decisions, decisions. See what I mean?"

He scrutinized her for a moment. "I see a lovely woman. What she wears doesn't matter."

"I'm a fake. If you saw me without my hair you'd have a heart attack." She'd said it intentionally to remind him who she was, and got out of the car. "Someday I'll lose it all again when I have to undergo another session of chemo, so I'll enjoy this momentary reprieve while I can. Thank you for this unexpected evening. I'll be waiting for you in the morning. Good night, Vasso."

She let herself in the back door, but was so out of breath it took a minute before she could climb the stairs. Even if her fairy godfather hadn't needed the reminder, *she* did.

Tomorrow has to be your last time with him, Zoe. Absolutely your last.

After a shower and shave, Vasso put on tan trousers and a silky, claret-colored sport shirt. While he fixed himself his morning cup of coffee, his phone rang. It was his brother.

He picked up. "*Yassou,* Akis."

"Where are you?"

"At the house."

"Good. Raina and I were hoping you'd come over this morning and have breakfast with us. We haven't seen you in two weeks."

"Thanks, but I'll have to take a rain check on that."

After a pause, "What's going on?"

"I'm off on business in a few minutes."

"We already closed the deal on the store in Halkidiki."

He rubbed the back of his neck. "This is something different."

"Then it has to involve Zoe Zachos. Talk to me."

Vasso let out a frustrated sigh. "I've been helping her settle in."

"And that includes taking her on a business trip?" His incredulity rang out loud and clear.

Vasso checked his watch. "I'm going to be late picking her up. I'll explain everything later. Give Raina my love."

The question Akis was really asking went to the core of him. But he couldn't talk about it. Once they got into a conversation, his brother would dig and dig. Zoe had said the same thing about him. They weren't brothers for nothing, and Akis wouldn't stop until he'd gotten to the bare bones. Vasso wasn't ready to go through that. Not yet...

Pieces of last night's conversation with Zoe had shaken him.

I'm a fake. If you saw me without my hair you'd have a heart attack. Someday I'll lose it all again, so I'll enjoy this momentary reprieve while I can.

Chilled by the possibility of the lymphoma recurring, Vasso started the car and drove to her apartment, unaware of the passing scenery.

When Chad heard I'd been told my disease would probably be terminal, he couldn't handle it. I told him I didn't want him to have to handle it and begged him to take the job offer in Boston and not look back. He took my advice.

Chad's pain would have been excruciating to realize he might lose her. But Zoe had to have been in anguish over so many losses.

Vasso's thoughts flew to his father when he'd been on the verge of death. The sorrow in his eyes that he wouldn't be able to see his sons grow to maturity—the pain that they'd never known their mother—the hope that they would never forget what a wonderful woman and mother she'd been—

Tears smarted his eyes. Not so much for the pain in his past, but for Zoe who didn't know what the future would bring. Their light conversations only skimmed the surface of what went on underneath. Her declaration that she never planned to marry was part of the babble to cover up what was going on deep inside of her.

All of a sudden he heard a tap on the window and turned his head. It was Zoe! He hadn't realized he'd pulled to a stop outside the apartment door. She looked gorgeous in a simple black linen dress with cap sleeves and a crew neck. The sun brought out the gold high-lights in her hair.

He leaned across the seat to let her in. She climbed in on those well-shaped legs and brought the smell of strawberries inside. Her lips wore the same color and cried out to be kissed. Her eyes met his. "*Kalimera,* Vasso."

"It's a beautiful morning now, *thespinis*. Forgive me for staring. You look fabulous."

Color rose into her cheeks. "Thank you. After getting caught off guard by the paparazzi in Athens, I thought I'd better be prepared to be seen in the company of one of Greece's major financial tycoons."

Vasso took a deep breath. "I hope that's not the case today. Have you eaten breakfast?"

"Oh yes. Have you?"

"Just coffee."

Her brows met in a delicate frown. "That's all you had last night."

Zoe managed to notice everything. He liked it. He liked her. *So much in fact he couldn't think about any-thing else.* "I'm saving up for lunch," he said and drove the car back along the tree-lined road to his house where the helicopter was waiting.

"Where are we going?"

"I've decided to let it be a surprise. You'll know when we land at the heliport."

Before long they'd climbed aboard the helicopter and lifted off. Vasso put on his sunglasses and turned on the mic. When he looked over his shoulder he saw that Zoe had put on sunglasses too. She was beautiful and could easily be a famous celebrity. But he was glad no one knew about her. He liked the idea of keeping his find to himself.

He gave her a geography lesson as they flew northward to Macedonia. She knew more Greek history than most people of his acquaintance. Once they neared the desired destination, the land became more mountainous. He could tell her eyes were riveted on the dark green landscape that opened up to half a dozen magnificent lakes. Further on a sprawling city appeared. The pilot took them down and landed in a special area of the airport. When the rotors stopped whirling Vasso said, "Welcome to Florina, Zoe."

She looked at him in wonder. "Are you serious?"

"When you told me your parents had wanted to bring you here for your graduation, it gave me the idea."

"So you don't really have business here?" she asked in a softer voice.

"I didn't say that."

Zoe shook her head and took off her sunglasses. "You do too much for me, Vasso."

"I'd hoped for a better reaction than a lecture."

"I didn't mean to sound like that. Forgive me."

"Come on. I have a limo waiting to take us sightseeing." He got out first then helped her down. The urge to crush her warm body in his arms was overwhelming, but he held back.

The limo was parked nearby. He helped her inside, but this time he sat next to her. "I've asked the driver to take us on a small tour. When I told him your great-grandparents lived here until the outbreak of the Greek

Civil War, he promised to show us some of the historical parts of Florina and narrate for us over the mic."

She looked out the window. "I can't believe this is happening."

"I'm excited about it, too. I've never spent time in this area and am looking forward to it."

"Thank you from the bottom of my heart," came her whisper. When he least expected it, Zoe put a hand over his and squeezed it for second. But as she tried to remove it, he threaded his fingers through hers and held on to it.

"I think I'm almost as excited as you are. The cycle of the Zachos family has come full circle today. Seventy years ago your ancestors left this town to get away from communism. Now their great-granddaughter is back to put down her roots in a free society. That's no small thing."

"Oh, Vasso."

In the next instant she pressed her head against his arm. While the driver began his narration—unaware of what was going on in the rear—Vasso felt her sobs though she didn't make a sound. Without conscious thought he put his arms around her and hugged her to him, absorbing the heaves of her body. He could only imagine the myriad of emotions welling up inside her.

After a few minutes she lifted her head and faced straight ahead. "I hope the driver can't see us. Here he's going out of his way to tell us about the city, and I'm convulsed."

"He knows this tour has more meaning for you than most tourists so he'll understand."

"You always know the right thing to say."

For the next half hour the driver took them past buildings and landmarks made famous by the prominent filmmaker Theo Angelopoulos.

"Since the last war I don't imagine the homes my great-grandparents left are even standing," she confided.

"Probably not." Vasso asked the driver to drop them off at a point along the Sakoulevas River. "Let's get out and walk to Ioannou Arti Street so you can get a better view of the twentieth-century buildings along here. There's an archaeological museum we can visit."

She climbed out and put her arm through his as they played tourist. It felt so natural with her holding on to him like this. He could wish this day would go on forever.

"This is fabulous, Vasso. I had no idea the city was so beautiful. To think maybe my great-grandparents walked along this very river."

"Maybe it was along here they fell in love."

Zoe looked up at him in surprise. "I had no idea you're such a romantic at heart."

"Maybe that's because you bring it out in me." Obeying an impulse, he lowered his mouth and kissed those lips he'd been dying to taste. It only lasted a moment, but the contact sent a bolt of desire through him. She broke the kiss and looked away before they walked on.

The limo met them at the next street and they got back in. "If you've had enough, I'll tell the driver to run us by a market the Realtor told me was for sale. He tells me there's a *taverna* nearby where we can try out *burek*. We'll see if it compares to your mother's recipe."

"I'd love that."

Vasso alerted the driver and soon they pulled up in front of a store selling produce. He got out and helped Zoe down. Together they walked inside the busy market. The city was certainly big enough to support one of their stores. But he was curious to know the figures and approached the owner.

"While I talk to him, take a look around and see if there's something you want to buy to take back to the apartment."

She smiled. "Take as long as you need."

Zoe strolled around, eyeing the fruits and vegetables brought in by local farmers. Vasso noticed the customers eyeing her, even the owner who could hardly concentrate when asked a simple question.

When Vasso had learned what he wanted to know, he went in search of Zoe and found her at the back of the market buying a bag of vegetables.

"Don't they sell peppers in Loggos?"

Her face lit up. "No. These are sweet Florina red peppers. My mother remembered her mother and grandmother cooking these. They aren't like any other peppers in the world. I have the recipe. When we get back to Loggos, I'll cook some for you with feta cheese and we'll see if they live up to their reputation. The eggplant looks good, too."

His pulse raced at the thought of going back to Zoe's apartment. "Then let's grab a slice of *burek* at the *taverna* two doors down now, and eat a big meal this evening."

"That sounds perfect."

She hadn't said no. Their day out wasn't going to end the second they flew back to Loggos. That was all he cared about.

After telling the owner he'd be in touch with the Realtor, Vasso carried her bag of precious peppers and eggplant as they walked along the pavement to the outdoor café. He ordered *burek* and Skopsko beer for both of them.

When she'd eaten a bite, he asked for her opinion.

"I'm more curious to know what you think, but you have to tell the truth. If you like it better than mine, it won't hurt my feelings very much."

He burst into laughter and ate a mouthful of the pie. Then he ate a few more bites to keep her in suspense. She was waiting for an answer. Those green eyes concentrated solely on him, melting him to the chair. "It's good. Very good. Yours is better, but I can't define why it's different."

She leaned forward. "You mean it?"

Good heavens, she was beautiful. "I don't lie, *thespinis*. Let's drink to it." They touched glasses, but she only drank a little bit of hers while Vasso drained the whole thing. Food had never tasted so good, but that was because he was with her and was filled with the taste of her. He wanted more and suspected she did too otherwise she wouldn't be talking about their spending the rest of the day together back on Loggos.

"Excuse me while I freshen up before we leave."

Two hours later they arrived back at Zoe's apartment. While she got busy preparing the peppers, Vasso followed her directions for *moussaka*. "I'm glad you're staying for dinner, Vasso. There's something important I want to talk to you about."

Vasso darted her a piercing glance. His heart failed him to think she had an agenda. Was that the reason he'd made it over her doorstep tonight, and not because she couldn't bear to say good-night to him?

"What is it?"

CHAPTER SEVEN

"I DIDN'T FINISH telling you about one of the patients named Nestor. The poor thing doesn't think he's going to get better. He's depressed, but it isn't just because he's undergoing chemo. He lives with the fear that because he was homeless when he was brought in, he has no work to go back to even if he does recover.

"I've discovered that several of the older patients are afraid they won't get their jobs back if their disease goes into remission. So I was thinking maybe in my off hours I could set up a service to help those patients find a job."

"A service?" One dark brow lifted. "Have you discussed this with Yiannis?"

"Oh no. This would be something I'd do on my own. But I wanted to see what you thought about it."

He put the *moussaka* in the oven. "It's a very worthy project. Maybe even a tough one, but you're free to do whatever you want in your spare time. Surely you know that."

"So you wouldn't disapprove?"

Vasso frowned. "Why would you even ask that question?"

She carefully peeled the skins off the roasted peppers. "Because the people I approach will ask what I do for a living and your foundation will come up. You're a modest man. I don't want to do anything you wouldn't like."

He lounged against the counter while she prepared the peppers to cook with olive oil, feta cheese and garlic. "You couldn't do anything I wouldn't like."

Her gaze shot to his. His compelling mouth was only inches away. She could hardly breathe with him this close to her in the tiny kitchen. "You shouldn't have said that. I'm full of flaws."

His lazy smile gave her heart a workout. "Shall we compare?"

"You don't have any!"

"Then I'll have to break down and reveal a big one."

"Which is?"

"This!" He brushed her mouth with his lips. "When a beautiful woman is standing this close to me, I can't resist getting closer." He kissed her again, more warmly this time.

"Vasso—" She blushed.

"I told you I had a flaw."

She turned from him to put the peppers in the oven. When she stood up, he was right there so she couldn't move unless he stepped away. "I'd like to spend the day with you tomorrow. We'll tour the island and go swimming on a beach with fascinating seashells. What do you say?"

He could probably hear her heart pounding. She'd promised herself that after today, she wouldn't see him again unless it was for professional reasons.

Thank heaven she had a legitimate excuse to turn him down.

"Thank you, Vasso. That's very sweet of you, but I can't. I'm going to Corfu in the morning with Olympia."

Those black eyes traveled over her features as if gauging her veracity. "I might have known you'd strike up a friendship with her. She worked in the food services industry before coming to us."

Zoe nodded. "We have that and more in common."

He took a deep breath and moved away. "I'm sad for me, but glad for you to be making friends so fast."

"I found out she bikes with her husband. So they're going to lend me one of their bikes and we'll take rides around the island after work and on our free weekends." She'd added that to let him know her calendar was full.

Another long silence followed, forcing her to keep talking. "Everyone here has been so friendly. I already feel at home here. After moving heaven and earth for me, your job is done. You don't have to worry about me anymore."

Still no response. Needing to do something physical, she set the little breakfast table. After making coffee, she invited him to sit down while she served him dinner. When he still didn't say anything, she rushed to fill the void.

"I'll never forget the gift you gave me today. Seeing the city of my ancestors meant more to me than you will ever know."

"It was a memorable day for me, too," he murmured. "I want to spend more days like this with you, Zoe. I'd love to go biking with you."

"Between our busy schedules, that could prove difficult." She put the *moussaka* on the table and stood at his side to serve him a plate of peppers. "Tell me what you think about Florina's most famous vegetable."

He took one bite then another and another and just kept nodding.

That was the moment Zoe knew she was in love with him. The kind you never recovered from. To her despair, the thing she hadn't wanted to happen *had* happened. She adored him, pure and simple. His kisses made her hunger for so much more. His touch turned her inside out with longings she wanted and needed to satisfy. *Oh, Vasso... What am I going to do about you?*

Before Zoe blurted that she loved him, she sat down and ate with him. "Um… These really are good."

"You're a fabulous cook, and I've never tasted better *moussaka*."

"You put it together, so you get the credit."

After Vasso drank his coffee, he flashed her a glance. "The next time we're together, I'll cook dinner for you at my house and I won't take no for an answer."

Zoe let the comment slide. The way he made her feel was toppling her resistance. As she got up to clear the table her cell rang. She reached for her phone lying on the counter.

"Go ahead and answer it," he urged her when she didn't click on.

She shook her head. "It's Kyria Themis. I'll call her back after you leave."

"Maybe it's important, so I'll go."

Much as she was dying for him to stay, she knew this

was for the best. Their friendship needed to remain a friendship, nothing more. The kiss he'd given her today had rocked her world. That's why the less they saw of each other, the better.

She walked him to the door. "Good night then, Vasso. This day was unforgettable."

So are you, Zoe.

Vasso got out of there before he broke every rule and started to make love to her. In his gut he knew she wanted him, too. Desire wasn't something you could hide. Whether in the limo or the car, the chemistry between them had electrified him.

Though he didn't doubt she'd already made plans for tomorrow, he sensed she was deliberately trying to keep their relationship platonic. But it wasn't working. Despite her determination not to go to his house, she'd invited him to the apartment tonight and had cooked dinner for him.

There were signs that she was having trouble being too close to him. He'd noticed the little nerve throbbing at the base of her throat before he'd moved out of her way in the kitchen.

While she'd stood next to him to serve dinner, he'd felt the warmth from her body. It had taken all his willpower not to reach around and pull her onto his lap. She was driving him crazy without trying.

On the drive to his house he made a decision to stay away for a few days and let her miss him. He had no doubts it would be harder on him, but work would help him put things in perspective.

Tomorrow he'd do a tour of the stores where he needed to meet with the new store managers to make certain they were following procedure. That would take him the good part of a week. In the meantime Akis would be free to meet with their food distributors in Athens for the critical monthly orders.

Once he was home he phoned his brother to tell him his plans. Before hanging up he said, "I met with the owner of a produce market in Florina today who wants to sell. The Realtor has named a figure that's too high. I think I can get the asking price down, but wanted to know your feelings about us putting up a store there."

"I always trust your judgment, but why Florina? What were you doing there?"

He gripped the phone tighter. "I flew Zoe there for her birthday. Her great-grandparents emigrated from there to America in the mid-forties. Before her parents could take her there for a college graduation present, they died in the fire."

His brother was quiet for a minute. "*Vasso—*"

"I know what you're going to say."

"Since you've already disregarded my warning to take it slow, I was only going to ask if there's a boyfriend in the picture."

"He bailed on her when he found out her disease would probably be terminal."

"That, on top of all her pain," his brother murmured in commiseration. "It would have taken a committed man."

He exhaled sharply. No one knew that better than Vasso. If Chad had loved her enough, he wouldn't have let her talk him into walking away. He could say the same for Sofia who hadn't had the patience to wait until things got financially better for him. Today he rejoiced that he and Zoe were still single.

"How is she working out with Yiannis?"

"They're trading off weekends and he lets her call him Yianni. That's how well they've hit it off. Let me tell you about her latest idea."

After he'd explained, Akis said, "I must admit a job referral service for the patients is a brilliant idea. When are Raina and I going to meet her?"

"I was hoping next Friday evening before she has to go on duty for the entire weekend."

"Do you want to bring her to our house?"

"I fear that's the only way it will work. She isn't comfortable coming to mine yet."

"Then you *have* heeded my warning to a certain extent."

Akis couldn't be more wrong. "Let's just say that for now I'm letting her set the pace. But I don't know how much longer I can hold out."

"Before you do what?"

"Don't ask that question yet because I can't answer it. All I know is I like being with her." *That was the understatement of all time.* "I'll talk to you later in the week. *Kalinihta.*" He clicked off and got ready for bed.

Once he slid under the covers, Akis's probing question wouldn't leave him alone. Until Vasso knew what Zoe really wanted, he couldn't plan on anything. She'd been hurt by Chad who hadn't seen her through her life-changing ordeal. To have a relationship with Zoe meant earning her trust. He'd begin his pursuit of her and keep at it until she had to know what she meant to him.

After a restless night, he flew to his first destination in Edessa and emailed her to let her know what he'd been doing. He did the same thing every night. By the time Friday came, he couldn't get back to Paxos soon enough. Before he drove to the center, he stopped by the number-one store to check in with the managers and buy some flowers.

"Vasso?" a female voice spoke behind him.

He turned around. "Sofia."

Her brown eyes searched his before looking at the flowers. "I was hoping to see you in here one of these days. Can we go somewhere private to talk?"

After she'd turned down his marriage proposal, there'd been times in the past when he would have given anything to hear her say that she'd changed her mind and wanted to marry him. How odd that he could look at her now and feel absolutely nothing. Meeting Zoe had finally laid Sofia's ghost to rest.

"Why not right here? I'm on my way to the center, but I can spare a few minutes. How are you?"

"Not good. I've left Drako."

Somehow that wasn't a surprise to him, yet it brought him no pleasure. Akis had told him he'd seen her in town a few months ago and she'd asked about Vasso. "I'm sorry for both of you."

Her eyes filled with tears. "Our marriage never took and you know the reason why. It was because of you. I've never stopped loving you, Vasso."

He shook his head. "I think if you look deep inside, you'll realize you were young and ambitious. Drako was already doing an impressive fishing business."

"I was a fool."

"I'm sorry for both of you."

"All this time and you've never married. I know it was because of me, and I was hop—"

"Sofia," he cut her off. "I moved on a long time ago."

"Are those flowers for someone you care about now?"

"They're for the woman I love," he answered honestly. Her face blanched. "You have children, and they need you more than ever. Now if you'll excuse me, I have to get to the center. I wish you the best."

He waved goodbye to the owners and hurried out to the car needing to see Zoe. By the time he reached the center he was close to breathless with anticipation. But first he went by Yiannis's office to let him know he was there. The older man told him she was out on the patio with several of the patients.

"When you have the time, I'll tell you about all the changes she's made around here for the better. We're lucky to have her, Vasso."

"I agree. Will it be all right with you if I steal her away for an early dinner?"

"Of course."

"Good."

Without wasting another second he hurried down the hall to find a container for the flowers, then he headed for the doors leading to the patio. She'd arranged four round umbrella tables to be close together with two patients at each one in their recliner wheelchairs. One man and one woman to a table. All wore some kind of head covering and all were playing cards. Zoe was obviously running the show using a regular chair.

She hadn't seen him yet. He stood watching in fascination for a few minutes.

All of them had to be in their late forties or were older, except for one man who looked to be in his twenties. He wore a red paisley scarf over his head like a pirate. As Vasso moved closer, he could tell the younger man was fixated on Zoe. Why wouldn't he be? She was by far the most beautiful and entertaining female Vasso had ever seen. Today she was wearing a soft yellow blouse and skirt.

They were all into the game and the camaraderie between them was apparent. This was Zoe's doing. He reached for a regular chair and took it over to put down next to her. "Can anyone join in?"

He heard her quiet intake of breath when she glanced up at him with those translucent green eyes. "Kyrie Giannopoulos—this *is* a surprise. Please. Sit down and I'll introduce you."

One by one he learned their names. They were profuse in their thanks for his generosity. "We're having a round-robin that's timed," Zoe explained. "Nestor here is on a winning streak." She smiled at the younger man.

"Then don't let me interrupt," he whispered, tamping down his jealousy. "I'll just sit here and watch. Maybe later you'll tell me why the emails you sent back to me were so brief."

For a moment their eyes met. He saw concern in hers. Before the night was out, they were going to talk.

It appeared Nestor couldn't take his eyes off her. When he could see that Vasso wasn't about to leave, the younger man glared at him beneath veiled eyes. The fact that he was recovering after chemo didn't stop the way he studied her face and figure. Was Zoe interested in him?

Vasso couldn't prevent another stab of jealousy, but when he thought about it that was absurd. If there was a bond between them, it had to do with the fact that both Nestor and Zoe had their illness in common. They had an understanding that drew them together. If she suspected the younger man's infatuation, she didn't let it show.

Soon a couple of the nurses came out to take the patients back to their rooms. But Nestor declined help and wheeled his chair out of the room.

"Don't forget movie night tonight!" she called to them. "I'm bringing a treat!"

"We won't forget!" said one of the older men.

Vasso watched her clear up the cards. She was nervous of him. Did he dare believe that she was equally thrilled to see him, and that's why she'd been caught off guard? He desperately wanted to believe she was in love with him, too.

"What's this about movie night?"

She nodded. "During my chemo, there were nights when I couldn't sleep and wished there were something to do. I asked Yianni about it and he told me to organize it. Anything that could increase everyone's comfort was worth it."

Zoe never ceased to amaze him. "You're already revolutionizing this place. What time is your movie night?"

"After nine-thirty. That's when the demons come."

He didn't want to think about the demons she'd lived through. "In that case I'd like you to have an early dinner with me first. Please don't turn me down. My brother and his wife want to meet the new assistant manager. They've invited us over. Maybe you can get Raina to unload about Akis's imperfections. Maybe he pecks at her, too."

She laughed, causing her nervousness to disappear for the moment. "As if I'd ask her a question like that!" There was green fire in her eyes. "I'll have to let Yianni know I'm leaving for a while."

"I've already asked if it's all right, but if you'd rather not leave the center, just tell me. We can arrange dinner with them for another time."

"No." She shook her head. "That sounds lovely. I've wanted the opportunity to thank Akis. How soon do you want to leave?"

"As soon as you're ready. We'll leave from the hospital roof."

"Let me just freshen up and then I'll meet you at the private elevator in ten minutes."

"Before you go, these are for you." He handed her the flowers.

"Umm. Pink roses. They smell divine."

"They smell like you. I noticed the scent the first time you climbed in the limo."

Color filled her cheeks. "Thank you, Vasso. They're beautiful."

"Almost as beautiful as you."

She averted her eyes. "You shouldn't say things like that to me."

"Not even if I want to?"

"I'll just run to my desk and put them on the counter, then I'll join you."

He could have no idea how much the flowers meant to her. She loved him... Too many more moments like this and all her efforts to keep distance between them would go up in smoke.

After receiving his newsy emails all week, to be given these flowers had her heart brimming over with love for him. It was clear he wasn't about to go away, and now he was whisking her off to his brother's villa.

She was filled with wonder as the helicopter flew over the tiny island next to Paxos. Vasso pointed out the vineyards on Anti Paxos. "If you notice the surrounding water, it's Caribbean green. Your eyes are that color, Zoe."

Every comment from him was so personal it made it harder for her to keep pushing him away. *That's because you don't want to, Zoe. You're in love and you know it.*

As they descended to a landing pad, she could see that the water *was* green, not blue, putting her in mind of emerald isles she'd never seen except in film. Vasso helped her down and kept a hand on the back of her waist as they made their way toward the small stone villa.

"Look at these flowers!" Zoe exclaimed. "It's breath-taking." They lined the mosaic stone pathway.

"Vasso?" she heard a female voice call out.

"Nobody else!" he called back.

In the next instant Zoe caught sight of the lovely American woman who'd married the other Giannopou-los son. She was a blonde, too. Zoe's first impression was that she glowed with health. Vasso had told her they were expecting a baby.

"Zoe? This is my favorite sister-in-law Raina."

"Your only one," she broke into English, rolling her violet eyes. "I'm so glad you could make it." Raina shook her hand before hugging Vasso. "Akis just got back from Athens and will join us after he gets dressed. Please come in. We've been excited to meet you."

Zoe followed her into the most amazing living room. A fireplace had been built in a wall carved out of rock. Between the vaulted ceiling and arches, the stone villa reminded her of pictures from the old family photos that had gone up in flames. The curtains and pillows added marvelous colors of blue and yellow to the décor. Zoe loved it.

"While Vasso goes to find Akis, come out on the terrace, Zoe, and have some lemonade with me."

They walked past the open French doors where the terrace overlooked a kidney-shaped swimming pool. Glorious shades of red, purple and yellow flowers grew in a cluster at one end. Beyond it the sea shimmered. "You live in paradise, Raina."

Her eyes sparkled with glints of blue and lavender.

"Every day I wake up and can't believe any place could be so beautiful."

"I know. When Vasso took me on a helicopter ride, I thought I had to be dreaming."

"May we never wake up." Raina Giannopoulos had a charming manner Zoe found refreshing. "Come and sit. I've wanted to meet you ever since we heard you were coming to Greece to work." She smiled. "Don't get me wrong. I love it here, but I miss talking to another American once in a while. Do you know what I mean?"

Zoe liked her very much already. "I know exactly. It's nice to speak English with you."

"I'm working on my Greek, but it's slow in coming."

"I may be Greek in my DNA," Zoe confided, "but I'm American in my heart."

"I thought I was, too, before I married Akis. Now the Greek part has climbed in and sits next to it."

Zoe laughed while Raina poured them both a glass of lemonade. "Before the guys come out, may I tell you how much I admire you for handling everything you've been through? My grandfather died of stomach cancer and my grandmother from heart failure. I watched them suffer and can only imagine your agony."

"It's over now."

Raina nodded. "You don't know it, but both brothers have been very touched by your story and are astounded by your desire to pay them back. Their father meant the world to them. Until you came along, I don't think either of them realized what good they've really done."

"I know," Zoe whispered, moved by her admission

about her grandparents. Raina had known a lot of pain too. "It's hard for Vasso to accept a compliment. I'm afraid all I do is thank him. I'm sure he's sick of hearing about my gratitude."

"If that were the case, you wouldn't be here now."

"That's the thing. He got me this job so fast he couldn't know how important that is to me. One day my lymphoma will come back, so I want to do all I can for as long as I can."

She saw a shadow pass over Raina's face, but before anything else was said, two black-haired men with striking features came out on the terrace, dressed in casual trousers and sport shirts.

Zoe stared at Vasso's brother, then turned to his wife. "I didn't realize how closely they resemble each other," she whispered. "I thought Vasso was the only Greek god flying around Greece in a helicopter."

"Do you want to know a secret?" Raina whispered back. "When I first saw Akis on the street in Athens, he seemed to be the incarnation of the god Poseidon come to life from the sea."

"I thought you met at a wedding reception."

"That's true, but we almost bumped into each other first on the street."

Zoe smiled. "And you never recovered."

"Never."

"Would you believe my first thought was that Vasso was the sun god Apollo? The statue in the fountain at the center looks just like him. With a husband like yours, it makes you wonder if you're going to give birth to a gorgeous god or a goddess, doesn't it?" After that comment they both laughed long and hard, cementing their friendship.

The men came closer. "What's so funny, darling?"

While Zoe sat there blushing, Raina smiled up at her husband. "We were discussing the baby's gender."

"What's funny about that?" Vasso wanted to know. His intense gaze had settled on Zoe. She knew he wouldn't let it go without an answer.

"Maybe Raina will give birth to a little Poseidon carrying a trident. That's why we laughed."

A knowing look entered Akis's eyes before he kissed his wife on the cheek. "My choice would be an adorable Aphrodite like her mother."

The two of them were madly in love. Zoe could feel it. She was terribly happy for them and about the baby on the way. Zoe would never know that kind of joy. To get married, let alone have a baby, when she knew her cancer could come back wasn't to be considered.

She could see the hunger in Vasso's eyes when he looked at his brother's family. It was killing Zoe, too, because marriage and babies weren't in the cards for her. They couldn't be.

"Akis, let me introduce you officially to Zoe Zachos. Yiannis tells me he doesn't know how they ever got along without her."

"So I've heard." Akis came around and shook her hand. "Apparently your round-robin card game was a huge hit today. We'll have to lay in some chips to make things more interesting for your future poker games."

"That would be fantastic! Thank you. Before another moment goes by, I have to thank you for allowing me to work at the center. I've been given a second chance at life and will always be indebted to you and Vasso." Zoe fought to hide the tears quivering on the ends of her lashes.

She put up her hands. "I'll only say one more thing. I know you're God-fearing men because of your father's example. Christ said that when you've done it unto the least of these, you've done it unto me. Well, I'm one of the least. It's my joy to give back what I can."

Vasso stared at her for the longest time before Raina told the men to sit while she put on an American dinner California-style in Zoe's honor. Fried chicken, potato salad and deviled eggs along with Raina's Parker House rolls recipe.

Zoe had never enjoyed an evening more. Vasso told them about their trip to Florina and discussed the wisdom of putting in a store there. The time passed so fast she protested inwardly when she looked at her watch and saw that she needed to get back to the center.

Raina walked her out to the helicopter. Zoe smelled a haunting fragrance coming from the flowers. "I've never seen Vasso this animated since I met him. He never used to laugh the way he does now. It must be your effect on him. We'll do this again soon," Raina promised.

No. There couldn't be another time. Zoe wouldn't be able to stand being around these wonderful people again when it hurt so much. "Thank you for making me feel welcome, Raina. I've loved it. Vasso told me how you two met. Apparently Akis was running from the maid of honor at the reception and asked you to dance."

"Did he tell you I'd just sprained my ankle and was on crutches?"

"No."

"I was glad I couldn't dance with him because I didn't want anyone to know I was there. The paparazzi were outside waiting. Chloe's wedding was the event of the summer for the media."

Zoe nodded. "They mobbed Vasso the day we went shopping at the department store in Athens. With them always being in the news, it doesn't surprise me that women are after those two brothers. It's really a funny story about you two. Akis is a lucky man. For your information, you could open up your own restaurant serving the food we ate tonight."

The other woman hugged her. "After I heard from Vasso what a great cook you are, that's a real compliment."

Vasso came from behind and opened the door so she could climb in.

"Thanks again, you two. It was wonderful meeting you."

He followed her in. Once they'd fastened their seat belts, the rotors whined and they climbed into the twilight sky.

Zoe could see Vasso's profile in the semidark. He was a beautiful man who'd taken over her heart without trying. She was prepared to do anything for him. That meant weaning herself away from him. He deserved to meet a woman who had a lifetime ahead to give him love and bear his children.

Because of the foundation, she'd been granted five

years, maybe a little more, to live life until her time ran out. But it would be a selfish thing to do if she reached out for love. It would be asking too much to deliberately marry a man and have his baby, knowing she would have to go through another period of illness before leaving them. Zoe refused to do that to any man.

"Zoe? We're back at the hospital." Vasso's low voice brought her back to the present.

She thanked the pilot and got out of the helicopter. When Vasso started toward the elevator with her, she turned to him. "I had a marvelous evening and loved meeting your brother and his wife."

"You and Raina really seemed to hit it off."

"She's terrific. Between you and me, your brother doesn't have anything to worry about. She's crazy about him. No talk of his pecking at her."

Vasso grinned.

"It's obvious they have a wonderful marriage. Now I need to go inside and set things up. You don't need to come all the way to make sure I'm safe."

His dark brows furrowed. "Why are you pushing me away, Zoe?"

After taking a deep breath, she folded her arms to her waist. "Let's be honest about something. Our relationship has been unique from the beginning. The normal rules don't apply. You've done everything humanly possible to help me relocate to a new life, but I'm acclimatized now. For you to do any more for me will make me more beholden to you than ever. I don't want that."

"What if I want to be with you, and it has nothing to do with anything else?"

Zoe lowered her head. "If that's true, then I'm flattered."

"Flattered," he mouthed the word woodenly. "That's all? So if you never saw me again, it wouldn't matter to you?"

"I didn't say that," she defended in a throbbing voice.

"Then what *did* you say?"

"You're trying to twist my words." She pressed the button that opened the elevator door. When she stepped in, he joined her.

"Why are you running away from me?

"I'm not! I'm supposed to be back at work."

"Work can wait five minutes. I want an answer."

"*Vasso—*"

"Yes? I'm right here. Why won't you look at me? I lived for your emails, but you didn't open up in them."

Her cheeks felt so hot she thought she must be running a temperature. "Because… I'm afraid."

"Of me?" he bit out, sounding angry.

"No—" She shook her head. "Of course not. It— It's the situation," she stammered.

"If you're afraid I'm going to desert you the way Chad did, then you don't know me at all."

"I never said that."

"But it's what you were thinking. Admit it."

"You've got all this wrong, Vasso."

"Then what are you worrying about?"

"*Us!*" she cried.

"At least you admit there *is* an us," he said in a silky

tone. In the next breath he reached for her and slid his hands to her shoulders, drawing her close to his rock-hard body. "You're trembling. If it's not from fear, then it means you know what's happening to us. I'm dying to kiss you again. But this time we're not standing in the middle of Florina for all to see."

She hid her face in his shoulder. "I'd rather you didn't. We'll both be sorry if you do."

"I'll be sorry if we don't. Would you deny me the one thing I've been wanting since we met?"

All this time?

"Help me, Zoe," he begged. "I need you."

His mouth searched for hers until she could no longer hold out. When it closed over hers she moaned. Thrill after thrill charged her body as they began kissing each other. One led to another, each one growing deeper and longer. She was so lost in her desire for him she had no awareness of her surroundings.

Vasso's hands roved over her back and hips, crushing her against him while they strained to get closer. She was so on fire for him it wouldn't surprise her if they went up in flames. This wasn't anything like her response to other men, to Chad. All Vasso had to do was touch her and she was swept away by feelings she'd never thought possible.

"Do you have any idea how much I want you?" His voice sounded ragged. "Tell me now how sorry you are." His mouth sought hers again, filling her with sensation after sensation of rapture. But his question made it through the euphoric haze she was in and brought her back to some semblance of reality.

"Vasso—we can't do this any longer," she half gasped, struggling for breath.

"Of course we can."

"No." She shook her head and backed away from him. "I don't want a complication like this in my life."

"You see me as a complication?" he ground out.

"Yes. A big one. You're my ultimate boss. I'm here because of you. We crossed a line this evening, but if we stop right now, then there's been no harm done. I look upon you as a blessed friend and benefactor. I don't want to think of you in any other light."

His face looked like thunder. "Don't make me out to be something I'm not."

"You know what I mean. I need to be here on my own and work out my life without any more help from you. I don't have to explain to you how much I already love it here. But when Father Debakis asked you to interview me, he had no idea what a kind and generous man you really are or how far you would go for the welfare of another human being."

"You're confusing my human interest in you with the attraction we feel for each other, which is something else altogether. Admit the chemistry has been there from the beginning."

"How can I deny it after the way we kissed each other? But it doesn't change the dynamic that I'm an employee of the Giannopoulos Foundation. It would be better if we remain friends and nothing more. You admit you've had other girlfriends. I'm positive there will be more. When another woman comes into your life who sets off sparks, you'll be able to do something about it without looking back."

His black eyes glittered dangerously. "What about you?"

She threw her head back. "I told you the other day. I'm not interested in romance. I want to make a difference in other people's lives. In ways, Ms. Kallistos had the right idea about me after all."

"What rubbish. You know damn well you don't believe what you're saying. I know you don't, but for some reason I have yet to figure out, you've decided to be cruel."

"Cruel?" Her face heated up. "I'm trying to save both of us a lot of pain."

She heard a sharp intake of breath. "You're so sure we'll end up in pain?"

"I *know* we will."

He shook his dark head. "What do you know that I don't?"

Zoe didn't want to say the words. "Think about it and you'll see that I'm right. There's another Raina out there waiting for you to come along. She won't be an employee and she'll be able to give you all the things you've been longing for in your life. Trust me in this. Your turn is coming, Vasso. You're a dear man and deserve everything life has to offer."

Frown lines darkened his handsome features. "Why do I feel like you're writing my epitaph?"

No, my darling. Not yours. Zoe swallowed hard. "I'm not the woman for you."

A haunted expression entered his eyes. "You're not making sense."

"In time, it will be clear to you. Good night, Kyrie Giannopoulos. From now on that's how I'll address you coming and going from the center."

He pushed the button that took them down to the main floor. "Since I'm your boss, I'll accompany you to the entertainment center to offer help if you need it."

Oh, Vasso…

When they reached the game room, there were twelve patients assembled with several nurses standing by. "We've been waiting for you, Zoe," one of the women called out.

Nestor shot her a glance. "Did you forget the treat?"

"Of course not. It's something we chemo patients enjoyed when I was convalescing at the other center. I'm curious to know if you'll like it. But you have to be patient while it cooks."

"What are you going to pull out of your magic bag now?" Vasso said *sotto voce*.

After their painful conversation, his teasing comment made her smile. She ached with love for him and moved over to the microwave. "See these?" Zoe picked up a packet of popcorn lying on the counter.

"They don't sell this in Greece," Vasso murmured.

"True. I brought a supply in my bag when I flew over."

She put a packet in the microwave and pressed the button. In a few seconds the kernels started to pop. Her eyes met Vasso's as that wonderful smell started to permeate the air. When it stopped, she opened the door and pulled out the filled bag. Taking care, she opened it.

Vasso had first dibs. After eating some, he started nodding and took a handful. He couldn't stop with just one and kept eating and nodding. Zoe knew it was a winner and smiled. "I'll let you keep this bag and I'll do another one."

She started cooking it. "Since you're the bird down in the mine and you're still breathing, they'll be willing to try it."

His burst of rich male laughter warmed her heart.

"You think it'll catch on?" she asked.

"Like wildfire. In fact we'll have to stock these in our stores."

"You'll have to tell your managers to cook a batch to entice the customers."

His black eyes smoldered. "You've enticed *me*, Thespinis Zachos."

The popping stopped, but her heartbeat pounded on. She hurriedly pulled out the bag. Vasso took over and opened it before passing it around to those who were willing to try it.

In a louder voice she said, "The popcorn helped some of us at the other center. But if you're too nauseated, then wait till next Friday night," she urged. "Now I'll turn on the film. It's the one that got the most votes to watch. *The Princess Bride* in Greek."

Everyone started clapping.

Vasso turned off the overhead light and came to stand by her with a lazy smile on his face. "Where did you find that?"

"When I went to Corfu with Olympia. This film is a winner with everyone. Have you seen it?"

"No. Any chance of my cooking another bag while we watch?"

If Vasso was trying to break her down, he was doing a stellar job. Those roses had been her undoing. "You don't have to ask me if you want more popcorn. You're the boss."

CHAPTER EIGHT

EVERYTHING HAD BEEN going fine until Zoe reminded Vasso that she worked for him. But that was okay because he wasn't going to let her get away with ignoring him. She would have to put up with him coming to the center on a regular basis. Little by little he would wear her down until she confessed what was going on inside her.

Throughout the entertaining film, he noticed Nestor watching her rather than the movie. One day the younger man would be better. Since Zoe had voiced her concern, Vasso had been thinking about him. Their company had two thousand and one store managers throughout Greece. On Vasso's say-so, any one of them would take Nestor on as an employee.

When the movie was over and the lights went on, the nurses started wheeling the patients back to their rooms. Vasso volunteered to take Nestor. He felt Zoe's questioning glance on him while she straightened up the room. He kept on going and soon they'd entered his hospital room where Vasso sat on the chair near the table.

"You didn't have to bring me," Nestor murmured. "Thank you."

"You're welcome. Before I leave, I wanted to discuss something with you. I know you're in the recovery phase of your illness. When you're ready to be released, I'm curious to know where you want to go."

"I was born and raised in Athens."

"But I understand you have no family now."

"No," he said, tight-lipped.

"If you could do anything, what would it be?"

"Anything?" Vasso nodded. "I'd like to go to college, but that would be impossible."

At Nestor's age, Vasso had wanted the same thing, but he and Akis were too busy building their business. There was never the right time. "Maybe not."

The younger man looked shocked.

"There are scholarships available for hardworking people. If I arranged for you to get a job in Athens, you could attend college at night."

Nestor's eyes opened wider. "That would be amazing, but I don't know if I'm going to get well."

"I understand you're better today than you were a week ago. Have faith and we'll talk again when the doctor okays your release."

He left Nestor thinking about it and headed for the private elevator. There was nothing he wanted more than to find Zoe and talk to her. But she needed her sleep so she could be in charge tomorrow and Sunday. The one thing that helped him walk away tonight was knowing she wasn't going anywhere. She loved her job and he would always know where to find her.

For the next week he kept busy coordinating work with Akis and continued to send emails to Zoe. He knew his brother wanted to ask him more questions, but Akis kept silent. That was good because Vasso didn't want to get into a discussion about Zoe. They debated the pros and cons of putting up a store in Florina, but didn't come to a decision. The city wasn't growing as fast as some other areas.

On Friday afternoon he flew back to Paxos. After a shower and shave, he put on casual clothes and headed over to the center. Seven days away had made him hungry for the sight of her. But first he checked in with Yiannis who sang Zoe's praises. "We can be thankful all is well with that young woman."

"Amen to that." He expelled a relieved sigh. "I'm going to go over the books with Kyria Lasko in accounting if you need to find me." Vasso knew he wasn't fooling the admiral, but he appreciated the older man for not prying into his personal life.

Two hours later he walked down the hall. When he couldn't see Zoe at the front desk, he headed for the entertainment center. Friday night was movie night. He had a hunch she was in there setting things up for later. But when he went inside, he only found a couple of patients with a nurse.

"Have you seen Thespinis Zachos?"

"She just left, but she'll be back at nine-thirty."

Vasso thanked her and left the hospital in his car. En route to the town center he phoned her. By the time she picked up, his pulse had jumped off the charts.

"Vasso?"

She sounded surprised. He'd missed her so much just the sound of her voice excited him. "I'm glad you answered. Where are you?"

After a pause, "At the apartment."

"No bike riding today?"

"No. Our plans fell through. Her husband hurt his leg biking, so she's home taking care of him this weekend."

"Sorry to hear that. I flew in earlier and worked with the accountant at the center. I didn't see you anywhere. Have you eaten dinner?"

"Not yet."

"I'd like to talk to you about Nestor. Would you like to meet me at Psara's? I don't know about you but I'm craving fish."

He could hear her thoughts working. "That's the *taverna* down near the parking area?"

"Yes. I'm headed there now if you'd like to join me. But if you have other plans, I'll understand."

"No—" she exclaimed, then said no in a quieter voice. "Nestor told me you talked to him last week."

"That's right."

"You…planted a seed."

Good. "If you want to discuss it, I'll be watching for you." Without waiting for a response, he clicked off and pulled into the parking. He got out and hurried toward the *taverna* to grab a table before the place filled up. Being that it was a Friday night, the paparazzi were out covering the waterfront. Celebrities from Athens often came to Loggos for dinner. Vasso couldn't escape.

In a few minutes, every male young or old stared at the beautiful blonde woman making her way toward him. She'd dressed in a leaf-green blouse with a white skirt tied at the waist. He experienced the same sense of wonder he'd felt when he'd seen her the first time. She was like a breath of fresh air and walked with a lilt on those fabulous legs.

When Vasso stood up to pull out her chair for her, several journalists caught her on camera. She couldn't have helped but see them. "Ignore them," he muttered. "Pretty soon they'll go away."

"Not as long as you're here." But she said it with a smile. "I knew I was taking a chance to be seen with you."

"You're a brave woman, but then we already know that about you." His comment brought the color flooding into her cheeks.

The waiter came to pour coffee and take their order. They both chose the catch of the day. Once they were alone again, he studied her classic features. "Thanks for answering my emails. You've kept me abreast of everything going on at the center. But you never share your personal feelings. How *has* your week gone?"

"Every day is different. I couldn't be happier," she said through veiled eyes. "What about yours?"

"I can't complain as you know from my messages to you, but thanks for asking."

Considering what it had been like to get in each other's arms last week, this conversation was a mockery. But he'd play her game for a while longer. "How much did Nestor tell you?"

Now that he'd changed the subject to something important to her, she grew animated. "He mentioned that you talked to him about a scholarship so he could go to night school. He's been in disbelief that you really meant it."

Vasso sucked in his breath. "I would never have brought it up if I weren't serious. Earlier this week I talked to the manager of our number-four store in Athens. He'd be willing to give Nestor a job. I have no idea if he would want to work in a convenience store after being employed at a hotel, but—"

"I'm sure he would!" she cried out excitedly. "Oh, Vasso—there's been a light in his eyes that hasn't been there until now. It's because of you."

No. That light had to do with Zoe. She ignited everyone she met. "How much more chemo does he have to go through?"

"He's had his last treatment. The doctor has high hopes for his recovery."

"In that case I'll come to movie night tonight and tell him."

His news made her so happy he realized she couldn't tell him not to come. "Hope will make him get well in a hurry."

The waiter chose that moment to bring their dinner. When he walked away Vasso said, "That's the idea, isn't it. We all need hope."

That little nerve at the base of her throat was pulsing again. She started to eat her fish. "Between you and Father Debakis, I don't know who will deserve the bigger reward in heaven."

"Your mind is too much on the hereafter," he teased. "I'm quite happy with life right here."

She flushed. "So am I. It's just that I'm so than—"

"Don't say that anymore, Zoe. I'm quite aware of how you feel. I want to talk about how we feel about each other. I can't stay away from you. I don't want to. So we need to talk about where we're going to go from here. I *know* you feel the same way about me."

Her head lifted and their gazes collided. "I admit it, but you'd have to be in my shoes to understand why it wouldn't be a good idea for us to get any more involved."

"I can't accept that."

Zoe's expression sobered. "You're sick of hearing the same thing from me, aren't you?"

If he dared tell her what he really thought, she'd run from him. He couldn't handle that. "I'm not saying another word while we're the focus of other people."

One journalist had stayed longer to get pictures of the two of them. Vasso shot Zoe a glance. "If you're through eating, let's head for my car and ruin that guy's evening."

Her sudden laugh always delighted him. He put money on the table and got up. She was still chuckling when they reached the Lexus and he helped her inside. Zoe looked over at him as he drove. "Even paradise has its serpents."

"They have to earn a living, too."

Her eyes rounded. "You feel sorry for them?"

"No, but I understand that the need to make money in order to survive makes some people desperate enough to take chances."

"You're right, of course. I've never been in that position." She glanced at him. "I've never gone to bed hungry in my life." There was a catch in her voice. "Because of your foundation, I've been taken care of in miraculous ways. Sometimes I'm overwhelmed by your generosity."

Vasso couldn't take it anymore. "Overwhelmed enough to do me a favor?"

"I'd do anything for you. Surely you know that by now."

"Then come to my house after movie night is over. There's something I have to discuss with you, but we'll need privacy."

He heard her quick intake of breath. "That sounds serious."

"It is. Don't tell me no. I couldn't take it."

Zoe trembled, wondering what had happened to put him in this cryptic mood. If he was unhappy with some of the innovations she'd made at the hospital, all he had to do was tell her up front. Maybe Yianni had confided that she wasn't working out, but he didn't have the heart to tell her to her face because he was such a sweetheart.

When they reached the center, he parked the car and they entered through the front door.

She saw the clock. "It's almost time. I need to hurry to the game room and set up."

"Go ahead. I'll be there in a minute."

Did he want to talk to Yianni again?

Zoe went to the restroom first so she could pull herself together. She had the idea he was going to discuss her future here at the foundation. Could he be going to let her go? Fear stabbed at her. Maybe coming to work for him hadn't been a good thing after all. The passion enveloping them last week had only muddied the water. Tonight things were crystal-clear.

If Father Debakis hadn't intervened, she wouldn't be in this precarious position now. It wasn't his fault, of course. If she hadn't been so desperate to repay her debt, she wouldn't have caused all this trouble.

That's what Vasso had been alluding to earlier. Desperation was responsible for all kinds of mistakes. Her biggest one had been to accept his offer to relocate to Greece and continue taking his charity for the rest of her life.

Of course she was earning a salary now, so she hoped that wasn't what it looked like to him. She buried her face in her hands, not knowing what to think.

She wished her mother were around to talk to her about this. The great irony about that was the fact that if her parents were still alive, Zoe wouldn't be thousands of miles away from home. She'd be finishing college and getting on with her life, never knowing of Vasso's existence. Instead she'd dumped all her problems on Vasso who hadn't asked for them in the first place.

Zoe was terribly conflicted. She'd acted besotted in his arms, but as he'd reminded her, the emails she sent back to him didn't say anything about her feelings. In her heart she'd been watching for signs of him all week. When he hadn't come to the center before tonight, she was desolate. But she couldn't have it both ways, not when she'd told him she wanted to keep their relationship professional.

What a laugh she must have given him. No doubt he saw her as the worst kind of needy female. If she kept this up much longer, he'd be forced to find her something else to do in order to get her out of his hair. But he was such a good man he would never fire her without a new plan.

When she'd washed the tears off her face, she headed for the entertainment center. Eight patients showed up. The other four had just been through another session of chemo and wouldn't rally for a few days.

Vasso had singled out Nestor. While he thrilled him with a job offer, she popped more popcorn and started a movie. This time it was the Greek version of an old film, *Zorba the Greek*. The audience would complain that Anthony Quinn was Mexican, not Greek then they'd pull the crazy plot apart. Hopefully it would entertain them enough for a little while to forget how sick they felt.

By the end of the film, no one wanted the evening to be over. It proved to her that movie night worked. While the nurses took the patients back to their rooms, she tidied the place. But when she followed Vasso out of the center to his car, her heart felt as if it weighed a stone. She dreaded what was coming and her legs felt like dead weights.

On the drive to his house she turned to him. "How did your conversation go with Nestor?"

Vasso let his wrists do the driving. "He sounded just like you when I told him I'd find him an apartment near the number-four store. That way he could walk to work and take the bus to the university after he was released. I don't think he could see the film through the tears."

No. Nestor's gratitude would know no bounds for their benefactor, but she refrained from saying anything because Vasso didn't want to hear it.

Zoe tried to gear up for what was coming. How awful that a conversation with him would take place in his house, the one personal area of his life she'd tried to stay away from. She loved it already just seeing it from the air.

He drove around the back of it. It had been built near the water's edge. They entered a door into the kitchen area with a table and chairs. Though small like a cottage, huge windows opened everything up to turn it into a beach home, making it seem larger. No walls.

Everywhere you looked, you could see the sea. All you had to do was open the sliding doors and you could step out on a deck with several tubs of flowers and loungers. Beyond it, the sand and water were at your feet.

A circular staircase on one side of the room rose to the upper floor. It had to be a loft. The other end of the room contained the rock fireplace with a big comfy couch and chairs.

"Would you like a drink?"

She shook her head. "Nothing, thank you."

"Let's take a walk along the beach. The sand feels like the finest granulated sugar. I do my best thinking out there. We'll slip off our shoes and leave them inside. You can wash your feet later at the side of the deck."

After she did his bidding, she followed him outside. Night had descended. A soft fragrant breeze with the scent of thyme blew at her hair and skirt. She knew it was thyme because there was the same smell at the center. Yianni had explained what it was. He was a walking encyclopedia of knowledge.

She could talk to him the way she did with Father Debakis. The wonderful man had great children who looked after him, but he'd loved his wife to distraction and talked to Zoe about their life together. How heavenly to have enjoyed a marriage like Yianni's.

When they'd walked a ways, Vasso stopped and turned to her. The time had come. Her body broke out in a cold sweat. To her shock, he cupped her face in his hands and lifted it so she had to look at him. Zoe couldn't decipher the expression in his eyes, but his striking male features stood out in the semidarkness.

"I want to start over."

She blinked. "What do you mean?"

"I mean, I'd like us to do what two people do who have met and would like to get to know each other better."

After everything she'd been thinking as to what might be the reason why he'd brought her here, Zoe was incredulous. "That's the favor?"

"I know it's a big one. Last week you made it clear you didn't want anything more than friendship from me, but we moved past that after your arrival in Greece. I want to spend this weekend with you and all the weekends you're available from here on out."

The ground shifted.

She was positive she'd misunderstood him.

"Did you hear me?" he asked in an urgent voice.

"You *can't* be serious." She grasped his wrists, but he still cradled her face in his hands.

"Why are you acting like this, Zoe?"

"Because you're carrying your sense of responsibility to me too far."

"Does this feel like responsibility?" He lowered his mouth to hers and kissed her long and hard until she melted against him. Zoe was delirious with desire after being away from him for a whole week. "Tell me the real reason you're fighting me," he said after lifting his head. They were both out of breath. "I know you're attracted to me. You told me there's no one else in your life." The warm breath on her mouth sent a fire licking through her body.

"There isn't, but Vasso—" she moaned his name, "I can't be with you. If I had known this was going to happen, I would have changed my mind and stayed in New York. I would have found another place to work."

His brows met. "You don't mean that. You're lying to cover up what's really wrong."

Making a great effort, she eased herself out of his arms. "You're a very intelligent man. If you think hard about it, you'll know why this won't work. My cancer is in remission, but no one knows when it will come back."

She heard him suck in his breath. "Guess what? Tomorrow I could go down in the helicopter and never be seen again. It could happen. But if I looked at life like that, nothing would get accomplished."

"A possible helicopter crash one day compared to a recurrence of cancer are two different things."

He raked his hands through his hair. "No. They're not. No matter what, life is a risk."

"But some risks are more risky than others, Vasso. To get close to you is like buying something you want on time. One day—much sooner than you had supposed—you'll have no choice but to pay the balance in full. It will be too heavy a price to have to come up with all at once. I won't let you get into that position."

This time his hands slid up her arms. "You honestly believe you're going to die soon? *That's* what this is all about?"

"Yes. But I don't know the timetable and neither do you. What I do know is that you watched your father die of the same disease. No one should have to live through the trauma of that experience a second time in life. You and your brother have fought too hard to come all this way, only for you to get involved with a time bomb, because that's what I am."

He drew her closer. "Zoe—"

"Let me finish, please? I saw the love Akis and his wife share. With a baby on the way they're totally happy. He doesn't have to worry that Raina is going to be stricken by the inevitable.

"Don't you understand? I want you to have the same life *they* have. No clouds on the horizon. To spend time with me makes no sense for you. I'm a liability and I made Chad see that. He was smart and did the right thing for both of us."

Vasso's features darkened. "How was it right for you?" his voice grated.

"Because I would have been more depressed to watch

his suffering over me when I could do nothing to alleviate it. Just think about what it felt like when your father was dying, and you'll understand exactly what I'm talking about. It would have been so much harder on me if Chad had been there day and night. I couldn't have handled it."

"I'm not Chad." His hands slid to her shoulders. "Did you love him?"

Vasso's question caught her off guard. "I...thought I did. There are all kinds of love."

"No, Zoe. I'm talking about that overpowering feeling of love for another person that goes so deep into the marrow, you can't breathe without it."

He'd just described her feelings for him and pulled away before he read the truth in her eyes. "I don't want to talk about this anymore. If it's all right with you, I'd like to go home."

She turned back and hurried toward the deck where she could wash the sand off her feet. By the time he'd caught up to her, she'd gone inside and had slipped on her shoes.

"Before we go anywhere, I need to tell you something important, Zoe. Will you listen?"

They stood in the middle of the room like adversaries. Spiraling emotions had caused her to shake like a leaf. "Of course."

"Something unprecedented happened to me when I flew to New York to interview you. I didn't ask for it, but it happened. I haven't been the same since. Like you with Chad, I thought I loved Sofia. She'd always been there. We'd been a couple for such a long time, it just seemed normal for us to get married.

"Luckily, she got impatient. While I was in the military, she couldn't wait for me. Though I didn't know it at the time, she did me the greatest service in the world because it was apparent she wasn't the one for me.

"After surviving that hurdle, Akis and I led a bachelor existence for years. When Raina came into his life, it was as much a shock to me as to him. He'd been with other women, but she knocked him sideways without even trying, and transformed his life. I can promise you that if she'd been a recovering cancer patient, it would have made no difference to him."

"That's what you say because it's what you want to believe." She shook her head. "I can see there's no way to get through to you on this."

"You're right. There's only one solution to end our impasse."

"Exactly. By ending it now."

"I have a better idea in mind."

Zoe couldn't take much more. "I need to get back to the apartment."

"I'll take you, but I want you to think very seriously about my next words."

She reached for her purse and started for the kitchen. "Will you tell me in the car?"

Without waiting for him, Zoe went outside and walked along the path to his Lexus. Afraid to have contact, she quickly got in and shut the door.

Vasso went around to his side of the car and started the engine. But before he drove them to the road, he slid his arm along the seat so that his fingers touched the ends of her hair. Immediately her body responded, but she refused to look at him.

"We need to get married."

Her gasp reverberated in the interior. "*Married*—"

"The sooner the better. According to your timetable, we might have five years together before everything comes to an end. I want to give you children. I'd rather take those five years and live them fully with you, than walk away from you now and leave us both in pain."

"I won't be in pain," she defended in a quiet voice while her heart ran away with her at the thought of having his baby.

"Well, I will." He tugged gently on her hair strands. "After the way you kissed me back tonight, I know for a fact you'll be in pain, too. I don't need an answer yet, but I'll look for one soon."

"No—" she whispered in agony. "You mustn't."

"If I'd let the *no*s and the *mustn't*s get in the way, I wouldn't be where I am today. You and I don't have the usual problems that beset couples. We know who we are and exactly what we're getting into. We've learned how precious life is. We've been made brutally aware that there are no guarantees for the future, only what we're prepared to build together."

She swallowed hard. "What it proves to me is how far you would go to honor the wishes of Father Debakis."

"He has nothing to do with this!"

"Then why would you be willing to make the ultimate sacrifice by marrying me and giving me a home when you know I have a very short life span."

"Because I love you."

"I love you, too, but I wonder if you remember the warning you gave me in New York. You said, 'Be sure it's what you want.' How sad someone didn't warn you to be sure it was what *you* wanted."

"You're putting up a defense because of your own insecurities." He drove the car to the road and they headed for the village.

"Vasso, you don't want to marry me. We're both temporarily attracted to each other. You're like any red-blooded bachelor might be, but you're not in love with me. I refuse to be your personal project.

"I came here to work and pay you back for your generosity. Wouldn't it be a great way to show my gratitude by becoming your wife? Then you'd be forced to take care of me for however long I have left.

"Forget children. No way would I want to leave a baby for you to raise on your own. Your father did that. I won't allow history to repeat itself. You and Akis have been through so much, you deserve all the happiness you can find.

"Sofia Peri didn't know what she was doing when she let the most marvelous man on earth slip through her fingers. If you'd married back then, you'd probably be a father to several darling children. I should never have come here."

Yianni had gotten along fine before Zoe had arrived. The center would run smoothly whether she was there or not. If she flew back to New York, she could get a job as a cook. When she'd saved enough money she could finish her last semester of college. Then she could get a job teaching school and send money to the foundation every month. It was the best plan she could think of under the circumstances.

When she got back to the apartment, she'd phone Father Debakis and have a heart-to-heart with him. He was probably at dinner and could talk to her when he was through. The priest would understand her dilemma and give her the guidance she needed because heaven help her, she couldn't make this decision without his blessing.

Vasso drove around to the back of the shop. She opened the door before he came to a stop. "Thank you for bringing me home. You made Nestor a happy man tonight."

"And what about you?"

"You already know what I think."

"We're not finished, Zoe."

"How can I convince you that this just won't work?"

"I didn't realize you were so stubborn."

"Then be thankful I'm not the marrying type. You've dodged a bullet. Good night."

CHAPTER NINE

FOR THE NEXT week Vasso worked like a demon, traveling from city to city to check on stores while Akis worked out of the Athens office. After the last conversation with Zoe, he knew she needed time to think about their situation without being pressured.

Now that it was Friday evening, he couldn't stay away any longer and flew to Paxos. She would be on duty this weekend and couldn't run away from him. After they watched a movie with some of the patients, he'd get her alone to talk until he convinced her they belonged together.

At five to six he tapped on Yiannis's half-open door and walked in. Zoe wasn't out in front, but he didn't expect her to be.

He found the admiral pouring himself coffee from a carafe brought in on a cart from the kitchen. The older man was using the cup Zoe had given him. He turned to Vasso. "Ah. You're here at last."

By his sober demeanor Vasso sensed something was wrong. "Did I miss a call from you?"

"No, no." He walked back to his chair. "Sit down so we can talk."

Not liking the sound of that, he preferred to remain standing. Yiannis looked up from his desk. "I have a letter here for you. It's from Zoe. She asked me to give it to you when you came by and not before."

His heart plummeted. He took the envelope from him, almost afraid to ask the next question. "Where is she?"

"She flew back to New York on Tuesday."

The breath froze in his lungs.

"On Sunday she came over, white as a sheet, and submitted her resignation. Zoe's the best assistant I could have asked for, but the tragic expression on her face let me know she's been suffering. She told me she was so homesick she couldn't stay in Greece any longer. The sweet thing thought she could handle being transplanted, but apparently it was too big a leap. Kyria Lasko is helping me out again."

His agony made it hard to talk let alone think. "I'll find a temporary accountant from headquarters until we can find the right person to assist you," he murmured.

"You'd better sit down, Vasso. You've gone quite pale."

He shook his head. "I'll be all right. Forgive me. I've got things to do, but I'll be in touch."

Vasso rushed out of the hospital and drove to the village at record speed. He parked the car and ran along the waterfront to the gift shop. The second Kyria Panos saw him she waved him over with an anxious expression. "If you're looking for Thespinis Zachos, she's left Greece."

He felt like he was bleeding out. "I heard the news when I was at the center earlier. Let me pay her bill."

"No, no. She paid me. Such a lovely person. Never any trouble."

Not until now, Vasso's heart cried out.

He thanked the older woman and drove back to his house. After making a diving leap for the couch he ripped open the envelope to read her letter. She'd only written one short paragraph.

Forgive me for accepting your offer of employment. It has caused you so much unnecessary trouble. I'm desolate over my mistake. One day I'll be able to start paying you back in my own way.

My dear, dear Vasso, be happy.

Blind with pain, he staggered to the storage closet and reached for his bike. He'd known pain two other times in his life. A young teen's loss of a father. Later a young man's loss of his childhood sweetheart. This pain was different.

Zoe thought she could spare him pain by disappearing from his life. But with her gone, he felt as if his soul had died on the spot. Vasso didn't know how he was going to last the night, but he couldn't stay in the house.

He took his bike out the back door and started cycling with no destination in mind. All he wanted to do was keep going until he got rid of the pain. It was near morning when he returned to his house and took himself up to bed.

The next time he had cognizance of his surround-ings, he could hear Akis's voice somewhere in the back-ground urging him to wake up. He couldn't figure out where he was. How had he made it upstairs to his bed?

His eyelids opened. "Akis?"

"Stay with me, Vasso. Come on. Wake up."

He groaned with pain. "Zoe left me."

"I know."

"Did you see her letter?"

"That, and your bike lying on the ground at the back door."

He rubbed his face with his hand and felt his beard. "How did you find out?"

"Yiannis called me yesterday worried about you."

"What's today?"

"Sunday."

He opened his eyes again. "You mean I've been out of it since Friday?"

"Afraid so." His brother looked grim. They'd been through every experience together. "You've given me a scare, bro. I was worried you might have driven your-self too hard and wouldn't wake up. Don't ever do that to me again."

Vasso raised himself up on one elbow. "A week ago I asked her to marry me. Friday night she left her answer with Yiannis. I wanted her so badly I pushed too hard."

"It's early days."

"No. She left Greece to spare me. Zoe's convinced the disease will recur."

Akis sighed. "Raina picked up on that the night you came for dinner."

"For her to give up the job she wanted was huge for her. There's no hoping she'll come back."

"Why don't you get up and shower, then we'll fly to my house. Raina has food ready. Once you get a meal in you, we'll talk. Don't tell me no. This is one time you need help, even if you are my big brother."

September 23, Astoria, New York

"Zoe? Come in my office."

She knew what the doctor was going to say and was prepared for the bad news. This was her first checkup since she'd left the hospital six weeks ago. The month she'd spent in Greece was like a blip on a screen, as if that life had been lived by a different person.

She'd decided not to call Father Debakis. No one at the church knew she was back in the US. Zoe prayed Ms. Kallistos hadn't seen her slip in the hospital and would never know about this appointment.

Zoe had made up her mind she wouldn't depend on the charity of others ever again. While she was staying at the YWCA, she'd been going out on temporary jobs to survive. There was always work if you were willing to do it. This was the life that had put Nestor in a depression. She could see why.

If any good had come out of her experience on Paxos, it had been to introduce him to Vasso who had not only saved his life through his charity, but had made it possible for him to go to college.

Vasso... Zoe's heart ached with a love so profound

for him she could hardly bear to get up every day and face the world without him.

"Zoe? Did you hear me?"

She lifted her head. "I'm sorry. I guess I was deep in thought."

He frowned. "You've lost five pounds since you were released from the hospital. Why is that?"

"With the recurrence of cancer, that doesn't surprise me."

"What recurrence?"

Zoe shook her head. "You don't need to be gentle with me, doctor. Just tell me the truth. I can take it.'

He cocked his head. She had to wait a long time before he spoke again. "I'm beginning to think that if I told you the truth, you wouldn't recognize it, let alone believe me. I *am* a doctor, and I've sworn an oath to look after the sick."

"I know," she whispered.

"But you think I'm capable of lying?"

She bit her lip. "Maybe not lying, but since you work with cancer patients, I realize you're trying to be careful how you tell a patient there is a death sentence in the future."

He leaned forward. "We all have a death sentence awaiting us in life. That's part of the plan. In the meantime, part of the plan is to live life to the fullest. Something tells me that's not what you've been doing."

Those were Vasso's words. It sent prickles down her spine.

"There's no recurrence of cancer, Zoe. I'm giving you another clean bill of health."

"Until another six weeks from now, then it will show up."

He made a sound of exasperation. "Maybe you weren't listening to me the first time I told you this. In people like you with none of the other complicating factors, the statistics prove that about ninety-one out of every one hundred people live for more than five years after they are diagnosed. And seventy-one out of every one hundred people live for more than ten years. Some even live to the natural end of their lives."

She'd heard him the first time, but she hadn't been able to believe it. *Was it really possible?*

"Since you're cancer-free and in perfect physical shape, I want to know the reason for your weight loss. It has to be a man."

She struggled for breath. "You're right."

"Tell me about him."

Zoe had refused to give in to her feelings since returning from Greece. But with the doctor who'd been her friend for a whole year pressing her for an explanation, she couldn't hold back any longer and blurted everything in one go. The tears gushed until she was totally embarrassed.

"Before I see my next patient who's waiting, do you want to know what *I* think, girl?"

Girl? He hadn't called her that in a long time. Surprised, she looked at him, still needing to wipe the moisture off her face. "What?"

"You're a damn fool if you don't fly back there and tell him yes. I don't want to see you in my office again unless you have a wedding ring on your finger!"

September 25, Athens, Greece

When the ferry headed toward the familiar docking point at Loggos, Zoe was jumping out of her skin with nervous excitement. She'd taken the cheapest one-way night flight from JFK to Corfu and caught the morning ferry to Paxos Island. While on board she changed into walking shorts and sneakers. Everything else she owned was in her new suitcases. Luckily the largest case had wheels, making it easier for her to walk along the waterfront to the gift shop.

Kyria Panos looked shocked and anxious when Zoe entered her store. "I didn't know you were back. If you want the apartment, I've already rented it. I'm sorry."

"Don't be. That's good business for you! I just wondered if I could leave my luggage here. I'll pay you and be back for it by the end of the day."

"You don't have to pay me. Just bring it behind the counter."

"You're so kind. Thank you."

"Did you know Kyrie Giannopoulos tried to pay me for your rental?"

"No, but that doesn't surprise me." There was no one in this world like Vasso. "I'll buy one of these T-shirts." She found the right size and gave her some euros. "Mind if I change in your bathroom?"

"Go ahead. Whatever you want."

Having deposited her luggage and purse, she left and was free to buy her favorite snack of a gyro and fruit at Vasso's number-one store. Once she'd eaten, she rented a bike from the tourist outfit at the other end of the pier and took off for Vasso's beach house.

Though she hadn't lived on Paxos for very long, it felt like home to her now. The softness of the sea air, the fragrance, it all fed her soul that had been hungering for Vasso. Raina had said it best. "I thought I was American too before I married Akis. Now the Greek part has climbed in and sits next to my heart." Zoe could relate very well.

She had no idea if Vasso would be home or not. If she couldn't find him, she'd bike to the center and drop in on Yianni. He was a sweetheart and would be able to help her track him down without giving her presence away. She wanted, needed to surprise Vasso. It was important she see that first look in his eyes. Just imagining the moment made it difficult to breathe.

The ride through the olive groves rejuvenated her. Every so often she'd stop to absorb another view of the azure sea and the white sailboats taking advantage of the light breeze. She removed her helmet to enjoy it. While she was thinking about Vasso, she saw the local bus coming toward her. It slowed down and a smiling Gus leaned out the window.

"Yassou, Zoe! Where have you been?"

"In New York, but I'm back to stay!"

"That's good!"

"I agree!"

After he drove on, she put her helmet back on and started pedaling again. She went through alternating cycles of fear and excitement as she contemplated their reunion. Zoe wouldn't allow herself to be bombarded with negative thoughts again. She'd weathered too many of them already. Because of a lack of faith, she'd wasted precious time, time she and Vasso could have had together.

Zoe stopped every so often to catch her breath and take in the glorious scenery. She had no way of knowing if he'd be at the house, but it didn't matter. This was his home. He would return to it at some point, and she'd be waiting for him.

Akis looked at Vasso. "What do you think about him?" The last person they'd interviewed for the assistant's job at the hospital went out to the lounge to wait. Over the last week there'd been a dozen applicants for the job before him.

"I think he's as good as we're going to get."

"His disability won't present a problem and he's ex-military. Yiannis will like that."

Vasso nodded. Neither of them wanted to admit Yiannis had been so unhappy about Zoe's resignation he'd found something wrong with anyone they'd sent for an interview. He'd rather do the extra work himself.

"Will you tell him? I need to get back to the house if only to find out if it's still standing." Since the Sunday Vasso had awakened to a world without Zoe in it, he'd been living at the penthouse when he wasn't out of the city on business. He got up and headed for their private elevator.

"Hey, bro." Akis's concern was written on his face. "Come over for dinner tonight."

"Can I take a rain check?" Akis and Raina had done

everything to help, but there was no help for what was wrong.

"Then promise you'll keep in close touch with me."

"Haven't I always?"

"Not always," Akis reminded him.

No. The Friday night he'd read Zoe's goodbye letter, everything had become a blur until Akis had found him on Sunday morning. By now he'd gotten the message that she had no regrets over leaving him. None.

While he'd waited in the hope that he'd hear from her, he'd gone through every phase of pain and agony. Maybe it would never leave him. Desperate for some relief, he flew to Paxos. When the helicopter dropped him off, he got in his car. After buying some roses in town, he headed for their family church on the summit.

A breeze came up this time of day, filling the air with the scent of vanilla from the yellow broom growing on the hillsides. He pulled off the road and got out. The cemetery was around the back. Sixteen years ago he and Akis had buried their father next to their mother. They'd been young and their grief had been exquisite. In their need they'd clung to each other.

Vasso walked around and placed the tub of roses in front of the headstone. Then he put a knee down and read what was inscribed on the stone until it became a blur. As if it had been yesterday, he still remembered a conversation they'd had with their father before he'd died.

"You're only in your teens and you'll meet a lot of women before you're grown up. When you find *the* one, you must treat her like a queen. Your mother was my queen. I cherished and respected her from the beginning. She deserved that because not only was she going to be my wife, she was going to be the mother of our children."

Tears dripped off Vasso's chin.

"I've found my queen, *Papa,* but her fear of dying early of the same disease as you has made it impossible for us to be together. I don't know how you handled it when our mother died, but somehow you lived through the grief. If you could do it, so can I. I'm the big brother. I *have* to.

"Wouldn't you know Akis is doing much better than I am because he's found the love of his life? They're going to have a baby." His shoulders heaved. "I'm so happy for them. I want to be happy, too. But the real truth of it is…I *have* to find a way for that to happen, *Papa,* otherwise this life no longer makes sense."

Vasso stayed there until he heard the voices of children playing on the slope below him. That meant school was out for the day. He'd been here long enough and wiped the tears with the side of his arm. It was time to drive back to the house and take stock of what he was going to do with his life from here on out.

Something had to change. To go on mourning for something that wasn't meant to be was destructive. He had a business to run. One day soon he'd be an uncle to his brother's child. Vasso intended to love him or her and give all the support he could.

After reaching the car, he drove home with the windows open, taking the lower road that wound along the coastline. As he rounded a curve he saw a cyclist in the far distance. It was a beautiful day. Vasso didn't wonder that someone was out enjoying the sea air.

But when the helmeted figure suddenly disappeared from sight, Vasso was surprised. There was only one turnoff along this particular stretch of road. It led to his beach house. Curious to know if he had a visitor, or if the cyclist was simply a tourist out sightseeing, he stepped on the gas.

When he reached the turnoff, he came close to having a heart attack. Despite the helmet, Vasso could never mistake that well-endowed figure or those shapely legs headed for his house.

It was Zoe on the bike!

He stayed a few yards behind and watched the beautiful sight in front of him, trying to absorb the fact that she was back on the island.

The way she was pedaling, he could tell she was tired. At some point she must have sensed someone was behind her. When she looked over her right shoulder, she let out a cry and lost control of the bike. In the next second it fell over, taking her with it.

Terrified she could be hurt, Vasso stopped on a dime and jumped out of the car. But she'd recovered before he could reach her and was on her feet. His eyes were drawn to the English printed in blue on her white T-shirt with the high V-neck. *I'd rather be in Greece.*

If this was a private message to him, he was receiving it loud and clear. The way she filled it out caused him to tremble.

"Zoe—I'm so sorry. Are you hurt?"

Those shimmering green eyes fastened on him. "Heavens, no. I'm such a klutz."

She looked so adorable in that helmet and those shorts, he could hardly find his voice. "Of course you're not. I should have called out or honked so you'd know I was behind you. But to be honest, I thought maybe I was hallucinating to see you in front of me."

He watched her get back on the bike. "I was coming to visit you."

His heart pounded like thunder. "This has to be perfect timing because I haven't been here for several weeks."

"I probably should have phoned you, but after I got off the ferry earlier, I just decided to come and take my chances." She flashed him one of those brilliant smiles that melted his insides. "Beat you to the house!"

He had a hundred questions to ask, but whatever the reason that had brought Zoe back to Paxos, he didn't care. It was enough to see her again. Something was very different. Her whole body seemed to sparkle with life.

She rode toward the house with more vigor than before, convincing him she hadn't hurt herself. He got back in his car and drove slowly the rest of the way. Zoe reached their destination first and put on the kickstand. She was waiting for him as he parked his car and got out.

"Where are you staying?"

"I don't know yet. Kyria Panos let me leave my luggage with her."

His mind was reeling. "You must be thirsty. Come in the house and we'll both have a soda."

Another smile from her turned his insides to butter. "You're a lifesaver."

They walked to the back door. Using his remote to let them in the house, he said, "The guest bathroom is behind that door at the far end of the kitchen."

"Thanks. I'm a mess."

The most gorgeous mess he'd ever seen. While she disappeared, he took the stairs two at a time to the loft and changed into shorts and a T-shirt. Before she came out, he hurried down to the kitchen in sandals and produced some colas from the fridge for them.

When she emerged she was *sans* the helmet. Her blond hair was attractively disheveled. Vasso wanted to plunge his fingers into it and kiss the very life out of her. Her flushed skin, in fact every single thing about her, was too desirable. But he'd learned a terrible lesson since the day she'd left Greece. He'd pushed her too hard, too soon, and wouldn't be making that mistake again.

He handed her a drink. "Welcome back to Greece." He clicked his can against hers and swallowed half the contents in one long gulp. "I like your T-shirt."

"The second I saw it, I had to have it and bought it from Kyria Panos earlier. She let me change shirts in her bathroom."

"You've made a friend there."

She sipped her drink. "Everyone is a friend on this island. Gus waved to me from the bus while I was riding on the road to your house."

"I take it you haven't seen Yiannis yet."

"No. If I couldn't find you, I was planning to bike to the center."

"You look wonderful in those shorts, Zoe."

She blushed. "Thank you."

"I'm used to seeing you in skirts and dresses."

"I know. They make a nice change. You look wonderful, too."

He didn't know how long he could resist crushing her in his arms, but he needed answers. "Shall we go out on the deck?"

"I'd love it."

They walked over to the sliding doors. She sat on one of the loungers while he pulled a chair around next to her. "Tell me what happened when you went back to New York."

He listened as she gave him an account. They were both circling the giant elephant standing on the deck, but he needed to let her guide this conversation if he wanted to know the reason she'd come back. If she was only here for a few days, he couldn't bear it.

"While I was there, I had to go in for my six-weeks checkup."

This was too much. Vasso broke out in a cold sweat and got up, too restless to sit still. He turned on his heel. "Were you given a death sentence and a date? Is that why you're here? To thank me one more time and say a final goodbye?"

"Vasso—" She paled and shot to her feet.

"Because if you are, I could have done without this visit. You know damn well why I asked you to marry me. Can you possibly understand the pain you've in-flicted by turning up here now?" The words had gushed out. He couldn't take them back.

"Do you want to hear the exact quote I got from my doctor?"

"Actually I don't." She seemed determined to tell him, but he couldn't go through this agony again and started for the doorway into the house.

She followed him. "He said, 'There's no recurrence of cancer, Zoe. I'm giving you another clean bill of health. In people like you with none of the other com-plicating factors, it's possible you'll live a full life.'"

Vasso wheeled around. "But you still don't believe him."

"You didn't let me finish. I told him about you and me."

He closed his eyes tightly. "Go on."

"The doctor said, 'You're a damn fool if you don't fly back there and tell him yes. I don't want to see you in my office again unless you have a wedding ring on your finger'!" Zoe moved closer to him.

"Little did he know he was speaking to the con-verted. After being the recipient of a miracle, I realized I would be an ungrateful wretch if I didn't embrace life fully. He reminded me that we are all facing a death sentence in life, but most of us don't have a time frame.

"Vasso—I came back because I want to spend the rest of my life with you. You have to know I love you to the depths of my being. I want to have children with you. I want the privilege of being called Kyria Giannopoulos, the wife who has a husband like no other in existence.

"You have no idea how handsome and spectacular you are. I lost my breath the first time I laid eyes on you, and I've never completely recovered. You're probably going to think I'm crazy, but I'm thankful I came down with the disease. It brought me to you. If you'll ask me again to marry you, I promise to make you happy because I'm the happiest woman alive to be loved by you."

He could feel the ice melting around his heart. "So you don't think I want you to be my wife because I feel responsible for you?"

"No, darling. I only said that because I was so afraid you couldn't love me the way I loved you. I know you're not perfect, but you are to me," her voice trembled.

"Then come here to me and show me."

She flew into his arms. When he felt them wind around his neck, he carried her in the house and followed her down on the couch. "*Agape mou*...I'm so in love with you I thought I was going to die when I read your letter.

"You're the woman my father was talking about. You're *the* one. I knew it when you walked in the center's office bringing spring with you. I'll never forget that moment. The fierce beating of my heart almost broke my rib cage. You're so sweet and so funny and so fun and so endearing and so beautiful and so kind and so compassionate all at the same time. I love you," he cried. "*I love you, Zoe.*"

He broke off telling her all the things she meant to him because her mouth got in the way. That luscious mouth that thrilled him in ways he'd never even dreamed possible. They couldn't get enough of each other. Her body melted against him. Their legs entwined and they forgot everything except the joy of loving each other at last.

If it hadn't been for his phone ringing, he didn't know when they would have surfaced. He let it ring because he had to do something else first.

"Maybe you should get that. It could be important," she whispered against his jaw.

"I'm pretty sure it's Akis calling to find out if I'm all right."

A frown marred her lovely features. "He loves you so much."

"I almost lost it when I read your letter. Akis found me here two days later. Just so he won't worry and come flying over here to find out if I'm still alive, just answer me one question, then I'll listen to the message. Will you marry me, Thespinis Zachos? We've already been through the sickness and health part. Will you be my love through life? I adore you."

Her eyes glistened with tears. "You already know my answer. I have a secret. The morning I got off the plane and found you waiting to pick me up at the airport, I wanted to be your wife. I couldn't imagine anything more wonderful." She buried her face in his neck. "You just don't know how much I love you."

He gave her another fierce kiss before getting up to find his phone on the table. "It's from my brother."

"Call him so he won't worry. I'll wait right here for you."

Without listening to the message, he called him back.

"Thanks for returning my call, bro."

"I'm glad you phoned. How would you like to be the best man at my wedding?"

"*What?*"

"She's back and we're getting married as soon as we can."

Akis let out a sound of pure joy then shouted the news to Raina who was in the background and gave her own happy cry. "Tell that Zoe I love her already."

Vasso stared down at her. "I will. She's easy to love."

"I only have one piece of advice. Remember what *Papa* said."

He knew. Treat Zoe like a queen. "I remember."

"Come on over for dinner so we can celebrate."

"You mean now?"

"Now! And you know why." Vasso knew exactly why. "We're expecting you." Akis clicked off.

Vasso hung up and leaned over Zoe. "We're invited for dinner."

"I don't want to move, but considering it's your brother…." She sat up and kissed him passionately. "You two have been through everything together. I get it."

He knew she did. "We'll go in the cruiser. I'll phone Kyria Panos and tell her we'll be by for your luggage later tonight."

CHAPTER TEN

October 16, Paxos Island

"IRIS!" ZOE CRIED out when she saw Akis help her old friend from New York out of the helicopter that had landed on the center's roof. She ran to her and they clung. "This is the best present I could have. You've been like a mother to me. I'm just so thankful you could come for the wedding."

"I wouldn't have missed it. Neither would Father Debakis."

Zoe's eyes lit on the priest who was getting out of the helicopter. The two of them had flown over yesterday and had stayed at the penthouse.

She left Iris long enough to run to the great man she owed her life to. "Oh, Father—I'm so glad you could come to marry us."

He hugged her hard. "It's my privilege. I had a feeling about the two of you a long time ago."

"Nothing gets past you."

Akis walked over to them. "Come on, everyone. Let's get on the elevator. Raina is waiting to help you into your wedding dress. Yiannis will drive you and Raina to the church. I'll drive everyone else in my car.

"Needless to say my older brother is climbing the walls waiting for the ceremony to begin. For his sake, I beg you to hurry, Zoe."

The best man's comment produced laughter from everyone and brought roses to Zoe's cheeks. She had to pinch herself that this was real and that she was getting married to Vasso.

When they reached the main floor, Zoe hurried along the hall to a private room where Raina was waiting.

"They've arrived!"

"Thank heaven! I've had three phone calls from Vasso. If he doesn't see you soon, he's going to have a nervous breakdown."

"Well we can't have that."

Zoe got out of her skirt and blouse and stepped into the white floor-length wedding dress. Raina had dared her to wear the latest fashion. It was strapless, something she would never have picked out on her own. But Raina insisted she was a knockout in it. This was one time she needed to render her soon-to-be husband *speechless*.

"Oh, Raina. It's so fun having you to help me. What I would have given for a sister like you."

"I feel the same way. Today I'm getting her. We're the luckiest women in the world."

"Yup. In a little while I'll be married to a god, too."

"They really are," Raina murmured. "But you've

still got your perfect figure while I'm beginning to get a bump."

"If you ever saw the way Akis looks at you when you're not aware of it, you'd know you and the baby are his whole world."

"Today the focus is on you. I have something for you, Zoe. Vasso asked me to give this to you."

With trembling hands, Zoe opened the satin-lined jewelry box. Inside lay a strand of gleaming pearls. A card sat on top. "*For my queen.*"

She looked at Raina in puzzlement. "He thinks of me as his queen?"

Raina nodded. "Akis gave me the same kind of pearls with the same sentiment on his card. When I asked him about it, he told me that his father had told them the women they would choose would be their queens and they needed to treat them like one."

"What a fabulous father he was. Vasso has always treated me like that."

"So has Akis. Now hold still while I put this around your neck."

Zoe's emotions were spilling out all over to feel the pearls against her skin. She'd already done her hair and applied her makeup. She wore pearl studs in her ears.

"Now for the crowning glory." Raina walked over and put the shoulder-length lace mantilla over her head. "When you get to the church, pull it over your face. You know? I think I'd better have an ambulance standing by. After Vasso sees you, anything could happen."

"You're such a tease."

"I'm only speaking the truth." She turned and opened

a long florist's box. Inside was a sheaf of flowers. Raina laid it in the crook of Zoe's arm.

"Aren't they lovely!" Her eyes took in the all-white arrangement: white roses, cymbidium orchids, hydrangeas and stephanotises. "My mother would have planned a bouquet just like this for me. She loved white flowers."

"Don't we all." They both breathed in the heavenly scent.

Zoe eyed her dearest new friend. "You look absolutely stunning in that blue silk suit." Raina wore a gardenia in the lapel.

"Except that I had to undo the zipper to get into it. I think I can get away with it for as long as we're at the church." She smiled at Zoe. "Ready?"

"Yes," she said emotionally.

They left the room and headed for the main entrance. When they walked outside by the fountain Zoe saw Yianni. He looked splendid wearing his former naval uniform. "You're a sight for sore eyes, Zoe."

"So are you. I can see why your wife grabbed you up the second she met you."

"You look radiant today." He kissed her forehead then pulled the edge of the veil down to cover her face.

"Thank you for standing in for my father."

"It's an honor. Now let's get you in the car and be off. Your fiancé is waiting for you. I've had two phone calls from Vasso. He's going to have a coronary if we don't arrive soon."

Zoe laughed and got in the rear of the limo. Raina helped her with her dress. Yianni checked to make sure everything was secure then he drove them through the olive groves and up the steep hillside to the glistening white church at the summit. It made an imposing sight overlooking the sea.

This was the church where Raina and Akis had been married by his family priest. Their parents had been buried in the cemetery behind it. This was the place where history had been made and was still being made today by another Giannopoulos son.

Father Debakis would be doing the honors with the other priest's help. This was right out of a fairy tale.

The closer they got, she could see dozens of cars lining both sides of the road leading to the church. Akis and his best friend Theo had taken care of the invitations. Zoe feared there wouldn't be enough room in the church to accommodate everyone.

Vasso had told her not to worry. The priest would leave the front doors open and set up chairs for those people who couldn't get inside. A real Greek wedding was a high point no one wanted to miss.

When they came around the bend she could see dozens of beautifully dressed guests seated at tables outside with white ribbons on the chairs. But that wasn't all. Behind the chairs were throngs of people willing to stand.

Raina and Theo's wife Chloe had made the arrangements for the food, which would be served on the grounds after the ceremony, followed by singing and dancing. She promised they wouldn't run out of food, but when Zoe saw the amount of people congregated, it shocked her.

Yianni drove past the cars and circled around to the front steps of the church. Suddenly all Zoe could see was Vasso. He stood at the open doors waiting for her in a formal midnight-blue suit with a white rose in the lapel. She couldn't hold back her cry when she saw him. No man was ever created like him.

Once the limo came to a stop, he walked toward her with a loving look in his black eyes that lit up her whole body. Yianni came around the door to help her out. But it was Vasso who grasped her hand and squeezed it.

Raina took the flowers from her and walked behind them with Yianni while Vasso led her into the church. She'd been in here several times in the last few weeks and thought it an exquisite jewel. The smell of incense and flowers greeted them as they moved toward Father Debakis, decked out in his priestly finery. The interior was so full people who hadn't found a seat were lined up against the walls.

Both she and Vasso wanted a traditional wedding to honor their parents. Her heart pounded so hard she knew he could feel its beat through her hand. When they arrived at the altar, he leaned over and lifted the veil. The love pouring from his soul was evident in those gorgeous black eyes.

If ever there was a time to faint, it was now. But she didn't feel light-headed. She felt a spirit of joy wash over her as they grasped hands and entered into this sacred ritual that would make him her husband.

They went through the different stages of the ring

ceremony until it came to the union of the bride and groom with the crowning. This was the part she'd been looking forward to. The priest took two crowns with ribbons from the altar table, blessed them, then put the crowns on their heads.

"Oh, Lord our God, crown them with glory and honor."

The other priest exchanged their crowns over their heads to seal the union. He read from the Gospel account of the wedding in Cana. After a prayer, he passed the common cup for them to take a sip of the wine. This was the part that meant they shared equally in the process of life. Father Debakis then led them around the table three times.

This was where her heart beat wildly as the two of them stared at each other while they made circles. A hint of a smile broke the corners of Vasso's mouth. Zoe felt this part of the wedding ceremony was terribly romantic, but she'd never admit it to anyone but him. He looked so handsome with the crown on she wanted a picture of him just like that.

When they faced the priest again, he removed their crowns. His eyes rested kindly on Vasso. "Be magnified, O Bridegroom, as Abraham." Then he looked at Zoe with such tenderness she was deeply moved. "And you, O Bride, be magnified as was Sarah, and live a long, fruitful life."

He'd added those words meant just for her. Once again she was overcome with gratitude that out of the shadows, she'd emerged into a light greater than the one she could see with the naked eye.

Father Debakis placed a Bible in both their hands and said a final prayer. He smiled at them. "Congratulations, Kyrie and Kyria Giannopoulos. Just think, Vasso," he whispered. "If I hadn't called you…"

"I don't want to think about it, Father," he whispered back. He put his arm around Zoe's waist and they faced the congregation. She'd never seen so many smiling faces in her life, but one stood out above the rest.

It was Akis. He and Vasso exchanged a silent message that was so sweet and said so much Zoe could hardly breathe with the love she could see between the two of them.

Suddenly Vasso lowered his mouth to her ear. "Let the fun begin."

Raina came forward to hand her the sheaf of flowers. After she stepped away, Zoe and Vasso started walking down the aisle. Everyone was here. Olympia and Nestor had come from the center. She smiled at Kyria Lasko, Kyria Panos, Gus the bus driver, Iris, and her doctor from the center in Astoria.

With each step, people said Vasso's name; they were the managers from some of their stores, family friends, their mutual friends, two of the helicopter pilots, the woman called Elpis who'd given the boys free sweets when they were young. The list went on and on. When they reached the rear of the church and stepped outside, there was cheering and music. People rushed to congratulate them.

The paparazzi were out in full measure, but Zoe didn't care. She was too happy to be married to her heart's desire to have a care in the world. They had their own videographer there to record the proceedings of the day.

"Give us a kiss with your husband, Kyria Giannopoulos."

"Gladly!" She turned to Vasso. There was a wild look in his eye before he caught her to him and kissed the life out of her in front of everyone. They were a little drunk with happiness. The taste of his mouth was sweeter than any wine. She would never be able to get enough of it. Anyone could see that.

Part of her felt a fierce pride at the turnout. If she had a megaphone and dared, she'd love to say, "Look at these poor Giannopoulos boys now! Eat your hearts out!" But of course she couldn't say or do that.

The caterers had arrived and had set up more tables to accommodate the huge crowd. With the musicians in place, the dancing began. Yianni grabbed Zoe's other hand and several dozen people joined to form a line. They danced through the tables while everyone threw rice. The excitement had made her heady.

Every time Vasso's fiery eyes met hers, her heart palpitated right out of her chest. She knew what he was thinking. It was all she could think about. Their wedding night.

Zoe had been waiting all her life for the time when she would marry. She actually wanted to call Ms. Kallistos one day and tell her that *she* was the person responsible for the miracle that had come into Zoe's life. But on reflection it wouldn't be a good idea.

Vasso had hired Alexandra and there was no doubt in Zoe's mind the manager had been crazy about him from day one. Through Akis she'd learned that Sofia Peri had left her husband and wanted Vasso back. Zoe couldn't blame her for that. Today she could feel sorry for every woman alive who wasn't married to her Apollo.

Today she'd met so many people who thought the world of Vasso and Akis. If their father were still alive, he would be so proud of them. *And their mother...*Zoe had seen the few pictures they had of her. She'd been a beauty. That's why the two brothers were so gorgeous.

Oh, Vasso. I can't wait until we're alone. Really alone.

The party went on several hours. Toasts were made to the happy couple. As Zoe danced with Akis, Vasso danced with Raina. Then she saw the brothers signal each other. The next thing she knew Akis whirled her toward the limousine where Yianni was parked in front of the church.

Akis opened the rear door and hurried her inside. Vasso came around the other side and slid in next to her. The second his door closed, the limo started moving. Everyone saw them leave and gave out shouts. But Zoe was caught in Vasso's arms. His mouth came down on hers and the world whirled away. When he lifted his lips, she realized the car had come to a stop outside Vasso's beach house.

He opened the door and stepped out. Then he helped her. The second she was on her feet he picked her up and carried her in his arms. "Thank you, Yiannis."

The car drove off, leaving them alone. "I've been dreaming about doing this for weeks, Zoe."

"So have I, darling."

Vasso unlocked the back door with the remote and carried her over the threshold. He didn't stop until he'd gained the loft. "I've never been up here before," she said as he twirled her around.

"That was the plan. Thank heaven the long wait is finally over."

"I love you, my darling Vasso. *I love you.*"

After they'd made love throughout the night, Vasso's beautiful wife fell asleep around five o'clock, but he was still wide awake. Adrenaline rushed through his system like a never-ending fire.

Her wedding dress lay over one of the chairs, her mantilla on the dresser with her wedding flowers. Their scent filled the loft. He'd thrown his wedding suit over another chair. The white rose was still in the lapel.

She was the most unselfish lover he could ever have imagined. For the next little while he lay on his side holding her loosely in his arms so he could study her beautiful features. He still couldn't believe she was his wife, all signed, sealed and delivered to be his, now and forever.

Her mouth was like a half-opened rose, lush with a red tint, like a strawberry. He needed to taste her again and again and never stop. As soon as he started to kiss her in earnest, she made a little moan and her eyes opened.

"Vasso—I dreamed I was kissing you, but I really *am* kissing you."

He laughed deep in his throat. "I wanted to kiss you

good morning. It wasn't nice of me to wake you up, but I'm so in love with you, I don't think I'll ever be able to leave you alone."

"Please don't, or I won't be able to bear it." She rolled over and kissed him so deeply that age-old ritual started again. They didn't come up for breath for several more hours.

Vasso finally lifted his mouth from hers. "Did I tell you yet how gorgeous you looked in that wedding dress? I could hardly breathe when you got out of the limo."

"Raina said I should wear it to give you a jolt."

"You did a lot more than that. Every man at the wedding would have given anything to be in my place. She has the right instincts. Raina's so good for Akis."

"I love her already."

"So do I."

"You kind of stopped traffic yourself. Have I told you yet how good you are for me? You make me thankful to have been born a woman. Seriously, Vasso, I'm so wild about you I think maybe there's something wrong with me."

"I'll never complain." He kissed every feature. "So you don't mind that I'm invading your space?"

"I must have been crazy when I said that."

"It's because you never lived with a man and didn't know it's the only way for a man and woman to experience true joy. These last few years I knew that the most important element in my life was missing. But not anymore." He crushed her body to his, kissing her neck and throat. "Where do you want to go on our honeymoon?"

"Right here with you."

"We could go anywhere," he murmured against her lips.

"I know. What do you say we wait to take a trip after we find out we're going to have a baby."

Vasso smoothed the hair off her forehead. "You want a baby soon?"

"You know I do. I'm so envious of Raina and Akis. There's no reason to wait. You heard what Father Debakis said. Be fruitful."

He rolled her over and looked deep into her eyes. "Maybe he already knows something we don't."

"I know. Exciting, isn't it?"

"In that case we'll just stay here until we get it right."

She cupped his face and pulled him down to press a passionate kiss to his mouth. "I was hoping you'd say that. If you think I'm shameful, I don't care. I need you with every particle of my being."

His expression sobered. He kissed her hands and moved them to either side of her head. "Don't you know you've made me whole? A thrill went through me when you circled the altar with me. I felt your love binding me tighter and tighter."

"I had that same wonderful feeling," she cried softly. "Our ceremony was holy, but it was also very romantic."

He smiled. "Only you could come up with the perfect description. That's because there's only one perfect you. You're the light of my life, *agape mou*. Kiss me again, Kyria Giannopoulos."

Three hours later he heard his cell vibrate. Only one person would be texting him.

Zoe smiled. "That has to be your brother. I love how close you are. Put him out of his misery and tell him we're deliriously happy."

Vasso reached for the phone on the bedside table. "He says to turn on the news. Do you want to watch?"

"No. I don't need to see my beloved husband on TV when I've got him right here in my arms."

"That's just another one of the thousand reasons I love you more than life itself." He buried his face in her neck, crying her name over and over again.

* * * * *

Praise for Marie Ferrarella

"A joy to read"
—*RT Book Reviews* on *Christmas Cowboy Duet*

"Ferrarella's romance will charm with all
the benefits and pitfalls of a sweet
small-town setting."
—*RT Book Reviews* on *Lassoed by Fortune*

"Heartwarming. That's the way I have described
every book by Marie Ferrarella that I have read.
In the Family Way engenders in me the same
warm, fuzzy feeling that I have come to
expect from her books."
—*The Romance Reader*

"Ms Ferrarella warms our hearts with her
charming characters and delicious interplay."
—*RT Book Reviews* on
A Husband Waiting to Happen

"Ms Ferrarella creates fiery, strong-willed
characters, an intense conflict and an absorbing
premise no reader could possibly resist."
—*RT Book Reviews* on *A Match for Morgan*

THE COWBOY
AND THE LADY

BY
MARIE FERRARELLA

Published in Great Britain 2015
by Mills & Boon, an imprint of Harlequin (UK) Limited,
Eton House, 18-24 Paradise Road, Richmond, Surrey, TW9 1SR

© 2015 Marie Rydzynski-Ferrarella

ISBN: 978-0-263-25164-7

23-0915

Harlequin (UK) Limited's policy is to use papers that are natural, renewable and recyclable products and made from wood grown in sustainable forests. The logging and manufacturing processes conform to the legal environmental regulations of the country of origin.

Printed and bound in Spain
by CPI, Barcelona

Marie Ferrarella, a *USA TODAY* bestselling and RITA® Award-winning author, has written more than two hundred and fifty books for Mills & Boon, some under the name Marie Nicole. Her romances are beloved by fans worldwide. Visit her website, www.marieferrarella.com.

To
Stella Bagwell,
who I always channel
when I go to Texas in my mind.
Thank you for your eternal patience,
and most of all, for your friendship.

Prologue

"You're going where?" John Kincannon demanded angrily.

A high school basketball coach, Deborah Winters Kincannon's husband had just come home to find her shaken and pale as she was terminating a phone call. Her next words to him had obviously taken him by surprise.

From the look on his face, it was rather an unpleasant surprise.

He glared at her. It was supposed to make her back down. But she couldn't. Not this time. If she did, she had a strong feeling the results would turn out to be fatal, if not now, then soon.

Debi felt almost numb as she replaced the receiver on the kitchen wall phone. Part of her refused to believe that the conversation she had just had was real, that it wasn't the product of some recurring nightmare she just couldn't seem to wake up from.

Another part of her knew that this was all too real—and something, frankly, she had been expecting even as she'd been dreading it.

When her husband didn't seem to absorb what she'd said to him, Debi repeated it. "I'm going down to the police station to bail Ryan out."

The simple statement—voiced for a second time—infused her husband with pure rage. His complexion actually reddened as he shifted, blocking her path to the front door.

"Oh, no, you're not," he declared heatedly. "This is it! I have *had* it with that kid, Deborah."

For a second, Debi closed her eyes, digging deep for patience. She wasn't up to another argument. She'd gotten home just ten minutes ago herself, after putting in a very long day in the OR with three back-to-back surgeries. It wasn't supposed to have been three, but one of the other surgical nurses had called in sick and she had wound up pulling an extra shift.

She was bone weary and this was just the absolute *very* last thing she needed to cap off a day that had dragged on much too long.

"Look, I know you're angry," Debi began wearily, "but—"

"No, uh-uh, no 'buts,'" John informed her firmly as well as loudly. "We've given that kid every chance and it's gotten us nowhere. He can stay in that jail and rot for all I care. You're not going down there to bail him out. I refuse to allow it, do you hear me?"

Debi looked at her husband, stunned. Had John always been this hard-hearted and she'd just missed it?

Upset and overwrought, Debi upbraided herself, knowing she had turned a blind eye to one too many signs when it came to John. He'd changed. This was *not* the man she had fallen in love with all those years ago on the campus.

"I can't just leave him there, John," she pointed out, struggling to curb her own anger.

John obviously didn't share her opinion. "You can and

you will," he informed her. "I think I've been pretty understanding about all this. It's not everybody who'll take his wife's brother into his home, but this is it, the proverbial straw. I don't want that kid in my house anymore!"

He was doing it again. John was making her feel like an outsider in her own home. A home she had helped pay for as much as he had. Why was he behaving like a Neanderthal?

"It's my house, too, John," she reminded him, her voice tight.

"Nobody said it wasn't," he snapped at her. "But you're going to have to choose, Deborah."

"Choose?" she repeated incredulously, her voice deadly still. John couldn't possibly be saying what she thought he was saying to her.

When had he gotten so cold, so unfeeling?

There were tears gathering in her soul, but her eyes remained dry.

"Yeah. *Choose*," he emphasized. "It's either Ryan or me, Deborah. You can't have both."

She stared at the man she'd loved all through high school and college. The man she thought she knew so well, but obviously didn't know at all.

Just to be perfectly clear, she put the question to him. "You're asking me to choose between my kid brother and you."

John continued to glare at her. His brown eyes were completely cold and flat, his stand unwavering. "That's what I'm doing."

"Ryan doesn't have anybody but me." Had John forgotten that?

It had only been three short years since Ryan and her parents had been involved in that horrific car accident. He was twelve at the time. The accident claimed her parents and came very close to claiming her brother, as well. It had taken close to six months of physical therapy before Ryan could get back on his feet.

The scars on his body healed. The ones inside his head were another story. Debi was convinced that they were responsible for her brother transforming from a kind, sweet young man who got straight As into a sullen, troubled teen who ditched more classes than he attended.

"That's not my problem," John informed her. "Him or me, Deborah. You have to choose."

If he could say that to her, then their marriage was already over, she realized. "I'm not leaving him in jail, John," she retorted, grabbing up her shoulder bag.

"Fine. Go." John angrily waved her toward the door. "Rescue that sad sack of wasted flesh. But when you get back, I won't be here."

Angry, hurt and exasperated beyond words that John could put her into this sort of a position when she was struggling to deal with the circumstances surrounding her brother's arrest, she glared at her husband. "That is *your* choice, John. I can't do anything about that," she informed him coldly.

"You're making a big mistake, Deborah!" John shouted at her back.

She squared her shoulders. "I think I made one four years ago," Debi said, referring to the length of their marriage. She didn't bother to turn around. She slammed the door in her wake, thinking that it might make her feel better.

It didn't.

She had a confused, rebellious younger brother who was, unless something drastic happened, on his way to a serious prison record before his eighteenth birthday, and a husband who was bailing on her at the worst possible time rather than offering emotional support.

She had hit rock bottom, Debi thought as she got into her car and started up the engine. Worse than that, she was in far over her head. What she desperately needed was to find a way back up to the surface before she drowned.

Chapter One

Standing just inside the corral, Jackson White Eagle leaned back against the recently repainted railing, watching three of the current crop of teenage boys, who lived in the old converted bunkhouse, put the horses through their paces.

They probably didn't realize that in actuality the horses were putting *them* through *their* paces, Jackson thought. Training horses trained *them*.

He felt the corners of his mouth curve just a little in satisfaction.

Whatever the reason behind it, even after all this time, it still felt odd to glance in a mirror or a reflecting window and realize that he was smiling. The first ten or so years of his life, there had been precious little for him to smile about. He had grown up with nothing but bitter words and anger erupting, time and again, in his house.

His parents were always fighting. His father, Ben White Eagle, was a great deal larger than his mother and Jackson had instinctively taken his mother's side. He'd appointed himself her protector even though at ten, he had been small for his age and his father had continually referred to him as "a worthless runt."

Despite that demoralizing image, he had tried his best

to protect the woman who had given him life. He went on being protective of his mother until the day that she walked out on his father—and him.

At first, he had convinced himself that it was just an oversight on her part. He'd told himself that his mother was too angry at his father to realize that she'd left without him.

Night after night, he waited, listening for her return.

But after two weeks had passed, and then three, and then four, he knew he had to face the truth. His mother wasn't coming back for him. That forced him to face the fact that the person who he had loved most in the world hadn't loved him enough to take him with her. His heart broke.

And then he just shut down.

By then, four weeks after his mother had taken off, his father was already preparing to get married again. He was marrying the woman he'd been having an affair with. The affair that had produced another son and had been the final straw for his first wife.

Like him, his stepmother, Sylvia, was only half Navajo. Sylvia was also the mother of his half brother, Garrett, who was five at the time of his parents' marriage.

The second his father brought Sylvia into the house, Jackson was certain that he was going to be locked out of the family. In his eyes, his father, Sylvia and Garrett formed a complete unit. That left him in the role of the outsider, unwanted and on the outside, looking in.

But Sylvia hadn't been the typical stepmother he'd expected. To his surprise, she reached out to him. She went so far as to tell him that she wasn't going to try to take his mother's place. But that didn't mean that he couldn't come to her with anything that was bothering him. Knowing that he'd gone through a lot, she said that she intended to be there for him, as well as for Garrett. To her, they were *both* her sons.

He'd appreciated the effort on Sylvia's part, but he was just too angry at the world, predominantly his mother, to allow Sylvia into his life. He began acting out, taking part in unacceptable behavior.

Things went from bad to worse.

His father's idea of fixing a problem was to take a belt to the cause. At first, he did it covertly, waiting until he got Jackson alone. But he soon tired of that and lashed out at him the moment his temper flared.

The first time Sylvia became aware of what her husband was doing, she quickly put herself between him and Jackson. Ben had shoved her aside, which caused Jackson to attempt to tackle him. It ended badly for Jackson, but he had gotten a few licks in before his father had gotten the better of him.

Sylvia had called the reservation police. Ben White Eagle took off for parts unknown that same night, before they came for him.

Jackson was relieved that his father was gone, but the absence of his father's salary made life very difficult for Sylvia, his half brother and him. Sylvia never blamed him, never threw the incident in his face. This didn't change the fact that he felt as if he was to blame for everything that had gone wrong.

Things got even worse.

He got arrested—more than once. And each time he did, Sylvia would go to the local law enforcement establishment on the reservation, pay whatever fines needed to be paid and bring him back home.

Jackson secretly felt sorry for what he was putting her

through, but even her tears hadn't gotten him to change. Angry at the world and with little to no self-esteem to speak of, for a while it looked as if his fate was predestined—and cast in stone.

And then his stepmother, in what she later admitted to him was one final act of desperation, turned to his father's older and far sterner, as well as far more stable, brother, Sam, for help. Sam White Eagle had pulled himself out of poverty and had, Jackson later found out, managed to survive personal tragedy, as well, although at the time it had been touch and go. His wife of less than eighteen months died giving birth to his son. Beset by a number of complications, the baby had died a couple of days later. Sam had them buried together. And then he had shut himself down emotionally, losing himself in bottle after bottle until he finally pulled himself up out of what he recognized would have been a death spiral.

Emotionally stoic, he did feel for his brother's sons as well as for Sylvia, which led to his taking her up on her plea.

Sam became the male role model for both him and for Garrett. Initially, his uncle put them both to work on his small horse ranch. His reasoning was that if they were kept constantly busy, they wouldn't have the time, not to mention the energy, to act out.

His uncle turned out to be right. Jackson knew that to the end of his days, no matter what he accomplished, he would owe it all to Sam. When his uncle died, leaving the ranch to him and to Garrett, Jackson decided that Sam's work should continue. He broached the idea to Garrett, who didn't need to be sold on it. His brother wholeheartedly agreed with him before he'd had a chance to finish a second sentence.

And that was how The Healing Ranch came to be. Five years after Sam had passed away, the ranch was still in existence, turning out top-quality quarter horses and transformed juvenile offenders who had learned to walk the straight and narrow.

Secretly, Jackson had thought that, after a while, this so-called crusade he had undertaken would get old for him. When he had first started all this, he hadn't realized that there was a part of him that actually enjoyed the challenge, that looked forward to that rush that came when he knew that the misdirected kid he was working with had turned a corner and no longer was interested in gaining notoriety for what he did wrong but for what he did that was right.

"Wish you were here, Sam, to see this," Jackson murmured under his breath. He glanced up at the all but cloudless sky. "This is all your doing, you know," he added.

"You know, they lock people up who talk to themselves with such feeling," Garrett said to his older brother as he came over to join him.

Five years younger than Jackson, and with only their father in common, the whole world could still easily identify the two as brothers. They almost looked alike, from their deep, thick, blue-black hair to their hypnotic blue eyes. Jackson's had come directly from his mother while with Garrett it was most likely someone somewhere within his family tree.

"Just your word against mine, Garrett. No one else is anywhere within earshot so there's no one around to back up your claim. They'll think you just want the ranch all to yourself and that you're looking for a way to get me out of the picture," Jackson told him.

So saying, Jackson eyed his half brother. They had gone through a lot together, he thought with affection. That didn't mean that either of them ever purposely missed a chance to zing the other.

Garrett grinned. "I guess you saw right through my plot." He snapped his fingers like someone acknowledging a missed opportunity. "Foiled again. Looks like I'm just going to have to come up with another way to take over the old homestead."

Jackson glanced at his watch. The latest applicant he had accepted at the beginning of the week should have arrived by now. He wondered if something had happened to bring about a change in plans. It wouldn't be the first time a teen's parent or guardian had backed out of the arrangement before it ever started. Total commitment was required and sometimes that didn't pan out.

"I take it there's no word yet on our latest resident 'bad boy'?" he asked Garrett.

Heaven help him, he needed a new challenge, Jackson thought. Needed to be given another teen to turn around and thereby rescue. With each and every one that he and Garrett rehabilitated, he was paying off a little more of the debt that he owed to Sam, a debt that he could never really fully repay. And although his uncle had been gone for a few years now, Jackson felt that somehow, Sam knew the good that was being done in his name by the boy he had saved from coming to a very an unsavory end.

Garrett climbed onto the corral, straddling the top rail.

"Not yet," he answered. "I just checked phone messages, emails and text messages. Unless the kid and his guardian are using smoke signals to communicate, they haven't tried to get in touch with us." Garrett shrugged casually. "Could be they just decided to change their minds at the last minute."

"Always possible," Jackson admitted—although he really doubted it. The call he had received from the troubled teen's guardian made him feel that the woman thought that the situation was desperate—just as desperate as she was. He'd heard things in her voice that she hadn't knowingly put into words, but he'd heard them just the same. Things that told him that even if he didn't have a ready bed for this latest applicant, he would have found a way to make room somehow.

Luckily, he hadn't had to get creative on that front. When he'd inherited the ranch, he and Garrett had renovated the bunkhouse so that it could handle eight boys with ease. Ten would have necessitated bringing in two extra twin beds and space would have been rather limited, but it could be done.

Currently, there were seven boys living on the ranch besides Garrett and himself. His latest success story, Casey Brooks, had graduated less than a week ago. Upon his initial arrival, Casey had been one seriously messed-up, lost sixteen-year-old. His parents had gotten in contact with him because they were genuinely afraid that their son would either be killed or eventually land in prison, where heaven only knew what would happen to him.

Casey had been so tightly wound up it was a wonder he hadn't just exploded before he ever came to The Healing Ranch.

Getting through to the inner, hidden, decent teen had required an extreme amount of patience and going not just the extra mile but the extra twenty miles. There were times when he was certain that Casey was just too far gone to reach. Those were the times that he had made himself channel Sam, recalling how his uncle had managed to get to him back when he was just like Casey.

It worked, and in the end it had all paid off. That was all he—and Garrett—were ever interested in. The final results. That made everything that had come before—the strategizing, the enduring of endless hostility and curses—all worth it. And he also kept in contact with former "graduates," taking an interest in their lives and making sure that they remained proud of their own progress—and didn't backslide.

So far, he hadn't lost a single teen. He intended to keep it that way.

"Hey, you think that's them?" Garrett asked. Shading his eyes with one hand, he pointed at something behind his brother's back with the other.

Jackson turned around to see a beige, almost nondescript sedan that had definitely seen better days approaching from the north. The road was open, but the driver refrained from speeding, something that tempted a lot of drivers around the area, whether they were tourists or natives.

The closer the vehicle came, the dustier it appeared. Jackson recalled that his new challenge hailed from the state of Indiana. Indianapolis to be precise. And unless the Dallas airport car rental agency was dealing in really beaten-up-looking vehicles these days, his latest boarder had been driven down to Forever rather than coming in by airplane.

Interesting, Jackson thought.

RESTLESS, IMPATIENT AND WORRIED, Ryan Winter shifted in his seat for the umpteenth time even though he had decided more than several hundred miles ago that there was no such thing as a comfortable position in his sister's beat-up, secondhand sedan.

Ryan glared out the window, sulking.

He'd always been able to get his sister to come around to his way of thinking. But the other morning, when she had told him—not asked, but *told*, something he was still angry about—that they were going to a place called Forever, Texas, he'd thought she was kidding. It wasn't until she'd marched into his room and thrown some of his clothes into a suitcase, then grabbed him by the arm and all but thrown *him* into the car after the suitcase, that he realized she was serious.

Dead serious.

He'd tried to reason with her, then he threatened, cajoled and pleaded, going through the entire gamut of ordinarily successful avenues of getting her to change her mind. But every attempt had failed. One by one, his sister had tossed them all by the wayside. She wasn't going to let him talk or con his way out of going to this stupid, smelly horse place, and he was furious.

He'd had all those miles to sufficiently work himself up.

He thought he knew why this was happening. Because he was the reason why her stick-in-the-mud husband had left. But just because her life was falling apart was no reason for her to take it out on him.

Making one last-ditch attempt to get her to turn the car around, Ryan said, "Look, I'm sorry about your marriage breaking up, but the way I see it, I did you a favor. John was a loser, and you're a hell of a lot better off without him. If you're dumping me here at this stupid prison ranch just to get even, it's not going to work because I swear I'm taking off the first chance I get," he added for good measure, thinking that would really get to his sister. Debi was very big on family and he was officially all she had. He felt confident that the threat of losing him would be enough to get his sister to back off about this prison ranch and give him the space he needed. "And if I do leave, you'll never find me."

DEBI'S HANDS TIGHTENED on the steering wheel. It had been a long drive from Indianapolis. She was hot, she was tired and she'd gotten lost half a dozen times during the trip down to this ranch. She fervently hoped this place dealt in miracles on a regular basis because she really, really needed one.

Badly.

Debi had a feeling that nothing short of a miracle was going to save her brother. And maybe even *that* wasn't enough.

She spared her brother a quick glance. He always had a habit of trying to turn things around, of putting her on the defensive. Well, not this time. She couldn't allow it.

"This isn't about my marriage, or lack thereof, this is about you. You're broken, Ryan, and I don't know how to fix you." Even saying it pained her, but it was the truth. Somehow, Ryan had lost his way and she had lost the ability to connect with him. She wasn't too proud to admit that she needed help in both departments.

"Drop-kicking me here to this dude ranch that's built out of horse manure sure as hell isn't going to do it, Debs."

She sincerely hoped that wasn't a prophecy. "I've tried everything else with you and it hasn't worked. Maybe the people who run this ranch will have better luck."

Even as she said it, she mentally crossed her fingers.
She'd been at her wits' end and more than desperate the
day after she had bailed her brother out of jail. True to
his word, John had been gone when she came home with
Ryan. The following morning, she'd broken down in the
hospital's fifth-floor break room. Trying to comfort her,
Sheila, another nurse on the floor, told her about The
Healing Ranch.

It turned out that Sheila's cousin had a son who was
well on his way to a long rap sheet and possibly life in
prison. She had sent him to The Healing Ranch in a last-
ditch attempt to save him from himself. According to
Sheila, it had worked. Three months later, she'd gotten
back the decent kid she'd always known was in there.

Debi had called the number Sheila had given her that
very day. She'd had to leave a message on the answering
machine, which didn't fill her with much confidence, but
that all changed when she received a call back that evening from the man who ran the place. She remembered
thinking that Jackson White Eagle had a nice, calming
voice. Just talking to him had made her feel that maybe
it wasn't really hopeless after all.

He hadn't made her any lofty promises, he'd just said
that he would see what could be done and invited her to
come down with her brother. Debi hadn't wanted a tour,
she'd wanted to sign Ryan up right then and there, afraid
that if this Jackson person had a chance to interact with
her brother first, he couldn't accept him into the program.

"You're sure you don't want to see the ranch and think
about it first?" he had asked her.

Her online research had told her that the man who
ran the ranch had a perfect track record so far. That was

definitely good enough for her—especially since she had nowhere else to turn.

"I'm sure," she had replied.

She'd taken a leave of absence from the hospital, gotten together what there was in her meager savings account, transferring it into her checking account, and driven down here with Ryan. John's divorce papers were tucked into her purse. She had no one to lean on but herself.

Ryan had put up a huge fuss about being taken away from his friends. He'd also threatened to run away the first chance he got.

He repeated the threat every hour on the hour in case she hadn't heard him the first half a dozen times.

Debi told herself that Ryan only threatened to run away because he wanted to frighten her into turning around and driving back to Indianapolis. Maybe a year ago, she might have, but what stopped her now was that she knew if she did, for all intents and purposes she would have been signing her brother's epitaph because as sure as day followed night, Ryan was on a path headed straight for destruction.

"Well, the clowns who run this place aren't going to get the opportunity to brainwash me because I'm taking off first chance I get. You know I will," he threatened again.

Debi sighed as she stared at the road before her. She wasn't all that sure the threats were empty ones. Ryan could very well mean what he said. That was why she wasn't going back home once she had finished registering him and got him settled in. If Ryan *did* take off, she wanted to be right here where she could go after him and bring him back. He was her brother and at fifteen, obviously still a minor. She was responsible for him, and she would have felt that way even if he were eighteen.

She prayed that it wouldn't come to that, but considering what she had already gone through with Ryan, she wasn't counting on it being easy.

"I mean it. I'm gone. First chance I get," Ryan repeated with emphasis.

"Yes, I heard you," Debi replied stoically. She also heard the fear in his voice. *God, let these people here reach him*, she prayed. She saw the cluster of people in and around the corral. "Okay, we're here. For my sake, try not to insult the man in the first five minutes."

Ryan's laugh had a nasty sound to it, and she knew this was not going to go well. "Hey, I don't want to spoil the man, now, do I?"

She didn't bother answering her brother. Anger and despair had grabbed equal parts of her. Anger that he had allowed himself to become this destructive, negative being and despair because she couldn't snap him out of it and had been forced to turn to strangers for help. She'd thought she was too proud for that but obviously pride had withered and died in the face of this situation.

There were two cowboys by the corral as she pulled up. Were they just workers, or…?

She saw the slightly taller of the two draw away from the enclosure and approach her car. Debi turned off the engine, carefully watching the approaching cowboy's every move. He strolled toward them like a sleek panther, with an economy of steps.

Debi got out of the vehicle. Ryan remained where he was. She wasn't about to leave him in the car, not even if she was only inches away and had the car keys in her hand. She knew her brother, knew that he could hot-wire anything with an engine and take off at a moment's notice. She had no doubt that he probably thought that he could propel himself into the driver's seat and just take off without a single backward glance.

Well, not today, she told herself. Bending down, she looked in through the open window on the driver's side. "Get out of the car, Ryan."

"No," he informed her flatly.

At fifteen, Ryan was taller than she was and while scrawny-looking, he was still stronger. The only time she ever managed to get him to move was when she caught him off guard.

That wasn't going to work here, she realized, looking down into his defiant face.

Jackson White Eagle chose that exact moment to enter into her life. "Trouble, ma'am?"

Chapter Two

"'Ma'am'?" Ryan echoed with a sneer. "Is this guy for real?" he jeered, turning toward his sister.

"Very real," Jackson assured him in an even voice that was devoid of any emotion. "Why don't you get out of the car like your sister requested?" he suggested in the same tone.

"Why don't you mind your own freakin' business?" Ryan retorted, sticking up his chin the way he did whenever he was spoiling for a fight.

"For the next month or two or three," Jackson informed him slowly with emphasis, "you *are* my business, Ryan," he concluded in the same low, evenly controlled voice with which he had greeted the teen's sister.

Jackson opened the door on the passenger side, firmly took hold of Ryan's arm and with one swift, economic movement, pulled his newest "ranch hand," as he liked to call the teens who arrived on his doorstep, out of the car and to his feet.

"Ow!" Ryan cried angrily, grabbing his shoulder as if it had been wrenched out of its socket. "You going to let this jerk manhandle me like that?" he demanded angrily, directing the question at his sister.

Before Debi had a chance to respond, Jackson told her brother matter-of-factly, "That didn't hurt, Ryan."

"How do you know?" Ryan cried, still holding his shoulder as if he expected his arm to drop off.

"Because," Jackson said in a calm, steely voice, "if I had wanted to hurt you, Ryan, trust me, you would have known it. To begin with, the pain would have thrown you off balance and you would have dropped like a stone to your knees." He released his hold on Ryan's arm, but his eyes still held Ryan prisoner. "Now then, why don't you get your things out of the car and come with me? I'll show you and your sister where you'll be staying for the next few months."

"Few months?" Ryan repeated indignantly. "The hell I will."

Jackson suppressed a sigh. He turned from the woman who he was about to escort to the ranch house and looked back at the teen she had brought for him to essentially "fix." This one, he had a feeling, was going to take a bit of concentrated effort.

"By the way," he said to Ryan, "I let the first two occasions slide because you're new here and this is your first day—"

"And my last," Ryan interjected.

Debi had stood by, quiet, until she couldn't endure it any longer. "Ryan!"

The smile Jackson offered to the woman who had brought the teen to him was an understanding one.

"That's all right. Ryan will come around." His eyes shifted to the teen. Under all that bravado was just a scared kid, he thought. A kid he intended to reach—but it wouldn't be easy. "There's a fine for every time you curse. You put a dollar into the swear jar."

"Curse?" Ryan mocked. "You call that a curse?" he asked incredulously.

"Yes, I do. While you're here you're going to have to clean up your language as well as your act," Jackson informed the teen.

Ryan rolled his eyes. "Pay him the damn fine so he'll stop whining," Ryan told his sister.

"That's three now," Jackson corrected quietly. "That one isn't free. And you're the one who needs to pay, not your sister. Time you learned to pull your own weight. Your sister can't be expected to always be cleaning up your messes."

"Yeah, well, a lot you know," Ryan retorted, an underlying frustration in his voice. "My sister's the one with all the money."

"That'll change," Jackson informed him. "You'll be earning your own money while you're here. Everyone at The Healing Ranch earns his own money by doing the chores that are assigned to him. You'll get yours after you settle in."

"Wow," Ryan marveled. "How lame can you get?"

Ryan shifted from foot to foot, eyeing his sister and obviously waiting for her to say something to back him up—or better yet, to spring him so he could stop playing this ridiculous game and go home.

Debi's cheeks began to redden. "I'm sorry about this," she apologized to Jackson.

Jackson waved away the apology. "Don't worry about it. We've had a lot worse here."

"Gee, thanks," Ryan sneered. "You know I'm right here."

"Wouldn't forget it for a second," Jackson assured him.

By then, Garrett had come over to join them. Behind

him, the three teens who were in the corral had stopped working with their horses and were now watching the newest arrival at the ranch try to go up against Jackson. It played out like a minidrama.

Garrett flashed a wide, easy smile at both the newest addition to the crew on the ranch and the young woman who had brought him to them.

"This is my brother, Garrett." Jackson made the introduction to Ryan's worried-looking sister. "We run the ranch together," he added rather needlessly, since the information was also on the website he'd had one of Miss Joan's friends put together for him, Miss Joan being the woman who ran the town's only diner and who was also the town's unofficial matriarch.

Taking the attractive young woman's hand in his, Garrett slipped his other hand over it and shook it. "Welcome to The Healing Ranch, ma'am," he said in all sincerity.

"Who came up with that stupid name, anyway?" Ryan asked. "You?" The last part was directed toward Jackson. "'Cause it sounds like something you'd say," the teen concluded condescendingly.

Garrett treated the question as if it was a legitimate one. He was attempting to defuse the situation. Once upon a time, Jackson had quite a temper, but he now prided himself on keeping that temper completely under wraps.

"Actually," Garrett told Ryan, "it was our uncle. He came up with the name. This was his ranch first," Garrett remembered fondly.

"Oh," Ryan mumbled, looking away. He shoved his hands into his pockets and shrugged, lifting up bony shoulders. "Still a lame name," he muttered not quite under his breath.

Jackson pretended not to hear. "The bunkhouse is right over there," he pointed out.

"Yeah? So what? Why would I want to know where the stupid bunkhouse is?" Ryan asked, the same uncooperative attitude radiating from every word.

"Because that's where you'll be staying," Jackson said. Inwardly, he was braced for a confrontation between the teen and himself.

Ryan's deep brown eyes darkened to an unsettling murky hue. "The hell I am."

"You'd better get to work soon, Ryan. You've already got several fines—and counting—against you," Jackson informed him. "Garrett, why don't you take Ryan here—" he nodded at the teen "—and introduce him to the others?"

"Others?" Ryan repeated. "Is this where you bring out a bunch of robotlike zombies and tell me they're going to be my new best friends and roommates? Thanks, but I'll pass."

"Ryan, apologize right now, do you hear me?" Debi ordered. Her words might as well have been in Japanese for all the impression they made on Ryan. Watching her brother being taken in hand had her looking both relieved and tense.

"Ryan, drop the attitude," Jackson told him. "You'll find it a whole lot easier to get along with everyone if you do."

Ryan drew himself up to his full six-foot-two height. "Maybe I don't want to get along with 'everyone,'" he retorted.

Jackson looked at the teenager, his expression saying that he knew better than Ryan what was good for him.

But for now, he merely shrugged. "Suit yourself," he

told Ryan. Jackson turned toward the distraught-looking young woman he had spoken to on the phone several days ago. He could feel that protective streak that had turned his life around coming out. "Why don't you come with me to the main house and we'll go over a few things?" he suggested.

She looked over her shoulder back to the bunkhouse. Garrett was already herding her brother over to the structure.

"Debi!" Ryan called out. It was clearly a call for help.

It killed her not to answer her brother. Debi worked her lower lip for a second before asking Jackson, "Is he really going to be staying in that barn?" she asked uncertainly.

"It's the bunkhouse," Jackson corrected politely, trying not to make her feel foolish for getting her terms confused. "And back in the day, that was where ranch hands used to live. It's been renovated a couple of times since then. Don't worry, the wind doesn't whistle through the mismatched slates." The corners of his mouth curved slightly. "The bunkhouse also has proper heating in the winter and even air-conditioning for the summer. All the comforts of home," he added.

Apparently, Ryan wasn't the only family member who needed structure and reassurance, Jackson thought. Ryan's sister had all the signs of someone who was very close to the breaking point and was struggling to hold everything together, if only for appearance's sake.

"If home is a bunkhouse," Debi interjected. It obviously seemed incongruous to her.

"A renovated bunkhouse," Jackson reminded her with an indulgent smile. "Don't worry, your brother will be just fine."

Well, if nothing else, Ryan had certainly proven that

he was a survivor, she thought—if only in body. His spirit was another matter entirely. But then, that was why she had brought Ryan here. To "fix" that part of him.

"Right now, I think I'm more worried about you and your brother," she said.

"Why?" Jackson asked, curious. This, he had to admit, was a first, someone bringing him a lost soul to set straight and being worried about the effect of that person on *him*. "Is Ryan violent?" The teen seemed more crafty than violent, but it paid to be safe—just in case.

"Oh, no, nothing like that," Debi was quick to clarify. "Under all that, he's basically a good kid—but I'll be the first to admit that Ryan is more than the average handful."

"If he wasn't," Jackson pointed out as they made their way to the main house, "then he wouldn't be here—and neither would you."

"True," Debi readily agreed—and then she flushed slightly, realizing what the man with her had to think. "I'm sorry if I sound like I'm being overly protective, but I'm the only family that Ryan has left and I don't feel like I've been doing a very good job of raising him lately." She looked over her shoulder again in the direction her brother had gone as he left the area.

She spotted him with Garrett. The two were headed for the bunkhouse. Garrett had one arm around her brother's shoulders—most likely, in her estimation, to keep Ryan from darting off. Not that there was anywhere for him to go, she thought. The ranch was some distance from the stamp-sized town they had driven through.

"He'll be all right," Jackson assured her. "Garrett hasn't lost a ranch hand yet."

"Is that what you call the boys who come here?" she

asked, thinking it wasn't exactly an accurate label for them. After all, they were here to be reformed, not to work on the ranch, right?

She looked at Jackson, waiting for him to clarify things. What he said made her more confused. The man seemed very nice, but nice didn't get things done and besides, "nice" could also be a facade. That was the way it had been with John. And it had fooled her completely.

"I found that 'ranch hand' is rather a neutral title and, when you come right down to it, the boys *do* work on the ranch. My office is right in here," he told her as he opened the door for her.

She was going to ask him more about having the boys work on his ranch—had she just supplied him with two more hands to do his bidding?—but when he opened the door to his ranch house without using a key, her attention was diverted in an entirely different direction.

"Your door's not locked," she said in surprise.

He heard the wonder in her voice and suppressed a smile. He knew exactly what she had to be thinking. "No, it's not."

"Do you think that's wise?" she asked. "I mean, if you and your brother are outside, working, isn't that like waving temptation right in front of the boys that you're trying to reform?"

"They're on the honor system," he explained, closing the door behind her. "I want them to know that we trust them to do the right thing. You have to give trust in order to get it. Around here, the boys keep each other honest. For the most part, the ones who have been here the longest set an example and watch over the ones who came in last."

She looked at him skeptically. "That sounds a little risky."

"We find it works," he told her. "And just for the record, 'I' don't reform them. What we do here is present them with the right set of circumstances so that they can reform themselves. Most of the time I find that if I expect the best from the teens who come here, they eventually try to live up to my expectations."

Debi looked around. The living room she had just walked into was exactly what she would have expected: open and massive, with very masculine-looking leather furniture, creased with age and use. The sofas—there were two—were arranged around a brick fireplace. The ceiling was vaulted with wooden beams running through the length of it. The only concession to the present was the skylight. Without it, she had a feeling that the room would have a dungeonlike atmosphere.

The rustic feel of the decor seem like pure Texas. Debi really had no idea why that would make her feel safe, but it did.

Maybe it had to do with the man beside her. There was something about his manner that gave her hope and made her feel that everything was going to work out.

She knew she wasn't being realistic, but then, she'd never been in this sort of situation before.

Realizing that she'd fallen behind as he was walking through the room, Debi stepped up her pace and caught up to Jackson just as he entered a far more cluttered room that she assumed was his office.

"Sounds good in theory," she acknowledged, referring to his ideas about trust.

"Works in practice, too," he told her with just the tiniest bit of pride evident in his cadence.

Sweeping a number of files, oversized envelopes and a few other miscellaneous things off a chair, Jackson nodded toward it. He deposited the armload of paraphernalia on the nearest flat surface.

"Please, sit," he requested.

Debi did as he asked, perching on the edge of the seat. She appeared as if she was ready to jump to her feet at any given moment for any given reason, he noted.

This woman was wound up as tightly as her brother. Maybe more so. Undoubtedly because she was constantly on her guard and vigilant for the next thing to go wrong. And he had a feeling that she was doing it alone. She'd said she was the teen's only family.

"So," Jackson began as he sat down in his late uncle's overstuffed, black leather chair. It creaked ever so slightly in protest due to its age. To Jackson, the sound was like a greeting from an old friend. "What do you think is Ryan's story?"

Debi blinked, caught completely off guard. His wording confused her. Did he believe she wasn't involved in her brother's life and could only make a wild guess as to why he was the way he was? Her problem was she was *too* involved in her brother's story.

"Excuse me?" she demanded, forgetting all about feeling as if she had failed her brother.

Jackson patiently explained the meaning behind his question. "Every parent or guardian who comes to us usually has some sort of a theory as to why the boy they brought to us is the way he is. They give me a backstory and I take it from there. Sometimes they're right, sometimes they're wrong. Not everything is black or white." He leaned back in the chair. The motion was accompanied by another pronounced creak. "What's Ryan's backstory?"

He *did* think she wasn't involved, Debi thought. She set out to show this man how wrong he was by giving him a summarized version of Ryan's life.

"As a little boy, Ryan was almost perfect," she recalled fondly. "Never talked back, went to school without a single word of protest. Kept his room neat, ate whatever was on his plate. Did his homework and got excellent grades. He was almost *too* good," she added wistfully, wishing fervently for those days to be back again.

No one was ever too good, but he refrained from commenting on that. Instead, Jackson gently urged the woman on. "And then…?"

It took her a moment to begin. Remembering still hurt beyond words. "And then, three years ago, he was involved in a car accident. He was in the car with my parents." A lump formed in her throat, the way it always did. "They were coming out to visit me—I was away at college."

She would forever feel guilty about that. Guilty about selecting her college strictly because that was where John was going. If she'd attended a college close to home, the way her parents had hoped, this wouldn't have happened.

"Except that they never made it," she said after a beat, forcing the words out. "A truck hauling tires or car batteries or something like that sideswiped them." She had no idea why it bothered her that she didn't have all the details down, but it did. "The car went off the side of the road, tumbled twice and when it was over…" Her voice shook as she continued. "My parents were both dead." Taking a breath, she continued, "And Ryan was in ICU. They kept him in the hospital for almost a month. Even when he got out, he had to have physical therapy treatments for the next six months."

Jackson listened quietly. When she paused, he took the opportunity to comment. "Sounds like he had a pretty hard time of it."

Debi took in a long, shaky breath. It hadn't exactly been a walk in the park for her, either. But this wasn't about her, she reminded herself sternly. It was about Ryan. About *saving* Ryan.

"He did," she answered. "He kept asking me why he was the one who got to live and they had to die." A rueful smile touched her lips. "That was while he was still talking to me. But that got to be less and less and then the only time we talked at all was when I was nagging him to do his homework and stop cutting classes." The sigh escaped before she could stop it. "I guess you could say that they were one-way conversations."

He was all too familiar with that—from both sides of the divide, he thought.

"What brought you here to The Healing Ranch?" he asked her. When Debi looked at him, confused, he explained, "It's usually the last straw or the one thing that a parent or guardian just couldn't allow to let slide."

She steeled herself as she began to answer the man's question. "I had to bail Ryan out of jail. He ditched school and was hanging around with a couple of guys I kept telling him to avoid. One of them stole a car." She had a pretty good idea which one had done it, but Ryan refused to confirm her suspicions. "According to what another one of the 'boys' said, the guy claimed he was 'borrowing' it just for a quick joy ride. The owner reported the car missing and the police managed to track it down fairly quickly. The boys were all apprehended."

Age-wise they were still all children to her, not young men on their way to compiling serious criminal records.

"But first they had to chase them through half the city." She didn't want to make excuses for her brother, but she did want Jackson to know the complete truth. "Ryan didn't steal the car, but he knew it didn't belong to the kid behind the wheel. He should have never gotten into the car knowing that." This time, she didn't even bother trying to suppress her sigh or her distress. "He used to make better decisions than that," she told the man sitting opposite her.

A lone tear slid down her cheek. She could feel it and the fact that it was there annoyed Debi to no end. She didn't want to be a stereotypical female, crying because the situation was out of her control. She couldn't, *wouldn't* tolerate any pity.

Using the back of her hand, she wiped away the incriminating stain from her cheek.

"Sorry," she murmured. "I'm just a little tired after that long trip."

Rather than comment on what they both knew was an extremely lightweight excuse, Jackson took the box of tissues he'd kept on his desk and pushed it over toward the young woman.

He watched her pull one out, his attention focused on her hand. Her left hand. There was no ring on her ring finger—but there was a very light tan line indicating that there'd been a ring there not all that long ago.

"Did your marriage break up over that?" he asked her gently.

Debi raised her eyes to his in wonder as she felt the air in her lungs come to a standstill.

How did he know?

Chapter Three

Debi stared at the man sitting across from her. Had Sheila called him to set things up for her? She hadn't mentioned anything, but if her coworker and friend hadn't called this man, then how did Jackson know about the current state, or non-state, of her marriage?

"Excuse me?" she said in a voice filled with disbelief.

Even as he asked the question, Jackson was fairly certain that he already knew the answer. Whoever this woman's husband had been, the man was clearly an idiot. Two minutes into their interview, he could tell that Deborah Kincannon was a kind, caring person. That she seemed to be temporarily in over her head was beside the point. That sort of thing happened to everyone at one point or another. It certainly had to his stepmother.

The fact that Ryan's sister was exceedingly attractive in a sweet, comfortable sort of way wasn't exactly a hardship, either. The more he thought about it, the more convinced he was that her choice in men, or at least in *this* man, left something to be desired.

"Did your marriage break up over that?" he repeated. Jackson could almost hear the way the scene had played out. "Your husband said he'd had enough of your brother's actions and told you to wash your hands of him, am I right?"

Debi could feel herself growing pale. The second this man said the words, she remembered the awful scenario and how it had drained her.

Her mouth felt dry as she asked, "How did you...?" Her voice trailed off as she looked at Jackson incredulously.

"Your ring finger," he answered, nodding at her left hand. "There's a slight tan line around it, like you'd had a ring on there for a while—until just recently."

Debi nodded and looked down at her left ring finger. It still felt strange not to see her wedding ring there. She hadn't taken the ring off since the day she'd gotten married, not even to clean it. She'd found a way to accomplish that while the ring remained on her finger. But now there seemed to be no point in continuing to wear it. If she did, it would not only be perpetuating a lie, it would also remind her that she had wasted all those years of her life, loving a man who was more a fabrication than real flesh and blood.

The John Kincannon she had loved hadn't existed, except perhaps in her mind.

Stupid, stupid, stupid, she couldn't help thinking. There had been signs. Why hadn't she allowed them to register?

She supposed the answer lay in the fact that she just couldn't admit to herself that she could have been so wrong about a person for so many years. A person she had given up so much for. A person who had inadvertently caused her to sacrifice her parents' lives. So when warning signs had raised their heads, she'd ignored them, pretending that they didn't exist. Whenever she found herself stumbling across another warning sign, she'd just pretended that it was a little rough patch and everything was all right. How wrong she'd been.

Debi cleared her throat and sat a little straighter in her seat.

"I don't see how that would matter, one way or another," she finally replied, sounding somewhat removed and formal.

Jackson pretended not to take notice of the shift in her voice and demeanor. "Oh, it does," he assured her. "It does. I'm not trying to pry into your private life. I just want to identify all the pieces that make up your brother's life. If your marriage broke up because of him, then Ryan might have that much more guilt he's carrying around."

The laugh that suddenly left her lips had a sad, hollow sound. "Oh, you don't have to worry about that, Mr., um, White Eagle—"

"Jackson," he corrected.

That felt easier for her. As if they were in this together.

"Jackson," she repeated, then continued with what she wanted to tell him. "If Ryan feels responsible for my marriage falling apart, to him that's a very good thing. He and John never got along and he never really liked him. The feeling, I'm sorry to say, was mutual. If anything, that's the one thing Ryan feels good about," she said ruefully. "Getting John to leave our house."

She seemed very sure of that, Jackson observed, but for his part, he wasn't, not at this point. "You might be surprised."

"Surprised? Mr. Wh— Jackson, I would be completely flabbergasted if this didn't thrill my brother to death," she said, waving her hand dismissively as if literally pushing this subject to the side. There were more pressing things she wanted to get straight. "Exactly how does your program work?" she asked.

Jackson had always favored an economy of words. "Very simply, we put the boys to work."

"In other words, free labor."

"No, not free," he corrected. "They earn a small salary. The exact amount depends on how well they do the job they're assigned."

Everything he was talking about was entirely new to her. "You *grade* their work?"

"Sure," he freely admitted. Seeing that she was having trouble digesting what he was telling her, he decided to try to clarify things for her. "Let me give you an example. If the job is to clean out the horse stalls and he does the bare minimum, his 'pay' reflects that. If, on the other hand, the stall is clean, there's fresh hay put out, fresh water in the trough, that kind of thing, then his pay reflects *that*. It gives them an incentive to work hard and do well. It also teaches them that doing a good job pays off. We want them feeling good about what they accomplish and, by proxy, good about themselves.

"What we're hoping for, long-term, is that the guys get used to always doing their best and trying their hardest."

"Why horses?" she asked.

The question seemed to come out of nowhere.

Jackson smiled, more to himself than at her. His first response was one he didn't voice. He was simply passing on the method that his uncle had used with him. For the most part, though he dealt with tough cases and teens that came with extrawide chips on their shoulder, Jackson was a private person who would have been content just to keep to himself. But after his uncle's death, he'd felt compelled to take his uncle's lessons and methods and put them to use.

Still, that didn't mean baring his own soul—or parts thereof—to someone he really didn't know.

"Easy," he answered. "I work with what I have. Besides, it's been proven that people bond more easily with animals than they do with other people. Having a hand in the care, feeding and grooming of these horses brings order and discipline into the boys' lives. It teaches them patience—eventually," he specified, recalling that the horse Sam had given him to work with had seemed to be every bit as headstrong and difficult to deal with as he was at the time. It had been a battle of wills before he finally emerged victorious.

The greatest day of his life had been when he finally got Wildfire to respond to his key signals. He'd felt high on that for a week. After that, he no longer had any desire to seek out artificial ways of escape—he'd found it in working with Wildfire.

Debi leaned forward, folding her hands before her—making him think of an earnest schoolgirl. "Do you think you can help my brother?"

He didn't answer her immediately. Instead, he had a question of his own first. "Is going along for a joy ride in the car his friend stole the worst thing he's ever done?"

"Yes," she answered with conviction, then realized that she had no right to sound that sure. "To the best of my knowledge," she qualified in a slightly less certain voice.

"Then it's my opinion that Ryan can be turned around," he told her. "Since you're here, I'll need to have you fill out some forms. Nothing unusual, just education level, how many run-ins with the police he's had, how long he's had an attitude problem, any allergies, medical conditions, where we can get in contact with you, that sort of thing," he explained, opening a deep drawer on the right side of his desk.

Digging into it, he found what he was looking for and placed the forms in question on his desk while he shut the drawer.

"To answer your last question, I'll be close by while Ryan's here at the ranch," she told him as she accepted the papers he handed her.

For the most part, guardians asked to be called and then returned home, wherever home happened to be. "Define 'close by,'" he requested.

It was Debi's turn to smile.

Even the slight shift in her lips seemed to bring out a radiance, just for a moment, that hadn't been noticeable before. Jackson caught himself staring and forced himself to look away.

An unsettled feeling in his gut lingered a little longer.

"Don't worry, I'm not going to be parked on some hillside, looking down and watching his—and your—every move if that's what you're worried about," she told Jackson.

"I just thought it might be uncomfortable for you to sleep in your car," he said. She had no idea whether or not he was kidding or serious. It shouldn't matter whether or not she was uncomfortable or not. "If you need a place to stay, Miss Joan is always willing to open her doors and temporarily take someone in."

"Miss Joan?" Debi repeated quizzically. The setup he mentioned sounded suspiciously like a brothel to her. When had she gotten so distrusting? she wondered. It had crept up on her when she hadn't been paying attention.

Jackson nodded. "She runs the local diner and is kind

of like a self-appointed mother hen to the town in general."

There was a fondness in his voice whenever he mentioned the outspoken older woman. Miss Joan had a nononsense way of talking and a big heart made out of pure marshmallow. When Sam had taken him under his wing, his uncle and Miss Joan were seeing one another. The relationship continued for a couple of years before they unexpectedly just went their separate ways. At the time, he was curious as to why they had split up, but when he brought the matter up, Sam merely gave him a long, penetrating look and said nothing. Any attempt to get information from Miss Joan went nowhere, as well. Miss Joan wasn't one to talk about herself at all.

Consequently, he'd never found out what had gone wrong, but whenever he did find time to stop by the diner for a cup of coffee, Miss Joan always told him it was on the house, adding that Sam would have disapproved if she charged him for it.

"Why would I stay with her?" Debi asked.

It didn't make any sense to her. After all, the woman didn't know her from Adam—or Eve. If she were in this woman's place, she certainly wouldn't take in a stranger. Things like that just weren't done these days. There was trusting, and then there was being incredibly naive.

She had a feeling that if she said as much to this cowboy, she'd offend him, so she kept her comment to herself. But it didn't change her opinion.

"I thought I saw a sign when I was passing by Forever that said something about a new hotel having a grand opening."

He'd forgotten about that. In his defense, he didn't get to town very often these days and the hotel was practically brand-new, having opened its doors less than five months ago. What he recalled was that building the hotel had been a huge shot in the arm for a lot of his friends on the reservation, providing many of them with construction work.

"It's not just a new hotel," he informed her. "It's Forever's *only* hotel, as well."

"You don't have any other hotels in town?" she asked in wonder.

That sounded almost impossible, Debi thought. Indianapolis had over two hundred of them. How could this town have just one—and recently built at that?

Maybe she had made a mistake in bringing Ryan here after all.

What choice did you have? she asked herself. And this wasn't about how big or little the town was. This was about the ranch's track record, which, according to Sheila, as well as the internet, was perfect so far.

"If you'd have come here a year ago, we wouldn't have had this one," Jackson was telling her. "The people in Forever don't exactly believe in rushing into things," he explained with a soft laugh.

Debi was unprepared for the sound to travel right under her skin, but it did, probably because she was vulnerable. Having the man she had once thought of as the love of her life walk out on her had sent her self-esteem crashing to subbasement level. It made her doubt all of her previous assumptions and had her feeling that she couldn't trust her own judgment. Everything that she had believed she'd had turned out to be a lie—why would anything be different from here on in?

"Apparently," she agreed, feeling as if she was moving through some sort of a bad dream—a dream she couldn't wake up from.

She glanced down at the forms he'd just given her and tried to shake off her mood. "Do you want me to fill them out now?" she asked. It might be easier for her to tackle the forms tonight, after she checked in to this new hotel and went to her room.

"If you don't mind, I'd like that, yes," he told her. "I learned that it's better not to put things off," Jackson explained. Rising to give her some breathing room while she filled the forms out, he asked, "Would you like something to drink? Coffee? Tea?"

Or me?

Now where the hell had that come from? Jackson upbraided himself. That had to be something he'd unknowingly picked up from a program that had been playing in the background, or that he'd seen as a kid. When his parents were arguing, he'd turn the TV up loud to block them out so he could pretend that everything was really all right and that they weren't screaming all sorts of terrible things to and about each other.

Jackson looked a little closer at Ryan's sister. There was something almost appealingly vulnerable about her that brought out the protector in him. He was going to have to be careful to keep that under wraps, he warned himself.

Debi stopped perusing the forms and looked up at him, clearly surprised. "You have tea?"

"Yes. We're not entirely barbaric out here in Texas," Jackson told her, amused by her surprised expression.

Realizing that she might have insulted the man, Debi did what she could to backtrack and remove her foot from her mouth.

"I'm sorry, I didn't mean to imply anything. It's just that, well, I can't visualize you actually drinking tea."

"I don't," he told her, then answered the question he knew she was thinking. "I keep tea around for guests. I like being prepared." He paused, waiting. But she didn't comment or make a request. He tried again. "So, can I get you that tea?"

Debi shook her head. "No, that's okay," she answered. "I'm good."

Yes, you are.

There it was again, he thought. Unbidden thoughts popping up in his head. This wasn't like him. Besides, the woman wasn't even his type. Any woman he had ever socialized with either came from the reservation, or had ties to it.

Maybe he'd been spending too much time with the horses in his off hours. Lately, he'd been devoting himself to the boys and the ranch to the exclusion of everything else. Maybe that had taken its toll on him and this was his body's way of getting back at him. It was reminding him that he needed to get out and mingle a little bit with people who didn't come with a list of problems and lives they needed to have turned around.

It was getting to the point that he was forgetting that there were people like that out there. People whose souls *weren't* troubled.

Jackson forced his mind back to the woman who regarded him as if he was her last hope in the world. At this point in time, he probably was.

"We've also got a couple of cans of diet soda and then there's always that old standby, water."

But Debi shook her head to that as she started filling out the forms. "No, really, I'm fine. Nothing to drink for me, thank you," she told him, sparing Jackson a quick glance before looking back at the questionnaire on the desk before her.

"Would you know of anywhere that I could get a job?" she asked.

If she needed a job, that was going to put an entirely different spin on matters, Jackson thought. Most likely, the woman wouldn't be able to afford the down payment for her brother's treatment.

Since he prided himself on never turning away anyone in need, he was going to have to come up with a way to fix that situation.

He approached the subject cautiously. "You're out of work?"

Her head popped up. "What? Oh, no, I have a job waiting for me back home. I just took a leave of absence so that I could be close by if either Ryan or you needed me."

Now that was a loaded sentence that he wasn't about to allow himself to touch with a ten-foot pole, Jackson thought.

"What kind of work do you do?" he asked her. "Because Miss Joan could always give you work at the diner. She's got a lot of part-time waitresses and a good many of them come and go, especially the ones who work at the diner just to get some extra cash that'll supplement their regular income."

"I'm a surgical nurse," she replied. "You wouldn't be hiding a regular hospital out here, would you?" She hadn't seen evidence of one when she'd driven down the town's Main Street, but that didn't mean that there wasn't a hospital around somewhere.

Jackson shook his head. "It's a real pity, but we don't

have one," he confirmed. "The closest hospital to For-ever is in the next town, some fifty miles down the road."

He made it sound as if it was just a hop, skip and a jump away—and it was a little more than that. She sup-posed it was all in how a person viewed things and where they grew up. Compared to where she came from—Indi-anapolis—Forever seemed incredibly tiny. Not only that, but the city had its share of hospitals, as well.

Why would anyone stay in a place like this where their options were so limited? she couldn't help wondering. It was a surprise to her that everyone didn't just pick up and leave town the minute that they graduated high school. She knew she would have. The pace here felt as if it had been dipped in molasses on the coldest day in January.

"We do, however," Jackson told her after a beat, "have a medical clinic, and the doctors there are always look-ing for more help."

A medical clinic. She could work with that. "They might just have found it," she told him with a relieved smile.

Chapter Four

Jackson thought of Daniel Davenport and Alisha Cordell-Murphy, the two doctors who ran the clinic, and the over-worked nurse at the desk, Holly Rodriguez. He'd had occasion to interact with all of them at one time or another. Not directly for himself, but he'd brought several of his friends from the reservation in to be treated there.

The clinic was definitely a godsend, seeing as how not all that long ago there hadn't been *any* doctor within fifty miles of Forever.

However, godsend or not, the clinic was woefully understaffed. He wasn't sure if Forever and its surrounding area was growing, or if the doctors had just become overwhelmed and slowed down. But it was clear that help was definitely needed.

The doctors would be thrilled at the mere thought of getting even temporary help for a short respite. He knew that for certain, recalling what Dr. Davenport had said when it had been just him running the clinic with Holly's help, and Dr. Cordell-Murphy—she'd been just Dr. Cordell at the time—had arrived in response to an open recruitment letter he'd sent to his old hospital in New York.

"After you finish filling out the paperwork," Jackson

told the nurse, "I can have one of the boys take you to the clinic."

Debi paused for a moment. "Is it in town?" she asked.

"Yes, ma'am, it is."

She winced at the word he'd used to address her. "Please, don't call me *ma'am*," she requested earnestly. "It makes me feel like I'm at least eighty years old."

"Just a sign of respect, nothing more," he replied. "And just for the record, you'd be the *youngest*-looking eighty-year-old on the planet," Jackson told her with a wink.

Debi felt something in her stomach flutter in response to the wink. Whether the man knew it or not, that was an extremely sexy wink.

Even so, she had no business reacting like that. She told herself that it was just because she hadn't really eaten in more than twenty-four hours.

This decision to drag her brother to a horse ranch almost fifteen hundred miles from home hadn't been an easy one for her. Neither had driving all the way to Forever by herself.

Ryan didn't have a license, but he did, she'd discovered, know how to drive. That changed nothing. There was no way she would have allowed him behind the wheel, despite the volley of curses he'd sent her way. Had she given in—there were exceedingly long, lonely stretches of road with nothing in sight—she had no doubt that he would have driven them to who-knows-where while she caught a few much-needed winks.

So she had loaded up on energy drinks and coffee and driven the entire distance by herself. Fast.

That left her exhausted and yet wired at the same time. The thought of being in the car with someone who had been sent to The Healing Ranch to be reformed made her somewhat uncomfortable. She would have no idea what to expect—or what could happen. What if, like Ryan, her would-be guide would use the opportunity to try to escape from Forever and the ranch?

"No need to take up anyone's time," she told Jackson. "I can get to the town on my own. But after we get all this paperwork squared away, I would like to see the bunkhouse, please."

"So you can see for yourself that it's not some primitive dungeon?" Jackson guessed, deliberately exaggerating what she probably assumed about the conditions in the bunkhouse.

Debi opened her mouth, then decided there was no point in trying to deny what he seemed to have already figured out. "Yes."

Her admission surprised him a little. But it also pleased him. She was brave enough not to try to divert or dress up the truth.

"Sounds to me like Ryan has a good role model to look up to once we get him straightened out and back to tapping into his full potential," Jackson observed.

"I don't know about that," she said as she continued filling in the forms. "If I'm such a good role model, why did he get to the point that I had to bring him somewhere like this or risk losing him altogether?"

Jackson had been doing this for a while now and it never ceased to amaze him how many different reasons there were for teens to act out. "It's not always clear to us," he told her. "Sometimes it takes a while to understand."

"So," Debi observed wryly, "you're a philosopher as well as a cowboy."

"A man wears a lot of hats in his lifetime," was Jackson's only reply.

Working as quickly as she was able, Debi filled out all the forms and signed her name on the bottom of the last one. After she was finished, she gathered all the pages together, placing them in a small, neat pile. She felt exhausted and was running pretty close to empty, but the espresso coffee she had saved for last on her trip here was giving her a final shot in the arm.

Pushing the pile of forms to one side, Debi took out her checkbook. Funds were growing dangerously low, thanks to John and the divorce he seemed to have processed at lightning speed. Bringing Ryan here was probably going to eat up every spare dime she had. That was one of the reasons she'd driven here instead of flying.

"I assume you prefer being paid up front." Turning to the next blank check, Debi asked, "What should I make it out for?"

If the woman was taking a leave of absence to be near her brother while he was here and if she was looking for employment, that meant she was probably living close to hand to mouth.

Jackson placed his hand over her checkbook, stopping her from beginning to date the check. "Why don't you hold off on that until he's been here a week?"

"Why? Because you might decide he's incorrigible and you'll hand him back to me? Won't you still want to get paid for 'time served' if that's the case?"

"Actually, I was thinking about you," Jackson said simply. "I figured that you might decide you're not happy with the program we have here and want to take your brother home."

She flushed, embarrassed for the conclusion she'd leaped to. Lately, she'd been too edgy, too quick to take offense where none was intended.

"I'm sorry, I didn't used to be this way," she apologized. "The last six months have taken a toll on…on all of us," she said, changing direction at the last minute. She'd meant to say that the past six months had taken a toll on her, but that sounded terribly selfish and self-centered to her own ear—even though arguing with John over Ryan had completely worn her down to a nub.

"All?" Jackson questioned, his tone coaxing more information out of her.

Debi obliged without even realizing it at first. "On Ryan, and me—and John." She saw the unspoken question in Jackson's eyes. "John is my ex."

"Oh." The single word seemed to speak volumes—and yet, how could it? she thought. Maybe she was just getting punchy.

She avoided Jackson's eyes and got back to her initial apology. "I apologize if I sound abrupt."

"No apologies necessary," Jackson told her, carelessly waving her words away like so much swirling dust. "I've heard and seen a lot worse than anything you might think you're guilty of."

Every time he dealt with the parents or guardians of one of the teens brought or sent to his ranch, it reminded him just what he had to have put his stepmother through. The woman had been nothing but fair and good to him when she didn't have to be, taking him in after his father had taken off. Heaven knew his own father never felt anything for him, neither affection nor a sense of responsibility.

Yet somehow Sylvia had, and in return he had treated her shamefully, putting her through hell before he finally was forced to get his act together, which he did, thanks to Sam.

She was gone now, but remembering her made him more considerate of the people who brought their troubled teens to him to be, in effect, "fixed."

"Okay, everything looks in order," he told Ryan's sister, glancing through the forms quickly. "Let me take you on that tour of the bunkhouse to set your mind at ease," he offered.

"I'd like that," she told him. She wanted to see the bunkhouse and felt that since he was the one in charge of the ranch and its program, he would be the best one to conduct the tour.

And if something turned out to be wrong in her eyes, he was the one to be held accountable.

Debi got up and immediately paled. She'd risen a little too quickly from her seat. As a result, she immediately felt a little light-headed and dizzy. Trying to anchor herself down, she swayed ever so slightly. Panicked, she made a grab for the first thing her hand came in contact with to steady herself.

It turned out to be the cowboy standing next to her.

Jackson seemed to react automatically. His free arm went around her, holding her in place. Thanks to capricious logistics, that place turned out to be against his chest.

The light-headedness left as quickly as it had appeared. The air in her lungs went along with it as it whooshed out the second she found herself all but flush against the cowboy's chest and torso.

Their eyes met and held for an eternal second—and then Jackson loosened his hold on her as he asked, "Are you all right?"

Yes!

No!

I don't know.

All three responses took a turn flashing through her brain as the rest of her tried to figure out just what had happened here.

Bit by bit, what transpired—and why—came back to her in tiny flashes. "Sorry, I got a little dizzy," she apologized. Dropping her line of vision back to the floor, she murmured, "I think I got up too fast." Looking at the arm she had grabbed, she realized that she must have dug her nails into his forearm. There were four deep crescents in his skin. "Oh, God, I'm sorry." She didn't need confirmation that she had done that. She knew.

"No harm done," he told her good-naturedly. Jackson took a step back from her slowly, watching her for any signs that she was going to faint. "We can stay here a little longer if you like."

"No, that's all right. I'd like to see the bunkhouse before your…ranch hands come back to use it."

The bunkhouse, for the most part, was used for sleeping and winding down in the evening after a particularly long, hard day filled with chores.

"The day's still young," he replied. "We have plenty of time." As he spoke, he studied her more closely. She looked exhausted, as well as a little disconnected. "Did you drive here?" he asked.

She started to nod and discovered that made the world spin again, so she stopped immediately.

"Yes."

"From Indianapolis?" He wanted to make sure that he had her starting point down correctly.

"Yes." Her eyebrows drew together in a quizzical expression. "Why?"

Jackson did a quick calculation. "That's roughly fourteen to fifteen hundred miles away," he estimated, impressing her. "How long did that take you?"

Debi had no idea why he was asking her this, but she saw no harm in answering. "A little more than twenty-four hours."

The "why?" was silent, but implied.

That meant she had to have driven straight through to get here that fast. "You were the only one driving?" He didn't expect her to say no—and she didn't.

"Yes, I was the only driver." If she didn't get moving soon, she was going to stretch out on top of his desk, clutter and all, she thought, feeling drained beyond belief.

"Why didn't you stop somewhere for a break—or to spend the night?" he asked.

"I like to drive—and besides, I wasn't tired at the time," she said, deciding not to tell him that she'd been wired for nearly half the trip, determined to get there before exhaustion caught up to her because she was afraid that Ryan would take off and disappear the second she stopped driving.

"When did you last eat?" he asked her, curious.

She'd found a tiny box of really old raisins at the back of her glove compartment. "Do raisins count?"

"Only if they're embedded in an apple crisp pie." His

own main flaw, the way Jackson saw it, was his weakness for all things sweet or bad for him.

No wonder the woman looked like a wraith in the making. She hadn't had any food in a day and probably didn't eat all that well before that. Worry did that to a person, he thought, remembering his stepmother.

"Why don't you come with me to the kitchen and we'll see what I can rustle up?" he suggested.

After standing for a bit, she felt steadier and definitely ready to walk wherever he wanted her to go. "I thought ranchers were against rustling," she said, tongue in cheek.

He pretended to take her seriously for a second. "Interesting. Hungry to the point of light-headedness and you still have a sense of humor. That bodes well as far as survival goes," he commented. "Did Ryan go without eating, too?"

Ryan had always been her first priority, now more than ever. He had to be saved. "I packed a couple of sandwiches and some fruit for him and we went through a couple of drive-throughs. He didn't want to eat." Her brother referred to it as "that junk." As for her, she'd had no appetite. "But he changed his mind when he got hungry."

"Why sandwiches just for Ryan and not you?" Jackson asked, trying to glean as much information as he could about the family dynamics of this newest "ranch hand" he was acquiring.

"I didn't have enough cold cuts available for any sandwiches for me. I just took it for granted that Ryan was going to need his strength when he got here. I could always eat later."

"Lucky for you, this is your 'later,'" Jackson told her.

And then he asked, "How long have you been Ryan's sole guardian?"

"Not sole," she protested. "John and I were both his guardians." At least, that was how she had tried to set things up.

It wasn't hard for Jackson to read between the lines. "And how often did your ex participate in anything that had to do with Ryan?"

"Often," Debi answered automatically as well as defensively. And then she flagged just a little when Jackson continued looking at her as if he was waiting her out. "Okay, not all that much…" Debi admitted reluctantly.

He had a better assessment of the situation. "How about not at all?"

Debi blew out a frustrated breath. "Do you do that a lot?" she asked. When he raised an eyebrow in response to her question, she went on to elaborate. "Just stare at people until you make them squirm mentally?"

The corners of his mouth curved just a hint at her observation. "I find it works pretty well on occasion, although," he recalled, "it never really had an effect on Garrett."

"By the way, you're right," Debi admitted out of the blue.

He stopped just short of the kitchen's threshold to turn around and look at her. The woman had lost him. Right about what? "About Garrett?" he asked.

"No," she shook her head. "About my ex. I made a lot of excuses for him in my head, including that he didn't say anything because he felt he didn't have the right to butt in between Ryan and me. But the truth of it was, he resented the fact that Ryan was living with us and that we—meaning me—were responsible for him financially, emotionally and, well, basically in every way."

Jackson took it all in. "And Ryan picked up on John's resentment." It wasn't a question. He knew how these teens acted and reacted because they were him fifteen years ago.

"I tried my best to shield him, to tell him that John cared, but had a hard time showing it—after all, men are like that," she told Jackson with an air of firm conviction.

"In general, yes," Jackson allowed. "But it's not a hard and fast rule around here. And there are a lot of ways for someone to demonstrate that they care without being blatant about it."

"Maybe," she agreed, only half-ready to concede that there might be some truth in what he was saying. "But John didn't." She was about to say something about the ultimatum her ex had given her, then decided that it was far too personal to share with a person she hardly knew. And besides, even though it was to be shared as a secret, secrets had a way of leaking out when you least expected them to. And she didn't want any of what she had just said to accidentally get back to Ryan. He needed to be protected and sheltered from hurtful things like that. If Jackson knew, he just might let it slip to her brother without even thinking. And that would be terrible.

"Sit." Jackson gestured in the general direction of the long, rectangular table where they took all their meals. There were ten chairs in all. Four on either side of the sturdy, scarred wooden table and one placed at either end. She guessed that the two end chairs were for Jackson and his brother and the others were intended for the teens they had staying on the ranch.

Eight. That many? She thought that Ryan might get lost in the shuffle.

"I'm taking you away from your work," Debi protested even as she complied with his invitation.

"It's all part of a whole," Jackson assured her in an easy tone. "We've got some hash browns and bacon left over from breakfast. I can make you some fresh eggs to go with that," he offered.

She really didn't want to cause any trouble—or work. She went for the leftovers—with one exception. "Bacon and hash browns will be fine. And a cup of coffee—if you have creamer."

Jackson acquiesced easily. "Garrett likes his coffee diluted so you're in luck. We have creamer."

Moving like a skilled short-order cook, Jackson put together a plate of food and had the coffee ready for her in a matter of a few minutes.

"Looks good," she commented. And then a thought hit her. "Won't your cook mind that you're giving away the food?"

"I'm the one who pays for the food, and besides, we don't have a cook," Jackson told Ryan's sister, sliding into the chair directly opposite hers rather than taking a seat at the head of the table. "We all take turns making meals."

"The boys, too?" she asked incredulously.

He saw no reason for her to look that surprised. After all, there were male chefs, damn good ones from what he'd heard. Not that anyone here was in danger of reaching that lofty level. Still, they hadn't poisoned anyone, either, so that was pretty good.

"Absolutely. It's all part of learning how to take care of themselves."

She was still exhausted, still wired, but nonetheless,

she felt a peacefulness tiptoeing forward. Jackson White Eagle sounded like a down-to-earth person. More importantly, he struck her as someone who could handle Ryan.

For the first time since she'd set the wheels in motion, Debi felt confident that she'd made the right choice coming here—no matter what the financial cost would ultimately wind up being for her.

Chapter Five

"That was very good."

Pushing her empty plate off to one side of the table, Debi set down her coffee mug after finishing off her second serving of coffee. She'd been prepared to be polite about Jackson's cooking efforts. What she hadn't been prepared for was that his efforts would actually turn out a meal that wasn't just passable, but really good.

Jackson's broad shoulders rose and fell in a quick, dismissive shrug.

"You were hungry," he pointed out modestly. "Most likely anything outside of three-day-old dirt would have tasted good to you."

Debi made a face at the thought of consuming something like that.

"I know it's not considered polite to contradict my host in his own home, but I wasn't too hungry to tell the difference between good and oh-my-God-what-have-I-just-eaten?" Debi assured him with enthusiasm. The more she thought about it, the more genuinely surprised she was by how good the man's cooking actually was. "Where did you learn how to cook like that? From your mother?" she guessed.

Your mother.

Jackson thought of the woman who'd never had time for him. The woman who had walked out on him and never once, in all these years, tried to get back in contact with him or reconnect in any way.

He shook his head and instead said, "Necessity really is the mother of invention."

Her dealings with Ryan and his recent penchant for secrecy and lies had taught her rather quickly to learn to read between the lines.

"Does that mean you were on your own a lot?" Debi asked.

Jackson knew, because of the nature of the ranch he ran, that he should be used to fielding questions. All sorts of questions. But the side of him that was left to deal with those questions was at war with the private side of him, the side that didn't want people knowing the details of his life—any of the details—because hearing them might just make them feel sorry for him.

There was nothing he welcomed less than pity.

For now, Jackson's answer was a vague "Something like that," hoping that would be the end of it.

Debi glanced over toward the kitchen. "Well, it does show a great deal of initiative. Most guys living on their own would have found a woman to cook for them."

That was what John had done. In John's case, he had found her. Debi couldn't remember a single time when John had offered to prepare something rather than leaving it all up to her. John's idea of serving a meal was opening a pizza box.

Just the smallest hint of a smile passed over Jackson's lips. "I would have wound up starving to death," he told her. "I'm pretty fussy—about everything," he added.

With his looks, she caught herself thinking, Jackson

White Eagle could well afford to be fussy. Women would probably fight with frying pans at ten paces for the right to feed him.

"It was just easier learning how to cook on my own," he told her. "So," he concluded, "you still want that tour of the bunkhouse?"

She struck him as a newly lit rocket that was dying to achieve liftoff. Hard to believe she'd seemed so out of it just a short while ago. She'd been attractive before, and now she was even more so, plus exceedingly sensual.

"Now that you've replenished my energy, I'm ready for that tour more than ever," she replied.

So saying, Debi rose from the table carrying her empty plate and coffee mug in her hands. Jackson watched her as she crossed to the sink and turned on the water. Following behind her, he leaned over and decisively shut off the faucet.

When she looked at him quizzically, he told her, "I'll have one of the hands take care of that."

"I don't mind," she responded in all sincerity.

"But I do," he countered. "The hands are here to learn the benefits of work. Cleaning up after a guest is all part of it. Ready?" he asked her again.

Since there was nothing left for her to do there, Debi quickly dried her hands and nodded. "Ready."

Jackson led the way outside. When he walked right past his truck, which was parked outside the front of the house, and kept on going, she was rather surprised. Back in Indianapolis, any distance that amounted to more than a few steps was traversed using a car. Walking was viewed as a pastime, as in taking a walk around the block. Anything other than that necessitated the use of a vehicle.

But apparently not here.

Not only that, but she discovered that in order to keep up with Jackson, she had to either lengthen her stride or break into a trot. She wound up doing a little of both.

When he realized that he was outpacing her, Jackson deliberately slowed down so that she could wind up walking beside him.

"Why didn't you say anything?" he asked as he fell back to join her.

"You mean like 'why are we galloping?'" Debi asked, amused. "It didn't seem polite."

He waved away her assessment of the situation. "I'm used to going everywhere on my own—occasionally with Garrett. Since he's the same height as I am, he tends to walk as fast as I do," he explained, then apologized. "Sorry, I didn't mean to make you trot."

Really good-looking, polite and he could cook. The man was almost too good to be true—which meant that this was probably just his public facade, Debi decided. No man was too good to be true. She knew that now.

She shrugged off his apology. "No harm done," she responded. "I think of it as burning off calories," Debi added. Whenever possible, she tried to look at things in a positive light. It was a coping mechanism that she employed.

Her last comment had him looking at her, his gaze lingering longer than he'd intended because he was verifying something for himself. "Why would you want to burn off calories?"

"Same reason every woman would, to noticeably slim down."

The way the female mind worked was nothing short of mysterious to him, Jackson concluded. "You slim down 'noticeably,' you'll have to be on the lookout for people wanting to run a flag up along your body." He paused for a moment right before the bunkhouse. "If something is already good, you don't mess with it," he told her matter-of-factly.

"Was that a compliment?" Debi asked, rather stunned if it was. He didn't strike her as someone who bothered with flattery, yet what else could it be?

"'That' was a bunch of words, signifying a thought and forming a conclusion," he answered. "If you feel it was a compliment, then fine, it was a compliment. But it wasn't intended as one. Make of it what you will."

And what do I make of you, Jackson White Eagle? she wondered. No immediate answer came to her.

Moving on, Jackson pushed open the door to the bunkhouse.

"This is it," he told her, acting as a guide. "This is where the hands on the ranch sleep and where they unwind at night after dinner."

Debi looked around slowly. She had walked into a very large communal room. Rather than the bunk beds she'd expected to see, there were two rows of equally spaced twins beds facing one another. Four on one side, four on the other.

Now that she thought about it, she hadn't recalled seeing that many teenage boys on the grounds, but they could very well have been within one of the buildings she'd noted as she'd driven onto the ranch.

Curious, she asked, "How many hands are there currently on the ranch?"

"If you'd asked me that question at the beginning of the month, I would have said we were full up with twelve." They'd had to bring in extra beds at the time, making it more crowded. "But since then I've had a few of them graduate and go back to their homes." It was easy to see that he was quietly proud of that accomplishment. "Currently, counting your brother, we have eight."

She moved about the room slowly, trying to get a feel, a vibration from the area. She would've said that no teens slept in the bunkhouse these days. The neat way the beds were all made was nothing short of impressive. "How many repeaters do you get?"

His eyebrows came together in almost a huddle as he looked at her, puzzled. "Excuse me?"

"How many of the 'hands'—" that word still felt very awkward in her mouth "—that graduate from here fall back into their old habits and wind up coming back to your ranch?"

He didn't have to think. Jackson's answer was immediate. "None."

He seemed pretty positive. "Is that because their parents take them elsewhere?" she asked bluntly. Being blunt had never been her way nor had she found it acceptable, but the situation Ryan had put her in had changed all that.

"No, it's because none of the boys who graduate from here wind up being repeat offenders. They wind up going on to finish high school and they either take up a trade or, in some cases, go on to college." He saw the doubt in her eyes. It was to be expected. He would have been suspicious if she'd been too trusting. "I've got letters from former ranch hands, catching me up on their lives, if you'd like to look them over."

The fact that he had volunteered the letters put a different sort of light on the matter. Jackson didn't know her and thus had no way of knowing whether or not she would take him up on his offer. Bluffing would have been a mistake. The cowboy didn't seem like the type to make mistakes.

She supposed she could say yes and see if that made him uncomfortable, but she already had a strong feeling that it wouldn't. The man struck her as being more than able to hold his own in a war of nerves.

Her gut told her that he wasn't a liar.

"No," she told him simply. "I'll take your word for it."

He nodded as he watched her roam about the room. "Suit yourself, but the letters are available if you ever want to, say, satisfy your curiosity—or put your mind at ease."

She looked around one last time before making her way over to what was a very large bathroom. The door was open so she assumed it wasn't occupied. Peering in, she saw that it had a number of shower stalls, a long counter with five sinks and the same number of bathroom stalls. Closer scrutiny showed that the entire area appeared to be clean enough to eat off. Just like the rest of the bunkhouse.

She found it almost unbelievable.

"Are you sure you have the hands *sleeping* in here?" she asked incredulously. This place was every bit as clean as her own apartment—perhaps even more so.

"Very sure," he answered. Then, to lighten the mood just a bit, he added faux-solemnly, "It's either that, or somebody has substituted some very lifelike robots for the guys who bed down here every night."

With nothing left to see within the bunkhouse, they walked back outside. Jackson pulled the door closed behind him. "Would you like to see the stables, as well?" he suggested.

It was as if Jackson had been expecting her scrutiny,

or at least scrutiny by someone conducting a close re-
view of the premises, but if the ranch was normally in a
state of chaos, there would have been no way to make it
this presentable in a few hours. This had to be the normal
state of affairs on The Healing Ranch, and that alone all
but left her speechless.

"The hay's probably been scrubbed clean," Debi
guessed.

Jackson shook his head. "Too time-consuming," he
deadpanned. And then he added seriously, "I just have
whoever's in charge of the stables that day replace the
old hay with new hay. It's a lot simpler—and cleaner—
that way."

What did she have to lose? It wasn't as if she actually
had a job interview waiting for her. Besides, she did like
horses, even though the closest she'd ever been to one was
in her living room, watching a Western on the TV screen.

"Okay, sure, I'll have a look," she told Jackson gamely.

As it turned out, the stables were close to the bunkhouse. All part of the so-called "hands" bonding process with the horses they were assigned to care for, Debi
surmised.

When she arrived, the doors to the stables were standing wide-open the way, Jackson told her, they were every
day during normal operating hours.

Since they had passed a number of hands working with
horses in the corral, Debi expected to find the stables as
empty as the bunkhouse had been.

But they weren't.

While there were no horses to be seen—they were
all out in the corral—the same wasn't true of the people
Jackson was working with. Specifically, the person he

was going to work with that day after he finished being her guide on the ranch.

Debi was stunned when she realized that the person dressed in jeans, boots and a plaid shirt, and manning a pitchfork as if he was trying to figure out how he was supposed to handle an oversize dinner fork, was her brother.

She'd overlooked him at first.

An involuntary little gasp of surprise passed her lips and had Ryan looking up. There was nothing but blatant hostility and anger blazing in his eyes when he realized that the sound had come from his sister and that she was here, looking at him.

"You come here to gloat?" Ryan demanded nastily. "Or maybe you just came by to tell me that this enforced slavery is for my own good."

"It's not 'slavery' and it is for your own good, Ryan," she said, feeling helpless and taken advantage of as well as angry at her brother's tone.

She'd put up with so much for so long that she was dangerously close to her breaking point. She was seriously worried that she would wind up breaking at the wrong time.

Ryan's eyes narrowed into small, angry, accusing slits. "Well, if it's so damn great, why aren't you in here, shoveling all this sh—"

"Careful, Ryan," Jackson warned, intervening. "You don't want to owe the swear jar more money than you're going to earn this week. If you do, you're going to find that what you ultimately wind up doing will be a whole lot worse than just mucking out the stables."

It wasn't a threat, but a promise. One that was vague enough to mean nothing—or everything. But Jackson

White Eagle did not look like a man to be antagonized without consequences.

Slightly intimidated, Ryan obviously bit back the insult he was about to hurl at both his sister, the betrayer, and the man she had sold him out to.

Ryan changed the wording, but not the tune. "I'm not staying here," he shouted to his sister as she was being escorted away by Jackson. Ryan thought of him as the dark soul who ran this place. "Just giving you fair warning," Ryan shouted even louder. "First chance I get, I'm outta here. I'm gone."

Debi turned and looked over her shoulder at her brother.

"Ryan, please, let them help you," she begged, afraid that her brother would carry out his threat. Afraid that he would wind up dead in some alley before the year was out.

"I don't need their help. I don't need yours, either," Ryan retorted with a nasty edge to his voice.

Each word just cut straight into her heart. There had been a time when they had been close, when she had known or sensed her younger brother's every thought, every need. Now she hardly recognized the angry being he had become.

"Ryan—" she began in a supplicating tone.

The next second, before she could find the words to even remotely try to convince Ryan that being here was a good thing, she felt Jackson taking her arm and leading her away from the stables.

"What are you doing?" she demanded, shaking off his hold.

Jackson released her only once they were outside and several lengths away from the stables.

"The longer you stay in there with him, the more he's going to rant and work himself up," Jackson told her mildly.

She gazed up at him, her concerns piquing. She only heard one thing. "You're telling me I can't talk to my brother?"

"I'm telling you that you can't talk to your brother *now*," he corrected in a voice that was almost maddeningly calm. "Give me a chance to work with him, to show him the right path and make Ryan come around on his own accord."

She was trying very hard to have faith in the process and in the man she was talking to. But in light of her brother's present attitude, it was very difficult for her. "You mean like finding God?"

"God doesn't have to be found. He's not lost," Jackson replied in a voice so mild she found it both soothing and maddening at the same time. "What Ryan has to find is Ryan. He has to stop feeling angry and guilty and all those other hostile emotions that are getting in the way of his own inner growth and evolution. We get him down to the very basics," he explained to Debi, "and then start rebuilding him into a person both you and he can be proud of."

She was beginning to doubt that was even remotely doable. "Sounds like a dream right now," she confessed.

Jackson smiled at her. "Then I guess I'm in the business of making dreams come true," he said before redirecting the conversation. "If there's nothing else that you want to see here, I'll drive you into town." Jackson began leading the way to his vehicle.

That wasn't what the rancher-slash-miracle-worker

had told her earlier. "I thought you said you'd have one of the hands take me."

"I did, but you turned that down, saying you could find the town yourself," he reminded her.

And nothing had changed since then as far as she was concerned. "I still can."

"I have no doubt," Jackson was quick to affirm. "But the way I see it, things'll go faster for you if I introduce you to Doc Davenport myself. Otherwise, you might have to sit out in the waiting room and wait your turn. I don't really recommend that," he added, specifying in a lower voice, "They're *always* busy."

She didn't want to be in his debt, but then, if the man actually managed to turn Ryan around and get him even marginally back to where he had been before things began falling apart, she knew that she would be *eternally* in Jackson's debt until the day she died.

This was a small deal in comparison to that.

"Then I guess," she told him, "you've made me an offer that I can't possibly refuse."

Jackson had no idea that she was paraphrasing a famous movie line. He took it seriously at its face value. "Not wisely, no," he agreed.

"Well, then I won't refuse it," she told him.

Chapter Six

As far as the size of towns went, Forever was more of a whisper rather than a long-winded speech.

While it was true that when it came to Forever's citizens, not everyone knew everyone else, it was a town where everyone at least knew *of* everyone else by name if not by association or sight. However, when it came to those necessary to keeping the town running smoothly and without mishaps, they became known to everyone. People like the town vet, the town doctors, and the store owners since their numbers were few, as well.

The sheriff and his three deputies were familiar faces to one and all even though Forever's worst offenders were a couple of men who preferred spending their time at Murphy's, the town's tavern, to coming home to their sharp-tongued, overbearing wives.

The one person that everyone knew without question was Miss Joan.

Miss Joan had owned and run the local diner for as far back as anyone in town could remember. The diner was the one place where everyone eventually came to meet as well as eat, either on a regular basis or once in a while. Because of this, and the fact that Miss Joan liked to stay on top of everything that was happening in Forever, be it eventful or of no consequence whatsoever, Jackson decided to bring the woman sitting in the passenger side of his truck to the diner first.

And to Miss Joan.

Debi was under the impression that the cowboy was taking her straight to the clinic. So when Jackson pulled up in front of what looked like a diner, the sunshine gleaming off its silver exterior like a lighthouse beacon, she was mildly curious. For a moment, she assumed that he was going to pass by the eatery—cutting it admittedly rather close.

But then he parked.

Debi was growing increasingly aware that the people in this area seemed to march to an entirely different drummer than she was accustomed to, but she just couldn't reconcile herself to the fact that the medical clinic was being run out of a diner.

But he was parking here, and this place was really different from anything she was familiar with back home.

The best way to find out, she decided, was just to ask.

"We're stopping?" She put the question to Jackson as he turned off the ignition and pocketed the key.

"Sure looks that way," he replied, an easy, laid-back drawl curling itself around each word.

Jackson couldn't readily explain why, but the way she seemed to be puzzled by the simplest things amused him—in a good way.

Still, he knew enough about women to know that they didn't like being the source of someone else's amusement, so he kept his reaction to himself. It was undoubtedly safer that way.

Getting out of the cab of his truck, Jackson rounded the hood and came over to her side. He saw that she hadn't opened the passenger door yet, so he opened it for her.

She appeared to be looking at the diner uncertainly.

"The doctors practice out of a diner?" Debi asked incredulously.

He thought of the time that Lady Doc, Alisha—the newest addition to the medical clinic—had treated Nathan McLane, the saloon's best customer, for a ruptured appendix. She'd examined the man on the floor of Murphy's, where he had collapsed.

"The docs practice wherever they're needed," he responded vaguely.

Jackson knew he should have set the record straight immediately as to why he'd stopped here, but he had a feeling that if he said, right off the bat, that he was bringing her here so that Miss Joan could meet her, Ryan's sister would balk at that. Not that there would be any harm done. He'd tell Debi soon enough.

Debi got out of the truck, but then remained where she stood, staring at the gleaming silver structure. "Are you telling me that the clinic is actually located inside a diner?"

"No, but I thought you might want to get a feel for the people in Forever before you offer your services to the docs. This way, you'll have an idea of what you're getting yourself into."

Was he warning her? Or trying to scare her off? She couldn't quite make up her mind about that.

"You make it sound like I'll be making a deal with the devil instead of just making a temporary arrangement to work." That was all she was after, something temporary, just until Ryan was ready to go home. Hopefully, it wouldn't be any longer than a month, tops.

"Oh, no, not with the devil," Jackson assured her. "But being part of Forever—even temporarily—takes commitment and hard work."

Did he think she wasn't up to that? She'd worked hard for every single thing she'd ever gotten. "I'm not a stranger to hard work," she informed him with a touch of indignation.

"Good to hear that," he said so casually, she wondered if he had heard her at all and was merely paying lip service. "C'mon," he went on, "I want to introduce you to someone."

Going up the two steps to the diner, he pulled open the door and held it for her.

Well, at least they didn't lack manners here, she thought.

The second she walked in, the noise level in the partially filled diner—it wasn't lunchtime yet—began to abate until, thirty seconds into her entrance, the noise factor went down to zero.

People seated at the counter as well as in the booths lining the windows turned to look at her.

The red-haired older woman behind the counter paused as she was setting down someone's order. For a split second, the customer appeared to be forgotten.

Sharp hazel eyes swiftly took in the length and breadth of the stranger.

"You brought me a new face, Jackson," the woman said, raising her gravelly voice in order to be heard across the diner.

Debi felt as if she was on display, but her instincts told her that there was no getting around this, not if she intended to remain in this small, backwater town for the duration of Ryan's stay.

And she did.

Debi found the thought of going back home to her empty apartment completely soul draining. Without anyone to talk to there, she would have nothing to do once she got back but dwell on her failed marriage and her failed efforts at raising her very troubled younger brother. Not exactly a heartening scenario.

And what if something went wrong on the ranch while Ryan was there?

Or what if Ryan ran away?

The thought of being almost fifteen hundred miles away at a time like that and being unable to immediately get involved in the search to find him and bring him back to the ranch was something she refused even to contemplate. It was completely unacceptable to her.

She had no choice but to remain in Forever. And if she was to remain here for the duration—however long that might be—then she needed to be able to earn a living. And that meant that she was going to be interacting with the citizens of this collar button of a town. Withdrawing into her shell was not an option that was open to her no matter how enticing it might be.

The woman with the bright orange hair beckoned to her.

"C'mon closer, darlin', I don't bite," the woman promised.

"Don't you believe it," someone within the diner piped up, then laughed at his own statement.

"Don't listen to him, honey. He's just sore because I made him finally pay up his tab." Hazel eyes drew in closer as Miss Joan continued to scrutinize the young woman with Jackson. "So, you passing through or staying?" she asked.

"A little of both," Jackson volunteered before Debi could say anything.

Miss Joan looked at him.

"What's the matter?" she asked Jackson sharply. It was a tone of voice almost everyone in Forever was familiar with. "The girl can't speak for herself?"

Debi straightened her shoulders as her eyes met Miss Joan's. "Of course I can speak for myself," she replied with just a trace of defensiveness.

The next moment, she upbraided herself for her lack of discipline. She was the outsider in this town. If she hoped to fit in, at least marginally, she was going to have to watch that.

Belatedly, Debi offered the woman behind the counter a shy smile.

"So you can." Miss Joan nodded her approval. "What's your name, girl?"

"Deborah Kincannon," Debi answered.

Again, the woman nodded in response. "I expect you already know who I am. So, Deborah Kincannon, what brings you to our town?" When the young woman didn't answer her immediately, Miss Joan glanced over at Jackson. "Guess it's your turn to play ventriloquist again." Although her expression never changed, this time around, her voice sounded far less gruff.

Jackson looked over in the younger woman's direction to make sure he wasn't stepping on anyone's toes before he answered Miss Joan's question.

"Her brother Ryan's going to be staying at the ranch for a while."

Miss Joan's hazel eyes softened as they regarded the new woman at the counter for a moment. "Oh, I see. Well, it's a damn fine place to stay," the diner owner said to no one in particular and everyone in general. "Some pretty worthwhile people have put in their time at The Healing Ranch."

As she spoke, Miss Joan placed an empty cup and saucer on the counter, then proceeded to fill the cup with coffee that looked blacker than a raven's wing.

With the cup three-quarters full—leaving room for cream if any was desired—she moved it in front of the young woman Jackson had brought in.

Debi looked down at the cup. She was husbanding every dime she had. She couldn't afford to just throw money around, even for something as relatively inexpensive as a cup of coffee. Until she was assured of securing that job at the clinic that Jackson had told her about, every penny was precious and counted.

"I'm sorry, there's been a mistake. I didn't ask for any coffee," Debi told her politely, moving the cup and saucer back.

Miss Joan offered her a steely glimmer of a smile as she gently pushed the cup and saucer back in front of her. "First cup is always on the house," Miss Joan told her. "House rules," she added in case more of a protest was coming.

Debi found the woman's smile a little unnerving. A frown looked to be more at home on the woman's lean face, she couldn't help thinking.

She gave it half a minute. The smile, such as it was, remained. Maybe the woman's offer was on the level, Debi decided.

"Thank you," Debi murmured, bringing the coffee closer to her. It smelled delicious.

"You can sit, you know," Miss Joan told her, gesturing

at the empty stools that were directly behind her. "There's no extra charge for that."

As if on cue—and to show her how it was done—Jackson slid onto the stool that was next to the one behind her.

At this point, standing there was beginning to make her feel awkward, so Debi slid onto the stool that was right behind her.

Miss Joan moved both the creamer and the shaker of sugar over to her. The brief flash of a smile seemed to say that the diner owner knew she was a cream-and-sugar person.

"So, where are you from?" Miss Joan asked without the slightest bit of hesitation, or even the hint of a preamble.

Debi took a long sip of coffee first before answering quietly, "Indianapolis."

Miss Joan's expression gave nothing away. "Nice place to be from," she agreed. "Dropping the boy off and going back?" she questioned casually.

Debi's immediate reaction was to say that that was no one's business except for the man who had brought her here, and that was only because he would need to know how to get in touch with her. But the survival instincts that had gotten her this far warned Debi that her words might give offense to the woman. She had the very strong feeling that Miss Joan was someone she would rather have on her side than not.

"No, I'm going to stay in Forever until Mr. White Eagle thinks Ryan can be taken home." God, but that made Ryan sound like he was a cake or something. When a cake was baked and cooled, then it could be transported.

Miss Joan looked over toward Jackson, then back to the young woman he'd brought with him. "Mr. White Eagle, eh?" Miss Joan chuckled to herself, clearly amused. And then she became more businesslike again. "You know, I could use a little help behind the counter," she said, approaching the offer she was about to make slowly and tendering it to Jackson as if he was the intermediary in this scenario. "Nothing major, just a few hours a day. Maybe some help with the inventory," she added, her eyes meeting Jackson's.

"Debi's a surgical nurse," Jackson told the older woman. "I'm going to bring her to the clinic since they could always use some help." His mouth curved into an easy, friendly smile, one she hadn't witnessed yet, Debi caught herself thinking. "But I thought she should meet the queen bee first."

Miss Joan leveled a long, scrutinizing gaze at the young man she had known since before he took his first step, thanks to Sam.

She pretended to be displeased with the label he had just given her. "Don't get sassy with me, boy. If I were 'the queen bee,' you can bet your bottom that I would have stung you a long time ago."

Debi looked from the woman to Jackson, wondering if this was an argument because of her, or if Miss Joan was just bandying words about. The woman didn't appear to be particularly annoyed. Then again, Debi really didn't know her at all. Maybe this *was* the older woman's annoyed expression.

Unable to decide, Debi took refuge in the cup of coffee that Miss Joan had placed before her. The coffee was light enough, but it still hadn't reached its maximum sweetness level. She added another teaspoon of sugar, then took another tentative sip. Satisfied with the results, Debi drank up in earnest.

Aware that the woman was watching her—and rather intently at that—she assumed that Miss Joan wanted to know what she thought of the coffee, so she offered her a smile and murmured, "Good."

The corners of Miss Joan's thin lips curved so slightly anyone with challenged eyesight would *not* have been able to detect the difference.

"I know," she replied as she went back to her other customers, leaving the duo alone.

For now.

"Did I pass inspection?" Debi asked in a whisper, holding the cup in front of her lips so that if Miss Joan looked over in her direction, the woman wouldn't see them moving. There was no doubt in Debi's mind that Miss Joan probably knew how to read lips.

Amusement glinted in Jackson's deep sky-blue eyes. "Yes."

He sounded convinced. However, she wasn't. Just what did he know that she didn't? Or was he just trying to placate her?

"How can you tell?" Debi asked.

Jackson smiled, his amusement very evident. For just a second, he felt like a guide, unveiling a national treasure. Had circumstances been different, he could have been talking to Debi about his aunt instead of just the very unique and unorthodox owner of the town's only restaurant.

"If you didn't," he told her knowingly, "you would have heard about it. Trust me." Having finished his own cup of coffee, he gave no indication that he was about to get up. Instead, he nodded at her cup. "When you're finished, I'll take you to the clinic."

Debi was eager to have her situation resolved and on an even keel—or as even a keel as her circumstances allowed. She drained the rest of her coffee with one long swig. Swallowing, she set the cup down in its saucer, and said, "Finished."

Jackson suppressed a laugh. He hadn't expected her to gulp down her coffee.

This woman might be interesting after all.

"Then I guess we're good to go," he responded.

Jackson finished the last of his own coffee and set the cup down. Looking about the diner, he saw Miss Joan and nodded at the woman as if to say goodbye.

The next second, he was leading the way to the door. He didn't expect to have Debi suddenly ease herself in front of him and go outside first.

Why was she in such a hurry? Was it merely because she was anxious about getting a job at the clinic—or was there another reason for her all but racing outside of the diner?

Debi squeezed past the cowboy and went through the exit first. When he joined her outside the silver structure, she turned around and blurted out, "Is she like that with everyone?"

Now he understood her hurry to leave the diner. For some, Miss Joan was an acquired taste. Even he would admit that the woman did take some getting used to.

When his stepmother had died, Miss Joan had stepped in, like family, and had taken care of details he would have never even thought to attend to. Without so many words, she was there to provide emotional support, as well, if either he or Garrett needed it. In Garrett's case,

Sylvia had been his mother, so making it through the first few days and then weeks had been difficult—and would have been even more so without Miss Joan.

"Absolutely," he was quick to assure her. "You always know where you stand with Miss Joan. She doesn't believe in playing games or fabricating stories. Miss Joan is the real deal," he told Debi. And then, as if reading her mind, he added, "She can come on pretty crusty at times."

Now *that* was an understatement if she'd ever heard one. "I'll say."

"But there's nobody I'd rather have in my corner," he said with conviction. "When she's with you, she's with you a hundred and ten percent. Not to mention that the woman has a heart of gold."

He could see that Debi needed convincing of that. Jackson thought of telling her about Sylvia, but that felt too personal. Fortunately, there was more than one story.

"One winter was particularly bad here. Crops had failed, a lot of people were out of work. And things were particularly bad on the reservation. Miss Joan made sure her food trucks made it there every week until things turned around. Wouldn't take a penny, either. Said they could pay her when they were back on their feet. Turned out she was losing money right and left. But, being Miss Joan, she didn't say a word about it. When someone found out and asked how she could get by, she said that wasn't anyone's business but her own." He smiled to himself as he started up his truck again. It wasn't far from the diner to the clinic, but, being tired, he figured Debi would prefer not to walk. "A lot of folks around here think of her as the town's guardian angel. Nobody says anything like that to her face, of course, because they know she'd probably let loose with a string of words that would more than fill up ten swear jars," he told Debi. "Still, I think she'd be secretly tickled to hear that we think of her that way.

"Looks like they've got another full day," Jackson said in the next breath as he drew near the medical clinic. There were all manner of vehicles parked in front of the single-story building as well as close by. "You are really going to make their day," he predicted as he looked for a place to park.

I hope so, Debi thought, mentally crossing her fingers.

Chapter Seven

Holly Rodriguez pushed a wayward, stubborn strand of dark blond hair out of her blue eyes. It just annoyingly refused to stay put and she had no time to fuss with it. The day felt as if it was spinning out of control and she barely had time to breathe, much less fuss with her hair.

As happened on a tediously regular basis, she'd wound up pulling double duty at the clinic. That meant that she had to periodically return to the front desk and act as what had once been referred to, generations ago, as a "Girl Friday"—which meant that she had to do whatever it took to keep the office, or in this case, the clinic, running as smoothly as was humanly possible.

The rest of the time, she was in the back, working at her true calling and recently obtained vocation, that of being a nurse. Achieving the status meant that her fondest dream had come true. Or, more accurately, her fondest dream right after marrying Ray, the youngest of the Rodriguez clan and the man she had been in love with for what amounted to most of her life—ever since elementary school.

Holly loved being a nurse.

Loved it so much that not even the most menial of tasks associated with the vocation daunted her enthusi-

asm. On a few rare occasions, since Forever had no hospital and the closest one was located in Pine Ridge, some
fifty miles away, patients who had to undergo emergency
surgery were placed in the room that served as the clinic's
recovery area. When that happened, Holly was the one
who gladly remained overnight and watched over the patient until he or she was strong enough to be transported
to Pine Ridge Memorial.

Holly had momentarily returned to the front desk less
than three minutes ago. She was in the middle of orga-
nizing the last batch of patients who had signed in while
she was in the back, assisting the two doctors. She had
to admit, if only to herself, that trying to split herself
equally between the doctors and working the desk was
really beginning to wear her down.

Right about now, she was very close to wanting to sell
her soul for some extra help.

The bell over the door chimed, indicating that yet another patient was coming in. Holly tried not to feel overwhelmed as she looked up to see who had come hoping
to be squeezed in to see one of the doctors.

It felt as if most of Forever had already been here
today.

Holly was surprised to see Jackson White Eagle enter.
To her recollection, the man had never set foot in the
clinic seeking medical help for himself. It was always
for whomever he had in tow.

Today was no different, Holly thought when she saw
that someone was with him.

Someone, Holly realized as she looked more closely,
who she didn't recognize at all.

Between working at the clinic and waitressing at the
diner, the job she'd held down while she was studying

for her nursing degree, Holly felt fairly confident that she knew everyone who lived in and around Forever, at least by sight if not by actual name.

But the person with Jackson was a woman she had never seen before.

"You picked a really bad day to try to see one of the doctors," she told Jackson the moment he crossed to the front desk. "I think we're well on our way to breaking the record for number of patients treated here in a single day. If you're not feeling too bad, maybe you could come back tomorrow," Holly tactfully suggested. She was addressing her words to Jackson, but due to past experience, the polite suggestion was intended for the person she assumed was the real patient, the woman he had brought in with him.

"We're not sick," Jackson assured her. "As a matter of fact, I'm actually here to do you and the docs a favor."

A rather mysterious smile played on his lips as he spoke.

Somewhat confused, Holly cocked her head, waiting for more of an explanation.

"Who's in charge of hiring?" Jackson asked her.

He assumed that it was Dr. Davenport, since Davenport was the one who had reopened the clinic after it had been closed for over thirty years. But just in case Dan had handed off that job to the new doctor, he didn't want to start Debi off on the wrong foot by accidentally stepping on any toes—or egos.

But he hadn't.

"That would be Dr. Dan. Why do you ask?" Holly asked. The words were no sooner out of her mouth than the answer hit her. Afraid that she'd probably made a mistake, her eyes still seemed to light up as she went on to ask, "Did you bring the clinic a sec— An administrative assistant?"

Her tongue had stumbled a little over the job title. At times it was hard remembering the correct terminology being used these days. Forever might be a very small town with its share of growing pains, but it wasn't exactly lost in the last century, either. People in the know did their best to remain current.

Jackson glanced at the woman with him before looking back at Holly. There was a spark of amusement in his eyes. "Not exactly."

"Oh." The single word was just brimming with disappointment.

Debi was quick to pick up on it—as well as to take in the fact that there was growing chaos on the front desk's surface.

"Do you need help out here?" Debi asked, ready to volunteer.

She knew what it felt like to be swamped. As far as she was concerned, what she'd just asked was basically a rhetorical question since she could see that the young woman behind the front desk was all but drowning in paperwork, files and patients.

"Oh, God, yes." The words slipped out of Holly's mouth before she could think to stop them. She could handle this, she knew she could. It would just take her half the night after the doors closed, that's all.

The young woman's response was all the urging Debi needed. "What do you need me to do?" she asked, coming around the desk.

Jackson watched the woman he'd brought to the clinic. It was his turn to be confused. "I thought you told me that you were a surgical nurse," Jackson said.

"I am, but I worked in the front office while I was studying for my nursing degree. You get a feel for how a hospital operates that way."

Holly's mouth dropped open.

"You're a nurse?" she cried, looking very much like a child whose every wish for Christmas had just been summarily granted. "Really?" Her voice trailed off in a thrilled squeak.

"Really," Debi happily confirmed, then added, "But I know my way around a desk and appointment ledgers. I don't mind working a desk, really."

Energized by this one piece of information and the promise that went with it, Holly sprang to her feet. "Wait right here," she instructed both of them.

Actually, it was more of a plea.

She began to dash to the back of the clinic when one of the patients in the waiting room lumbered to his feet. A big man with a gravelly voice, Ralph Walters wasn't shy about voicing his displeasure.

"Hey, I've been waiting to see the doctor for almost an hour," he complained, then jerked his thumb in Jackson's direction. "How come they're getting to see him before I do?"

"Because they're about to make life a whole lot better around here," Holly promised. Turning around to look at Jackson and the young woman he had brought with him, she said, "Don't go anywhere."

The next moment, she ducked into the second exam room.

Less than three minutes later, Holly was back out and at the desk. "Dr. Dan said not to go anywhere. He's finishing up with a patient and he'll be right out to see you."

Debi realized that with all this going on around her,

she hadn't introduced herself to the very pretty, harried young woman behind the desk. Leaning forward, she extended her hand to the nurse.

"Hi, I'm Debi Kincannon," she told her.

Holly grinned. "I'm Holly Rodriguez," she responded, gladly taking Debi's hand and shaking it.

"And I'm getting damn impatient," Ralph grumbled, glaring at the two women.

Holly suppressed a sigh. "Mr. Walters, please. The doctors are working as quickly as they can, but they don't want to be careless or overlook something just in order to save time," Holly told him, doing her best to reason with the man.

Jackson turned around and looked at Walters, who had a couple of inches and a great many pounds on him. Seeing what appeared to have all the earmarks of a confrontation, Debi held her breath as she waited to see just what was going to happen next.

"Nobody likes waiting, Mr. Walters," Jackson pointed out. "But complaining about it just makes it unpleasant for everyone."

Walters appeared as if he was about to say a few choice words in response, but then the older man looked up into Jackson's face. It was obvious that the rancher realized that Jackson was younger, stronger and far more capable of subduing him than the other way around.

Muttering under his breath rather than voicing his opinion out loud, Walters sank back down into his seat again.

Holly seemed both impressed at the interaction and relieved that it hadn't escalated. "Bless you," she mouthed to Jackson.

Jackson nodded in reply.

Just then, the door to the second exam room opened

and Alice Ledbetter, one of Miss Joan's waitresses, walked out. The woman was smiling. "My back and neck feel much better already," she was saying to the tall, striking man who walked out with her. "I don't know how to thank you, Doctor."

"That's what I'm here for," Dan replied genially. Sending off his patient, Dan quickly took in the duo standing by the front desk. "Jackson," he said heartily, shaking the man's hand, "Holly tells me that you've brought someone to make our lives here a little less hectic." Dan focused on the young woman standing beside Jackson. "I take it Jackson and Holly were talking about you."

Flattered and a little floored, Debi wasn't exactly sure just what to say or even where to begin. Did she thank the man for seeing her? Modestly brush aside the fact that any sort of compliments were implied? Or did she give him a litany of her accomplishments and focus on explaining why he should be hiring her?

In general, she had never been the type to oversell herself. Too much of a buildup left too much of an opportunity for a letdown. She could only go with the simple truth.

"I'm a surgical nurse and I'm going to be here in Forever for at least a month." She glanced toward Jackson. Maybe she was being too optimistic about Ryan's progress. "Maybe longer. I was wondering if you—"

"You're hired," Dan told her.

Debi stared at him, stunned. She was good and she deserved to be hired, but there was no way the man could know that, not without verification.

"Don't you want references, to see my work records, my—"

Dan stopped her right there.

"I'm sure they're all in order. If they're not, that'll come to light quickly enough," Dan told her. Putting out his hand to her, he said, "I'm Dan Davenport and I'm very happy for any help you can give us, as, I'm sure, is Holly. We'll discuss terms later after the clinic closes for the night. When can you start?" he asked, not bothering to hide the fact that he was eager for her to join the team.

"I was thinking tomorrow, but I can stay and help Holly if she needs me to." Debi was exhausted and the thought of getting a room at the hotel and just sleeping through until tomorrow morning had a great deal of appeal, but becoming part of the team, even a temporary member, was important. She didn't want to begin by shirking off responsibility.

"And risk having you quit before you ever get started?" Dan asked with a laugh. "No, tomorrow will be fine," he told her. About to go into exam room one where yet another patient was waiting for him, Dan paused for a moment longer as a question occurred to him. "Do you have a place to stay? Because if you don't, my wife and I have a spare bedroom—"

"I'm taking her to the hotel," Jackson told him, cutting the doctor's offer short.

Dan nodded. "Good—but if you decide you don't like it there, the offer's still on the table," he told his new nurse before finally leaving the reception area.

Holly was about to bring another patient into the room that Alice Ledbetter had just vacated. But first she paused for a moment by the woman she looked upon as a candidate to become her new best friend.

"Ray and I have plenty of room on the ranch if you decide you want something a little quieter than a room at the hotel," she offered. "No charge," she promised. "Just let me know."

Debi nodded, somewhat caught off guard by the displays of generosity aimed in her direction. It overwhelmed her.

"You look a little confused," Jackson observed as they walked out of the clinic again. Despite the Stetson he wore, Jackson found he had to shade his eyes as he looked in her direction. "Something wrong?"

She wouldn't have put it quite that way. "Not wrong, exactly…"

Inclining his head, he asked her patiently, "But what, 'exactly'?"

She wasn't used to being on the receiving end of this sort of selfless generosity. It didn't exactly make her feel uncomfortable, but it did make her feel a little…strange, for lack of a better word to describe her reaction.

Debi did her best to explain how she felt about being offered all of this to Jackson.

"Where I come from, people go out of their way *not* to take you in if they don't have to, especially if they don't really know you. Being offered a place to stay not once but twice in the space of a few minutes, well, it just seems…"

Her voice trailed off as she lifted her shoulders in a vague shrug.

"Unusually generous?" he supplied when she stopped talking.

Debi nodded. That was as good a way to phrase it as any, she supposed. "That wasn't exactly what I was going to say, but I guess that's a good way to describe it."

"I guess people are a little more cautious about opening up their homes to other people in Indianapolis," Jackson guessed.

"Yes."

Was he looking down at Indianapolis? She could feel herself automatically getting defensive. When had defensiveness become a way of life? she wondered. It hadn't always been that way.

"People tend to march to a different beat in a big city. In a town, especially a town as small as Forever is, people look out for one another." It was the same way on a reservation, Jackson thought. Because they had more than their share of missing parents and incomplete family units, the inhabitants that were there became one large extended family. "It's the usual course of events. They want to help, they get involved. Anonymity and minding 'your own business' just isn't a factor in a small town like Forever."

"Maybe not, but it does take some getting used to," Debi confessed.

He thought about it for a moment. "I suppose that it does. If you're raised to be suspicious and to examine everything, then taking things at face value takes some effort."

Something in his voice caught her attention. "You sound like you've been through something like that yourself."

She regarded him in a whole new light. Initially, she'd thought that Jackson was born somewhere close by if not directly in Forever. But for him to know why she might have misgivings about the offers that had been made, he had to have experienced something along the same lines as she had at some point.

"I might," Jackson acknowledged, then closed the topic in the next moment. "Here's the hotel," he announced needlessly.

The hotel had been finished less than a year ago and it was still a surprise to see it standing there whenever he came into town. Getting used to having the building as part of the town's backdrop was going to take some doing, Jackson surmised.

"You know, if you're worried about money," he began abruptly as he pulled up in front of the hotel, "you're welcome to stay on the ranch."

"Your ranch?" she asked, half convinced that he had to be referring to another one.

"Yes," he answered. Why would she think that he would offer up someone else's home?

"Where?" To the best of her knowledge, any extra people on the ranch slept in one communal place. "In the bunkhouse?"

Now *that* would have definitely been asking for trouble, Jackson thought.

"No, we can't have you staying there with the guys. If nothing else, that sends the wrong message to them and having you there would definitely distract them from any lesson they've been sent here to learn. No, I was talking about the ranch house," he told her. "We do have a couple of spare bedrooms in the ranch house. Nothing fancy, just a bed, a small bureau and one nightstand." He came full circle back to the reason for the offer. "But if you're pressed for money—"

Debi looked at him, surprised and somewhat uncomfortable.

"Who said I was pressed for money?" she asked.

"No one," he replied simply.

He wasn't making his offer based on words he had actually heard. What had prompted him to make the offer was a feeling he'd gotten from the way she talked more than from what she actually said. She'd said she was taking a leave of absence from her job, but she had seemed eager to go to work at the clinic. If money was of no consequence, she would have been content just to stay at the hotel and observe Ryan at a distance.

Money, however, *was* of consequence.

"But no one likes to spend money if they don't have to…" he said vaguely.

She had a difference of opinion on that, an opinion that was probably the direct opposite of the one that Jackson had, she thought. She knew of several people who loved spending money and they did it as if it was going out of style.

In addition, one of those people—John—was actually spending money he didn't have. That had come to light thanks to the divorce proceedings. Spending money recklessly was definitely something she would absolutely *never* do. However, she wasn't about to be the object of pity, either. If she actually did have that job at the clinic, then the charge for the hotel room wouldn't be a problem. She wasn't looking to save money while here, she was attempting to pay her bills while she stayed close enough to be within shouting range for Ryan if it turned out that he needed her.

"If I'm going to be working at the clinic, it's easier for me to be staying in town, as well, which in this case means having a room in the hotel. But thanks for the offer," she told him with feeling.

Jackson shrugged. "Don't mention it. Anytime I can

make you an offer you don't want to take me up on, just let me know."

He noticed that her eyes crinkled as she laughed softly to herself. "I'll be sure to do that," she told him.

Chapter Eight

Jackson walked into the bunkhouse, the heels of his boots echoing within the all but empty room.

He'd been expecting this.

Expecting the challenge from the newcomer. The contest of wills that pitted the newcomer against the authority figure—in this case, him. New "ranch hands" always envisioned the clash they felt was coming, the one they always built up in their minds because it was all they had to cling to. It was crucial to their so-called hot-shot reputations which made them the king of the hill.

Or so they believed.

Debi Kincannon's brother, Ryan, struck him as being no different from all the other boys he had taken on at the ranch since he'd started his program. Boys who arrived with attitude to spare stuffed into their suitcases because their self-esteem was nonexistent.

Oh, there were nuanced differences to be detected, because every boy was different in some way. But when it came to the overall big picture, all the boys were basically alike. They felt neglected, ignored, belittled, and they were all bent on doing something to be noticed, something that would gain them a measure of respect, even in a cursory, shallow way.

It was better than nothing.

And every troubled teen who, one way or another, found his way to The Healing Ranch would challenge his authority, sometimes immediately, sometimes a little later, but most of the time sooner than later.

Ryan, apparently, wanted to start that way right off the bat.

As he crossed the bunkhouse floor, making his way to the two rows of beds facing one another, Jackson spotted Debi's brother immediately. Ryan was sitting on his bunk with his back against the wall.

His arms were crossed before his thin, shallow chest, a bantam rooster biding his time and waiting for the fight to start.

Jackson could feel the teen's dark brown eyes on him, watching his every move.

Waiting.

So it was up to him to break the silence, Jackson thought. He obliged. "Garrett said you refused to leave your bunk."

Ryan's lower lip curled in a smirk. "Yeah, he's smart that way," the teen quipped. Something flickered in his eyes. Fear? "Don't think you can get me up, 'cause I got ways to hurt you."

"I'm not about to drag you out of bed," Jackson told the teenager. "Although I could if I wanted to," he informed him in a steely, unemotional voice. Letting him know the way things could be. "But if that's what you want to do, lie in bed all day, be my guest."

"Why are you being so nice?" Ryan asked suspiciously, pressing his back even harder against the wall, as if bracing himself for a sudden move.

Jackson shrugged indifferently. "I'm not being nice. Just the opposite."

More suspicion, if possible, entered Ryan's eyes. "How do you figure that?"

"Well, if I was being nice," Jackson said, coming to a stop directly in front of Ryan's bunk bed, "you'd be able to eat lunch and dinner."

Ryan scowled at him. "Why can't I eat?" he asked.

Jackson's tone indicated that the answer was self-explanatory. "Because you've elected to lie in bed. You don't work, you don't eat. It's as simple as that. There are no free rides here, Ryan. You have to earn everything, just like in the world that exists outside these walls."

Ryan raised his chin. "My sister's not going to let you starve me," he cried.

"She has no say in it," Jackson said in a soft voice that was all the more terrifying for its lack of volume. "Your sister signed over all rights over you to me. While you're here, I am your sole guardian." He was stretching things, but he knew that Ryan had no way of knowing that. "I decide what you do, what you wear, if you eat. I decide *everything*."

Clearly, Ryan's fear was escalating. "I don't believe you," he cried. "Deb wouldn't do that."

Jackson didn't bother trying to convince him, didn't waste so much as a single breath arguing, cajoling or convincing. Instead, he took a folded, legal-looking document out of his back pocket and held it out for Ryan to see.

"That's your sister's signature, isn't it?" he asked calmly.

Ryan's breath shortened and caught in his throat, and he looked to be on the verge of a screaming fit. Jumping up out of the bunk, Ryan looked around for something to throw, to break.

Grabbing the first thing he saw, a lamp, he was all set to throw it when Jackson informed him, "You break it, you pay for it. And if you have no coinage because you refuse to work here, you'll wind up spending a few days in jail as a guest of the county."

"You can't do that." Ryan's voice cracked as he spat out the retort.

"Oh, but I can," Jackson countered.

On his feet, the teen looked like a caged wild animal, scanning the room as he tried to figure out his next-best move.

There wasn't one.

Undoubtedly, he hated conceding, but it appeared that he had no choice. "So if I work, I eat?"

"That's the deal," Jackson agreed.

"And this 'work' you're talking about," he said, approaching the subject warily, "just what is it that I do?"

"It varies. Whatever is on your schedule to do that day," Jackson told him.

Muttering something unintelligible, Ryan stomped toward the door, anger smoldering in his eyes.

"Oh, and if you don't put in a full day," Jackson added as Ryan passed him, "you get docked for each half hour you miss."

Ryan swung around to glare at his jailer. "You've got this damn thing rigged, don't you?"

"You owe another dollar to the swear jar," he said mildly. "And as for what you just said, it works both ways," Jackson answered, his tone as mild as when he had begun talking.

While The Healing Ranch was still in its early days,

he'd discovered that the boys he had undertaken to turn around behaviorally had a great deal in common with wild animals.

And as with wild animals, if he spoke in a non-threatening, even an almost monotone, sort of way, there would be far less miscommunication between them.

"But all we can hope for is the present and the future. There is no changing the past," Jackson murmured under his breath to himself as he walked out of the bunkhouse behind Ryan.

Out in the open, the teen turned around and looked accusingly at him. "So where am I supposed to be today?" he asked in a nasty tone.

That was an easy enough question to answer. He had checked all the teens' schedules first thing that morning, before he had even gotten dressed or sat down to his own breakfast. "You have stable duty."

"Wow, what a surprise," Ryan sneered. He looked around the area and saw some of the other teenagers he had bunked with last night. They were in the corral, each of them working with the horse that had been assigned to them. For a moment, it appeared as if interest had sparked in his eyes before he reassumed his bored, sullen stance. "Hey—" he swung around to look at Jackson "—when do I get my own horse?"

"When you've earned it," Jackson replied matter-of-factly.

Lengthening his stride, he passed Ryan and made his way over to the corral to see how the teens there were doing.

"And how do I accomplish that great deed, oh Fearless Leader?" The sarcasm fairly dripped from Ryan's lips as he asked the question.

"I'll let you know when it happens, Ryan," Jackson told him.

Frustrated and obviously feeling helpless, Ryan raised his voice and shouted after Jackson, his tone threatening, "I'm going to tell my sister that you're just yanking me around!"

Without breaking stride, Jackson turned for a split second and calmly called back, "Won't make any difference, remember?"

The next minute, Jackson behaved like a man who was completely out of earshot, even though in reality he could actually hear everything that the teen was shouting at him.

He'd made himself immune to words the likes of which Ryan was hurling at him a long time ago.

"How long?" Garrett asked him, joining his brother as Jackson reached the perimeter of the corral.

Jackson knew exactly what Garrett was asking. He barely paused to think. His response at this point, after all the boys he and Garrett had worked with and managed to turn around, was close to a science and his assessments were all but automatic.

"A week, week and a half if he's particularly stubborn."

"A week and a half before he drops that abrasive attitude." Shaking his head, Garrett sighed. "Tell me again why we keep beating our heads against the wall, trying to make model citizens out of a bunch of thugs, future con men and thieves?"

"We're banging our heads against the wall because we want to keep them from becoming those future con men and thieves. We make a difference, Garrett," Jackson stressed. "And we're banging our heads against the wall because when *we* were these rotten know-it-alls, Sam was there for us. And *because* he was—and because he turned us around—now it's our turn to be there for all those others who don't have an Uncle Sam—no word-play intended," he added when he realized what that had to sound like.

Leaning against the corral railings, Jackson momentarily allowed his thoughts to drift back to his much earlier days. He'd lived on the reservation then and all he had wanted back in those days was to fit in, to be accepted.

"Besides," he continued as if this, at bottom, had been the answer to Garrett's question all along. "Weren't you the one who said he liked that good feeling inside when he realized he'd turned another kid around and kept him away from a life of crime?"

"Maybe." Garrett shrugged his shoulders carelessly. "I guess I must have had one too many beers when I said that."

Jackson played along. "Doesn't matter if you did or not. The point is that you said it and since you did, it can't be unsaid. You're committed to this way of life, same as I am." He was well aware of the fact that he couldn't have done nearly as much as he had if Garrett hadn't been there right next to him, sharing the load. "Repeat after me," he coaxed Garrett. "It's nice to make a difference."

"'It's nice to make a difference,'" Garrett parroted. "It would be even *nicer* to be well compensated for it," he added with a bit more feeling than he had intended to begin with.

"We are," Jackson told him in all sincerity. "It just doesn't happen to be in coinage."

"Ever try to buy dinner with non-coinage?" Garrett

asked him. He frowned slightly as he went on to say, "Doesn't work very well."

Jackson stopped watching the teens in the corral and looked at Garrett more closely for the first time during their conversation. "You're serious, aren't you?" He eyed Garrett with concern. "Are you burned-out?"

Garrett shrugged.

"Let's just say, it's more like tapped out."

"We're not in this for the money," Jackson reminded him.

Garrett laughed shortly. "Hell, don't I know *that*," he said.

Jackson had always believed in tackling a problem head-on, before it became a major disaster. If nothing else, he wanted to be prepared for whatever this problem might happen to kick up.

"You thinking of leaving the ranch?" Jackson asked, hoping he'd managed to successfully hide his deep concern.

"I'm *always* thinking of leaving," Garrett confided to his brother.

He supposed that wasn't exactly a secret, Jackson thought. Hell, there were times when he was all set to pack his own bags and go himself. But the good accomplished on the ranch far outweighed the bad he had to endure. It always did, which was why he was hopeful about continuing their work.

"Well, before you act on it, Garrett, come talk to me," Jackson requested.

"Right, because you're really talkative and everything." Garrett laughed, shaking his head.

"Good point," Jackson responded. He certainly couldn't dispute his brother's image of him. He'd always believed in an economy of words. The world was already far too littered with words uttered by people who just liked to hear the sound of their own voices.

"I said come talk to me, I didn't say I'd talk back. Sometimes you just need someone to listen and use as a sounding board, nothing more."

"And you can be as wooden as the best of them," Garrett guessed, laughing heartily.

"Now you've got it," Jackson told his brother with an affectionate grin. But, being Jackson, the grin vanished even before it fully registered on his lips.

Just another day at the ranch, Jackson thought, leaving Garrett and moving on to interact with the teens in the corral.

DEBI REALIZED THAT she had never totally appreciated what "putting in a full day's work" actually meant until today.

She had definitely put in a very full day at the clinic.

It was a little like being thrown headfirst into the deep end of the pool—except in that case, even if she were a nonswimmer, she'd still had reasonable expectations of survival.

Here at the clinic, it was a somewhat different story. Midway through her first day, she wasn't all that sure about her odds of surviving until sunset.

The pace at County General, the hospital where she worked back in Indianapolis, had always been rather hectic with very little downtime, but there *was* downtime on occasion. She had a very strong suspicion that "downtime" here at the clinic would have to involve some sort of an injury that would normally keep her off her feet—and even then the doctor in charge, Dan Davenport, would probably urge her to keep on going, injury or not, cast or no cast.

It wasn't that Davenport was a slave driver—he seemed like a very nice person. As was everyone else who worked at the clinic.

The second she walked into the place, believing herself to be twenty minutes early, she saw a line of people beginning at the door and spilling out onto the street. It just became worse once the clinic doors opened. The people just kept on coming.

Eventually she decided that there had to be an endless supply of sick people within the town because for every one examined, two more came to take his or her place.

Try as they might, the doctors still couldn't get to all of the patients during normal working hours. But rather than send them away the way she assumed that they would, the doctors had her lock the front doors as an indication that they weren't accepting any more walk-ins. Then the patients who were still in the clinic, despite the fact that the hours of operation were over, were seen, each and every one of them. Neither doctor gave any indication that they would leave before the last of the patients were examined and diagnosed.

Dedication like that could be truly wonderful when there was no one waiting at home for you to come through the door. In that case, it allowed a person to give as much of themselves as they wanted to.

However, she quickly learned that was not the case for either of the doctors, or Holly for that matter. All three had spouses and children at home waiting for them.

She was the only one who had no one.

Coming "home" to the hotel room held no allure for her. Oh, the room itself was quite lovely. And it was also small, the perfect size for one occupant, not so much for two. She supposed she was given this one intentionally so as not to emphasize the emptiness of both the room and the life of the person who temporarily occupied it.

She had gotten so used to being someone's wife, to thinking in terms of two rather than just one, she found herself missing being married. Not missing John, just missing the concept of being married.

Which was why, she silently reminded herself, she needed to work, to keep occupied. To that end, Jackson White Eagle had done her a huge favor by bringing her to the clinic.

But she had reached her saturation point. Although she'd wanted to be a nurse for as far back as she could remember, right now she knew if she saw one more patient, applied one more cuff to measure blood pressure or called in one more prescription to be filled, she was going to run into the streets, screaming out words that the children in the area did not need to hear.

Before she had become a surgical nurse, she had worked in the ER. She had been convinced that working in the ER had been rough. But compared to the day she had put in here at the clinic, a day in the ER seemed to her like a day spent at an amusement park.

Every bone in her body was beyond tired.

The doctors had finally removed their white lab coats and resumed their civilian lives. Holly had stayed to lock up and, as the "new kid on the block," Debi felt that she needed to remain, as well.

They were the last two to leave the building.

"You did great for your first day," Holly told her with weary cheerfulness.

Debi thought there was no harm in pushing the envelope just a little further. "How would you have said I did if this hadn't been my first day?"

Holly looked at her as if she thought that was a very odd question.

"Good, still good," she answered with as much enthusiasm as she could muster. "Glad to have you on our team for as long as you're going to be here in our area," Holly tacked on.

Everyone at the clinic—the doctors, Holly and the patients, as well—had made her feel welcome.

Exhausted, but welcome, she thought with a weary smile on her lips.

She and Holly parted at the door. Their cars were parked facing opposite directions. Holly was headed out of Forever to the ranch where she lived with her husband, her niece and her mother, while Debi had a far shorter drive to the hotel.

When she drew closer to her dusty car, Debi saw that there was someone leaning against the hood, his arms folded before his chest.

The arms gave him away. Standing like that, he looked more like a fierce warrior than a teacher schooled in brokering a peaceful coexistence between the teens sent to his ranch.

"Jackson?" she asked, almost hoping that it wasn't. If he was here, waiting for her, that meant that something had gone wrong with Ryan. That was the way she thought these days—because she was usually right. "Did something happen to Ryan?"

Jackson straightened up. "Other than learning that he can't have his way, no, nothing happened."

She didn't understand. "Then why are you here?"

"I just came by to see how you survived your first day at the clinic," he explained amicably.

It was a perfectly plausible excuse for his being here. Why she suddenly felt butterflies fluttering in her stomach was something she didn't feel she could explore. Not safely, anyway.

Chapter Nine

The next moment she looked at Jackson warily, not certain if she really believed his initial disclaimer. Maybe he was just trying to break something to her gently because he thought she might be the type to come unglued if something bad happened, like Ryan taking off without warning.

"And you're sure that this doesn't have anything to do with Ryan?" she asked, watching him carefully.

"Well, you wouldn't be here in Forever if it wasn't because of Ryan, so in a way it *is* related to Ryan—but only in the loosest sense of the meaning." By now, he was pretty aware of the way a parent's mind worked and the kinds of concerns that sprang to their minds. "If you're asking me if he's run off or done something to get thrown off the program—"

"Has he?" she asked almost breathlessly.

God, but her eyes were green. They had opened so wide, he felt as if he could just fall into them and then try to wade his way back to shore.

The next moment, Jackson upbraided himself sternly. *Get a grip*, he chided himself silently. *Remember your place. She's the sister of one of your charges. That means keep your distance.*

Doing anything else, he knew, would just be asking for trouble.

"No," he answered Debi quietly. "I left your brother on the ranch with the other ranch hands."

"Who's watching him?" she asked.

She knew Ryan. He could take off at a moment's notice—although where he could go in an area that had nothing to offer for miles in any direction was beyond her. But if Ryan felt wronged and was angry enough, he wouldn't think things through that far.

He'd just go.

"The other ranch hands," Jackson repeated. He sounded as calm as she was panicked. "They watch out for one another."

"Are you crazy?" Debi demanded, stunned. "They're all teenage boys. Having them watch each other, that's like throwing a match into a factory that makes fireworks."

"I'd give them a little more credit than that," he told her. For the most part, the teens had earned his complete trust. "Relax. I also left Garrett with them."

"Oh." She breathed a huge sigh of relief. "That's better."

He watched her, debating whether or not to point out the obvious. He decided that it was worth it—for her own good. "If the ranch hands were as bent on running away as you think, Garrett wouldn't be able to stop them. The odds would be against him."

From what little she'd seen, Garrett seemed as if he could handle himself. But Jackson, in her estimation, looked to be even better equipped to cope with the boys. "But not against you," she guessed.

"Fortunately for us, nobody's ever tested that theory.

And right now, after the day they've all put in, I'd say they're all too tired to lift their feet, much less make a break for it."

She could certainly relate to that, Debi thought.

"In any case, I didn't come to talk about the ranch," he reminded her. "How did it go?"

Debi turned so that she could see the darkened clinic from where she stood. It looked deceptively quiet—now. "It went," she remarked. "Someone said that the clinic hasn't been here all that long."

"It hasn't," Jackson confirmed.

"Where did the doctors practice, then?"

"They didn't," he told her. He liked the way surprise added a touch of innocence to Debi's face. "Dr. Dan came out here a few years ago. Something about taking his brother's place because his brother was supposed to come here but died in a car accident the night before he was supposed to leave." He paused for a moment to think. "Lady Doc's only been here less than a year."

"Lady Doc?"

"That's what her husband, Brett, called her the first time he met her. It kinda stuck," Jackson explained. "Holly's the only native from around here," he said, referring to the lone nurse.

Debi was still having trouble processing what he'd told her to begin with. "If neither of the doctors have been here all that long, what did the people do before that?"

"Well, they either drove the fifty miles to Pine Ridge, or they toughed it out. You hungry?"

The man changed topics fast enough to give her whiplash. She didn't answer his question one way or the other. Instead, she gave him a rather neutral reply. "I thought I'd just grab something at the hotel."

In some ways, the hotel was still evolving. The actual structure had been completed months ago. However, some of the extras that Connie Carmichael-Murphy had envisioned had yet to become a reality.

"Unless you were planning to chew on a pillow," Jackson said, "you're out of luck."

Debi stared at him quizzically. "Why's that?"

"Well, the hotel's a work in progress and they haven't gotten around to building a restaurant inside. Everyone kind of feels that would be an insult to Miss Joan."

"Why's that?"

"Right now, the diner's the only place anyone can get a meal."

"Are you sure? I thought I saw this other place." She thought for a moment, remembering a bright neon light forming a name. "Murphy's, I think the sign said." She'd caught a fleeting glimpse of the place. It looked more like a tavern than a restaurant, but to the best of her knowledge, taverns served food.

"Murphy's is the local saloon," Jackson told her. "The Murphy boys have got a standing agreement with Miss Joan. She doesn't serve beer or any other kind of liquor in her place of business and they don't serve food—other than the standard peanuts at the bar."

"And the hotel really doesn't serve anything?" she asked incredulously. She hadn't bothered to check it out last night when she'd registered, and as for this morning, with her stomach all tied up in knots, the thought of breakfast had just made her want to throw up.

After having put in a very long day, Debi was no longer too nervous to eat, but now her choices were rather limited.

She played devil's advocate. "And if I don't want to eat

at the diner?" The diner was perfectly acceptable, but the idea that she didn't have a choice didn't sit well with her.

Jackson mulled over her question. "You could either drive the fifty miles into Pine Ridge," he told her, "or go to the local general store and get yourself something to put in between two pieces of bread." He gave her his advice on the matter, for whatever it was worth. "The diner's got a better selection and at least the food'll be hot."

The thought of something warm hitting her stomach did have its appeal. She supposed that it wouldn't hurt to go to the diner again. There was just one thing she was still unclear about.

"Are you offering to come with me?" she asked.

The shrug was completely noncommittal. "Thought you might want to have someone to talk to until you got to know some of the regulars."

After the day she had just put in, silence was more welcome than conversation, but she didn't want to seem rude. Jackson was obviously putting himself out for her—besides, if she was standoffish and rude to him, the man might decide to take it out on Ryan.

For a second, she thought about asking him if there were any consequences to turning his offer down, but then decided that doing so just might put the thought into Jackson's head if it hadn't occurred to him before.

So she forced a smile to her lips and murmured, "That's very thoughtful of you."

And, if she was being strictly honest with herself, sitting at a table across from Jackson White Eagle couldn't exactly be considered a hardship. The man was exceptionally easy on the eyes.

His facial features were all angles and planes with strong cheekbones. And he was fit, she couldn't help noting. His arms, even through his work shirt, looked as if they were as hard as rocks.

It was easy to see that the man didn't just sit back and let the others do the heavy labor. He worked the ranch just as hard as, if not harder than the boys who were in his care.

"My truck's right over there," he told her, pointing it out for her benefit. "Don't worry, I'll bring you back to your car after dinner."

"I wasn't worried," she protested, secretly wondering how he could possibly know that she had been.

"Sorry, my mistake," he replied, letting her have her way.

It took less than five minutes to get to Miss Joan's diner. The entire area around the silver structure was filled with cars. Jackson parked in the first spot he could find.

Debi took in the scene. It looked as if half the cars in Forever were parked near the diner. Business was obviously booming.

"I guess when you've got a monopoly, people don't have much of a choice where they go to eat," she commented.

"There's that," Jackson allowed, although he was fairly convinced that if the cooking was bad, all but the people most inept in the kitchen would choose to remain home. "And Angel's cooking."

"Angel?" she asked, curious.

"Angel Rodriguez," he told her. "That's one of Miss Joan's two cooks." He was fairly convinced the woman could make dirt appetizing. He spared Debi a quick half smile. "She's from out of town, too. Like you."

"So people actually come here and stay?" Debi asked in surprise.

Not that she exactly had a wild social life back in Indianapolis, but she was fairly certain that the people in Forever rolled up the streets after ten o'clock.

The entire town struck her as the last word in boring.

Jackson watched her as if he was making a judgment based on what she'd just said. "Hard to believe, but true."

After exiting the truck, Jackson moved around to her door and opened it before she had a chance to get out on her own.

Debi glanced down at the hand he was extending to her. Taking it, she curled her fingers around it and got out. The hint of a tingling sensation that undulated through her felt oddly arousing and comforting at the same time.

Just her mind playing tricks on her.

"Your mother taught you well," she commented. When his eyes narrowed, she explained, "Your manners. Your mother did a good job teaching you manners."

It took effort not to sound bitter. Every so often, the emotion would raise its head unexpectedly, taking a chunk out of him when he least expected it.

"My mother didn't teach me anything at all," he corrected.

Her head jerked up just a beat before she realized her mistake.

"Oh, I'm sorry. I didn't mean to dig up any painful memories." Her shoulders rose and fell in a careless, helpless motion. "I have a habit of saying the wrong thing at the wrong time," she apologized, shifting uncomfortably.

"Who told you that?" he asked sharply.

Maybe she had picked the right man for the job of turning Ryan around. He certainly could intuit things.

"My ex," she told him after a beat. "He said I was a verbal klutz." She could almost hear John's voice in her head, saying something disapproving. Looking back, she wondered why she hadn't caught on to John's subtle self-esteem bashing sooner—before he had done such a number on her.

"I can see why he's your ex," Jackson commented. "He didn't exactly have very much going for him in the flattery department, did he?"

It wasn't loyalty but a need to not be pitied that had her being defensive. "John liked to call them as he saw them."

"As he saw them, huh?" Jackson questioned skeptically. "He was obviously myopic so I wouldn't give a lot of credence to what he said if I were you."

Debi was going to counter what he had just said to her but she was headed off at the pass and never got the chance.

"Well, look who's decided to give us another try," Miss Joan said heartily by way of a greeting as she passed the duo. Personally making the rounds to refill her customers' coffee mugs, Miss Joan was carrying a pot that was filled to the brim. "Grab a dinner menu," she instructed Jackson. "I'll be right with you. Two seats right over there." Miss Joan pointed to a cozy table for two over in the corner. "Grab them while you can. This time of the evening they're going fast."

With that, Miss Joan went to complete her rounds and fill every cup that required filling.

"Are you getting used to her yet?" Jackson asked her as they sat down at the table that Miss Joan had pointed out.

Debi had her doubts that that was possible.

"Does *anyone* get used to her? Ever?" Debi asked, trying as discreetly as possible to keep observing the red-head while planting herself on the seat that Miss Joan had singled out for them.

"Oh, sure," Jackson answered. "It'll happen without you even realizing it. One morning," he predicted, "you'll wake up and it'll seem as if Miss Joan has always been part of your life."

"I sincerely doubt I'll live that long," she replied.

She could protest all she wanted, Jackson thought. He knew better because he'd seen it happen time and again. Miss Joan had a way about her—and a heart of gold. The latter was not on display and only became evident after a sufficient amount of time had gone by and her gruff exterior had faded.

"You'll see," Jackson said more to himself than to her.

"Besides, you're forgetting that I'm only here as long as Ryan's on your ranch. Once you've straightened him out, my brother and I'll be going back to our old way of life."

Why was she so eager to get back to the scene of everything that had gone wrong for her? Jackson wondered. "And your old stress triggers."

"You're getting ready to tell me that Ryan's 'magical cure' only sticks if he stays here?" she guessed. "That once he leaves, he'll go back to his old habits?"

Jackson behaved as if he was actually considering her theories. "I suppose it could happen," Jackson allowed. "But what I'm saying is to be vigilant. When you initially get back, you'll need to go to great lengths to make sure he avoids whatever it was that set him off and down that path he'd taken."

"I don't know all his triggers, but I do know that John

was one of them—and that, at least, won't be an issue anymore."

"Good." Why hearing that the man was out of her life had Jackson smiling to himself bothered him—but not enough for him to stop smiling. "But remember, you can't give up your own life in order for Ryan to have his. And you can't wrap him up in Bubble Wrap and watch over him 24/7. What you're shooting for," Jackson told her, "is to get to a place where you know he's watching out for himself. That he's doing the best he can for himself. He needs to grow, Debi."

She inclined her head. "Sounds good in theory," she acknowledged.

Jackson offered her his killer smile—at least that was what she had labeled it in her mind.

"Works well in practice, too," he assured her. "Keep in mind that it just doesn't happen all at once. It happens slowly, gradually. Baby steps," he emphasized for her benefit. "If you expect baby steps, then you won't be disappointed."

Miss Joan came up to their table, an old-fashioned pad and pencil in her hands. She didn't like getting away from the basics.

The smile she tendered to Jackson was one filled with affection. "I don't see you in forever and then you pop up twice in two days. I guess I have Debi to thank for this." She looked at the young woman and smiled. "Thanks for bringing Jackson around."

Debi was not one who had ever taken someone else's credit. "He brought me," Debi corrected politely.

Miss Joan didn't miss a beat. "As long as the two of you found each other here, that's all that really counts for me."

Debi had the very uneasy feeling that Miss Joan was attempting to communicate something that made precious little sense to her at the outset. The woman made it sound as if they were an item, Debi suddenly realized. Nothing could be further from her mind. For her, relationships—other than the one she had with Ryan—were all toxic. Well, she didn't have time for toxic, didn't have the time or the patience to feel her self-esteem being slowly shredded to pieces.

The old Debi wanted to be loved. This new version of her felt that love was unrealistic. The best she could hope for was to be happy if her brother could be saved.

She could live with that.

Chapter Ten

"She means well."

Debi blinked, suddenly realizing that Jackson must have said something to her, something she was apparently supposed to comment on. She'd been so lost in thought for a moment that all she had heard was a faint buzzing sound around her. She'd just assumed that it was due to the noise level in the diner.

Obviously, it wasn't.

Embarrassed, she said, "I'm sorry, what?"

"I said she means well. Miss Joan," he threw in for good measure. It occurred to him that he was trying to explain something to Debi that obviously hadn't gotten through to her. He needed to explain something else first. "Once upon a time, Miss Joan and my late uncle used to see one another on a really regular basis. That's why I think Miss Joan feels obligated to try to pair me off with someone."

"Meaning me?" Debi asked in wonder. She was an outsider. If this Miss Joan was into playing matchmaker, wouldn't the woman have picked someone she knew? Someone who lived here in this little button of a town?

But Jackson shook his head. He didn't want her to feel

intimidated. "Meaning anybody who happens to be female, unattached and within five feet of me."

"Oh."

Debi supposed she should be relieved that she wasn't giving off any particular signals that would have made the older woman think that she was fair game. Because she wasn't. Despite the fact that she was very vulnerable and lonely these days, she was determined never to put herself in that sort of a position again.

She would never allow someone else to almost literally break her heart as well as her spirit the way John had done.

In the year before her parents had been killed, she would have sworn to anyone who would have listened that she had found the kindest, most caring man on the face of the earth. Looking back, she now realized that he'd behaved that way because she had put herself at his beck and call. Time and again, she had deliberately gone out of her way to make sure that John was always happy and that if he needed something, she would fill that need for him, sometimes even before he could put that need into actual words.

In essence, without really being consciously aware of it, she had sacrificed herself, her personality and her own needs in order to make sure that John was always happy.

She only realized how much of herself she'd been giving when she had to stop giving so much of her time and effort to John. In essence, her whole life had been restructured in order to bring Ryan into her home.

Shortly after that, the kindest man in the world turned into a moody, self-centered narcissist. And he only got worse with each week that passed. As a result, she became more and more stressed.

Until the final straw came with his ultimatum.

Nope, she would never be in that kind of position again, Debi promised herself for the umpteenth time since her marriage had dissolved right in front of her like a wet tissue.

And if she was feeling more than a little attracted to the man sitting across from her, well, there were all sorts of psychological reasons for that which didn't revolve around the fact that he was probably the handsomest, sexiest man she had ever seen up close and personal.

She was just feeling sorry for herself. She'd been part of a couple for so long, it was hard for her to get used to being single again.

"Why would Miss Joan feel she had to do that?" Debi asked him after a waitress had come to take their orders and then retreated. "I mean, I'm sure that you can have your pick of willing women." Did that come out right? she silently questioned. She had a feeling that it hadn't. All she could do was hope that Jackson didn't think that she was flirting with him. "The town isn't *that* small, is it?"

Jackson watched as a faint shade of pink climbed up on her cheeks. Until this moment, he thought the idea of a woman blushing was some sort of a myth. Yet the woman he was talking to was doing just that.

Blushing.

And he found it strangely appealing.

"Not when you combine it with the number of people who are on the reservation," he acknowledged.

She'd forgotten about the reservation. About to say as much, Debi caught herself just in time. She didn't want Jackson to think she was insulting him or his heritage. It was just that the concept of a reservation was so foreign to her.

"So then, why aren't you 'spoken for'?" she asked, trying to appear as if she was asking him tongue in cheek even though part of her was genuinely curious.

Jackson shrugged carelessly. "I guess I never found the right person. That and my time's pretty much taken up with the ranch and the boys." There was another reason why he had never ventured into the marriage field. Both of his father's marriages had fallen apart because his father had cheated on one wife then just ran on another. So, not only didn't he have a decent role model to emulate, he had his father's blood running through his veins. In his eyes, that gave him less than a fighting chance of having a decent marriage.

What was the point of trying if failure was more than just a fleeting option?

Debi thought over the excuse he'd given her. It was flimsy at best. "I'd think that the boys would probably be the ones to do whatever it is that needs doing on the ranch—and that you're one of those people who can get people to do what you want them to just by looking at them a certain way."

Now that sounded like fiction, pure and simple. Jackson laughed softly at her supposition. "You spend a lot of time reading, don't you? Escapist fiction, am I right?"

There'd been a time when she could get lost in a book. But not lately. Between her longer hours at work and her time spent either looking for Ryan or fighting with him to change his behavior, she had precious little downtime to herself.

"I don't get much of a chance to read anything these days. Work and Ryan have kept me pretty busy." Mentioning her brother brought something else to mind. She didn't like putting Jackson on the spot, but she needed to know if she was being overly optimistic about the present situation. "Full circle now, do you think he can be straightened out?"

About to answer her, Jackson saw the waitress approaching with their orders. He paused, waiting for the young woman to finish and then leave. When she did, he realized that by waiting, he had dragged the moment out for Debi. He hadn't meant to.

"I never met a boy who couldn't be straightened out," he told her.

"Is that a slogan on your brochure, or do you really believe that? Tell me honestly," she pressed, her eyes never leaving his face. Aside from being extremely handsome, he had one of those faces that weren't expressive. Thus she had no idea what he was thinking, she could only hazard a guess and then hope that she was right.

"Honestly?"

Jackson repeated the pertinent word as if he was mulling his options over. What he was actually doing was stalling, stretching out this dinner so that it lasted a little longer. He told himself it was because he was just trying to find out what sort of a life Ryan had had before coming to the ranch. But if he was being honest, he was certain that he already knew the answer to that. Although she was definitely nervous, Debi struck him as a caring person. She would have tried to make things easier on Ryan, not tougher. That's all he really needed to know about her relationship with her brother.

"Of course honestly," she responded.

He paused to take a few bites of his dinner before answering. "It's both."

"Both?" she questioned. Was she putting her faith in the wrong person after all? Her gut told her no, but then her gut would have maintained that John was a decent person she could always count on, no matter what. Look how wrong she had been there.

He explained it to her. "It's the slogan I sometimes use, but it's also something I really believe to be true. The teens who come to The Healing Ranch aren't hardened criminals or sociopaths. In most cases, they're not even terminally bad. They're just 'troubled' teens in a very real sense of the word.

"My job is to get them to think past themselves, to realize that they have a lot to give and that it's okay not to be a tough guy all the time. In order to do that, I need to find out just what caused them to want to break all the rules, to act as if a jail cell was in both their immediate and their permanent future—and to act as if they didn't care if it was.

"In Ryan's case, the reason for his behavior looks to be fairly simple." He saw the questioning look enter her eyes. He doubted if he was telling her anything that she didn't already know. Most likely, she was wondering how he had figured it out so quickly. "He blames himself for being alive."

She'd come to that conclusion herself, but each time she'd tried to approach her brother about it, Ryan shut her down, blocking any successful communication.

But she had come to that conclusion after a few months. Ryan had only been there for a couple of days. She was curious what had triggered Jackson's theory.

"Why?"

"Because there were three of them in that car that day and only he survived. Survivor's guilt is pretty common actually," Jackson told her. He found it to be rather an appalling truth. "Not that there was anything your brother could have done to prevent your parents' deaths, but that doesn't change the fact that he thinks there should have been *something* he could have done. I'm sure he's gone over the seating arrangement dozens of times in his head. Maybe if he'd sat in the front passenger seat and your mother was in the back, she'd be alive instead of him, that kind of thing."

Jackson was putting into words what had secretly been haunting her all this time, as well. To have someone else verify it, to believe that Ryan was actually going through this, just tore at her heart.

Debi stifled a helpless sigh. "You really think he thinks that way?"

Jackson nodded in response. "I'm as sure of it as I can be without having him say the actual words. But what I need to do now is to get him to open up and talk about it."

"You mean like a group therapy session?" She couldn't see that happening. She'd tried to sign Ryan up for that, but he'd refused to go. And when she literally dragged him to the psychologist's office, Ryan had shut down completely. If anything, Ryan's hostility level increased. After two attempts—and failures—she gave up trying to get him to attend the sessions.

"In a manner of speaking," Jackson allowed. The way he said it sparked her curiosity. The half smile on his lips did a little something more. "Except that in this case, the 'group' consists of horses."

"Horses?"

He nodded. "You'd be surprised what kind of things people get off their chests 'talking' to the family pet dog, or their goldfish as they're feeding it." The skeptical expression in her eyes told him she needed to be convinced. There was a time he wouldn't have believed it, either.

But Sam had showed him differently. "It's a safe way to share something that's eating away at them. After all, an animal isn't about to betray a trust and spill the secrets it was entrusted with."

"So then what?" she asked. "Do you have a recorder hidden somewhere on the horse or in the stable so you can gain some insight into the teenager you're dealing with?" She knew it was the most logical way to proceed, yet doing that seemed somehow underhanded.

She was surprised to discover that Jackson agreed with her.

He shook his head in response to her question. "Having a hidden recorder in the vicinity is just begging to destroy any sense of trust that might have been built up. That would cause more damage than good in the long run."

She hardly noticed what she was eating and did it automatically, her attention fixed on what Jackson was telling her. "So then how—?"

He liked the fact that she was questioning his procedures. So many parents would just deposit their offending offspring and wait to be called back at some future date. Ryan was a lucky kid.

"If the boy talks to his horse, that's the first step. Sharing what's weighing so heavily on them brings a sense of relief—sometimes minor, sometimes more. But letting it out—whatever 'it' is—is definitely healthy and brings with it a feeling of well-being, however minor it might be. The next time that happens, the feeling will last longer.

"In the long run, it's healing to unload the burden of whatever offense they feel they're guilty of. Sometimes it's just the offense of living when someone else isn't anymore," he told her pointedly.

That was obviously what Ryan was experiencing, she thought. "What school did you go to?" she asked, clearly impressed. When he looked at her quizzically, she added, "To get your degree in psychology."

The smile that curved his mouth created a strange, fluttery sensation within her. It left her feeling somewhat confused. Was she reacting like this because she was grateful to Jackson, or—?

"The school of hard knocks," he told her.

Was that just his modesty kicking in? "No, seriously, because you're making a lot of sense."

"Well, I'm glad that you think so," he said, finishing the last of his meal and moving the plate to one side, "but it's still the school of hard knocks."

"You didn't go to college?" she asked, surprised at the extent of his insight without any formal textbook training.

Jackson laughed shortly. "I didn't graduate high school," he confessed. "At least, not the first time around."

He had gone back to get his GED once he had decided that returning Sam's favor was going to take him in a far different direction than he had initially foreseen for himself. He'd gotten the high school diploma not to impress anyone, but to satisfy his own needs. There'd been no money for college at the time. By the time there was, he was too busy rescuing young boys' souls to take the time to go for a degree.

Debi was surprised. She came from a world where in order to accomplish anything, a person had to go to college—it was one of the things she worried about when it came to Ryan.

It was also something she and John had argued about before his ultimatum. He definitely didn't want her using "their" money to send her brother to college someday.

"Seriously?" she asked Jackson.

"It's not something I'd joke about," he replied. He looked at her empty plate. "Would you like anything else? Dessert?"

He got a kick out of the surprised look that passed over her face when she looked down at her plate and saw that it was now empty. This was a woman who could never play poker successfully, he mused. Everything was there for the world to see, right on her face.

He liked her openness, he decided. Encountering it was not an everyday occurrence.

"I'd love dessert," she confessed once she made peace with the fact that she had consumed an entire meal without even realizing it. "But I shouldn't. I don't need the extra calories."

Jackson's eyes washed over her. The woman was slender but it wouldn't take all that much to get her to look "thin"—as in skinny. "I'd say you most definitely need a few extra calories. Either that, or bricks to put in your pockets."

That didn't make any sense to her. Why would she want to carry around bricks? "Excuse me?"

"The winds kick up here every so often. Right now, I'd say that you're slender enough to blow away in a good stiff breeze." He grew serious, saying something he felt that she needed to hear. "Ryan can't afford to lose you, too."

"You twisted my arm," she conceded. She had always had a weakness for sweets. "I'll have whatever you're having."

His response was automatic. "Apple pie." Of all the various desserts that the diner offered, apple pie was a staple and also his favorite.

Her mother used to make the very best apple pies, Debi thought as a wave of nostalgia as well as sadness washed over her.

"Sounds good to me," she told Jackson.

Jackson held up his hand to get their waitress's attention. Before the young woman turned in their direction, Miss Joan saw him. In short order, she presented herself at their table.

"Everything all right?" she asked. The question appeared to be intended for both of them, but it was obvious that Miss Joan was looking pointedly at her.

Debi nodded. "Everything's very good, thank you, Miss Joan."

Miss Joan inclined her head in acknowledgment—as if she had expected nothing less.

"We'd like a couple of slices of apple pie," Jackson told the older woman.

Miss Joan glanced from one to the other. "You like the same things." There was approval in her voice. "That's good. Two pieces of apple pie, coming right up," she promised, withdrawing.

Jackson exchanged glances with Ryan's sister as Miss Joan walked to the rear of the diner. The older woman usually tried to make newcomers feel at home, but even so, Miss Joan was behaving unusually accommodating, he thought.

"Hard to believe that woman was a free-living hellion in her younger years, or so people tell me. It wasn't until she got married that she started looking at unattached people as people in search of their soul mates."

Debi thought of her own failed marriage and the dreams she'd had at the outset. She had been incredibly naive.

"I really doubt if there's any such thing as a soul mate."

The sadness in her voice had him wondering about the extent of what she had gone through. "I think Miss Joan would argue with you about that."

"She's that happy?" It wasn't that she didn't believe him, it just went against what she'd experienced. There had been a time when, if asked, she would have said that she had found her soul mate, as well.

"Yes, she is," Miss Joan said, reappearing with two servings of apple pie. She slid the two plates from the tray onto the table.

"That makes what you have very special," Debi told her, feeling somewhat awkward at being caught talking about the woman.

"I'm aware of that, honey. I'm also aware that I can't be the only one who's found someone special. The trick," Miss Joan told her, "is not to give up if you did happen to wind up with a lemon your first time out of the gate." The woman winked at her. "If you know what I mean." She smiled broadly at both of them. "Enjoy your apple pie. It's on the house."

"You can't make any money if you keep giving things away, Miss Joan," Jackson protested.

"Not just in it for the money these days. Don't need to be," she added. "Henry would turn me into a kept woman if I let him, but I like being here, watching the good people of Forever grow and evolve. Now, eat your pie and don't argue with your betters, boy," she said with a pseudo-stern expression on her face.

The next moment, Miss Joan had turned her attention to a couple seated at another table.

"Like I said earlier," Jackson said, sinking his fork into the still-warm slice of pie, "Miss Joan means well.

She does have this tendency to come on strong. But if you've got a problem, she'll be right there to help. There's nobody better to have in your corner than Miss Joan," he assured her.

"Well, with any luck, I won't be here long enough to actually *have* a corner," Debi said. And then she realized how that had to sound to him. That she was putting him on notice as to the speed she expected him to use in bringing about her brother's transformation. "No pressure," she added.

"Didn't feel any," he replied casually.

And he didn't feel pressure. For the moment, all he wanted to do was to enjoy the pie—and the company.

Chapter Eleven

He enjoyed watching the way Debi savored her dessert down to the last crumb. The look of sheer pleasure on her face made him think of total contentment.

Jackson couldn't help wondering what that was like. He'd come close, but never managed to snag that particular brass ring. To him, there was always something more that could be done, the next teen to turn around and "fix."

When Debi was done and retired her fork, Jackson looked around for Rhonda, their waitress. Spotting her, he beckoned the young woman over.

"Something else?" Rhonda asked, her glance taking in both of them.

"Just the check. For all of it," Jackson specified, indicating both Debi's order and his own by waving his index finger back and forth between them.

"But Miss Joan said not to charge you for any of it," Rhonda protested.

"What would this have cost if I *was* paying for it?" he asked.

Looking at him a little warily, the waitress did a quick tally and told him the sum. "But—"

"I know," he said, digging into his pocket and taking out his wallet. "Miss Joan said not to charge for the dinners." He extracted the amount Rhonda had mentioned, plus a good-size tip on top of that. "I pay my own way," he told the young woman.

Jackson left the waitress looking rather apprehensive as she took the hastily written-up bill and his money to the register at the front of the diner.

Jackson deliberately did *not* look in Miss Joan's direction. Instead, he held the door opened for Debi, then slipped out himself.

The night was still warm, the silken air wrapping itself around her. Debi realized that for possibly the first time in a long time, the tension that had become part of her every waking moment was missing.

Enjoy it while it lasts. Because it never lasts, she warned herself.

Turning to Jackson as they walked to his truck, she asked, "How much do I owe you?"

He took a moment before he answered. "I'll settle for a smile."

Smiles didn't pay the bills. She was fairly convinced that, based on what he was charging her for Ryan's room and board at the ranch, Jackson wasn't exactly rolling in excess cash.

She wanted to pay her fair share, even if this was an indulgence. With her temporary job at the clinic, she could breathe a little easier when it came to her available cash.

"No, really," Debi insisted.

"Really," he assured her. Coming to a stop by his vehicle, he made no move to open the door. "I'm waiting."

It took her a second to remember what he was referring to. The smile she offered came from the very center of her being. Despite the doubts she'd harbored, she'd had a nice time. Jackson was an easy person to talk to.

"You make it very hard to argue."

Her comment in turn coaxed a wide smile from him. "I've been told that."

"Like you, I'm not comfortable with not paying my own way." The man couldn't fault her for that, she thought. "How about if I work it off?" she suggested. "Maybe this weekend. I can come to the ranch, do some work for you."

"Can't think of anything that needs nursing offhand." Her work ethic was similar to his, Jackson thought. He found the thought oddly comforting.

"Then I'll do whatever it is that people do on a ranch."

Jackson cocked his head. Moonlight was beginning to tiptoe in all around them. Streaks of it wove itself through her hair, highlighting its blondness. Things began to stir within him that he had to struggle to shut down. Things he didn't want to have stirred.

"So you're offering to sit on the porch in a rocking chair and rock?" he asked teasingly.

She was prepared to work as hard as she had to. A rocking chair was not part of that plan. "Maybe after a full day's work."

Jackson looked at her knowingly. She probably hadn't realized that he'd already caught on. "You know, you don't have to go this roundabout route. You could just come straight out and ask me," he told her.

Her eyes widened, like two cornflowers turning their faces up to the sun, their source of warmth. "Ask you what?"

He could almost buy into the aura of innocence she was projecting, but she was a city girl and surviving in the big city took a certain amount of savvy. "Ask if you can come to the ranch to see Ryan."

She blew out a breath. She supposed, at bottom, that was the main reason for her being so adamant about "paying her own way."

"Am I that transparent?"

Jackson laughed. She was *utterly* transparent, but he didn't want to come out and say it so bluntly. He decided to soften the blow a little. "Well, let's just say that I wouldn't be volunteering for any spy missions if I were you."

The smile his comment roused from her was shy and all the more charming for it, Jackson thought.

"Fine, I won't." She paused for a moment, then went full steam ahead. "So it's all right? Coming to the ranch to see Ryan?"

"Sure. Go ahead. Any time." He opened the passenger door for her and held it open. "I'm not running a prison camp in the middle of Siberia." He waited as she slid in and then pulled her seat belt taut, offering it to her. "The only rule is if your brother's in the middle of doing something, wait until he's finished before taking him aside for a visit."

"Sounds reasonable," she replied.

He got in on his side, buckled up and started the engine. "That's what I always try to be," he told her. "Reasonable."

She had no idea why, since she barely knew the man, but listening to him talk made her feel that everything was going to be all right with Ryan in the long run.

Now all she needed to do was survive the short run.

HER DAYS WERE filled to the point of nearly bursting. From the moment she set foot inside the clinic until the time that she closed the door after the last of the patients finally went home, Debi felt as if she was going ninety miles an hour. Sometimes more.

At the end of the week, after the last patient of the day had left, she looked wearily at Holly. The other woman still looked relatively fresh rather than wilted, the way Debi felt.

"How can you stand it?" Debi asked.

"'It'?" Holly asked, not quite sure she understood what was being asked. She lowered the blinds, cutting off the clinic from any view of the outside world.

"The pace," Debi clarified. "It feels like we're always rushing around like crazy."

"That's probably because we are," Holly said with amusement. Moving to the coffeemaker that was set up at the rear of her reception desk, she made sure that it was off. There were times when she and the doctors ran on nothing but coffee. "And I 'stand' it because I love it. Ever since I was a little girl, all I ever wanted to be was a nurse."

She had become a surgical nurse almost by accident. It was intriguing to her to meet someone who had set their sights on the vocation right from the beginning. "A nurse, not a doctor?"

Holly shook her head. "Doctors have to be willing to leap out of bed at a moment's notice, sharp as a tack and ready to go. I'm not much good half-asleep," she confessed. "Regular hours are more my style. I get that here."

Debi could understand that. "Having regular hours is great, but it's the pace that's really killing me."

"You get used to it," she promised.

Debi had her doubts, but she didn't want to be impolite and argue the point with the other woman. "If you say so."

Getting her purse out of the bottom drawer, Holly slung it over her shoulder. "Got any plans?" she asked Debi.

Debi had just retrieved her own purse. The clinic felt oddly quiet and still. She attributed it to the fact that Holly had just shut off the main lights. "Plans?" she questioned.

"For your first weekend in Forever," Holly explained. "Ray wants to have a barbecue tomorrow, invite a few friends, that kind of thing. It'll be mostly his family, but we'd love to have you." Holly's smile was warm and inviting. "A new face is always welcome."

It sounded tempting, but she had already committed herself. "Thank you for the invitation, but I'm going to have to pass on it. I already made arrangements with Jackson to come to The Healing Ranch, visit with Ryan and see how he's getting along." She realized that even as she said it, she felt her stomach tying itself up in a knot. Why? Was she afraid that Ryan wasn't doing as well as she'd hoped? Or was it something else that pricked at her nerves and caused a tingling sensation to zip right through her?

"Your brother's been on the ranch how long now?" Holly asked, trying to remember what Debi had said to her when she first came to the clinic.

"Ryan's been there a whole week. I'm not hoping for a miracle," she added quickly so Holly didn't think she was being unrealistic. "To be honest, I think it's a miracle that he hasn't taken off by now—or at least tried to."

She assumed that if that had occurred, Jackson would have notified her. But there hadn't been any communication between her and the cowboy since he'd taken her to dinner that evening. She had no idea why she kept looking over her shoulder, expecting him to just pop up. The Healing Ranch wasn't located at the end of the earth, but it wasn't exactly right on the outskirts of town, either.

"Well, I don't doubt that your brother's figured out pretty quick that there really isn't anything to run off *to* outside of Forever." Holly smiled to herself. "There's nothing but miles and miles of miles and miles."

Her brother could be pigheaded when he wanted to be. "Ryan's stubborn. If he gets it in his head to take off, he will, surrounding area be damned."

Holly frowned slightly. "Well, the area might not be, but he will if he's not careful. The weather can get downright brutally hot this time of year. Best not to go wandering off without a destination."

"Thanks for caring," she told Holly, flashing a grateful smile. "With any luck, Ryan'll come to his senses and realize that it's in his best interest to stay put, behave and do what Jackson tells him." She didn't want to think about what the alternative would mean to him—or her for that matter.

"I hope you're right," Holly said, locking the front door. "For both your sakes."

"YOU GOTTA GET me outta here," Ryan cried the moment he saw his sister coming toward him. It was ten o'clock Saturday morning and the weather was already too hot to bear. Back home he and his friends would be sneaking into an air-conditioned movie theater. Instead, he was here, sweltering in the heat. "This is nothing more than a stinking labor camp. I hope you're not paying these guys anything. They're working my tail off."

She noted that her brother wasn't cursing up a blue streak as had become his habit in the past year. She wondered if that was due to one too many encounters with the "swear jar."

Pretending to crane her neck to glimpse his rear, she said, "Your tail looks pretty intact to me."

He might not be spouting profanity, but the look in his eyes was saying censorable things. "I knew you'd take their side."

She tried to put her hand on his shoulder but he shrugged her off as if she'd just burned him. "The only side I'm on is yours."

Ryan's scowl deepened. "You sure got a hell of a way of showing it."

Okay, so maybe he hadn't been completely cured of cursing. "You're not supposed to swear, are you?" she reminded him.

If possible, he looked even more sullen than he had a moment ago. Sullen and angry. "Oh, great, now you're going to be a snitch, too?"

She was tired of tiptoeing around Ryan in order not to set him off. "Ryan, I only want what's best for you."

Ryan raised his voice, then quickly lowered it. It was obvious that he didn't want to attract any attention since it looked to him as if his sister wasn't going to rescue him the way she should. "What's best for me is getting the hell out of here and going back to Indianapolis." He looked at her plaintively. "You gotta take me!"

"Eventually," Debi agreed. "But not now—"

Frustrated anger all but radiated from every pore as Ryan accused, "He's brainwashed you. That damn cowboy brainwashed you."

She wasn't going to allow her brother to talk that way about Jackson. The man didn't deserve it. "That 'cowboy' has given me hope for the first time in a very long time."

A look of hurt betrayal passed over Ryan's face.

The next moment, he shrugged as if what his sister felt didn't matter to him. "If you're into him, fine. But don't offer me up like some kind of sacrifice just so you have something to talk about with him."

His words stung, and she struggled to convince herself that Ryan didn't mean any of it. That his low self-esteem had triggered the outburst and hurtful words.

"Ryan, I'm only going to say this once. You are here for one reason and one reason only—to turn your life around before it's too late. Now, I know you didn't steal that car, but you're a bright guy. You had to know that Wexler stole it."

Ryan's thin shoulders rose and fell in a careless, dismissive shrug. "He said it belonged to his cousin."

Ryan had to be smarter than that, she silently argued. "If it did, there was no way a relative would trust him to drive it. I wouldn't trust Wexler to drive a grocery cart down the produce aisle."

Her brother avoided her eyes, a clear sign to her that he knew she was right. "At the time it seemed okay."

"Until it wasn't," she said forcefully. "Ryan, you've got a brain in there. Please, use it."

He threw up his hands. "Fine. Great. I'll use it. I'll do anything you say—just get me out of here! Now!" he insisted.

Their voices were both raised so loud, neither one of them heard Jackson approach until he said, "Shouldn't you be getting back to work, Ryan?"

Ryan swung around, glaring at the man who was in charge. After a beat, he bent down to pick up the pitchfork he'd tossed down.

"I didn't hear you come up," Debi said, unconsciously

trying to draw his attention away from her brother until Ryan got back to work.

"It's the hay, mostly," Jackson explained. "It muffles sounds."

"Yeah, so when the bodies start dropping, you can't hear them," Ryan muttered belligerently under his breath as he went back to spreading out the hay.

Hearing him, Jackson looked far more amused than annoyed. "You found me out," he quipped. "When you finish mucking out the stalls, you get another fifteen-minute break."

Ryan merely glared at him and said nothing as he got back to work. "Yeah, right. Fine." It was hard to figure out if he was answering Jackson or just venting.

"See that?" Jackson asked her as he guided her away from where her brother was working. Ryan continued to animatedly mutter under his breath.

"See what? A surly teenager? I'm afraid I've seen way too much of that in the past couple of years or so." Ryan hadn't been like that right after the car accident, she recalled. His current behavior had evolved slowly, growing worse as time went on rather than the other way around.

"No," Jackson corrected, "what you're seeing is progress."

"Progress," she repeated. She shook her head, rather mystified. "Just how do you see that as progress?" she asked.

"The first day Ryan got here, he wouldn't budge from his bunk bed until he was told that if he didn't work, he didn't eat. He thought I was bluffing and he held out for a number of hours before he realized that I wasn't. It's amazing what a growling stomach will compel a teenager to do. Hasn't missed any work since," Jackson informed her.

"Well, that's heartening—but I think you should know, he asked me to get him out of here."

The news didn't surprise him. "I would have been suspicious if he hadn't," Jackson told her. "I've found that teenagers are a lot more prone to do something they *don't* talk about than something they keep threatening to do. It's been my experience that the ones who threaten to get involved in some sort of retaliation, for instance, generally don't do anything. They just like to talk. It's their way of knocking off steam."

She looked over her shoulder, back toward Ryan. A second teen had joined him and they seemed to be working in tandem. "Who's that?"

Jackson paused to look back. "That's Alan. He's one of the 'old-timers.'"

"Old?" she echoed, taking a closer look at the tall, thin, blond teen. "He looks like he might be all of eighteen."

"Eighteen and a half," Jackson corrected. "He first came to the ranch when he was fifteen. Like Ryan."

"And he's still here?" she questioned. Had Jackson's method failed the boy, then? Was he trying to brace her for her brother's failure down the line?

Jackson grinned. "It's not what you think. Alan successfully graduated from the program in a couple of months. I couldn't have asked for better results. But it seemed that his mother wasn't a very patient woman. She took off with her boyfriend just before Alan was set to leave here, saying that it looked to her that Alan had found a good home and should stick with it." Jackson shook his head as he thought back to the incident.

"I guess I knew something was off when her check bounced."

But the teenager was still here, Debi thought. "What did you do?"

"About the check? Wasn't very much I could do. And if you're asking about Alan, I had a choice. I could call the proper authorities and let him be absorbed by social services—and just possibly wind up in jail again—or I could take him in, have him live here on the ranch." He shrugged, downplaying the fact that, in her opinion, he just might have saved the other teenager's life. "I went with option number two."

"So you're what?" she asked, curious as to the relationship between Alan and him. "His foster parent?"

"I was until he turned eighteen. Kids automatically opt out of foster care and the system when they turn eighteen."

She glanced back toward the stable. "But he's still here."

Jackson smiled. "He likes it here and I like having him here. It all works out," he told her. "Alan's kind of the living embodiment of how the program works successfully."

Everything that Jackson was saying seemed so admirable to her. He came across as really caring about the boys who were sent here. She'd just assumed that he did it for both the money and, as Ryan had accused, for the free labor around the ranch. But after listening to Jackson, she had the feeling that this was a calling for him—and that he was aware of all the good he was accomplishing.

He was making a difference. That had to be nice.

"You know, I don't have anything planned for today and I'm sort of at loose ends. If there's anything you need doing, I'd love to pitch in." She saw a glimmer of doubt in his eyes. "I can do more than just sew up a wound and put a Band-Aid over it."

He had no doubt that she could do more, Jackson thought. A lot more.

He stopped himself. Taking that thought any further would be bringing him to a dangerous area that he had absolutely no business traversing.

But he didn't exactly want to just send her back to the hotel, either. If nothing else, being out in the fresh air was good for her—and watching her breathe, well, that was good for him on so many levels he couldn't even begin to admit to.

"Okay," he told her. "We'll put you to work. Consider yourself officially pitching in."

She smiled up at him. "I'd like that." And she didn't have to pretend she meant it, because she did. Whole-heartedly.

Chapter Twelve

"So? How's he doing?" Debi tried not to sound too anxious as she asked the question.

Ryan had been at The Healing Ranch for a little more than two weeks. To her regret, by the end of her days at the clinic, she was too tired to drive to the ranch and back in order to touch base with Jackson about her brother's progress. Today was Saturday and she was determined to make up for missed time.

Arriving at the ranch early, she looked for Jackson and was directed to the ranch house. Specifically to the cubbyholelike room that Jackson had had to turn into his office in order to keep up with the way his ranch was evolving.

Jackson put down his pen.

"The kid's coming along. We gave him his own horse to take care of. He's still trying to put up a front, complaining about the extra work, but I can tell that he's enjoying the fact that he's like everyone else now."

"His own horse?" She knew that was a badge of trust on the ranch. Debi was both happy and relieved at this turn of events. But despite what this meant, she could see that it came with its own set of problems. "That's wonderful, but is he really ready for that? I mean, the only horses Ryan's ever seen were in the movies. I don't know what he might have said, but he doesn't know how to ride one," she warned.

"Don't worry about that," Jackson told her. "Riding— and any necessary riding lessons—comes in due time. Right now, he's learning how to care for the animal, how to read signs."

"Signs?" She wasn't sure she understood what Jackson was referring to.

Jackson nodded as he leaned back in his chair. It had been Sam's favorite chair in his last few years. The subtle creak whenever he moved reminded him of his uncle and he unconsciously smiled.

"The kind that the horse gives off," he told her. "The bond between a horse and its master can be very strong if it's nurtured correctly. Ryan learns to relate to horses, then people aren't far behind."

She remembered that he'd told her that when she and Ryan had first arrived. "Sounds good to me. And just between us, it can't be happening fast enough for me."

Why that bothered him was something else he wasn't going to explore. Instead, he made the natural assumption. "Anxious to leave our tiny dot of a town?"

The question surprised her. She hadn't realized that her statement could be taken that way. "Actually, no, I'm beginning to like it here."

He looked at her quizzically. She had lost him. "Then why…?"

She was, for the most part, a private person. But she felt as if she knew this man who was working miracles in her life. And at this point, she could admit to herself that she needed to be able to share the parameters of her situation with someone. Jackson seemed like the natural choice.

"Things are getting a little tight," she confessed. "I'm running low on funds even with the job you got me at the clinic."

"I didn't get you the job," Jackson corrected. "I just brought you to the clinic. *You* got you the job." He paused a moment, carefully thinking through what he was about to say next. "You know, not to take anything away from the town's new hotel, but we've got a spare bedroom here at the ranch. You're welcome to stay in it until your brother completes his course here."

Not having to pay for the hotel room for another two to four weeks would be a huge help. But then again, she felt as if she was taking unfair advantage of Jackson's generosity.

"I can't impose on you like that," she protested.

"*Imposing* is if you declared you were moving in without first being invited to do it," Jackson pointed out even as a small voice in his head whispered that he was asking for trouble. He deliberately ignored it. "You're not imposing."

She still didn't feel right about this. "But Garrett lives here, too, right? Won't my staying at the ranch house bother him?"

Jackson laughed softly. "Garrett's the easygoing one in the family. And it would be nice to hear a female voice once in a while, so you'd actually be doing us a favor by staying here."

She readily admitted that there were areas she was still naive about, but this was taking it to an extreme. She did, however, appreciate what he was trying to do. "And if I believe that, there's a bridge you want to sell me, right?"

"Fresh out of bridges," he told her. "But I still have that bedroom."

Debi looked at him, debating, and sorely tempted to take the man up on his offer. It would solve her most immediate problem.

It took her less than two minutes to resolve her internal argument. She nodded, accepting his generous offer. This way, though she'd have to drive back and forth for the job at the clinic, she'd get a chance to be close by for Ryan, which was, after all, the entire reason she had remained in this town in the first place.

And maybe, just maybe, her proximity might even speed his progress along. She just needed to know one thing. "How much?"

"How much?" Jackson echoed quizzically.

"Yes. The bedroom," she specified. "How much is it per week?" She imagined that would be the best way to go since she wasn't sure how long it would take to bring Ryan completely around, back to the caring, sensitive and intelligent person he had once been.

"Well, I don't really know," Jackson replied, his expression entirely emotionless, "but when I figure out what bedrooms are going for, I'll let you know."

"Very funny. I meant how much rent would I be paying for the bedroom?"

He'd been like her once, suspicious and wary of any offer of kindness. In a way, there were a lot of similarities between Debi and the boys in terms of what they were all going through. And because he could remember and relate, that gave him the confidence that came with knowing that the situation could be reversed. Not easily, but definitely with effort.

"You wouldn't be," he answered. "I'm offering you

the room for the duration of your stay in Forever free of charge."

"Why?" He didn't really know her. She'd been a stranger less than a month ago, before she'd gotten in contact with him about his program. Why would he take a stranger into his house?

"Because it might help Ryan to know that you're somewhere on the premises. I think he feels that you have his back."

"He certainly doesn't act like it. The last time I talked to him, he sounded angry because I wasn't springing him and taking him home."

"Trust me. He's glad you're here and having you that much closer might just help him."

"Well, I know it would help me," she freely admitted to Jackson.

He didn't need to hear any more. "Then it's settled. I'll have the room ready for you by the time you get back from the hotel with your things."

This hunk of a cowboy was an answer to a prayer, she thought. Not only was Jackson making headway with Ryan when she couldn't, but he'd just found a way to keep her from slipping into a Chapter 11 situation. Between paying a lawyer to handle her divorce and paying for Ryan's stay here, her small life savings had been wiped out.

For that matter, she wasn't even sure if the position at the hospital that she had taken a hiatus from would still be there waiting for her when she got back. They'd said they'd hold it for her, but times were tough and situations changed. To know that she would have a little something to tide her and Ryan over until she could find another job was at least comforting to some extent.

"You're serious?" she asked, scrutinizing his face just to be sure.

To reassure Debi, he smiled as he said, "Completely." It was impulse that had her all but chattering as she thanked him profusely. And impulse was also to blame for what she caught herself doing next.

She had no memory of thinking this through. On the contrary, all she remembered, after the fact, was that one second she felt a huge sense of relief and joy surging through her, the next, she found her arms around the back of Jackson's neck and her lips directly on his.

It was supposed to be a spontaneous kiss between friends to say thank-you.

It was supposed to be just a quick, uncomplicated kiss with a life span of a second.

Maybe two.

It turned out to be, and say, a whole lot more than that.

First contact told her she was getting much more than she had bargained for.

He made her blood rush and her heart pound hard, the way it did when she poured it on for the last quarter mile of a run.

But a run had never made her head spin.

Jackson did.

The man's kiss packed a punch she wasn't prepared for. Until just now, she considered herself well-versed in the world of male/female relations. But now she realized that she was just a novice. Nothing she had *ever* experienced with John held a candle to what had just happened here with Jackson.

Certainly she'd never felt this kind of fire erupting within her.

He knew he should stop.

Knew he shouldn't have even allowed it to happen in the first place. But she had managed to catch him by surprise. In more ways than one. The second she'd thrown her arms around his neck, he'd known what was coming.

Or thought he did.

For a little thing, she could really bring him down to his knees. As it was, the aforementioned knees felt rather unstable for a moment or two, like they could collapse at any second.

This was a compromising situation, one he didn't want any of the teens on the ranch to be aware of. Luckily, when he'd checked recently, they were all in the corral. To the best of his knowledge, no one had witnessed what had just transpired. But he still didn't believe in taking chances.

And he was going to put a stop to this...any second now.

The truth of it was, he found himself enjoying this intimate contact far more than he thought he would.

Far more than he should.

And yet, there was no denying that it—and she—were having one hell of a dynamic effect on him.

Debi stepped back first.

"I wanted to thank you," she told him with feeling.

"I think you just did," Jackson responded. Pulling himself together, he made a suggestion, not realizing that he'd already said the same thing until the words were out of his mouth. That kiss had temporarily scrambled his brain. "Why don't you go back to the hotel, check out and come back with your things? After that, if you're still bent on helping with the chores—"

"I am," she told him eagerly. "Now more than ever." If he wasn't going to take money for the room, then she *had* to do something around the ranch that could be seen as payment.

"—I'll make up a list for you, if you insist," he said. "But just so you know, while the boys all have to pull their own weight around here, that doesn't apply to you. You've already got a full-time job. As far as I'm concerned, you're a guest here, which means that you don't have to do anything."

"I've never known how to do nothing," she confided.

"Well, you certainly can't be accused of doing nothing, not when you're working at the clinic. The way I see it, every hour there is equal to at least two hours in the real world. I'd think that it would leave you pretty exhausted."

"It did, but I've had a full night's sleep to recharge," she told him. "I feel pretty energetic, so your wish is my command."

His eyes drew together as he tried to remember something. "That's from a fairy tale, right?"

"Even fairy tales are based on a grain of truth," she reminded him.

Looking at her now, standing on the other side of his desk, he really felt as if he was in a fairy tale. The troubled kid he had once been could have never foreseen his life evolving this way.

I owe you, Sam. Big time, Jackson thought.

"Want me to drive you to the hotel?" he offered out loud.

"No, that's okay. I definitely know the way back. I'll be fine," she assured him. "You go do your ranching things," Debi said, her words deliberately vague since she really didn't know what needed doing on this sort of a ranch. "I'll try to be back as fast as I can," she promised.

"You don't have to hurry," he told her, moving back

behind his desk and sitting down again. "The room's not going to go anywhere."

He was making her feel safe, she realized. There was a danger in that. She'd let her guard down at some point and then that would leave her wide-open and vulnerable. She couldn't allow that to happen.

And yet, there was something almost seductive about not having to worry, about feeling protected and safe.

She was just deluding herself, Debi silently insisted. Squaring her shoulders, she replied, "You never know. Someone might make you a better offer than getting nothing for your trouble."

"Not everything comes down to a matter of dollars and cents," he told her. Picking up his pen again, he said, "See you later," and got back to work.

HE WASN'T AWARE of Garrett immediately.

Debi had hurried off and he forced himself to return to the part of running The Healing Ranch that he hated: filling out reports, keeping logs. He managed to cope with it because he knew that there was no way around the requirement. The sooner he got to the monthly endeavor, the sooner he would be done with it and free.

He'd made his peace with the fact that the reports were a necessary evil.

Somewhere into this storm of papers and recently released hormones running rampant through his system his brother walked into the office.

Jackson had no idea how long Garrett had stood there, in the rear doorway, observing him. All he knew was that he'd started to sense his brother's presence. Looking up, he saw that Garrett had on that strange, bemused expression that he sometimes sported.

He was also grinning.

From ear to ear.

"What?" he asked when he and Garrett made eye contact.

Garrett merely shrugged, dismissing the question. "Nothing." The grin, however, remained. If possible, it grew even wider.

"Nothing my eye," Jackson retorted. He didn't feel like playing games. "Out with it. You don't grin like that over nothing," he maintained.

Jackson had the uneasy feeling that maybe he and Debi hadn't gone unobserved after all. How long had Garrett been standing there?

Coming all the way into the room, Garrett perched for a moment on the edge of the desk. His brother pointedly looked into his eyes. "I was just beginning to get used to the idea that I was never going to see you attracted to anyone."

"And you still haven't," Jackson replied curtly.

"Okay," Garrett allowed. "Then I hate to tell you this, Jackson, but you have a perfect clone and he's alive and well and practically living right on top of you—or at least in your shadow."

"What are you doing here, anyway? Aren't you supposed to be out at the corral?"

"I just came in to get a book." Moving over to the narrow bookcase, he extracted a worn book that had once belonged to their uncle. It contained illustrations of all the different breeds of horses that existed.

"Well, you got it. You can go now," Jackson told him dismissively. He deliberately looked back down at the reports he was filling out.

"Okay." Garrett began to take his leave, then turned

around for one last word. "Don't get me wrong, it's really nice to see a spring in your step. That means—I think—that you're not selling Ryan on the idea of leaving, say, within the next week."

"You know better than that," Jackson replied. "If he stays, it's because he might need a little more work before he can be put back into the so-called general population—otherwise known as everyday society," Jackson told his brother. "It's nothing personal."

Garrett grinned, something he was far more given to doing than his older brother. "Of course it's not."

Rising from behind his desk, Jackson crossed to the open doorway and looked around. There was no one there. This time. Closing the door, he turned his attention back to his brother.

"Garrett, you know we both take this job seriously. If someone had just overheard your tone, they might take things the wrong way and that just might undermine all the good we're doing here."

Garrett dismissed the idea with a wave of his hand. "All anyone has to do is call on any one of the 'ranch hands' who got through this 'course.' They'll see the good you've done."

"*We've* done," Jackson corrected him.

But Garrett shook his head. "I was right the first time. I'm just following your lead, big brother. You're the one who decided to do this after Sam died. I guess everything happens for a reason," he continued. "If you hadn't been such a big screw-up, Mom wouldn't have called on Sam to come help her and we would have never inherited this ranch."

Jackson sincerely doubted that. "He had no next of kin, remember?"

"He had Dad," his brother reminded him, his own smile fading.

Neither one of them had good memories of the man even before he'd walked out on them. "That's taking it for granted that our illustrious father is still alive somewhere. Just between you and me, I don't think his kidneys could have held on for very long. The man went through booze like other people go through water."

Garrett didn't realize that he'd winced. "He was a mean drunk."

Jackson laughed shortly. His eyes were somber. "He wasn't exactly a walk in the park when he was sober, either," he recalled. Years ago he'd come to the conclusion that in their case, they were far better off with an absentee father than living under the same roof with someone who was volatile, unpredictable and lashed out with his fists without any warning.

Garrett nodded. Opening the door, he started to go when something occurred to him. "Oh, and Jackson?"

He was never going to finish wading through this annoying paperwork, he thought, looking up. "Yeah?"

"She's a honey. The girl I saw you lip-locking with. Ryan's sister, right?" he recalled, although her name escaped him at the moment. "She's a honey."

Jackson blew out a breath. Served him right for giving in to a flash of desire. "Spare me the fifty-cent analysis and get back to work like the helpful brother you're not being."

"I'll get right on it," Garrett said perhaps a bit too quickly in his estimation. "Oh, and when the big day comes—"

"*What* big day?" Jackson demanded, confused. What was Garrett babbling about?

"*The* big day," Garrett repeated with more emphasis. The look he gave his brother clearly said that he should know what the reference was regarding. "Just remember, I get dibs on best man."

"If I find a best man," Jackson deadpanned, putting a literal meaning to his brother's words, "I'll be sure to send him along to you."

He ducked his head as Garrett threw the book he'd come for at him.

Chapter Thirteen

"Hey Debs, I bet you never thought you'd ever see me doing this!" Ryan called out to her in a loud voice.

Debi's heart swelled. He sounded excited, just the way he used to before that horrendous car accident had changed everything.

She silently blessed Jackson before she even turned toward the sound of Ryan's voice. Any change for the better with Ryan was because of him and the man had earned her undying gratitude.

Another two weeks had passed.

Two weeks during which time she drove into town in the morning and back to the ranch at the end of her day. Two weeks of a routine that she was surprised to discover herself liking more and more.

Who would have ever thought that was possible? Certainly not her.

Another surprise was that she was becoming entrenched in this low-key town life. Her transformation was happening so easily, so effortlessly, it all but took her breath away.

Because of the steady and usually heavy traffic of people through the clinic, she was getting acquainted with a great many of Forever's citizens. Some of whom had taken to bringing her things—cookies, fudge, a crocheted poncho—to either say thank-you to her, or in some cases "welcome to Forever."

To the latter group, she tried to gently but tactfully explain that she wasn't planning on staying, but they would look at her with knowing looks and just smile. Eventually, she gave up. They would realize the truth once she was gone, she decided.

She had no idea why that thought brought a strange tinge of sorrow with it.

And following her routine, when she came home at night—and The Healing Ranch *had* become home to her—she became part of that life, as well.

Maybe even more so.

The teenagers in Jackson and Garrett's care ate dinner at the house every night and Jackson made sure that there was always a place set for her.

The first night she'd come to the ranch, thinking that she would just quietly slip in and go to the room he'd set aside for her, Jackson had derailed her plan. He'd been waiting for her on the front porch. The moment she'd arrived, Jackson had taken her by the hand and drawn her into the dining room.

"I'm thinking you haven't had dinner yet," he had said to her.

Which was when she'd held up the bag she'd picked up on her way back. "I picked up something to go at the diner," she'd explained.

Jackson had paused to take the bag from her, saying, "It can just 'go' to the refrigerator. Don't worry, it won't go to waste. You can have it for lunch tomorrow."

Gesturing toward the empty chair remaining, he'd coaxed, "Why don't you sit down?"

Even with all those faces turned toward her, watching her intently, Debi was still going to beg off, thinking that she'd feel awkward eating in their midst and that Jackson was only asking her to join them because he felt sorry for her.

But then she saw that Ryan was sitting just two seats down. He said nothing, but the look in his eyes asked her to stay.

That was enough for her.

Offering Jackson and Garrett a smile, she said, "Okay," and sank down into the chair.

That had been her first step in becoming part of The Healing Ranch's daily life.

In an odd way, the ranch did as much healing for her as it was supposed to be doing for all the troubled teens who had been sent here by desperate parents and relatives in hopes of bringing about some kind of miraculous transformation.

Every night she hurried home for dinner a little more quickly than the last, a sense of anticipation spurring her on. Having parked her car a ways from the ranch house, she was quickly walking toward it, passing by the corral on her way.

That was when she heard Ryan calling out to her. Happy that the sullen tone was absent from his voice, she turned to look in his direction. Her mouth dropped open.

She hardly remembered cutting across the rest of the distance. All she was aware of was smiling at him, broadly. *Yes, Debi, there is a Santa Claus*, she thought to herself. Had Jackson been there, she would have kissed him. The spark was returning into Ryan's eyes.

"You're right about that," she answered. Ryan was sitting in a saddle, astride a beautiful palomino. "You look like a natural," she told him.

Out of the corner of her eye, she saw that Garrett and Alan, the teen who Jackson had taken into his home, were both mounted on their horses, as well, and though they were good at masking what they were about, they were both paying very close attention to her brother.

"Wanna see me jump Jericho?" Ryan asked her eagerly, his body language indicating that he was all set to act on his offer.

"Isn't it almost dinnertime?" she asked, avoiding commenting directly on her brother's question. "Shouldn't you be getting ready?"

"She's right, Ry," Garrett told him. "Time to put our horses away."

Ryan appeared somewhat crestfallen, and she fully expected him to argue with Garrett. When he didn't, she was stunned.

Progress! Debi thought triumphantly. Three weeks ago, her brother would have argued, hurled curse words and pouted until he got Garrett to give in—or, more likely, was sent to the bunkhouse without dinner. This new, respectful Ryan restored her hope for the future.

Maybe by the time this was all over, she *would* have the old Ryan back. Permanently.

It was something to hope for.

"Someone certainly looks like she's happy," Jackson commented. Entering the living room, he caught the look on her face as she walked into the house.

The word *happy* didn't even begin to cover the way she felt. Seeing Ryan behaving like his old self filled her with a euphoric high that was almost dizzying.

Before she could think through her next action, Debi

crossed over to the man she held responsible for her brother's metamorphosis, braced her hands on his shoulders, raised herself up on her toes and brushed her lips against his cheek. "Someone is *very* happy," she told him.

The feel of her lips fleetingly brushing against his skin stirred an entire cauldron of dormant emotions that were simmering just beneath the surface, awakening a longing within him that he hadn't even known was there. It took effort to stop himself from just taking her into his arms and kissing her back.

Really kissing her.

He did his best to hide his feelings as he asked, "Good day at the clinic?"

"The day at the clinic was good," she confirmed, then added, "But this evening at the ranch is positively great." When Jackson cocked his head slightly as if waiting for an explanation, she filled in the blanks. "I just saw Ryan *riding* his horse. He looked happier than I've seen him in a long, long time." She blinked back tears of joy. She'd all but given up hope that Ryan could be reached this way. "When did he learn how to ride?"

"It's an ongoing thing," Jackson told her matter-of-factly. "I mean, what's the point in having a horse if you can't ride it, right?" He paused, as if deciding whether or not to say anything. And then he did. "You're crying. Are you upset?"

She shook her head. "No, I'm happy."

Digging into his back pocket, he took out a handkerchief and offered it to her. "I'll *never* understand women," he freely confessed.

She wiped away the tearstains on her cheeks, then handed the handkerchief back to him.

"This is like a miracle. Ryan never showed much interest in animals. Never begged for a pet dog or anything like that. Now it looks like your brother's going to have to all but peel him out of the saddle." She glanced over her shoulder toward where the corral would have been if there was no ranch house separating her from the view. She caught her bottom lip between her teeth for a moment, thinking. "Maybe Garrett needs my help." Saying that, she did an about-face in the living room, and began heading for the front door.

Jackson caught up to her in two strides and took hold of her arm, stopping her. "Stop worrying," he told her. "Garrett knows how to handle the situation. Ryan will be okay."

"I'm not worried about Ryan, I'm concerned about Garrett," she confessed.

That amused him, given that his brother was six-one with a body built by ranching and her brother was around five-ten and might tip the scales at one thirty-five if he carried rocks in his pockets.

"My brother hasn't met a boy he couldn't get along with. Stop worrying," Jackson repeated. "Go back to being happy," he coaxed. "It looks good on you."

Jackson was right, she thought. She had to back away and let things play themselves out.

Hanging up her purse on the coatrack by the door, she followed Jackson into the kitchen.

"Need any help with dinner?" she offered. The next moment, she felt it was only fair to tell him how limited her abilities in the kitchen were. "I can stir ingredients with the best of them."

"Not necessary," he told her. "Everything's all under control." Grabbing two towels, one in each hand, Jackson opened the oven door and slid out the pan of pork tenderloin that was to be the main course. "Ryan, by the way, is a natural. I watched him earlier in the corral," he explained. "You never took him horseback riding?"

Debi shook her head, then brushed away the hair that insisted on falling into her eyes. "Not even on one of those things that gives you a three-minute ride if you feed it enough quarters."

"How about you?" he asked. "Did you ever ride a horse?"

She didn't see the connection, but she answered, "Not too many occasions for that in the city. There aren't exactly a lot of horses wandering around Indianapolis."

"There are stables around if you know where to look for them," he told her, placing the pan on top of the counter. "They might not be smack-dab in the middle of the city, but they're around." He shut off the oven, then turned off the vegetables that were being cooked on top of the stove. "Not interested in riding?" he asked.

She hadn't really thought about it one way or another—until just now. "No, it's just not something I ever got around to. But I wouldn't mind learning someday."

The corners of his mouth curved ever so slightly. "Someday," he repeated.

"Uh-huh. Someday." Debi wanted to do *something*, be useful in order to show him her gratitude. She glanced into the dining room. The dishes weren't out yet. "Let me set the table for you," she offered.

Not waiting for Jackson's response, she went into the cupboard and began taking down the necessary plates and glasses as well as gathering the utensils out of the drawers.

Watching her, Jackson smiled to himself. "Why don't you do that?" he agreed as he went to strain the vegetables.

THE TENDERLOIN ALL but melted in her mouth. She was quickly coming to the conclusion that there was *nothing* that Jackson White Eagle couldn't do once he set his mind to it.

The boys at the table polished off both the tenderloin and the generous servings of corn, carrots and mashed potatoes that had been placed beside the main course. Fresh air and the day's work gave them all healthy appetites.

When the meal was over, Debi rose from the table and began clearing away the dishes. She might not be any help when it came to the actual cooking, but she at least knew how to clean.

But as she turned with a stack of dinner plates in her hands, Jackson put himself in front of her. Before she could say a word, Jackson took the dishes from her. The next moment, he turned to the first teen seated at his right. "Jim, you and Gabe take care of these for me. Nathan, you've got the glasses. Jerry, the knives and forks. Ryan, you've got the serving plates. That leaves the pots and pans to you three," he said, addressing the last three teens in his care.

"They can't all be at the sink at the same time," Alan pointed out.

"Work it out," Jackson instructed in a tone that told the boys he knew they would.

Debi frowned as she saw the teens complying immediately. She wasn't accustomed to just standing back and letting someone else do all the work. In this instance, several someones.

"I can do that," she protested to Jackson.

"Right now, you're going to be busy dealing with

something else," Jackson told her. Placing his hand to the small of her back, he guided her out of the dining room.

"I don't understand," she told him.

"Easy," he explained as they reached the front door. "'Someday' is here."

Okay, now he had really lost her. "What?"

He paused right outside the front door. "You said that you'd like to learn how to ride someday. You're going to need someone to teach you. I'm volunteering, which means that 'someday' is here."

She looked at him uncertainly. Her uncertainty increased as he laced his fingers through hers and ushered her off to the stables.

"Wait, I didn't mean that I wanted to learn immediately."

"That's good, because you don't learn how to ride immediately. You learn how to ride slowly, in stages," he outlined as they arrived at the stables. "Today," he told her as they walked inside, "we're just going to get you to mount a horse."

"Right after dinner?" she asked nervously.

"Riding a horse is not like swimming," Jackson informed her with a laugh. "And anyway, you're not going to be riding tonight. I just want to get you comfortable *sitting* on a horse."

Suddenly, the animals that were in the stalls looked prohibitively large to her. Larger than they had an hour ago. She didn't know about this.

"If you really want me to be comfortable," she told him, "maybe we should start out with a rocking horse."

Jackson thought he heard a quaver in her voice. "Debi, are you afraid of horses?" he asked her.

"No," she protested instantly, then, flushing, she reversed her statement. "Yes." But that wasn't the answer she wanted to settle on because what she was feeling was complicated. "I mean— Well, maybe. I guess I'm not quite sure yet."

This wasn't some kind of deep-seated fear caused by a traumatic incident in her childhood. He saw none of that in her eyes and was convinced that had there been something like that in her past, he would have been able to pick up on at least some of the signs. There were none.

Which meant he was free to proceed in making her come around.

"Come here," he requested. When she did, albeit somewhat hesitantly, he took her by the hand and drew her closer to the horse in the stall. "This is Annabelle," he told her. "She's the gentlest horse on the ranch. Why don't you try petting her?" he suggested.

"You're sure it's all right?" she asked. "I mean, it won't bother her?"

"None of the animals feel threatened if they're petted," Jackson promised her seriously. "Most animals don't," he added, looking at her significantly.

When she still hesitated, Jackson took her hand, cupped his own over it and then brought it up to the mare's muzzle. He then went on to slowly pass her hand over Annabelle.

"Do it just like this," he urged as he guided her through the motions. He could almost see her heart pounding in her throat. "See how easy it is?" he asked quietly, soothingly.

She had to admit that the muzzle felt almost silky beneath her fingers. The longer she stroked the mare, the more she found that she enjoyed the contact.

"I'm just a little worried that she might be too tired," she told Jackson.

"Just for the record," he told her, tongue in cheek, "I've never met an animal who was too tired to be petted. As a matter of fact, they perk up when you do that. Keep it up," he urged.

Taking his hand away from hers, he reached into his back pocket. Finding what he was looking for, he extended his hand out and opened it. There were a couple of lumps of sugar in his palm.

"Here, give her these."

Taking the lumps of sugar from him, Debi looked down at them, and then raised her eyes to his. "Are we bribing her?"

"Yes, we are. Bribing her to like you," Jackson explained, then added in a slightly lower voice, "Not that that's actually necessary. I doubt if anyone, man or beast, ever had to be bribed to like you," he said, momentarily thinking back to her enthusiastic kiss that first evening she had joined his household. It felt as if it had only happened a moment ago—and yet, at the same time it seemed so far in the past. Having her brush her lips against his cheek earlier had just stirred up his reaction to her.

Jackson shook himself free of the memory, but not nearly as quickly as he would have liked to or felt that he should have.

It also didn't help that while the memory had flashed through his mind, he had savored it.

"When do I get to ride her?" Debi asked.

"Maybe in a few days." Jackson didn't want to rush things. Given her extreme inexperience, there was a risk of Debi possibly falling off and getting hurt. He didn't want to take that chance.

"A few days?" she echoed in surprise—and disappointment. "I have to wait that long?"

"It's not that long," he assured her. But she didn't look convinced. "Like I said, we take this all very slowly, a little bit at a time. You master one step, we go on to another," he promised.

She rested her hand on the mare's muzzle. "And what am I mastering now?"

Jackson grinned, his blue eyes crinkling. "That's easy," he told her. "Petting."

Green eyes met blue. "I think that I've got that part down pat at this point," she told him quietly.

"Great." Jackson nodded his head, more to himself than to her. "Tomorrow you get to lead your horse around the perimeter of the corral."

"Is that when I get to ride her?" she asked, hoping for the green light.

Obviously she had missed the word *lead*, he thought. "No, you get to walk right alongside of her while *she's* walking, hence the word *lead*."

She didn't quite understand why she'd be walking around the perimeter of the corral, holding on to the horse.

"Are we going to be looking for something?" she asked.

"Yes," he replied. "Patience. To be a good rider, you have to have patience. Patience to build up a relationship with the horse."

"I don't want to marry the horse, I just want to ride her," she protested.

He watched her for a long moment. She was almost pouting. Jackson had to admit that it got under his skin, but not in an irritating sort of way. That was happening far too often It was just unsettling enough to cause what amounted to upheavals in places that were better left unaffected and alone. He could afford to have feelings for Debi.

Too late for that, Jackson thought.

What he needed was a battle plan. One where he could come out the victor.

The next second, he realized that was *not* going to be as easy as it might sound.

Chapter Fourteen

Jackson thought over his options. He wanted to keep Debi safe, but he didn't want to do it by shutting down her spirit. He came up with a compromise.

He thought it was a good compromise, but then, he *was* the one who had come up with it.

"Okay, tell you what. There is a way that I can let you get up on that horse tonight."

She looked at him for a long moment and realized that she trusted him. Maybe that was naive of her, especially after what had happened with the last man she had trusted—John had made her doubt herself and everything she had ever believed in.

But there was something honest—for lack of a better word—about Jackson, something that told her he had her best interests at heart because he had *everyone's* best interests at heart.

"Okay, I'm listening," she said, gamely waiting for him to tell her the terms he had come up with.

"You can get into Annabelle's saddle, but I'm going to be the one holding on to the reins and leading you around the corral." He looked at Debi to gauge her response to his idea.

"You mean like a pony ride in an amusement park?"

She could almost envision it. To her mind, the whole thing seemed painfully ludicrous.

Thinking it over, Jackson inclined his head. "In a way, I guess you hit it dead-on. Yes, like a pony ride in an amusement park—except a lot quieter because the other kids won't be around."

They obviously had different opinions of pony rides and amusement parks. Being taken to one—which he never had—symbolized caring parents and a happy childhood—something else he'd also never had.

His eyes met hers. He could see Debi's natural resistance. He sensed that she liked being independent and that was all well and good, except that wasn't going to work in this particular situation.

"It's the only way," he informed her, his voice quiet but nonetheless firm. The last thing he wanted was for her to get hurt. Annabelle was gentle, but like any horse, she could be spooked. He wasn't about to take chances. His reason for that went far beyond not wanting his insurance premiums to rise.

"I'd feel like a kid," Debi protested. She was a grown woman, which meant she could hold her own reins. Or rather the horse's, she silently amended.

"No, you wouldn't," Jackson corrected. "Because all the kids at The Healing Ranch have to show that they can master every step before they can move on to the next step. An inexperienced novice to the sport wouldn't ask to leap from being that to riding like a moderately experienced horsewoman in one step," he pointed out. Jackson crossed his arms before him and studied her face. "Now, what'll it be?"

Debi knew there was only one answer she *could* give him. Otherwise, she had a very strong feeling that her horseback experience would be put on hold, maybe even indefinitely.

Still, she wasn't above trying to persuade him to see it her way at least once.

"Tell you what, I'll do it the right way starting tomorrow evening—if I can ride Annabelle on my own for five minutes tonight." She followed up the proposition with a wide, hopeful smile. "Please?"

Jackson ignored her smile—for her own good. It wasn't exactly easy, but then, he could be stoic when he had to be.

"My way," he reminded her.

Her smile vanished, replaced by a frustrated frown. "You're being overly cautious."

Maybe he was, but it was far better to be safe than to be sorry. He knew what the latter could feel like. "My way."

Debi blew out a breath, fairly convinced that there was no way she was going to change his mind. She might as well give up gracefully.

"Your way," she said with a quick bob of her head as she conceded the point—and game—to him.

To her surprise, Jackson didn't gloat or look smug for having won, the way she'd expected. Instead, he merely nodded and immediately got started. "Okay, let me show you where we keep the saddles and the rest of the gear you'll need."

She followed right on his heel to the closet. When he opened the doors, she saw that there were stacks of saddles, blankets and bridles.

Collecting what was needed, Jackson proceeded to demonstrate to her the proper way to saddle a horse. Debi watched, making mental notes for when he had her do it—as she was completely certain that he would. Jackson led by example—but he expected that example to be closely followed to the letter.

"Wait, doesn't that hurt her?" Debi asked, concerned, when she saw Jackson start to put the bridle bit into the mare's mouth.

Quite honestly, she had never given what was involved in preparing a horse to be ridden any thought one way or the other. But being so close to the animal as it was taking place made Debi so much more aware of the process.

"They fight against it at first, but not because having the bit in their mouths hurts. They fight it because they instinctively know that it means the intended rider is exercising dominance over them. The horses resist that at all costs in the beginning. It's only natural," he emphasized. He saw the way Debi was eyeing Annabelle and guessed at what was going on in her head. "She's used to me, that's why she doesn't fight anything I do. She trusts me," he added proudly. "For the most part, once a horse is broken in, they pretty much put up with being bridled and saddled without a fuss—unless whoever's doing it mishandles them or treats them cruelly."

Finished, Jackson took hold of the bridle with one hand, holding on to it lightly.

"Ready?" he asked Debi.

She was a little nervous, but Ryan had done this, she told herself. If he could do it, then she could. After all, she was the older sibling, not Ryan. And as the big sister, she had an obligation to always be the one whom Ryan looked up to, the one who would always be an example for him to model himself after. That meant jumping into the deep end of the pool even if all she had was one swimming lesson under her belt. She had to be fearless so that her brother would never entertain fear.

She had to be good so that he didn't fail. There it was, all tied up in a bow. The philosophy that helmed her life.

"I was born ready," she answered him.

Jackson tried not to smile at that. Just as he tried not to smile as he watched her attempt to put her foot into the stirrup and mount Annabelle.

And fail.

Then fail again.

"Would you like a little boost?" he finally suggested after her third unsuccessful attempt to swing herself into the saddle.

Debi hated admitting defeat. "How do the boys do it?" she asked, frustrated.

"Simple. They're taller than you. And they're used to this. Now, about that help?" he asked her, waiting.

At least he didn't say the teens were more agile than she was. Looking back at Jackson, she knew she wasn't going to get any help from him until she officially asked him for it. Resigned, she gave in.

"Yes, please," she said grudgingly, wary about just what that so-called "help" from Jackson might ultimately wind up being.

To her surprise, Jackson stood before her, laced his fingers together and then bent down, holding his inter-laced hands right in front of her.

The implication was clear, but when she continued to just stare at his hands, Jackson spoke up to encourage her.

"Go ahead, put your foot right here." To move things along, Jackson bent down even farther so that she could easily comply with his directions. "Grab hold of the saddle horn with one hand so that you can pull yourself up.

Meanwhile, put your foot right here in my hands," he instructed again.

Feeling a little strange, not to mention rather wobbly, Debi did as she was told. Liftoff was less than smooth, but she did manage it, which was all that counted.

"Hey, it worked," she cried happily.

"Yeah, how about that." Jackson pretended to be just as surprised as she was. He secretly enjoyed this display of enthusiasm he saw.

Taking the reins in his hand, he proceeded to lead her horse out of the stables and into the corral.

"Hold on to the saddle horn," he advised.

"Again?" While happy, she still wanted reasons for everything. "Why?"

"So you don't fall off," he answered simply.

"I *do* have a sense of balance, you know," she protested, then added, "You know, you worry too much."

"Keeps my insurance premiums down," he quipped without looking over his shoulder at her. He just continued walking as he led her horse in a circle.

She hadn't thought of that. Just because this was a rural area of the country and he was running a ranch didn't mean that they were separated from all the annoying, so-called finer points of civilization. Like needing insurance for protection against circumstances that could bring about the loss of the ranch.

After all, Jackson ran a ranch that took in troubled teens. Myriad troubles could befall one of those teens—or be caused by them. Things he needed to be insured against—just in case some relative suddenly turned up to cite a violation that had in actuality never occurred.

She saw Jackson in a whole new, far more complicated light. He wasn't just a simple cowboy or even just a laid-back, drop-dead-gorgeous rancher. He was all that plus a businessman.

"Do you ever feel like chucking it all and going back to just being a rancher?" she asked him, curious.

Jackson continued walking along the perimeter, tedious though it seemed.

He thought her question over.

"Sometimes," he admitted. "But then I watch a kid get turned around and suddenly it all seems worth it. And, if you want to be technical about it, I was never really a rancher. What I did was help my uncle on the ranch after he straightened me out, but I never had a place of my own to run, at least not one that didn't involve working with hostile young guys who felt they'd been dealt a bum hand." He thought about his initial answer to her. "Seeing one of those get turned around, well, there's really nothing like it," he reiterated with feeling.

He'd been guiding Annabelle around the corral, keeping very close to the edges of the corral's perimeter as he talked with Debi and answered her questions. Before he knew it, he realized that he had come full circle and they were back at the entrance to the stables where they had started.

Not that he minded spending time with her like this, but it *was* getting late. Besides, he had a feeling that there were more than a couple of pairs of eyes watching him and Ryan's sister. He didn't want the boys to have anything more to talk about than he assumed they already had.

"How about calling it a night?" he suggested to Debi. "I think Annabelle's tired."

She had no idea how he could tell, but she wasn't about to argue or question his judgment. He had indulged her and she really appreciated it. "Whatever you say, Jackson," she answered.

Whatever he said. Jackson had to admit that he liked the sound of that.

The problem was, there were a lot of things he felt like saying to her.

A lot of things he felt like *doing* with her, as well. Neither of these impulses, he knew, was safe to act on. Not when he thought of the direction that either could take him or, for that matter, the consequences that lay at the end of either line.

Bringing Annabelle and her passenger back into the stable, he stopped just short of putting the horse into the stall.

Debi looked down at him. "Something wrong? Why did you stop?"

"Nothing's wrong," he told her, letting the end of the mare's reins touch the ground. The horse knew enough to remain where she was, as steadfast as if the reins had been tightly tied to a post, physically tethering her. "But it might be easier all around if you dismounted now, before I put Annabelle into her stall and take her saddle off."

"Sure," Debi said, more than happy to comply. But then she glanced down to the ground. Gauging the distance from where she was sitting to where she was supposed to step, she hesitated. It killed her to ask, but it was either that, or risk falling flat on her face in front of him.

Literally.

"Um, I think I might need a little help getting down," she said in a small voice.

Annabelle remained standing perfectly still. At least the horse was being cooperative, Jackson thought. Moving closer to the center of the mare, he raised his hands up toward Debi.

"Lean forward," he told her. When she did, he slipped his hands around her waist.

Debi sucked in a breath without meaning to. Her heart did a little dance within her chest, creating havoc.

No, she amended, *Jackson* was creating the havoc. She sincerely doubted that she would be reacting this way if she was being helped off her mount by someone who looked like an ogre out of a Grimm's fairy tale.

The next second, as she leaned down and put her hands on his shoulders for leverage, she felt Jackson's strong, capable hands gently tighten about her waist just before he eased her down.

That was when her body all but slid against his in one continuous motion.

She was only vaguely aware of her feet touching the ground. She was far more acutely aware of the fact that her body had made contact with his.

Soft against hard.

Warm waves went shooting not just up and down her spine but pretty much along the rest of her, as well. Her hands left his shoulders, but rather than falling to her sides, the way she had intended, they went in the other direction and somehow wound up going around the back of his neck.

Their eyes met and held. It seemed to her like things were being said without a single word being uttered.

Her breath caught in her throat. At the very least, she should be pushing him away—not pulling him in closer. This wasn't her. This wasn't the way that she normally behaved.

But nothing about this moment in the moonlight resembled her normal existence.

Debi had no idea who initiated the next move. Whether she was the one who tilted her head back, inviting his mouth to visit hers again, or if he made the first move, lowering his head—and his mouth—to hers.

She *shouldn't* be doing this, *couldn't* be allowing herself to get involved with a man, even *this* man. Her judgment was beyond poor. She couldn't risk using it and making another awful mistake.

The way she had with John.

Once a fool was *more* than enough, she knew that. And yet, somehow, she couldn't find it in herself to even *attempt* to resist.

She was drawn to this man who had done such miraculous things with teens—with Ryan—who everyone, including the system, had given up on.

Including?

Especially, she silently emphasized. Especially the system.

And even, secretly, her. She'd been precariously close, fractions of an inch away, to giving up on her brother.

Jackson had saved her from that. From the *despair* of that.

Jackson was at once her Lancelot, riding to the rescue, her miracle worker, and quite possibly the most compellingly sexy man she had ever met.

Debi melted into him, surrendering to the moment, to the kiss and to the man.

DAMN IT, HE KNEW this was wrong, knew he had no business being out here with her like this.

No business *doing* this.

She was technically a client, the guardian of one of his charges, for God's sake, and he was jeopardizing his standing by dropping his guard and going with his demanding needs.

What the hell was he *thinking*?

The sad truth of the matter was, he wasn't thinking. Not for one second. But oh, was he feeling. After being dead inside for so long, he was *feeling*.

He kissed the woman in his arms over and over again, living inside of the moment before the moment was somehow cruelly snatched away or just mysteriously disappeared into thin air.

But perversely, rather than satiate him, each kiss just made him that much hungrier for more.

Made him want *her* more.

Pulling Debi so close to him that they were in danger of fusing into one being, for one short moment, he allowed his imagination to go to places he'd never allowed it to venture before.

But then the common sense that had taken Sam so long to drill into his head reluctantly—but stubbornly—rose to reclaim its hold on him. They were inside the stable, but for all intents and purposes, they were still out in the open, still exposed.

He couldn't allow that to happen. She would suffer for it and he, he could lose at least some of the respect he had worked hard to build up.

She was worth it, a small voice whispered in his head.

Even so, he couldn't sacrifice the boys to his need for gratification.

Forcing himself to step back, he broke contact with Debi.

He said nothing. Protests filled his mind, scrambling

over one another, blotting out beginnings, blocking endings. He took a deep breath to try to regain control of himself.

"Good first lesson," Debi mumbled to him. "But I need to get back to the house. I'm very tired now and I should get an early start in the morning."

She was hoping he wouldn't ask her why because the second the words were out of her mouth, they sounded lame to her. Lame because she was making up the excuse. She shouldn't have allowed herself to surrender to this, to something that she knew had no future, that barely had a life expectancy.

Certainly not beyond a week.

"I'll walk you," Jackson offered.

"No," she said a bit too quickly. "You take care of the horse. I'll be fine. It's not like the house is in the next county."

She was already crossing the stable's threshold, moving outside as she said it.

Chapter Fifteen

She couldn't sleep.

It wasn't because of the heat. Granted, the day had been almost uncomfortably hot, but the heat had long since abated. The temperature in the world outside her open window had dropped by some fifteen degrees in the past few hours and there was even a rather sweet breeze coming in through the bedroom window.

Or, at least it wasn't because of the heat that existed *outside* of her. The heat inside of her was an entirely different story.

That heat had its roots in what had happened that evening in the stables, and rather than fading away after she had hurried back into the house, it clung to her.

Clung to her and blossomed.

Tired of tossing and turning, she got up and crossed to the window, hoping that if she stood there, eventually the breeze would cool her off.

It was a good theory. In execution, however, it fell flat—and almost painfully—on its figurative face.

This was absurd, Debi thought, disgusted with herself as she moved away from the window. She felt wide-awake and insanely restless. There was no way she was going to fall asleep like this.

How was she going to go to the clinic in the morning? She needed to be alert when she went to work. She owed as much to the doctors at the clinic, not to mention to the patients that came in.

But she wasn't exactly going to be fresh as a daisy by morning if she spent the night wide-awake because she was too wired to fall asleep.

By tomorrow morning, Debi thought in despair, she would be a zombie, not exactly someone thought to be an asset when it came to the medical field.

Pacing back and forth around the room and her rumpled bed, Debi dragged a hand through her tousled hair, frustrated and completely at a loss as to how to wind down.

But there was nothing she could do about it. Nothing that would help her resolve her situation or where her head was at…

Unless…

She stopped pacing and looked at the wall to her left. The wall that separated Jackson's bedroom from the one she was in.

Unless she retraced her dilemma back to its source.

Debi stared at the wall, thinking.

Maybe if she just talked to Jackson, she could also wind up talking herself down out of this strange, disconcerting place where her equally agitated mind and soul were currently residing, giving her no peace.

Summoning her courage—something that took her a bit of doing—she slipped on her robe, essentially a light, short scrap of blue that matched her equally short, equally blue nightgown.

She left her room, glancing up and down the hall to

make sure no one was around to witness this, then stood, waffling, in front of Jackson's door.

Twice she raised her right hand, her knuckles poised to knock, and twice she dropped her hand to her side, never having made contact with the door.

This is insane, she told herself in disgust. *Go lie down. Maybe you'll bore yourself to death and fall asleep that way.*

Turning on her bare heel, Debi started to go back to her room.

"Debi? Is something wrong?"

The sound of the deep voice behind her caused her heart to leap into her throat before she even turned back around to look at the man she was trying so hard to get out of her system.

He was bare-chested, the all but worn-out jeans he had on hanging seductively low on his taut hips. Breathing became a conscious effort for her. And having her heart lodged in her throat like this temporarily got in the way of her answering.

"I heard you pacing," Jackson told her when she said nothing. "Is something wrong?" he repeated.

Clearing her throat, Debi responded in a shaky voice, "Yes—and no."

"Multiple choice?" Jackson asked.

Her heart was back in place and pounding. Her fingertips felt almost damp and they were tingling.

She'd been a *married* woman for heaven's sakes. What was the matter with her? Why was she behaving like some adolescent girl facing her first teenage crush?

Because, for one thing, the man in front of her had a chest that seemed carved out of stone, and just looking at him made her pulse accelerate.

Taking a breath and trying to steady her capricious nerves, she moved closer to Jackson in order to speak quietly. "Listen, about what happened earlier…"

"I know," he told her, wanting to spare Debi the discomfort of talking about it. "You don't know what you were thinking," he said, taking a guess at what her excuse for kissing him with such intensity would be.

When he put it like that, when he handed her a readily crafted excuse for what she'd allowed to happen between them, it seemed to suddenly strip her of her indecisiveness and make the path before her almost crystal clear.

"Actually," she said softly, stepping into his room and then closing the door behind her without bothering to turn around or even spare it a single glance. "I do," she assured him softly. "I knew exactly what I was thinking then.

"Exactly what I'm thinking now," she added, her eyes on his. Suddenly, she felt as if she had been created with just this moment in mind.

The robe slipped from her shoulders, drifting to the floor and pooling there like a sigh.

Watching, mesmerized, he held back a ragged sigh.

How he wanted her.

And yet…

And yet he couldn't do this, couldn't allow this to happen. Not for the reasons he suspected lay at the very core of this for her.

Jackson framed her face with his hands, wanting her beyond belief, struggling to keep himself from acting on that feeling while blocking all those finely honed instincts that always rose to the forefront. The instincts that were so deeply entrenched in protecting lost souls and saving them.

Lost souls came in all sizes and shapes.

Some, he thought, belonged to big sisters who worried about their younger brothers caught in endless cycles of delinquent behavior.

The desire to protect this woman was tremendous. He realized that he needed to protect Debi from doing the wrong thing.

Needed, in this case, to protect her from himself.

Talk about being consigned to hell...

"I don't want this happening because you're feeling misplaced gratitude because of Ryan," he told her. That would be tantamount to his almost *preying* on her.

Debi placed a finger to his lips to keep Jackson from saying anything further.

"You saved Ryan and I'd have to be a robot not to feel something for you because of that," she whispered. "But it's not *just* that." She tilted her head back, bringing her mouth temptingly closer to his. "It's more. So much more."

What she was experiencing wasn't misplaced gratitude. Yes, it had sprung into being because of gratitude, but it was so much more than that.

What she felt for him intensified because he was trying to dissuade her. The man was incredibly selfless.

Her heart swelled.

"You're lonely," he guessed. Loneliness caused people to do foolish things they lived to regret. "Your jackass of a husband made you choose between him and Ryan— and when you did, he was outraged and insulted, so he left." Jackson searched her eyes for more insight as he spoke. "He didn't try to compromise or to negotiate, he just left. That had to hurt."

He wasn't given to violence, but he would have throttled the man for having hurt Debi this way.

Especially when he saw the tears.

She blinked back the tears that were now laced through her eyelashes. He had gotten it almost all right. "I'd forgotten. You know everything about what happened, don't you?"

"You did tell me some of it," he reminded her. "I looked into the rest." He'd done it to make sure that there wasn't something she was keeping back, something she was ashamed of. To his relief, she hadn't been physically abused. "Sheriff Santiago's got a deputy that knows her way around computers and search engines," he confessed. "She's gotten to be practically a wizard at it." Jackson paused, struggling between doing what he felt was the right thing—and taking what she was so generously offering him. "I just don't want you waking up tomorrow morning with regrets."

"If I do have regrets, it won't be because I made love with you," she told him softly. "It'll be because I didn't."

All the words he should have said to talk her out of this frame of mind fled as if they had been caught in a windstorm and swept out to sea. The next thing he was aware of was wrapping his arms around Debi, then feeling the soft contours of her body as it pressed up against the hardened, unyielding ridges of his.

But he was feeling far more than that.

Feeling guilt because he was unable to pull back, unable to lead her back to her room.

Unable to save her from herself—and from him, heaven help him.

But her mouth was so sweet, her body beyond tempting—and he was just a man.

A man with desires and weaknesses. A man who had gone through life, changed himself more than once, and when he'd finally got it right, had been so strict and demanding of himself that there had been—and was—no room for anything but the purpose, the calling that he had chosen: saving young lives by turning them around.

Companionship, romance and love, that was all for other people, people who didn't have something to atone for the way that he did. Who didn't have a debt to repay the way he did.

But this woman that fate—and her wayward brother—had brought to him, she made him forget all the rules that had been set in stone, all his silent promises to himself—and to the late uncle he would forever be grateful and indebted to.

This woman was, he felt quite simply, the fever in his blood—and his pending downfall as sure as day followed night.

Just kissing Debi gave him a rush, made his head spin.

Her nightgown—the bright blue scrap on her body—quickly became an afterthought as it found its way to the floor.

Jackson memorized her body with his hands before he ever actually laid his eyes on it. When he did, when he actually *looked* at her, he froze for a moment, stunned by how truly beautiful she was to him.

She had the body of goddess.

And a mouth that was made for sin, he thought the next moment.

His frayed, all but paper-thin jeans disappeared moments later. His body was totally primed for the final conquest, but he wanted her to derive as much pleasure from this as he could possibly give her. That meant placing more foreplay ahead of his own gratification.

Accustomed to all forms of self-denial, Jackson held

himself in check for as long as he could, making love to each part of her as if it was a separate entity as well as part of a greater, completely enticing whole.

He kissed her eyelids, the hollow of her throat, the nape of her neck before eventually working his way downward.

Using the tip of his tongue, he caressed her breasts, hardening the tips, finding a thrill in the way she moaned and shuddered in response before he worked his way to her belly, making it quiver.

And then, as the path took him ever lower, Jackson created a fire within her very core with teasing thrusts of his tongue.

Her movements beneath him grew in ever-increasing intensity and urgency.

Debi bucked and arched, grabbing fistfuls of the quilted cover beneath her on his bed. She all but bit through her lower lip to keep from crying out in sheer ecstasy as peak after peak rippled through her body that was so damp with sweat.

No ONE FELT like this and lived, she thought, falling back against the bed, exhausted, after yet another climax had seized her and then burst apart like so many fireworks. She had no idea exactly what she had been doing those years she'd been married to John and they had purportedly been making love. But whatever it was, it didn't hold the *hint* of a candle to this.

This was what dying and going to heaven was all about, she couldn't help thinking.

And it wasn't over. Because the next moment, Jackson was there, his handsome, rugged face looming over hers, a soft, gentle look in his sensually seductive eyes.

A very strange sensation darted into her. And stayed.

She reached up, placing her hands on either side of the hard planes and angles of his face. The next moment, she craned her neck so that she could reach his lips and press a kiss to them.

His arms closed around her, gathering her to him as he kissed her over and over again until she was more than ready—

Until she couldn't hold back anymore.

The next moment, he entered her, carefully, as if trying not to hurt her while giving in to what felt like an overwhelming need to possess her, to be one with her.

This was her other half.

This was how it was meant to be.

One whole from two halves.

Moving with urgency, Jackson increased his tempo by degrees, going faster and faster as she met him, movement for movement. Absorbing his rhythm.

They raced to the summit of the highest peak that stretched out before them. Raced until they came to the very top and then, still joined, still together, they experienced the inevitable mind-blowing explosion that embraced them in a cloud of ecstasy.

Pulses pounded like thunder as euphoria rained down on both of them. And when euphoria receded, he held on to her instead of the ebbing sensation, listening to the way her breathing slowed and became regular. Listening to her heart do the same.

But the feeling of well-being that had been created remained.

He smiled as his arms tightened around her. Jackson leaned over just slightly, kissing the top of her head, a deep affection spilling through him.

Tomorrow would come, as it always did, with its own set of problems, its own set of challenges. Very possibly, with its own set of regrets—hers, not his—no matter what she'd said. But tonight, tonight the warm glow of making love to a woman, of *loving* a woman for what he knew was the first time in his life, wove through his body, making him feel that everything else was secondary. That any obstacles would work themselves out because, after all, he had made love with what had turned out to be the perfect woman as well as his soul mate.

He had touched heaven.

"You okay?" he asked Debi. She'd been so quiet, he thought that she'd fallen asleep.

But she hadn't.

Debi smiled then, feeling far happier than she could remember being in a very long, long time. She turned her body into his.

"I'm perfect," she answered with a contented smile, all but intoxicated, tipsy on the giddiness still churning through her veins.

"Yes," Jackson agreed, wrapping his arm around her and drawing her closer still, "you are."

Chapter Sixteen

Jackson deliberately took the long way around the ranch house to avoid being seen. He made his way into the stables. He knew he'd be alone here this time of day and he really had to be alone to work out the tension and conflicting feelings that were even now doing battle inside of him.

One of the saddles needed mending and he put his mind to that.

Except that his mind was elsewhere and wasn't cooperating. A lot had happened in such a very short amount of time. Life-changing things. And it was all going to stop by tonight.

He stared at the saddle, not seeing it. Seeing something else entirely.

It had been a good run while it lasted, as Sam had been fond of saying toward the end.

Jackson pressed his lips together, saddened beyond words.

He'd had no examples to fall back on or to guide him when it came to male/female relationships. He never saw or heard anything but hot, angry words and cold silences exchanged between his own mother and father. No loving glances, no forgiving moments. None for each other and certainly none for him.

And both had left him, first his mother, eventually his father, neither one stopping to spare so much as a second glance in his direction or a word in parting. A byproduct of their marriage, he hadn't mattered to them just as their marriage hadn't mattered to them.

His father had cheated on his first wife with his second wife—the woman who had become his stepmother. And then he had cheated on her. And while his stepmother had done what she could to create a loving home for him and for his brother, that wasn't the same thing as being in a home with parents who loved and respected each other at its core.

While he had no example to guide him, he knew that Debi had a relationship that had failed her even though she had invested all of herself into it. She hadn't been able to see what was right in front of her and somehow wound up living a lie for more than a few years.

And yet, somehow, with all that holding them back, Debi and Jackson still seemed to trust one another, still reveled in what they had accidentally stumbled across and enjoyed.

Hesitantly, cautiously, they'd approached one another the morning after their first encounter with barely contained hope in their hearts. Hope that was quickly rewarded by the first word, the first smile. The first caress.

The first encounter turned out not to be an isolated one. Its existence bred another. And another. The night, Jackson felt, was their friend. And the calendar turned out to be their enemy because each day that went by brought him closer to the end.

The one he was facing now, he thought, his hands tightening on the fraying saddle cinch he was supposed to be repairing.

The boys who were brought to him had an average time in which their behavior would come around, if that was actually in their cards—and so far it always had been.

Some took more time, some took less, but a reversal in behavior usually occurred somewhere around a total of four weeks.

Ryan took less time to begin to come around. It was longer than two, but slightly less than three. Slightly less than three weeks to see that there was not just hope, but a definite reversal of behavior in the offing.

So Jackson braced himself. He knew in his heart that Debi would be leaving soon. Leaving because he had restored her brother to his former self.

Leaving because he had a knack for what he did, was good at it, so there was no longer an excuse for her to stay.

It was in his power to prolong the process, to drag it out and say things that would create stumbling blocks to reaching the desired final goal. But that would be unfair and selfish and he had learned not to be that way because years ago a good man had made him change his ways and his outlook.

Stretched, Ryan's complete return to decent behavior took a little more than four weeks. Jackson couldn't honestly pretend he needed any longer than that.

And now his honesty was going to cause him to lose the only complete happiness he'd ever known.

Jackson bit off the curse that rose in his throat then tried to focus in on his work.

He failed.

"You look like you've just lost your best friend." Garrett commented.

"What?" Preoccupied, Jackson stared at his younger

brother uncomprehendingly. It took a couple of moments to replay Garrett's words so that they registered in his head. "Oh, no, not yet anyway."

"But you're going to?" Garrett questioned, then re-phrased his question. "You're going to lose your best friend? Hey, I didn't know I was going anywhere," he kidded.

Jackson didn't smile.

"You want to talk about it?" Garrett gently prodded, drawing closer.

Jackson avoided making eye contact. "No."

"Worse than I thought," Garrett said, leaning against the stall right next to his brother and giving the impression that he wasn't about to go anywhere. "Look, don't play the noble, stoic Navajo warrior with me, you're only half Native American. The other half of you is Caucasian. That's the talkative half," Garrett instructed. "What's bothering you?"

This time Jackson *did* look at his brother. "Other than you?"

"Yeah, other than me."

Jackson turned his face away from him and looked back to the saddle repairs he had barely made a dent in. "I don't want to talk about it."

Garrett shrugged. "You want to play hard to get? That's fine by me." He shifted so that he was in front of Jackson and his brother was forced to look at him. "I've got all day."

Jackson took a step, only to have his brother emulate it, matching him move for move. "You're just going to stand there, blocking my way?"

Garrett's laid-back grin seemed to spread from ear to ear. "Yup."

Jackson drew himself up. He was taller, although Garrett was the more muscular one. "What makes you think I'll let you? That I won't just pick you up and toss you out of my way?" Jackson challenged.

Garrett shrugged nonchalantly, unfazed. "Because you're not a bully anymore. Because that's not who you ever really were, at bottom. So spill it," he ordered in a relatively quiet voice. "What's got you all pensive and sullen like this?" Garrett asked.

Jackson debated pushing his brother aside and storming away, but Garrett was right. This wasn't him. And while he had never been one to consciously spill out his insides—or want to—he knew Garrett. His younger brother was nothing if not persistent. He would keep after him until he got the answers he was looking for.

There was nothing to be gained by holding out on him. So he didn't.

"She's leaving."

"You saw her packing," he concluded, his tone compassionate.

Jackson's was both resigned and frustrated. "Yeah."

"Have you talked to her?"

There was a long, exasperated pause before Jackson finally replied, "No."

Garrett stared at his older brother as if Jackson had just grown another head.

"No?" he questioned in disbelief. "You didn't talk to her?"

"I said no," Jackson snapped, irritated.

"Let me get this straight. You obviously care about the woman—and from what I and the immediate world can see, the feeling is mutual—and you *haven't talked to her about staying*?" he demanded, his voice rising an octave, possibly two.

"What part of 'no' don't you understand?" Jackson shouted back.

"All of it," Garrett retorted. "Go, talk to her," he ordered Jackson. "Tell the woman you don't want her to leave."

But Jackson stubbornly remained exactly where he was. He was *not* about to beg—especially not when he felt it wouldn't do any good.

"If she didn't want to leave, she wouldn't," Jackson maintained.

Garrett could only shake his head in completely frustrated wonder. "Women are right, some men can be so dumb."

Jackson's eyes narrowed as he glared at his younger brother. "Are you calling me dumb?"

"Yes, I am," he shot back, going toe-to-toe with Jackson. "Did it ever occur to you that she's leaving because you haven't asked her to stay? That she feels that as far as you're concerned, this was just a nice little interlude, but now it's over and it's time for her to go back home the way you always knew she had to?"

"She doesn't think that," Jackson protested angrily.

"How do you know?" Garrett challenged. "You never talked to her about this."

A malevolent look washed over Jackson's features, then gave way to the realization that his brother was right. "You're annoying," he told Garrett.

The corners of Garrett's generous mouth curved. "You're only saying that because you know I'm right."

Jackson opened his mouth, then shut it again. Exasperation all but seeped out of every pore as he glared at his younger brother. Glared at him until Jackson abruptly turned on the heel of his boot and stormed out of the stable.

He had somewhere else to be.

"Remember to use your words, Jackson," Garrett called after him. "The woman's not a mind reader."

Jackson made no parting comment. He was too busy framing what he was going to say to Debi. He had to get this right.

Because he felt as if his very life depended on it.

DAMN HIM, ANYWAY.

Jackson knew she was leaving today and he hadn't said anything about it.

Not one single word.

Last night, he'd come to her bedroom, the way he had every other night since they'd first been together, and they'd made love. Wonderful, glorious love, the way they always did.

But afterward, when they lay there and he'd held her in his arms, Jackson didn't say anything. Didn't talk about what they both knew was happening today. Didn't even comment on Ryan and his complete about-face from being the angry, troubled teen who'd first crossed The Healing Ranch's threshold.

Nothing.

Not one single word.

He'd acted just like the next day—*this* day—was just another day instead of her last one here with him. Hers and Ryan's.

What that told her was that she had an unblemished track record, she thought bitterly. She *still* couldn't pick 'em. Couldn't pick a man to care about who would ultimately care about her.

Pick a man? Debi thought, mocking herself. Damn it, she didn't just "pick" him, she fell in *love* with him. In love with a man who didn't even care enough to come to see her today.

She stared down at the suitcase she'd finished packing more than an hour ago and blinked. A teardrop fell, landing on her tank top. It darkened the strawberry color as the moisture sank into the material.

"Stupid, stupid, stupid," she admonished herself, angrily wiping away the wet stain left on her cheek. Why was she crying? He wasn't worth it. The entire male species wasn't worth it.

Except for Ryan, she reminded herself. She had to think of her brother, not herself, she silently lectured. She had to remember that leaving here was going to be hard for him, too. He'd made friends here, worthwhile friends. Friends she knew he was going to remain in contact with.

Unlike Jackson with her.

The sigh shuddered through her as she let the suitcase lid fall into place. She snapped the locks closed one at a time. She had to stop stalling, Debi upbraided herself. The drive back to Indianapolis was a long one.

She was already tired.

Dragging the suitcase off the bed, she deposited it on the floor just as she heard the light knock on her door.

Ryan, she thought.

He'd finally found his manners. She could thank Jackson for that, too.

Debi pressed her lips together, struggling to bank down the emotions that threatened to burst through. She told herself not to think of Jackson. Not now. She wasn't strong enough to deal with that now.

The knock came again, more forcefully this time.

"It's open," she called to her brother. "I'm almost read—"

She didn't finish the word because she forgot it. Forgot everything.

Everything but the man standing in the doorway.

"Jackson."

He had no memory of crossing the threshold, or of entering the room. The sound of her voice just pulled him in, blotting out everything else but her, and his overwhelming need for her.

All the carefully selected words he'd rehearsed in his head walking here completely vanished, leaving him with only two.

"Don't go." He took her hands in his, his eyes pleading with her. "I know I have no right to ask this. I know that your whole life is back in Indianapolis. But if you go, you'll take my whole life with you. Because you *are* my whole life and if you leave, I won't have a reason to breathe.

"I won't be *able* to breathe," he emphasized. He pressed the hands he was holding against his chest, to his heart, his eyes still not leaving hers. "Is there anything, *anything* I can say to get you to reconsider and stay?"

For a second, she didn't say anything. *Couldn't* say anything. She'd wanted this so much, had longed for it so hard, that now that it was actually happening, that she was actually *hearing* him say it, it didn't seem real and the ability to form words, let alone the right words, momentarily deserted her.

"I can't, can I?" Jackson said, guessing at the reason